DRA'KAEDAN'S COVEN

JESSAMYN KINGLEY

Editing: Flat Earth Editing
Cover Design: 2017 © L.J. Anderson, Mayhem Cover Creations
Dragon Artwork by © Dimitri Elevit

CONTENTS

To my husband, Michael, for always believing in me and listening to me talk about all the D'Vaire men constantly.

To Hope and Jess for editing each D'Vaire book with such exceptional care. None of these guys would be the same without you.

To LJ for making each cover of the D'Vaire series extraordinary.

Dear Reader,

Brogan and Dra'Kaedan's story was my first book. Although I was proud of it when it was initially published, it's not up to par with the rest of the series. So, after completing nearly a dozen novels, I finally sat down and took on the task of writing something more deserving of such a special couple.

If you read the original book, I hope you enjoy this new spin on their love story. And if you are picking up Brogan and Dra'Kaedan's tale for the first time, welcome to D'Vaire.

Sincerely,
   Jessamyn

1

1367 AD, Castle Leolinnia

"Dra'Kaedan," his brother called out. Dra'Kaedan quickly stuffed what was left of the sweet treat one of the servants, Hilanore, had given him into his mouth. It was too large a bite, and his eyes teared as he chewed. Since he was busy trying not to choke, he didn't say a word as his twin strode toward him.

Unaware of the struggle Dra'Kaedan was having trying to survive, Dre'Kariston reached his side and asked, "What plans have you? I thought to accompany you."

After a gulp that did little more than lodge the piece of pastry in his throat, Dra'Kaedan offered his sibling a shrug. The color rushed to his face as his lungs burned from the inability to breathe comfortably.

Dre'Kariston cocked his head to the side, then shook his head slightly so his dark curls fell over his forehead. "You must get over this penchant for cakes. You've been to the kitchen again, haven't you? If Mother finds out, you will face her wrath."

With no way to verbally respond and lacking any remorse for his desire to eat constantly, Dra'Kaedan rolled his eyes. He was on his way out of the castle; he had no intention of running into his lady mother.

"Go on...swallow it down," his brother encouraged. He was likely growing weary of having a one-sided conversation, and Dra'Kaedan did his best to fill his belly with all that he'd jammed into his mouth.

When he was finally able to speak, he treaded carefully. Dra'Kaedan's mission was a secret one, and his best friend would not approve. "Mother need not know unless you tattle."

"When have I ever tattled?" Dre'Kariston demanded.

"Rest easy. I know the truth of your words," Dra'Kaedan said as he reached out and patted his brother's arm. "You have ever sought to be good to me."

"You've donned your heaviest cloak. Are you planning a journey?"

"Not far. Just past the castle gates."

"You're planning on watching for the dragons again, aren't you?" Dre'Kariston accused. They were recently told dragons existed beyond storybooks. Though not everyone believed the sorcerers who'd come to the castle with the news, Dra'Kaedan did. He had a simple plan: he was going to find them and when he did, Dra'Kaedan was sure his mate would be amongst them. It was a feeling deep inside his soul; he had grown so enamored of the idea that he'd decorated his chamber and clothing in dragons. It was a bone of contention between him and his twin as Dre'Kariston was a skeptic who insisted upon seeing things with his own eyes before believing them.

"It is not a crime, Brother."

"It is the height of foolishness. Were the beasts real, we'd see them flying over the castle itself."

"Will you come with me?" Dra'Kaedan asked. He was counting on his sibling's doubt of dragons to work in his favor. Dra'Kaedan was on a mission and although he loved his brother dearly, if Dre'Kariston was aware of his true destination, he would disagree vehemently with his plan.

"I will not waste my time staring at the sky because of some

nonsense given to us while we supped," Dre'Kariston retorted with
an irritated expression.

Dra'Kaedan's smile was one of relief. "I'm off," he said, then
hugged his brother and dashed away.

"You should make better use of your time," Dre'Kariston hollered
after him. Dra'Kaedan raised a hand to acknowledge he'd heard, but
he did not stop to offer a reply.

He raced toward the stables and since he'd sent word ahead, his
horse was waiting for him. Throwing himself up on Draco's back,
Dra'Kaedan thanked the stable boy and set his horse into motion
with a clicking sound. Dra'Kaedan kept him at a civilized trot until he
cleared the castle gates. Leaning forward, he and Draco galloped
toward a familiar spot. It was a cove of trees shaped naturally like a
hut—a favorite place of his family. He'd spent many an afternoon
picnicking there, but this day he was not planning on eating.

After the midday meal, he'd gone up to his room and found a
note lying on a trunk close to his bed. It was left unsigned, but the
writer had professed to know where to find the dragons Dra'Kaedan
was so desperate to set his eyes on. In an instant, he'd made his decision to meet the mysterious stranger who had promised to fulfill his
wildest dreams. As the hooves of his horse ate up the distance toward
his destination, Dra'Kaedan had no concern other than missing his
engagement.

When the canopy of trees came into view, he slowed Draco to a
stop and slid off his back. Securing his reins around a stout trunk,
Dra'Kaedan smoothed one hand over Draco's side, then walked past
him toward the clearing. The long grass under his feet made little
sound as he searched for anyone, only to find himself alone. With a
frown, he wondered if he'd been sent on a fool's errand. He had no
idea why it hadn't occurred to him beforehand that this could be
nothing more than a child's prank. Dra'Kaedan was thinking it now,
and his temper grew most angry.

Trying his best to remain calm, Dra'Kaedan surveyed the scene
around him and found nothing beyond the trees swaying in the wind.
Resigning himself to be patient and wait for someone to show their

face, he took three steps forward, so he was in the center of the circle. Seconds later, a whoosh of air reached his ears as crushing pain registered in his skull. It was so intense; the world around him grew dim at the edges. As his body slumped to the ground, Dra'Kaedan feared he might very well have been lured here to his death. He was given no time to grieve over his own demise as the blackness took him.

When Dra'Kaedan tried to open his eyes, his first thought was to be glad he was still on the right side of the veil that separated life from death. His head pounded ferociously and when he tried to move, he found that both his hands and feet were tied down. Dra'Kaedan's heart pounded as he struggled against his restraints.

"Ah, finally, you've decided to awake," a mocking voice said. Dra'Kaedan recognized it but could not place the name. It was of great import to know what danger he'd fallen into, so he forced his lashes up and glimpsed Carvallius of Mallent in the dim light of a stone room.

"What do you?" he asked.

"Dra'Kaedan of Leolinnia. Here in my humble home. I can hardly believe my eyes," Carvallius taunted as he stepped close to Dra'Kaedan. "I have big plans for you."

"Release me," Dra'Kaedan demanded as he ignored his throbbing headache. "Release me before you find yourself answering to my parents."

"Right...*them*. I have no fear of Grand Warlock T'Eirick or Grand Summoner Saura. For too long, they've ignored me....But rest easy, I have plans for them as well. Now I do apologize. This will be quite painful, but there's no danger to your life," Carvallius said.

"You cannot hope to take on the entire Coven of Warlocks," Dra'Kaedan snapped. He was clearly in a room with a madman, so he would not mince his words nor quell his fiery disposition.

"Don't you worry over them either. I told you...I have plans," Carvallius retorted as he rubbed his hands together. "We must take care of you first. I do wish Latarian would hurry down. I do not have all day to go about this."

"Damn you, Carvallius. Untie me."

"Rather haughty of you to start tossing out demands. I think you'll find that I am in charge. Are you unable to teleport away? Do you feel that drain upon your power? It's the secret of the Cwylld elven. Have you heard of them? A rather brutal and primitive tribe... but they do have their benefits—such as the ability to nullify magic."

"You fool. If you're draining me, you also do the same to yourself," Dra'Kaedan snarled as he struggled against his restraints.

"Do stop moving around. The noise of those chains is quite annoying. Do not worry over me, dear Dra'Kaedan. I've got all but where the stone touches you covered in copper. Somehow the metal interrupts the effects of the stone. Is it working? I do hope so. I was only able to steal the one."

Dra'Kaedan was in real danger. His magic, normally so strong and reliable, was failing him. "Let me go," he shouted.

"Grandfather, I got your message," a female voice called out as a woman came into view. Like Carvallius, she had red hair and green eyes. Only, hers were a pale green; this warlock was not one of great power.

"I sent for you some time ago. Is this whole plan not for your benefit? Why would you tarry?" Carvallius demanded.

"I am sorry, Grandfather."

"Lazy girl," Carvallius muttered. "Have a seat, Latarian. It will take some time to complete our task."

"This will work? I have a great wish to be more powerful," the woman called Latarian responded.

"Let me out of this room this instant," Dra'Kaedan ordered.

"Boy, I would suggest you keep your mouth shut if you know what's good for you. No matter how we go about this it will be painful, but I can make it worse if you annoy me," Carvallius snarled back.

"I have no fear of you," Dra'Kaedan sneered. He let out a scream as pain tore through his shoulder blade. It was as if someone had stuck a sword through him.

"I did warn you," Carvallius admonished. "That was the first step. How did it make you feel?"

The agony was so intense that Dra'Kaedan could not speak. A tear leaked from his eye as his back bowed. Carvallius cast a second spell, this one not as excruciating as the first, but it left him drained of power.

"Latarian, come and check on our guest. I've already begun the process of making him your familiar. Do you feel more strength in your magic?" Carvallius asked.

"I do. It is most glorious. You are simply the best grandparent one could ask for," Latarian replied jovially. As Dra'Kaedan panted and tried to push away the pain of Carvallius's continuous spells, he wondered over his fate. No one had known where Dra'Kaedan was headed when he'd left the castle. Would anyone know where to begin the search for him? Could he escape this wicked pair before his life was irrevocably changed?

Latarian approached the bed, and Dra'Kaedan noted that her green gaze was already darker. Her mouth twisted in scorn. "He looks rather strange with red hair."

"Better than those ridiculous golden ringlets," Carvallius muttered. Dra'Kaedan did not want to know what they were discussing. There was no way his tresses had morphed from blond to scarlet. He refused to believe it.

Dra'Kaedan let out a roar as the black magic in the room filled his view. Another symbol was etched into his skin and it pulled at his soul, tugging him closer to this creature staring so intently at him. His eyes burned as the bones of his face shifted and contorted. The sweat seeped from his pores as he endured the torture of Carvallius's spells.

"Grandfather, can you not add something to have him heal us both constantly?" Latarian asked without turning her glance away from the pain being inflicted upon Dra'Kaedan's poor self.

"It is simply cast. You will have plenty of power."

"It is one less thing to weigh upon my mind, Grandfather," Latarian pleaded.

"Very well," Carvallius agreed.

"Let me go," Dra'Kaedan pleaded in a whisper. "If you do not, when I return to my family, I will tell them of this atrocity."

"No, Dra'Kaedan of Leolinnia. You will not. Did I forget to mention, you will have no memory of your former life?" Carvallius asked. "Which reminds me. Latarian, you must remove his necklace."

Without a word, Latarian reached down and yanked off the necklace Dra'Kaedan was given eighteen years earlier, only hours after his birth. Fashioned by his father, it contained an essence of his twin, so they would always be able to find each other. He had no strength to struggle. Instead, Dra'Kaedan gritted his teeth as a new spell was cast and wracked his body with agony.

"Hand over the necklace, dear granddaughter, for I have use of it. Say farewell to your future, Dra'Kaedan. The title of Grand Warlock will never be yours," Carvallius taunted as a darkness settled over Dra'Kaedan, and the pictures in his mind were wrenched away. "Instead, that will be how you'll address me. I will see your family dead."

Dra'Kaedan let out a tortuous cry as the last of his identity was ripped asunder. Unable to cope with all that was being forced upon him, everything faded to black once again. The last words that echoed in his skull were in the callous voice of the woman he was now bound to. "We shall call him Ayden."

2

Several weeks later, Castle Mallent

The wind howled and moaned outside the large castle as Latarian wandered toward the curved stone staircase. A chill pervaded through the scant protection of her shoes, and she shuddered. She braced a hand against the wall and made her way carefully down to the darkest part of her home. Her grandfather had requested her presence, and she knew better than to make him wait. Besides, he had her favor now that there was such incredible power coursing through her veins. For one hundred and fifty years, she'd dealt with a negligible amount and had taken no interest in learning the craft of spells. She was finding catching up with her sorcery a tedious task.

Finally at the bottom of the steps, she held her candle aloft as she traipsed lightly through the darkened hall. At the end was a large wooden door, and it took the weight of her entire body to open it. Latarian was grateful she'd managed the task without setting her dress aflame. She stepped into the dim room, her spirits rising as her eye immediately caught the welcome visage of the man who was the center of her world.

"Grandfather, I was so happy to receive your summons. I was not expecting you to return for many months," Latarian exclaimed.

"You know I always long to see you, my dear, but I'm afraid I've brought you bad tidings," Carvallius told her as he took her cold hands and bussed her cheek. A powerful and busy man, Latarian was always appreciative of his infrequent visits. The last time he stayed at the castle was when he'd bound her to Ayden.

"Bad tidings? What is amiss?" she asked as he released her and paced the barely lit room.

"It's the Cwylld elven. They are demanding tribute from the Grand Warlock. Should he not give them the land and gold they seek, no doubt it shall come to war."

"I believed you to be an ally of the Cwylld. You will go to Grand Warlock T'Eirick? Surely you can make him see that a war with the Cwylld elven would not favor the warlocks?" She'd not been privy to any of his meetings with the tribe he often described as ruthless. Carvallius kept her ignorant of most of his plans, and Latarian was grateful. She preferred her time to be her own, and Carvallius was often traveling from one distant spot to another; Latarian had no desire for such adventure in her own life.

"The Cwylld will obey me—I am sure. I am headed to T'Eirick directly. I hope to arrive before he leaves to take this dire news to the Council of Sorcery. The other leaders should not be burdened by the failure of the Grand Warlock to protect his people," Carvallius sneered. He had no fondness for the Council of Sorcery, even though their rulers, T'Eirick and his mate, Saura, were the ones who'd created it. The goal was to unite willing magical races with the hope of bettering them all.

Thus far, the leaders were unwilling to cede any of their power, which left the Council with little progress. They had not even managed to provide a treaty to protect anyone. Grand Warlock T'Eirick was the only one prepared to yield his authority to the Council, and Carvallius believed that showed weakness. Of course, Carvallius had little nice to say about T'Eirick or Saura on any occasion, and Latarian believed he was correct in his poor opinion of the pair.

"The Cwylld elven have never found any fault with the warlocks before. Why are they making demands of us now?" Ayden asked as he entered the shadowy room.

"Your familiar is impertinent, Latarian. A lash or two from the whip will teach him not to ask questions of his betters," Carvallius admonished, the contempt in his voice for Ayden unmistakable. He might have been willing to increase Latarian's power at her suggestion and bring Dra'Kaedan into their home with his identity concealed, but he could not disguise his revulsion.

"Ayden, you know better than to question Grandfather without first gaining his permission. He is too important of a warlock to be troubled with the likes of you. You know nothing of the Cwylld elven nor about anything else," Latarian scolded as she shoved him behind her.

Bowing his head, Ayden muttered an apology to them both and lowered his dark green eyes to the stones beneath their feet. It was becoming quite the task to teach Ayden his place. Latarian was already growing weary of correcting his behavior and dealing with his incessant questions. While she lacked interest in books and other such nonsense, Ayden was forever reading. He expected Latarian as his better to answer his queries, and she found his ignorant view of the world a chore to endure.

"Will you stay here and have a night of rest before your journey, Grandfather?"

"There is no time, child. It is only my concern for your safety that forces me to delay my journey to T'Eirick. I fear for the fate of our people should he not listen to my counsel. I must know that you are taken care of. I want you to go to the small cottage that I once took you to as a child after the unfortunate passing of your father and mother."

"I do remember a cottage during those tragic days after you brought me the news of their deaths. It was quite small, but the garden vast." Latarian hadn't enjoyed her time there, but her grandfather had insisted it was the best place to recover from her grief.

"It is small enough that servants will not be needed—they cannot be trusted in this time of peril. I have enchanted it, making it impossible for the world to see. You will be protected there and remain undetected. I will send word when it is time for you to return to the castle." Her grandfather's words rang with urgency, and he once again grasped her hands as he spoke.

"What of Ayden?"

"Of course, he will travel with you. You know it would cause him great pain to be separated from you. Have you any other questions before I must leave?"

"You have my thanks. How long do you believe I will need to endure life at the cottage?"

"Latarian, how am I to know how long it will take to talk sense into the Grand Warlock and the Grand Summoner? You know from my tales what a stubborn lot they are. Once again, I find myself being forced to act in the best interests of our people, with no reward other than a clean conscience."

"They have no idea how fortunate they are to have you as an advisor," Latarian said soothingly. "May I have your promise you will send word once it's safe to return? I know I will pine for my home as soon as we leave."

"No more of your silly questions. I have already promised to do so. I must journey on, and you must make your way to the cottage. Do not return until I command it."

Latarian threw her arms around her grandfather and clung to him as he patted her back. She had no wish for him to go, but her race was doomed without him. Someday he would be Grand Warlock, though she had no knowledge of how he planned to attain the title. Carvallius had managed to kidnap Dra'Kaedan, so she was sure he would meet his goal. It would be a new beginning for the Coven of Warlocks, and Latarian herself would be able to reap the benefit of being Carvallius's only living relative. People would wait on her, and she would have to lift naught a finger to have her needs met.

"You will write?" Latarian asked. After releasing him, she allowed her tears to have full reign. She could not abide the thought of staying at that horrid little cottage with no one but the annoying

Ayden to accompany her. The only consolation was that it would keep Dra'Kaedan from finding his mate. The lone instruction Carvallius gave her when Dra'Kaedan had submitted to his spells was to keep him from finding his other half, though she was given no explanation as to the consequences. She shrugged off her thoughts; that kind of tedious detail was not going to prey upon her mind.

Carvallius raised the hood of his cloak over his head, clearly anxious to be on his way. His words were rushed. "I will have your promise that you will not return until I send word."

"I promise, Grandfather," Latarian whispered as he faded away to nothing. A sigh slipped through her lips as desolation overtook her at the thought of being forced to care for herself without servants.

"Think you he will be successful?" Ayden asked.

With a roll of her eyes, she landed her gaze on the short man her grandfather had changed into her familiar. His red hair had not fully straightened from his former riot of curls, and now they were both forced to endure tresses with disobedient waves. When she strained her vision, the navy of Dra'Kaedan's orbs peeked through the green of Ayden's. It annoyed her, as she had no wish to remember what a glorious life Fate bestowed on him while she was granted a pittance. His very presence both thrilled her, for his power, and irritated her due to the force of his personality.

"Ayden, you are too often asking questions you have no business thinking. If we're to get along, you will obey me. I've been easy with the whip thus far, but my arm will no doubt grow stronger if you should continue with your defiance."

"I did not mean to be insolent. It's nothing more than a simple question. Am I not to worry over our fate or that of your grandfather? You are both the only family I have."

Satisfied his concern was for her and Carvallius, she smiled. "Come, we must obey Grandfather, though I will tell you I have no wish to while away my time at a cottage. Go to our chambers, and pack what we'll need. Then see if Cook has some food to spare. You'll need to learn to grow crops and prepare our meals while we are away. I have no wish to starve."

"Of course, Latarian," Ayden responded softly as he turned and walked toward the stairs. His words were just what she'd expected, but his eyes were full of boldness, and his strong will was hardly subdued. It was a good thing she was willing to thwart it at every opportunity. It would not be an easy task, so she would reserve her energy and do naught else while they waited for Carvallius to send word.

She longed for the day he would find the crown of the Grand Warlock upon his head. With a grin, she made a note to ask him for a title and coronet of her own when the time was right. Following in Ayden's wake toward the top of the castle so she could oversee his packing, Latarian wanted to make sure he collected all her favorite dresses. As for her familiar, she would allow him to pack as many books as he desired. She had no wish to converse with him and should he have activities, he might give her some peace. *A body could hope*, she thought derisively as she resigned herself to her future. Not so long now and she would be the envy of every woman in the Coven of Warlocks. She would keep that thought close at hand and enjoy her newfound power. Latarian wished it was enough to keep her desolation at bay.

3

1369 AD, Castle Draconis

Fully dressed, Brogan lay on a pallet, admonishing himself for acting like a scared boy. The last day of his life had been a tumultuous one. For a century he'd waited to go from drakeling to dragon, and it finally happened the previous morn. To his shock his best friend, Prince Aleksander Ethelindraconis, had shifted into a beast so large and rare, he still could not wrap his brain around it. King Ethelindraconis had not suffered from the same malady. He'd demanded his only son return to his human form and remove himself from the Draconis Court of Ethelin.

Brogan hadn't needed any time to decide what his fate would be. Aleksander was a constant in his life and since the death of Brogan's parents, his only ally. He would not allow his closest confidante to venture forth into the world alone. Only taking the time to gather his belongings, Brogan had sought out a pair of mates stifled under King Ethelin's rule. The two young dragons were both female, and Aleksander's father had no tolerance in his heart for couples of the same sex. It was one of the very reasons Brogan had to go—other than his friendship to Aleksander.

Like Madeline and Larissa, he favored his own sex. He'd warily agreed to allow the three to follow him, though Aleksander's reluctance had only to do with his fear for them. There was little coin— only a few gold pieces King Boian's first, Duke Drogo, had handed over—and he worried they made a mistake in leaving the safety of Castle Ethelin. Aleksander's cousins Noirin and Dravyn had caught up with them and insisted on leaving as well.

The six dragons had only just attained their beasts, but they would have to find a way to make it on their own. Duke Drogo bade them go to Castle Draconis, and so they made that their destination. They'd just passed the castle gate and were prepared to fly when Aleksander doubled over in pain. Once he managed to right himself, they grasped that Fate had once again altered his life. She'd made him a king by placing a silver ring around the pupils of his exotic blue-black eyes. In her wisdom, she had also placed a golden one, though only the emperors were supposed to have such. None of them understood what it meant, but now they were able to go to their rulers and ask for a kingdom for the new Court D'Vaire. It was the name Fate had splashed onto Aleksander's forearm for a few precious moments.

Merrily they'd headed to Castle Draconis, but their good cheer hadn't lasted long. After they'd dined in the opulent Great Hall, a sense of foreboding crept over them, and the D'Vaires retreated to the safety of the guest chambers. Brogan could not explain his trepidation, but danger lurked within the walls. So, he lay trembling like a boy too afraid to blow out his candle for fear tragedy would befall him. He had no idea how long he'd languished when there was a scratch upon his door.

Either it was a welcome respite from his dire thoughts or bad luck had truly found him, he mused. Aleksander had made him a duke, so Brogan had to be brave. Rising from his bed, he crossed the room and opened the door. He came face-to-face with a pair of female dragons.

"Is aught amiss?" he asked two of the women he was sworn to protect.

"May we come in?" Larissa requested.

Brogan allowed them entry into this room. When he closed the door behind them, he smiled as he noticed a change between the two. "You've sealed your matebond. Good tidings on you both."

"Thank you. We thought such a happy thing would settle our minds, but it has not. Something's amiss," Madeline replied as she hugged her other half close. Larissa's orange eyes were terrified.

"I thought the feeling would be easier to bear the longer we stayed, but I find myself growing more concerned," Brogan stated.

No words were spoken as there was another knock on Brogan's door. He offered Madeline and Larissa what he hoped was a reassuring nod and then turned to open it. In the hall was the only other D'Vairedraconis duke and his older sister.

"Come in," he urged Dravyn and Noirin.

"Oh good, it is not only me who is starting at every sound," Noirin said as she took stock of everyone in Brogan's room. None of them knew each other well. Though Noirin and Dravyn were cousins to Aleksander, they'd been servants in Castle Ethelin after the deaths of their parents when they were young. Brogan only met Larissa by chance and she'd turned out to be the friendly sort who confessed all to him regarding her relationship with Madeline. They'd only recently discovered each other, and she'd bumped right into Brogan while crying over their bleak future under the rules of King Ethelindraconis, who would never allow them to mate.

"No, I do not know how anyone finds their rest under this roof," Brogan told her.

A third knock sounded, this one louder and more aggressive. With a roll of his eyes and wondering how many more people they could squeeze into his small bedchamber, he yet again whipped open the door. On the other side was the newly crowned King D'Vairedraconis.

"Brogan, we need to wake the others. I must leave," Aleksander stated. His jaw was clenched, and his exotic eyes were full of sorrow.

"Come on in. They are with me. It is the middle of the night—you wish to leave now?" Brogan asked as Aleksander walked stiffly into the crowded room.

"It is not my wish," Aleksander revealed. "Rather, an order."

"The Emperors have demanded you leave? That is strange. You said they were most helpful when you met with them earlier. Did they give a reason for the change of heart?" Dravyn asked.

"I am afraid I have grave news," Aleksander said. He swallowed thickly. "The Emperors are dead."

Gasps filled the space, and Brogan's was added to the rest. "Dead? How?"

"I do not know. Imperial Duke Bernal came to my bedchamber to apprise me of their deaths. He didn't say how it came about."

Noirin propped her hands on her hips. "But he had a reason to ask you to go? What was it? Why did he wish for us to venture out in the dark?"

"His Grace feels I'm to blame. My dragon's strange coloring and therefore my own has cursed this castle and invited murderers into our midst."

"That's absurd," Brogan shot out. "How does a mix of blue and black invite in assassins? Has the man taken leave of his senses?" He simply could not fathom how the only bi-color dragon in their realm could lead to the death of their rulers.

"It does not matter. We must leave. No doubt he will become more insistent if we tarry," Aleksander replied. Brogan could hardly believe the Emperors were gone. How were two men killed in the middle of the night in their own castle?

"Aleksander, how did this happen?" Noirin asked, as if reading Brogan's mind.

"I do not know, but I'm a king. I should've done all I could to protect Emperor Drystan and Emperor Conley," Aleksander responded.

"We have all just shifted for the first time. You cannot be expected to see to their defense," Brogan insisted. He did not like the guilt and hurt weighing upon his best friend.

"I cannot absolve myself of duty simply because I am new to my role. His Grace has given me directions to a small bit of land where

I'm to go. I think it's best if you return to my father's castle. He will see to your comfort," Aleksander said.

"Do not be a fool, Aleksander," Brogan countered with a stern glare at his new king. "We have sworn our fealty to you. We will be following you to the patch of grass His Grace was kind enough to bestow upon you."

"You do not understand. He has deemed me cursed. I'm not to have anything to do with other dragons," Aleksander argued.

"And you will do what, cousin? Live there with no one and nothing? You've done nothing wrong. I have spent the last century in the kitchens. I will see us fed," Noirin stated calmly.

Dravyn gave a small smile. "My century of life has passed in the fields. I have a talent for growing things. I will see that Noirin has plenty of crops to make her dishes."

"I was an apprentice to my father. He's a blacksmith for King Ethelin. I will see to weapons and anything else we may need to survive," Madeline added.

"My mother was a fine tailor before her death a few years past. I learned at her side. I will see us clothed and fill our home with tapestries," Larissa told them.

"I will make sure none of these dragons who've so cruelly judged us as cursed bring us danger," Brogan said. "We can put a roof over our heads and despite the dragons, we'll find a way to prosper."

"I can promise you nothing," Aleksander whispered. It was the same excuse he'd tried to use to keep them all from following him the previous day, and it was just as inconsequential to Brogan now.

"Fate has chosen you as a king. She gave you the name D'Vaire. We shall see it is a noble one by our deeds. You're an honorable man. Did we not meet because you saw fit to stop those other drakelings from pounding on me when we were but sixteen?" Brogan demanded.

"You did nothing wrong. There's no shame in kissing a boy. They had no cause to fight you," Aleksander replied. Unlike his father, Aleksander found no fault with those that preferred their own sex. It was something Brogan was immensely grateful for, and it was why he'd made a fast friend of him some eight decades ago.

"Aleksander, you're going to be a great king. You have everything inside you already for that. We shall be at your side to see to your survival. Fate will remedy this situation in time," Noirin stated brusquely.

Aleksander studied each one of their faces, then grinned. "Very well. Return to your rooms and grab your belongings. We'll fly tonight to our new home. Tomorrow, we'll begin the process of building a roof over our heads. Together we will forge D'Vaire into a name of honor and nobility, even if it means we do so in isolation. Thank you for having faith in me. I have the same belief in all of you. If we move forward, we do it as more than simply the Draconis Court of D'Vaire. We do it as a family."

Brogan smacked his shoulder in a friendly gesture. "Already you speak with the silvered tongue of a king."

"We must go. His Grace will grow angry, and there's a great deal to do, I'm sure, to plan for the funerals," Aleksander said.

"I can still hardly believe the Emperors are dead," Dravyn replied as he strode toward the door with his sister's arm looped through his.

Since he had not unpacked a single thing in his small bag of belongings, Brogan fetched it from the floor and slung it over his shoulder. "It is indeed a sad day for dragonkind. They ruled but fifty years. I do not want to spend another moment under this roof. If a curse lives here, it resides in the hearts of those who cut down our rulers."

"I wish you'd all had the chance to meet them. Emperor Conley was the most extraordinary gold dragon, and they looked to be very much in love. Let us hope Fate picks a worthy successor. Come, I've already gathered my things. I need only grab my bag. Brogan, you will go with Larissa and Madeline, won't you?" Aleksander asked as he pulled open the door.

"I'd already tasked myself with the duty," Brogan assured him. He followed the two women down the hall and wondered what would happen to the D'Vaire dragons. How long would they languish, forced away from dragonkind? Brogan had to believe Fate would spare them the solitude, given time. He took a moment to ask her to guide Emperor Drystan and Emperor Conley as they made their journey across the veil. Though he'd not met the pair, he mourned their passing all the same. However, their deaths came to be, he hoped the culprits were soon found. He wished that when they were, it would clear Aleksander of his supposed curse. Being different should not have led to them being sent to the far edges of dragonkind, and he worried over what consequence it would have on Aleksander. He had no wish for his best friend to feel like an outcast. As Brogan waited for Larissa and Madeline, he made a vow he would never stray from his duties as duke. No matter what, he would protect his family. Their lives and their honor were all the D'Vaires had left.

4

Some centuries later, Mallent Cottage

Ayden gritted his teeth as the lash connected with his back. Latarian had obviously thrown her weight into the swing, because his skin tore. Seconds later, one of the spells Carvallius had carved into him healed the wound. He did not know which was more agonizing, the woman punishing him or the fight of magic inside him. Supposedly Carvallius had used sorcery somewhere between light and dark to make Latarian's life easier but whatever it was, it left Ayden in constant pain.

Again the leather slapped against him, and his jaw clenched as he absorbed the blow. He hated when Latarian decided a verbal reprimand was not enough to convince him of the errors of his ways. A grunt was all the warning he got before the whip assailed him once more.

"Have you learned your lesson?" Latarian panted out. He might be the one being disciplined but since his warlock rarely lifted a finger beyond beating him regularly, Ayden suspected she grew weary of the strenuous activity.

"I should not have made anything sweet to go with our meal,"

Ayden stated calmly. He wanted to lose his temper and tell her it was insane to punish a man for wanting something besides the bland foods she insisted upon, but he knew better. As ever, he choked down the desire inside him to rage and rally against her.

"I do not know how you can stomach such things," Latarian replied. "Here, take this."

She nudged the handle of the whip into his side and he released the grip he had on the tall poster of her bed to take the instrument of his pain from her. Briefly he thought about calling his magic to torch it, but Fate only knew what form of torture she would think of then, so he stifled his feelings. It was something which should have come easily to him after so much time with her, but it did not. Ayden didn't know why he was not a proper familiar. Since the day he was summoned, he'd struggled to understand his place. Without any other familiars to speak with—he had never known another—how was he to know if it was something all his kind battled with?

"Ayden, gather your tunic and go on," Latarian demanded. "You have a new meal to prepare so we may eat."

Bending over, Ayden scooped up his clothing and tugged it over his head. Then he strode over and replaced the lash onto its hook beside her bed. "We have no more bread," he regrettably informed her as he left the room.

"What do you mean?" she asked as she followed him. "I was to sup with it."

"You threw the last of it to the floor when you saw the pastry I made," Ayden informed her calmly. He had planned on making more bread after the evening meal, but she would only regard that bit of information as an excuse and accuse him of shirking his duties.

"How very clever of you to tell me that after I've finished your lashes. Had I known that to be the case, you can be assured I wouldn't be finished with your punishment."

Trying to find the humble side of himself, Ayden turned and offered her a placid look. "You have my apology."

"You are without a doubt the very worst of familiars. Why do you vex me so? You know I wish for us to be close as intended for a warlock and their familiar. You're an extension of my own magic. I have no wish to quarrel with you. I take no pleasure in whipping you," Latarian said, which made Ayden feel no higher than a lump of dirt. She spoke often of her great desire to call him friend, and he could not understand why he failed each day to please her.

"I do wish to be close to you."

"I know it, Ayden. How could you not want to be? I simply don't understand why you cannot do your duties each day without running afoul of me. Are my demands so great?"

"Of course not, Latarian. I don't know what's wrong with me. You know I've always had this struggle. Fate created me while she was decidedly wrong-headed. I must fight with myself to stay in my place. I've confided such things to you. All the books I've read don't speak of troubles such as this. Why do I feel as if I should be more than a familiar?"

"Clearly, I am too good to you. You forget yourself and suddenly believe you are my equal. You'll do better, Ayden. I will do all I can to aid you. Now run off so we might eat. You'll stay up the night making bread, so we have plenty," Latarian replied.

Ayden hated when she did not allow him to sleep. It made it impossible during those few breaks in his day to sit down and read. He would fall right to sleep and miss out on his opportunity to learn a new spell or be educated on magickind. Latarian had no head for such things, but her grandfather had used one of the rooms in the small cottage as storage for many of his tomes. After all the time that passed since their arrival, Ayden had studied much of them but found he gained more knowledge when returning to them for a second or third pass.

"Of course, Latarian," he responded as he slunk out of the room. He was sad over the tiredness that would plague him on the morrow, and he grappled unhappily with his inability to be a proper familiar.

"How long until the meal is prepared? I'm famished," Latarian said from behind him. He hadn't heard her approach, so her voice had him nearly jumping out of his skin.

"Not long. I made plenty, thinking it could be warmed for tomorrow. It won't take me but a moment to heat it," Ayden told her once his heart stopped galloping in his chest over his fright.

"First, you'll clean the mess on the floor. I have no wish to eat in such filth."

Ayden's belly grumbled, but he did not argue. He grabbed the pail from inside the door and went outside to the well. There was a chill in the air, and he wished he'd taken the time to get his cloak, but he ignored it as he filled his bucket. Full and terribly heavy for a small familiar, Ayden trudged back inside. He would have liked to use magic to make his burden easier, but Latarian forbade him to use any unless she commanded it. After setting the large vessel down, he snatched a brush, kneeled on the floor, and scrubbed. Across the room, Latarian muttered to herself as she took up her needle. The warlock was a horrible seamstress and struggled to do even the most basic mending, but she needed something to fill her days, Ayden supposed.

As he made quick work of the mess she'd created, he wondered how long they'd languished at the cottage. They had no way of know- ing. There were no visitors, and everything around them was enchanted so nothing changed. Seasons did not pass; it was the same autumn weather they experienced upon their arrival. Only two notes had come from Carvallius, and they were devoid of details. He simply told them he was doing all he could to prevent a war. Carvallius had not mentioned the Cwylld or the Grand Warlock, and Ayden wasn't given permission to pen him back.

"Ayden, did I not tell you I was suffering from hunger pains?" Latarian asked crossly. "Hurry up."

Straightening up, Ayden put the brush away and left the bucket to be taken care of later. The entire floor needed a good scrubbing, so perhaps he could attend to it while he was waiting for some of the bread he was required to bake overnight.

"Ayden, answer me."

"I am sorry. I was hurrying and forgot you could not read my thoughts. I've finished with the floor. It won't be but a few moments until your pain is eased," Ayden assured her as he unwrapped the cooked meat he'd placed in a cloth.

"I could think of nothing worse than knowing the meanderings of your small mind. I don't know how you manage as a familiar. Do you simply wake up each morn and wish you were a warlock? Perhaps a great one like my grandfather?"

Ayden smiled as he stoked the fire underneath the foods he'd chosen for their second evening meal. "I do think being a warlock would be a grand thing. Can you imagine wearing a crown and carrying the responsibility of your people? What a great honor that would be to make decisions for their best interests. I think about it more often than I'd like, if I'm being honest."

"You have it all backward. It is the people who should be honored to have a ruler above them. When Grandfather becomes Grand Warlock, the Coven of Warlocks will prosper—I can assure you of that. Imagine all the finery we'll have at the castle. Think on it, Ayden. We'll have servants to do much of your chores, and you'll be able to while away the hours reading those dusty tomes you enjoy."

Ayden had no idea how Carvallius thought he could find himself bearing the title of the Grand Warlock, but he certainly wasn't going to argue the point. He'd been punished enough for the day and was already expected to give up his entire night, so he let it pass....But Ayden did allow himself to fantasize about an existence outside of the cottage. "I do believe a life where I had more time for books and spells would be a wondrous thing. Come, this should be warm enough. I'd barely set it aside to cool before I prepared our first meal."

Latarian bounded across the room to sit down on the wooden bench. She swallowed several bites while Ayden waited for her to speak again. "I do not understand your desire to read. It seems a dreadful waste of time."

"I like to know of spells and of history."

"History is over. Why do you need to know of it? I have knowledge already of all the spells I need know."

Ayden tried not to eat too quickly. Latarian would get angry at him if he took too much from their shared trencher, and she only allowed so much to be served to them both. He often found himself just as hungry when he was done as he'd been when they sat down to dine. "I find myself yearning to know as many spells as I can. I've even tried to craft a few of my own with varying degrees of success."

"I must not give you enough to do in a day if you have such time to do all that," Latarian quipped. Ayden wondered what in the world she could do to add to his duties. *The only thing I don't do is tuck her into her bed at night*, he thought wryly.

"I think on new spells while I am attending to other tasks."

"That would explain why I often find your duties done in a haphazard way," Latarian stated with a pointed look at him.

Deciding a subject change would benefit him, Ayden asked, "Have you by chance received another missive from your grandfather?"

Latarian's bottom lip poked out slightly. "I have not. I wish I knew what was keeping him from giving me news. I grew weary of this dreadful place the moment I arrived."

"It is difficult to know how much time has passed since we made the journey."

"It feels as if it's been an eternity."

On that Ayden could agree. Each day seemed to last forever before blending into another endless night. Ayden would give anything to find something to break up the monotony of his life. "It would be nice to see beyond these four walls."

"Damn that Grand Warlock T'Eirick for making us wait so," Latarian grumbled. "It will be so much better when Grandfather's in charge. We won't ever be cast aside to the ends of the earth again. I hope Grandfather makes him pay for all the misery we've spent here."

"He will ensure the warlocks aren't troubled by the Cwylld elven."

"Let us just hope Grandfather does it soon. I do not know how much longer I can bear this cottage."

Like Latarian, Ayden was fed up and wanted a return to having time of his own. He wanted space from Latarian and to speak to another soul besides her. Then he could find out if the struggles he dealt with inside him were a fault of his own or if all familiars found themselves with an ongoing war in their heart and mind. He didn't know if Carvallius would reach his goals, but he had to hope he did, so someday Ayden's life would change—and the sooner the better.

5

Present Day

"Have you managed to clean my best dress?" Latarian demanded as she walked up to where Ayden was scrubbing it in his wooden bucket.

He pulled it from the water and examined it. "I believe so. I can see none of the stains."

"I cannot stomach the idea of wearing a garment with your blood upon it. Use a cleansing spell on it."

Ayden stifled his sigh. She had purposely told him not to use magic when his blood had splashed onto her lavender day dress as she beat him. Determined not to let his temper fly and lead him into more trouble, he chanted a few words to remove all stains from the fabric. "Shall I put it outside to dry?"

"Have you not a spell to do that?"

Without giving an answer, he gathered a bit of power and seconds later, it was bone-dry. He carried it to her room and put it in the trunk along with the other purple clothing she preferred to wear. It was her favorite hue, and she refused to consider any other color. When he returned to the main area of the cabin, he found his warlock staring out the window.

"Is aught amiss?"

She turned to stare at him with a quizzical expression upon her face. "How long do you believe we have languished here?"

Ayden shook his head as he could offer her no clear answer. "Centuries."

"I know Grandfather has a great many duties, but I grow weary of this life. Surely he's quelled whatever nonsense rose between the Cwylld and the warlocks by now."

Feeling bold despite his recent punishment, Ayden offered a suggestion. "Perhaps we should scry and ask Fate to give us some insight on what is going on in the world."

"Go and get my mirror."

Ayden wasted no time and dashed back into her chamber. Finding the object lying on the table next to her bed, he snatched it up. Racing into the living space, he handed her the silver looking glass. "Shall I use my magic?" he asked. Despite her great wealth of power, she always insisted Ayden be the one to cast anything.

"We shall pool our resources, I think. I've decided I wish to leave the cottage. We shall ask Fate to send us to a safe place. I don't want to burden Grandfather with our presence, but if I stay another day here, I shall go mad."

"A safe place. That's where I will put my focus. After all, we don't know if something has befallen your grandfather, and that's why he's kept his silence for so long." As soon as the words left his lips Ayden regretted them.

Latarian's eyes narrowed; then her hand connected strongly with his cheek. "He is fine. There is no living soul powerful enough to harm him."

"My apologies," Ayden replied, ignoring the sting of her slap.

"Now let us focus," Latarian demanded as she laid the mirror on the floor. They both kneeled next to it across from one another. She closed her eyes and placed her palms just above it.

Ayden did the same and then whispered, "A safe place."

Their combined magic tingled over his skin as he focused on finding a haven, and he lifted his lashes. The looking glass turned black as a strange structure came into view. It was an enormous dwelling, and Ayden had no idea what to make of it. Then it disappeared, and a single word appeared.

"What is a D'Vairedraconis?" Latarian blurted out.

"Perhaps an ally of your grandfather?"

Latarian dropped her hands to her sides, and her face was strained. *Perhaps she's trying to recall if she had ever heard the name before*, Ayden thought as he waited for her to answer. "It is a possibility, I suppose. Fate believes we will be safe there."

"Perhaps he can give us your grandfather's direction."

"I would rest easier knowing how his life is going as Grand Warlock."

"Shall we travel to the dwelling?"

"Rather strange home this D'Vairedraconis has," Latarian mused. "Did you see how large? Adorned with so many windows, he must be very rich. Go, Ayden. Gather our things. Let us not anger Fate by not going to visit Grandfather's ally."

Springing to his feet, Ayden once again found himself scurrying to her bedchamber to gather her things. His own were kept in the living area where he slept—so he need not worry over that, he mused as he carefully removed her dresses from the trunk. The beloved books that kept him company would stay at the cottage. Latarian would grow angry should he wish to take them. She barely tolerated him reading the tomes.

He grinned as he packed. For an untold number of centuries, he'd been forced to stay within the four walls of the tiny cottage. It would be good to meet others and see the world. There was no way of knowing what waited for them or how Carvallius would react to them disobeying his orders, but if Latarian were willing to leave, Ayden would not gainsay her. After all, it was his greatest wish to speak to other familiars—or anyone else for that matter. Ayden had no idea why Latarian came to the decision to make this day different, but he was exhilarated. It had taken an eternity for this moment to arrive.

Ayden stood at Latarian's side as they stared up at the massive structure. "I can feel no warlock or familiars inside," he whispered to her.

"Grandfather has a great many allies, not all of them warlocks."

"It's bigger than I would've believed possible."

"Not as grand as Castle Mallent."

Deciding not to comment since he didn't agree, Ayden shifted his weight from one foot to the other. "Shall we see if anyone dwells inside?"

Latarian marched up to the two large doors and pounded her fist on it. Ayden lifted her trunk and came to stand at her side. She offered him a dark look that promised retribution when the door whipped open. Turning, Ayden found himself peering up at a tall woman with strange orange eyes that had scales in their midst. She was wearing breeches in a coarse fabric he did not recognize and a shirt with no tunic over it. It was most unusual for a woman to be dressed in such things, but Ayden liked her bright smile.

"Hey, can I help you?" the woman asked; then her gaze widened in surprise. "Your clothes are incredible. They look like genuine fourteenth-century stuff."

Latarian said not a word, and Ayden couldn't address the stranger without her permission. He gave Latarian his attention only to observe her standing there, slack-jawed. Ayden didn't know if it was due to the woman's shocking attire or if Latarian had another bug plaguing her mind. Perhaps she was regretting their decision to call upon Fate, but Ayden wasn't. Deciding upon a discreet cough to help Latarian gather her wits, Ayden waited patiently for her to do or say something.

Instead, it was the woman at the door who broke the silence. "Your throat sounds dry. Did you need a drink of water? Come on inside. Noirin made cookies earlier. We'll eat a few and wash them down with milk."

The stranger grabbed Ayden's arm, and he nearly dropped the trunk still in his hands. It bobbled but he secured it as he did his best to keep up with the woman's long strides. She pulled him down a short hallway, and then the space opened into an enormous room full of windows. What caught Ayden's eye was a second woman even taller than the first.

"Hey, Noirin, can we have those cookies you made earlier? We'll need milk too since I think the little guy here's got a sore throat," the lady who had a hold on his arm said.

"Larissa, who the hell are these people?" Noirin asked as Larissa finally released Ayden. His burden was heavy, and Ayden was interested in tasting the cookies, so he set the trunk down. Latarian walked toward him, and she did not have a happy expression upon her face.

"I'm not sure," Larissa responded with a shrug. "They were outside, so I invited them in." She opened a door and light spilled from it. Ayden had no idea how she managed it as he sensed no magic inside her.

"Brogan's going to lose his mind when he finds out," Noirin stated dryly, then turned to where Ayden and Latarian were standing. "I'm sorry. We're being very rude. I'm Noirin—or Noir, and this is Larissa."

"I am Latarian, granddaughter of the great Carvallius of Mallent, and you need not know his name," she said, pointing to Ayden. "He is of no consequence."

One of Noirin's jet black brows rose, and she pursed her lips slightly. "I'm not sure how to respond to that, but it's nice to meet you, Latarian. I can't say I like the idea of yelling 'Hey you' whenever I need to ask him a question."

Feeling bold and deciding he wished to know these strangers better, Ayden lifted his chin and hoped he didn't pay too dearly for his actions. "Ayden. I am called Ayden."

Latarian examined him through narrowed eyes. "Always, you forget your place."

Ayden's gaze dropped down to the gleaming board in front of him where Noirin had set down a plate with the round cookies piled upon it. Larissa set down two clear vessels full of milk. "My apologies."

"Eat up," Noirin invited. "Is there anything we can do for you besides give you a snack?"

"I seek D'Vairedraconis. I believe him to be an ally of my grandfather. I wish for news of him, and we were told this was a place of safety," Latarian said.

"This is the Draconis Court of D'Vaire. Everyone under this roof is D'Vairedraconis," Noirin replied as she leaned against the stone surface in front of Ayden. His mouth watered as he fixated upon the treats and milk, but he knew better than to avail himself of them without Latarian's permission.

"How many call this castle home? If I must have speech with all of them to learn of my grandfather, then I am up to the task," Latarian stated haughtily. Ayden sincerely hoped she did not anger the helpful women who called themselves D'Vairedraconis.

"It's not a castle. It's just a house, and there are only five of us here right now. Usually, it's six, but Brogan's traveling again," Noirin supplied. Ayden got a whiff of the cookies and nearly swooned at the tantalizing scent.

"Brogan. I take it he is your leader. I assume the rest of you are his servants. I must know of his whereabouts," Latarian retorted. The treats were turning into a siren for Ayden, and he subtly moved closer to them.

"Actually, none of us are servants, but we do have a leader, King Aleksander. Brogan's one of his two dukes."

"A king? Are you human, then? This must indeed be a mistake. My grandfather would not ally himself with a mere human."

"We're not human. We're dragon shifters," Noirin said stiffly.

"What is a shifter?" Latarian demanded.

"A shifter's someone who shares their soul with a beast and can transform into that beast whenever they want. For us, that's a dragon. Which is why Draconis is tacked onto our last name," Noirin explained.

"Truly, you share your soul with that of a dragon?" Ayden asked in astonished wonder. He was fascinated by tales of the legendary beasts, but he'd believed them to be fables, even though he possessed a dragon mirage of his own. It was a secret he'd kept from Latarian since the day of his summoning. Instinctively he understood; she would not be thrilled to know Ayden had an ability that didn't exist in a single book he'd ever read.

"Yep. Dragons. We're the coolest shifters ever. Our Emperor rules everybody. He leads the Council of Sorcery and Shifters," Larissa boasted.

"I thought it to be the Council of Sorcery," Latarian retorted, her tone suggesting disbelief at all the news that these dragon women had imparted.

"It was until about two hundred years ago when basically all the cool people left Europe and came here. Shifters were invited to join, and Emperor Chrysander Draconis was put in charge," Larissa enlightened them.

"A king leads you. He must have great power amongst the Council. Surely this is how he became an ally of my grandfather."

"I am indeed a king, but I'm afraid I have no power to speak of. I'm considered cursed amongst dragonkind, and the world at large ignores the six of us. You're looking for your grandfather?" A man even taller than the dragon women entered the large room where they stood. He was dressed similarly to the women and had black hair, with what appeared to be a layer of dark blue underneath that fell in varying lengths to just past his shoulders. The dragon king had eyes that bore the same mix of black and blue found in his sleek tresses. They too had scales and around the pupils, a tiny ring of silver and one of gold showed in their depths.

"Cursed? What kind of curse has befallen you?" Ayden blurted out.

"It's a long, boring story of misunderstandings, bad timing, and superstition. Not really all that interesting. I'm Aleksander, by the way," the exotic D'Vairedraconis offered.

"It is indeed a pleasure, Your Highness," Latarian replied with a curtsy. She tugged on Ayden's sleeve and he bowed. He hoped to make a good impression on King Aleksander D'Vairedraconis, so he might help them find Carvallius and if they could not join Latarian's grandfather, perhaps this dragon shifter would give them refuge. Anything was preferable to returning to the cottage.

6

"We don't really use titles around here. Call me Aleksander," the king said.

"Thank you, Aleksander. I hope you will be able to offer me the information I seek," Latarian said. Her tone had become increasingly superior, and Ayden hoped it did not get them banished back to their tiny home.

As he worried, he took one step closer to the plate of treats. His fingers itched to grab a cookie and taste it. His mind was convinced it was not something to be missed. It wasn't decent for him to ask many questions of the king or his kin, so Ayden concentrated on his rumbling belly instead of the people around him.

"Latarian is the granddaughter of Carvallius of Mallent," Noirin told her king.

Aleksander's face worked its way into a scowl; then he burst out in gales of laughter. When he was done with his hilarity, he gave Latarian his attention. "Okay, the outfits are pretty good, but if you want to parade around pretending to be from the fourteenth century when Carvallius of Mallent was still alive, I'd suggest you pick someone more popular."

"What say you?" Latarian demanded.

"Carvallius of Mallent died in what? 1367? 1368? Something like that? And trust me, nobody misses him. He was a traitor to his own people—he tricked the Cwylld elven into attacking the Coven of Warlocks. Apparently, he thought somehow that would make him Grand Warlock. Instead the Cwylld killed *all* the warlocks," Aleksander explained.

"My grandfather was no traitor," Latarian bit out.

"Look, I don't know what this is all about, but Carvallius made no secret of his intentions, and he also left behind his journals. He was a madman hell-bent on destroying Grand Warlock T'Eirick and Grand Summoner Saura of Leolinnia. The only mystery left is what happened to their two sons. They had teenage twins whose bodies weren't found. They were said to be the most powerful warlocks ever born and were destined to take over their parents' roles at some point. Occasionally some rumor will surface that they're alive somewhere, but shit like that is inevitable," Aleksander said. "The Council does keep the story fresh, so history doesn't get repeated."

"The destruction of the warlocks led Arch Lich Chander Daray, who took over the Council after Grand Warlock T'Eirick died, to resurrect a race called the Order of the Fallen Knights to defend us all and enforce laws," Noirin added.

Ayden's head was spinning, and this time it was not because of the intoxicating smell of the cookies. It was no secret in the Mallent household that Carvallius was an ally to the Cwylld and that he coveted the title of Grand Warlock. The words of the dragons were plausible and terrifying to Ayden.

"This cannot be true," Latarian shrieked as the skin on her face mottled with color in fury.

"Larissa, will you grab the history book of races from the library?" Aleksander asked, and the brunette hurried out of the room. "Maybe if you read it for yourselves, you'll believe me. Now tell me who you really are."

Latarian's expression was pinched and she gave Ayden's back a push. "Tell him."

"I am Ayden of Mallent and this is my warlock, Latarian. We were sent to a cottage by Carvallius of Mallent in the year 1367. He bade us stay safe while he tried to stop a war between the Cwylld and the Coven of Warlocks," Ayden whispered.

Larissa returned with the book and handed it to Aleksander, who flipped through the pages, then set it down on the counter.

"Go on, read it for yourselves," he said.

Ayden and Latarian leaned over to do as the king requested. By the time Ayden's eyes skimmed over the words—a repeat of everything Aleksander had already told them—he was weak in the knees.

"These are lies," Latarian stated. "Horrible, *terrible* lies. My grandfather was a wondrous man. It was T'Eirick who was ever ignoring him and not paying heed to his words. I cannot believe this of the man who raised me. I must clear his name. Fate has brought me here for this purpose."

"Have you really spent over six centuries in a cottage with no clue about the outside world?" Larissa asked.

"It's enchanted. Not even the seasons pass. We had no notion of how much time we'd lost nor did we know the fate of our people. I can barely convince myself of these truths, and yet I do not know why anyone would fabricate such a story," Ayden explained.

"Come on, you haven't even helped yourselves to the cookies and milk," Noirin encouraged as she pushed the platter closer to Ayden. "We'll have a snack and figure out what to do."

"Latarian, might I have one of these cookies?" Ayden asked.

"My grandfather's dead, and all you can think of is food," Latarian snarled as she swiped her hand through the air. Her eyes filled with tears. "Oh, who cares if you eat yourself sick? I shall simply stand here as my heart breaks."

It was not that Ayden lacked compassion for the loss of Latarian's grandfather, but he could do nothing to lessen her pain. "I'm sorry, Latarian. I would not see you suffer."

She sobbed into her hands, and Ayden grew bold enough to offer her a pat on the shoulder. Just as quickly as the storm began, she lifted her head and her eyes blazed with fierce determination. "I will clear his name. If it is the last thing I do, I shall make sure this world knows what an incredible man Carvallius of Mallent was."

"We'll help how we can," Aleksander assured her softly. "I can contact the Emperor's office and see if he might be willing to meet with us."

Since he'd secured permission, Ayden snuck a hand out and slowly slid a cookie off the plate. The bottom of it was rough against his fingers and when he inhaled, his eyes nearly crossed with the pleasure. Biting into it was pure bliss, and he purred his delight as he chewed.

"Good, right?" Larissa asked.

"Most delicious," Ayden said, though his mouth was still full.

"Noir, will you show Latarian and Ayden to a couple of guest rooms?" Aleksander asked.

"Sure," Noirin responded. "Follow me, guys. We'll finish our cookies later."

With a great deal of regret, Ayden left the sweet treats and hefted Latarian's trunk. He fell into place behind her as she sniffled her way after Noirin. Once there was some distance between them and the dragon shifter, Latarian spoke softly to him. "You will unpack my things, beginning with the whip."

Ayden gave a nod of acknowledgment. He was not pleased to start his life in King D'Vairedraconis's home with a beating, but there was no way to change her mind, and his heart was full of misery for her. The loss of Carvallius had to be a great one, and perhaps if she were to vent some of her frustrations out on his poor self, it would lessen her grief. It was, after all, his duty as her familiar to see to her comfort.

~

For several days, Ayden and Latarian adjusted to life outside their cottage. The world had changed drastically, and Ayden was doing his best to catch up. He'd started by crafting a spell to allow him to speak like the dragons. Ayden offered to cast it on Latarian, but she'd refused. She preferred not to change anything about herself, including her mode of dress. Larissa had made it her mission to help them acclimate and purchased all sorts of jeans, T-shirts, and sneakers for Ayden and Latarian. The dragon also made Ayden an entire drawer full of brightly colored pajamas. Latarian turned her nose up at all of it, but Ayden was more than willing to adapt.

Latarian hadn't been thrilled, and blood had splattered all over his pale denim the first time he'd worn them, courtesy of her lash. The next day when he returned to his old clothing to please her, the D'Vaires asked him about his decision to revert, and Latarian pretended to be as clueless as they were. Then she'd whipped him that night for forcing her to allow him to do what the dragons wanted. Ayden was caught between the kindness of the shifters and Latarian's anger, which made him apprehensive of each decision he made or word he said.

While it was great not to be confined to a tiny stone house, Ayden still struggled to understand why he was unable to be a good familiar. A weight settled over him as it was a problem without a remedy. The warlocks and their familiars were all dead—and history believed it to be the direct responsibility of Carvallius of Mallent as well as the Cwylld elven. The tribe hadn't survived the war unscathed; only perhaps a dozen or so still lived. Ayden could not say he had many kind feelings toward them though—they'd murdered women and children. It embarrassed Ayden that he was part of the family that led the Coven of Warlocks to their doom.

To begin Latarian's mission, he was preparing to travel to the Council of Sorcery and Shifters Headquarters in a place called Las Vegas to plead the case of Carvallius. He hoped the dragon emperor did not kick them out of his office or decide they needed to pay with their lives for being Mallents. After securing the D'Vaire sash Aleksander gave him, Ayden tugged on a long cloak. Some traditions had carried over from his time, and magickind still wore them. They were required by the Council, and Ayden was proud to represent the Coven of Warlocks.

Ayden smoothed a hand over his unruly red locks and left the sanctity of his bedroom. It was the best thing about the D'Vaire household—he had a refuge where Latarian refused to tread and the softest mattress he could have imagined. Walking into the living room, Ayden found everyone waiting for him.

"Hey, Squirt. Nice suit," Aleksander greeted him.

Knowing the dragon was teasing, Ayden grinned. "Squirt, is it? Well, at least I'm not freakishly tall."

"Ayden, mind your manners," Latarian snapped and the irritation on her face promised retribution.

Aleksander chuckled. "It's okay, Latarian. I encourage a laid-back atmosphere under my roof. Ayden's free to say whatever he likes."

"Of course, Aleksander. I understand this is your court, and I would not gainsay a king," Latarian said prettily, but Ayden wasn't fooled. He was going to do his best to spend as much time around Aleksander as he could, so she was unable to berate him.

"All right, ready to go?" Aleksander asked. "I have a picture of the teleportation area closest to the Emperor's office. The druids have a large company called Dérive which they use to teleport people, so they built these areas everywhere and all magickind can use them."

"Ayden, teleport us," Latarian ordered.

Giving her a nod and asking the dragons to close their eyes so they wouldn't get dizzy or queasy, Ayden cast the spell to the place in Aleksander's picture. When he lifted his lashes, they were in an opulent building with people rushing all around. There were shifters in suits with sashes and magickind in luxurious cloaks. Ayden thought it was beautiful, and his smile was brilliant.

"Okay, let's figure out how to find the Emperor," Aleksander commanded as he led them down a long hallway. After he found a directory to get them on the right path, they were hassled slightly— going through two security checkpoints with only guest passes. The D'Vaires were ostracized from not only the dragons but the entire Council of Sorcery and Shifters. After a torturous ride up an elevator, they were asked to take a seat in a stunning waiting area.

Ayden parked himself on a smooth dragonskin couch. "Isn't it strange for you to sit on dragon scales?" he whispered to Aleksander.

"Nope. Our beasts shed them regularly. Some people every few weeks, others take months or longer. It's how you've got that sash with my dragonskin. I'm the only bi-color dragon on the planet. If I didn't shed them, it'd be impossible to recreate it."

"Thank for telling me. I like learning new things."

Aleksander winked at the same time the assistant at the enormous desk informed them that the Emperor was ready to see them. Ayden stood and waited for Latarian to get in front of him; then he followed her into the Emperor's office. Safely tucked behind her, Ayden took stock of his surroundings.

Once they entered, a dark-haired man with black eyes rose from a comfortable-looking chair. Under his suit he wore a dress shirt without a tie, and his dragonskin sash had the word "Draconis" embroidered on it in bold, white letters. A few feet away was the Emperor, whose regal bearing commanded everyone's attention.

As tall as Aleksander, who stood at six inches over six feet, his coloring was similar to the first man, but the gold ring around his pupils proclaimed his rank. The Emperor's gleaming crown glinted on a high shelf behind him. It appeared he did not bother with it in the confines of his office.

Coming around a modern desk of mostly glass, the Emperor walked toward Ayden and the rest of their group. He smiled and extended his hand in greeting. "King Aleksander, I apologize that it's taken so long to meet you in person, but you certainly haven't made it easy on me. Why has it taken you so long to visit Council Headquarters?"

"Your Majesty, it's a pleasure to meet you. Thank you so much for taking the time to see us. I wasn't sure I was welcome. It's pretty common knowledge that everyone thinks I'm cursed," Aleksander explained after their handshake.

"I think it's been a few hundred years since I've even heard the word curse, let alone met anyone who still believed in them. This is my brother, Imperial Duke Damian Draconis," he said with a wave toward the man in all black. The rest of the introductions were made, and Ayden was careful not to overstep his bounds, so he greeted them and never made eye contact.

After they were invited to sit, the Emperor returned to his desk. He was flummoxed to learn about Latarian and her connection to Carvallius of Mallent. His eyes grew wide with surprise when Latarian hopped to her feet.

"I have read what history thinks of my grandfather, but it simply holds no truth. He was not the type of man to betray his race in such a manner," she informed him.

"Unfortunately, your people died before I met a single sorcerer. All I know comes from the same history books you've read. I think your best bet would be to visit the offices of the Spectra Wizardry. They should be able to help you start your search to clear your grandfather's name if history has indeed treated him unfairly," Emperor Chrysander replied.

"History has been most unfair. Thank you for your guidance. I will go to the Spectra Wizardry and find the evidence I need." Latarian's eyes glowed with zealotry, but she did return to her seat.

"Thank you, Your Majesty. It's very important to Latarian that she learns all that she can about the war between the warlocks and the Cwylld elven," Aleksander added.

"From what I've read, it was brutal. The Cwylld elven didn't stop until every man, woman, and child with warlock blood was dead. If you like, I can call the Prism Wizard and see if he has time to meet with you this afternoon," Emperor Chrysander offered.

"That would be much appreciated, Your Majesty," Latarian responded.

Emperor Chrysander made a quick call to the Prism Wizard and after resting the phone back in the cradle said, "He'd love to meet with you. King Aleksander, you need to arrange to have your entire family properly registered as members of the Council. Those visitor passes we sent aren't going to continue to allow you to get through security. Court D'Vaire was somehow lost when we went from paper to electronic records. Your Highness, I think it's best if Latarian and

Ayden are recognized as permanent members of Court D'Vaire. I trust that's okay with you?"

Ayden held his breath. He wanted to stay with the dragons and hoped Aleksander would keep them under his roof.

"Of course, Your Majesty, it would be an honor to add Latarian and Ayden to our family," Aleksander said. Ayden was so pleased, he was smiling like an idiot. He would dearly love to have the D'Vaires as family and hoped someday he could forget the word Mallent—especially if Latarian's quest to find some scrap of information to clear Carvallius's name went unfulfilled.

"King Aleksander, before you leave I must say, I'm quite intrigued by your eyes. I've never seen a king with gold in them before," Imperial Duke Damian commented.

"It appeared at the same time as the silver and just like the blue in my scales and hair, I can't explain it," Aleksander said quietly.

"I assumed you'd added the blue. It grew that way after you shifted for the first time?" the Emperor asked curiously.

"Yes, and we even tried dyeing it black to match the rest, but my hair refused to cooperate."

"I find it quite striking, and I plan on convincing Chrysander to take a trip to your home in Arizona to see you shift," the Imperial Duke responded.

"No need to talk me into it—I'd consider it an honor to see the world's only bi-color dragon," Emperor Draconis said. An open invitation was extended by Aleksander, and Ayden hoped it meant his new king was no longer ostracized by his people. In the brief time he had known the D'Vaires, he'd found them all welcoming and kind. He could not imagine anyone finding fault with his new family.

7

I t only took a few minutes for their small group to find the Spectra Wizardry. Ayden practically salivated over the large library attached to it. He wondered if he would ever get the chance to go inside—Ayden sincerely hoped so. When they reached the door to the Prism Wizard's office, the man himself was waiting for them. Ayden was shocked at his snow-white hair and his wrinkled visage.

It was unusual for magickind to appear so elderly, and Ayden didn't know what caused the change. His senses told him it was not due to his age; he was only a few centuries old. Without a word, the Prism Wizard waved them into his cluttered office. Ayden followed behind Latarian and marveled over all the books scattered around the space.

"I must say, I was in disbelief when I received the phone call from His Majesty telling me that he had a warlock in his office, but I could sense your magic as soon as you got to the outer office. Of course, technically you're not a warlock," Prism Wizard Vadimas Porfyra said after they were closed inside.

"I most certainly am a warlock," Latarian countered angrily and propped one hand on her hip.

"No, most decidedly not. You see, you're the only known representative of your race, but you are a woman. Though men ruled warlocks for thousands of years, there were female leaders at one time. Those ladies were called Grand Witches, and your people were known as the Coven of Witches. To be historically accurate, you should now be called a witch. May I see your wrist?"

With a bewildered expression, Latarian lifted the hem of her sleeve to display her arm for the Prism Wizard. "What do you expect to find on my wrist?"

"Most unusual that Fate didn't mark you as the leader of your race. If she had, there would be a gold circle here on the inside of your wrist in a design selected by Fate. Grand Warlock T'Eirick had a lion's head and before him, the warlocks were represented by a bird thought to be a raven. The Grand Summoner, who was just below the Grand Warlock and his mate in rank, bore the same mark but in silver. Grand Summoner Saura had a unique one in both colors since she was the mate of the Grand Warlock as well as the Grand Summoner. King Aleksander, your eyes are both gold and silver. Fate must have some special authority to bestow on you," Prism Wizard Vadimas remarked as he released Latarian and peered up at the tall dragon king.

Aleksander let out a choked laugh. "Fate certainly hasn't explained to me what that authority is, and I've had the gold for centuries."

"Perhaps that authority hasn't been bestowed upon you yet, but I'm sure things will work out as they are meant in time. Latarian, your familiar seems quite shy standing there behind you."

"Ayden, stand next to me so the Prism Wizard can have speech with you. There is no need to fear him."

Ayden wasn't scared of Vadimas, but he had a healthy amount of respect for Latarian's lash. He obeyed her words and took a step so he was at her side. He offered Vadimas a smile.

"Your eyes don't match that of your witch. They're similar in color, but yours are a darker green. Is that perhaps some blue peeking through?" he asked as the Prism Wizard took two strides to put him only inches from Ayden's face.

"I've noticed it myself," Ayden confided. "When I cast strong spells, the navy almost takes over the green."

"Most interesting. There's something else strange, but it's hard to determine if my feeling is correct with the two of you standing so close together. Ayden, would you be kind enough to join me near the window?"

Ayden glanced at Latarian, who nodded. Vadimas had already crossed the width of his office, and he beckoned Ayden to follow him. When Ayden did, Vadimas once again ventured into his personal space. He was so close that Ayden noticed the brown of the Prism Wizard's irises shrink when Vadimas squinted.

"Definitely a blue, a navy, nearly black," he muttered; then the Prism Wizard cast his inquisitive gaze in Latarian's direction. "The green appears almost an overlay of color, as if it's masking the blue. Very strange indeed. I've never seen the like, and even the elemental familiars have the exact same eye color as their summoner, but that's not the reason I've asked you to join me over here. It appears my hunch was correct. Your power is stronger than Latarian's. I have no way to explain such a phenomenon."

"Surely you must be mistaken," Latarian stated starchily.

"I rarely make such mistakes. Perhaps you've recently restored his power, and I'm sensing an overflow of magic?"

The Prism Wizard's words confused Ayden. Clearing his suddenly dry throat he said, "Latarian doesn't restore my power. She doesn't need to, I have plenty of my own."

Vadimas's bushy brows rose in surprise. "That simply defies logic. You're a familiar—you were summoned from Latarian's magic. You should lack the ability to create your own power, which is why you would need her to resupply you. I can't make sense of this. Most odd indeed."

"I assure you if there's anything odd, it is due to Ayden himself. He's struggled his entire life to fit into his proper role. I find him adequate on only his best days," Latarian responded as she straightened her spine as if ready to battle.

"It is also interesting that, Ayden, you're male while your witch is female. Normally familiars are the same sex as their caster," the Prism Wizard stated.

"How many witches have you known, Prism Wizard?" Latarian asked sharply. "I have no desire to continue discussing Ayden and his failures. I wish to speak to you regarding my grandfather."

"I see...you are of course, the first witch I've met. I'd be happy to discuss your grandfather. I can mull over the reasons why Ayden differs from other familiars after you leave," he replied. Vadimas strode away from Ayden and sat at his desk. He poked at the keys on his computer. "We've spent the last few years creating a computerized database of all known magickind, both living and dead. Let's see what it says about you and your family."

"All that information's in the computer?" Ayden asked. He was finding it more difficult to stifle his curiosity when around others and luckily, Latarian barely glanced at him. Hoping she was too wrapped up in her search to reprimand him, he stepped closer to the desk.

"No worries, Squirt. We'll get you a laptop when we get home," Aleksander promised.

"Thanks. I'd be very grateful to have one. Latarian too," he said, remembering his warlock—*witch* he mentally corrected himself.

"Truly Ayden, what would I do with such a contraption?" she asked. Ayden didn't respond to her; he was thrilled she hadn't forbidden him to get one just because she wasn't interested.

"Ah yes. Latarian. There you are," Vadimas interjected. "I'm glad your parents were thoughtful enough to give you such a unique name —there's only a single record. Carvallius was indeed your grandfather, but for some reason you're listed as a novice. Strange, novices can't summon familiars, and I can feel your magic. It's quite above that rank. It doesn't appear to be a clerical error. The warlock elders recorded you that way in three different censuses. You were listed at the age of one hundred and fifty-seven at the time of your presumed death."

"My magic developed later in life than most," Latarian snapped.

Vadimas stopped muttering to himself and stared at her in amazement. "That's intriguing. I'd certainly love to hear about your transformation. Your story would be an inspiration to those born with little power."

Ayden agreed; it was a tale he hadn't heard. He'd always thought he was the one with oddities, not Latarian.

"I'm afraid I must remain focused on fixing my grandfather's good name. Mayhap when the world knows the truth, I can inspire those less fortunate," Latarian retorted.

"Carvallius is the one who left the proof behind in his journals and correspondence, which explained his plans. He tricked the Cwylld, and they became fixated on annihilating the warlocks. If you wish to see the originals, you'll have to contact the Arch Wizard in the Consilium Veneficus. I wish you the best of luck....They aren't fond of anyone within the Council," Vadimas responded as he got to his feet. His eyes were full of pity—Latarian was unlikely to be successful on her quest.

"Consilium Veneficus?" she asked.

"Yes, I'm afraid two hundred years ago when the Council decided to relocate, many wizards and some small pockets of magickind and shifters chose to stay in Europe. They started their own government and cut off all communication with those who chose to travel to North America," Vadimas informed them.

Latarian lifted her chin. "I shall write to them. I must see these supposed journals and letters. How would anyone beyond his beloved granddaughter be able to say if it is even written in his hand? Carvallius of Mallent was the envy of many, and I can well see any number of them leaving behind this nonsense to lay the blame upon his shoulders."

"I hope they'll be amenable to your request," was all the Prism Wizard said.

"Thank you for your time, Prism Wizard. I am fully prepared to do whatever it takes to clear my grandfather's good name."

They said their farewells to the kind wizard and left his office. Luckily for Ayden, Aleksander was starving, and they stopped to have a delicious meal at a buffet inside Council Headquarters. Ayden simply stared for two minutes straight as he studied the bounty in front of him. Since Latarian couldn't stop him, he filled three consecutive platefuls with nothing but cake—which he decided was his favorite thing on the planet. As he gorged, Latarian chattered on and on about Carvallius and her plans to rewrite history.

It gave Ayden a great deal of respect for Aleksander as the D'Vaire king offered polite responses and a promise to help, however he could. But he was clear that he was not familiar with the Council, let alone the Consilium Veneficus. When Aleksander and Latarian were finished eating, their king suggested they leave for the teleportation area. Before they headed out, Ayden promised his belly he would find a way to return to the restaurant next time they were in town.

Busy gawking at all the smartly dressed people around him as they strolled down the hallway toward their destination, Ayden stumbled over a large object in his path. He barely managed to break his fall, but Ayden was pleased he hadn't landed on his face.

"I'm so sorry," the object said. Ayden glanced down in surprise as the "object" turned out to be a beautiful redhead with gray eyes full of tears.

"Ayden, mind your feet," Latarian snapped. "Look what you've done to this poor creature. She must be in considerable pain—she's crying terribly. You'll feel the bite of my lash when we return home."

His face burned as it flushed with color, and he mumbled an apology to the floor.

"Oh no, I'm fine. Really. I—"

The petite woman was wringing her hands and searching for words when Aleksander gently interjected. "Latarian, calm down. It was an accident, Ayden tripped over her. We're terribly sorry, ma'am." He stretched out a hand to help the lady from the floor, but she was oblivious to his attempt. Though Latarian didn't comment, her face was pinched with anger.

"No really, it's my fault. I was totally in the way. I'm sorry. You could've been hurt. I'm glad you didn't fall," the woman with the tear-stained cheeks said.

"I didn't mean to cause you any harm. I'm terribly sorry," Ayden offered.

"No harm done, I promise. My name's Blodwen, by the way. I'm really sorry about being in the way. It's just...well, I got fired."

Latarian's brows met in the middle in disbelief. "Someone set you ablaze?"

"No, it's my job. They told me I no longer work there. That's why I'm sitting here crying. What am I going to do without a job?" she asked. "It's my fault. Everyone in the Order of Necromancia hates me because I refuse to summon my sentinel. I've been fired from so many jobs. They always have an excuse, but that's the real reason." She wrapped her arms around her knees and sobbed in earnest. Unable to watch anyone suffer, Ayden ignored Latarian and sat down on the floor next to Blodwen.

"I'm sorry you've lost your job," he said. Using a bit of magic, he created a handkerchief for her tears, which he handed to her as soon as she lifted her head.

"Thanks. You're sweet. I hope you didn't hurt yourself tripping over me," Blodwen replied.

"I'm not hurt."

She craned her head to peer up at Latarian and Aleksander. "You guys don't have to sit here and listen to me whine. I'll just have to find another job somewhere else."

"Have you always worked here at Council Headquarters?" Aleksander asked.

"For the last three decades anyway."

"Allow me to introduce you to Latarian D'Vaire, formerly of Mallent. She needs someone who can help her with a history project. No one in our family knows where to start or anything besides the most basic Council stuff. We've been isolated for the last six centuries or so. Maybe you'd like to work for us? My name is King Aleksander D'Vairedraconis. The little guy next to you is Ayden D'Vaire," Aleksander said. Once again, he held out his hand to Blodwen, and this time she allowed him to help her stand.

"I'd love to work for you, Your Highness," Blodwen exclaimed.

Ayden grinned and got to his feet. He loved the sound of D'Vaire after his name, and he wanted to get to know Blodwen; she seemed very kind. Aleksander and Blodwen exchanged contact information, and the D'Vaire king promised to find out what he needed to do to secure her employment with them. Blodwen was all smiles as she assured him she'd assist how she could and that she would contact the Order of Necromancia to get permission to transfer to a dragon court.

"I'm really sorry I tripped you, Ayden," Blodwen said.

"Don't worry about it," Ayden assured her. They said their good-byes to the necromancer and finished their walk to the teleportation area. Once there, Ayden cast the spell to return them to the D'Vaire living room.

Latarian's haughty voice hit his ears right away. "Ayden, your punishment awaits. Come to my room so I can reacquaint you with my lash."

Hanging his head after a nod, he took two steps but was stopped by Aleksander's hand on his arm.

"Wait a minute, Ayden," Aleksander directed. "Today, the Emperor made you both official members of my Court. I understand you guys aren't familiar with how things work within dragonkind but from this point on, there won't be any punishments in this house unless I dole them out. Tripping over someone is an accident, so Ayden won't be lashed. In fact, that went out of style a few centuries ago. I know it's going to be a struggle for you both as you adjust to your new lives, but you will obey my rules. You've spent the last six and a half centuries together, and I think you could both benefit from some distance. Ayden, feel free to do whatever you want in this house. I'll let you know if you're doing something wrong or inap-propriate."

Latarian's eyes went dark with fury and her jaw clenched, but her only response was a stiff bob of her head; then she stalked out of the living room.

Ayden smiled gratefully at Aleksander and received a smirk in return.

"Let's go get changed, Squirt. I think we could both use a beer."

"Sounds great," Ayden responded as he raced past him toward his new room. He hoped Aleksander would able to keep him from Latarian, but only time would tell how they'd coexist. Deciding to focus on the positive, Ayden wondered how long it would be before Blodwen joined them. Ayden planned on staying out of Latarian's way and if luck was on his side, she'd find better things to fill her day than berating and beating him.

8

Ayden's sneakers had barely hit the wooden deck when Duke Dravyn D'Vairedraconis appeared out of nowhere.

"Pears," the dragon shifter said as he thrust his hand toward Ayden with two pieces of fruit in his palm. "For your walk."

"Thanks so much, Dravyn," Blodwen enthused as she grabbed both and handed one to Ayden.

Dravyn smiled shyly, then strode off toward the massive garden he spent most of his waking hours in.

"That's the first time I've heard him talk," Ayden said once the duke was out of earshot.

Blodwen bit into her pear and nodded. After she swallowed, she looped her arm through Ayden's. The pair strolled across the deck, so they could wander over Aleksander's expansive grounds as they did most days. "He's got a very gentle way about him."

"Yeah, it was nice of him to give us these pears for our walk."

"I can't believe how incredible the dragons are," Blodwen commented. "I mean when I emailed the Arch Lich's office to get permission to live here, I had no idea what I was getting into. I needed a job, and this was perfect. I know I've only been here a few days, but I'm not ever leaving."

"Me either. Not only are the dragons kind but they're so generous."

"Right? Aleksander's like a super-hot genie. You want something? He'll make sure you get it," Blodwen replied as they munched on fruit and wandered over the desert landscape. "And no one cares that I don't want to summon my sentinel."

If asked, Ayden would've loved to have an elite assassin at his beck and call, but he was taught necromancy went against Fate, so he could relate to Blodwen's desire to stay far from her undead warrior. "Those stories you told me about are scary. I wouldn't want a sentinel murdering me."

"I don't know why someone created them and bound one to every necromancer. It's insane. I don't want some bloodthirsty sentinel who's been trained for nothing but killing hanging around."

"It's okay. You don't have to. No one here cares if you refuse."

"Speaking of people stuck with us, how's your witch?" Blodwen asked. The necromancer had taken an immediate dislike to Latarian after arriving at Court D'Vaire a few days ago. Latarian was difficult to deal with, but Ayden was reluctant to gossip about her.

"Okay, I guess. We've been keeping our distance from each other at Aleksander's request," Ayden stated. He steered as clear from Latarian as he could, and she was content to continue to stay buried in the fourteenth century. Blodwen helped her send emails to the Consilium Veneficus, but Latarian still refused to change her clothing or mode of speech. Ayden wasn't sure why; nothing was going to turn back time or return Carvallius to life.

"It must be a relief not to deal with her as much as you used to. She's so rude."

"It's very difficult for her to deal with the fact that everyone believes her grandfather destroyed our people because he wanted to be Grand Warlock."

"Which is the only reason I haven't told her off. I feel bad for her. I don't think she's going to get a response to her emails, and I don't see any way for her to change people's minds about Carvallius. He was a horrible person."

Ayden hadn't known Carvallius well. He was summoned a few weeks before they'd gone to the cottage, and Latarian's grandfather wasn't at Castle Mallent with them in that brief time. Latarian had spoken often over the centuries of Carvallius's wish for power, but now she denied those words. "I'm just sorry all our people are dead. In some corner of my mind, I wanted a mate. Now I'll never have one."

Blodwen stopped in her tracks forcing, Ayden to do the same. "What do you mean? Of course, you will. All magickind and shifters get one."

"Yeah, but familiars were always mated to other familiars. I'm the only warlock—*witch* familiar," he responded. He was still struggling with the change from warlock to witch.

Giving him a bright smile, Blodwen set them back in motion. "Well, that was how it used to be done. Fate will figure out someone else who's perfect for you. Don't worry."

"I guess," Ayden replied though he was not convinced. "I don't really think about it that much. I mean, where would I even meet my mate? This place is fantastic, but our dragons have been ostracized for the same amount of time I spent in that cottage with Latarian. Sure, the Emperor was nice, but you don't see anyone beating on the door to join the D'Vaire family."

"It's too bad they don't. You're right—this place is incredible. The dragons have the biggest hearts. They've taken in the last living witch and her familiar as well as a necromancer who defies her brethren by refusing to summon her sentinel. Do they make us feel bad for being strange or unique? Nope, they just treat us with kindness and do everything they can to make our lives richer."

"It's too bad they can't do that for more people. It'd be wonderful if they could invite other folks to the house who don't fit in or are different from the others of their race."

Blodwen threw her head back and laughed. "Oh Ayden, you're perfect. That's a brilliant idea, but I don't think the Council would allow it. There aren't any multi-race sanctuaries."

"Why not?"

"Most races keep to themselves."

"I think we should talk to the dragons about it and see if they want to do that. I mean, we could ask the Council for permission. The worst thing they could say is no," Ayden argued. The more he toyed with the idea of a sanctuary for odd people in his head, the more he liked it. Every D'Vaire—except for maybe Latarian—would open their hearts to make them feel wanted. Since Aleksander's decree a week ago that Ayden keep space from Latarian, his happiness had grown. For the first time in his life, he was being embraced for the person he wanted to be. No one corrected the things he said or lashed him if he ventured outside Latarian's stringent rules of behavior.

"You're right. It certainly can't hurt to ask, but I don't want you to get your hopes up too high. Doing this would be revolutionary within the Council," Blodwen cautioned.

"Tonight's our family meeting. I'll bring it up to Aleksander then."

"Thanks, everybody, for taking the time to meet tonight," Aleksander said.

"It's so exciting that we actually have things to talk about now. Before our family grew, we'd spent Monday nights talking about how much toilet paper we have in the house and trying to figure out who forgot to replace the roll in the bathroom right off the living room," Larissa responded.

"One time. *One time* I forget to replace the roll, and it was ten years ago. Do you think we could let it go now?" Aleksander asked.

"The mighty King D'Vaire brought down by his failure to make sure there was paper on the roll," Noirin teased.

Aleksander's expression was unamused. "If I haven't said it enough already, I just want to extend another warm welcome to our newest D'Vaires. We're so glad to have the three of you here. I'd like to start with you guys. Latarian, do you have any concerns or issues?"

The witch lifted her chin. "I would like to know the status of Carvallius's good name."

"Latarian, I told you. I emailed hundreds of people. Any wizard's name I could find on the Internet who belongs to the Consilium Veneficus or is old enough to have been alive in that time got our request to discuss history with them. So far, I've received zero response," Blodwen supplied.

"I cannot understand how there is no one willing to stand up for my grandfather. He had so many allies in life."

"Perhaps they died too," Ayden suggested.

"You should offer no comment. This has nothing to do with you," Latarian snapped.

"I'd appreciate if everyone could treat each other with kindness under my roof," Aleksander stated with a hard look at Latarian.

"Of course, Aleksander, my apologies. I just cannot believe no one will help me get the truth out about my grandfather. It leaves me rather short-tempered."

"I know it's important to you, but I'd like you to respect my rules. Is there anything else you need to discuss, Latarian?" Aleksander asked.

"That is all."

"Great. Ayden, it's your turn. Any questions or concerns?"

Ayden squirmed a little on the sofa. He liked the idea of a sanctuary but was nervous at the prospect of sharing it with the entire D'Vaire family. "Blodwen and I were talking on our walk today about how wonderful everyone here is, and we thought it would be great if more people got to call D'Vaire home. What if we asked the Council to allow us to turn Court D'Vaire into a sanctuary for outcasts like us?"

"I am no outcast," Latarian countered.

"You're the only living witch," Blodwen responded. "You don't even have a leader for the Coven of Witches. I'm pretty sure that makes you an outcast. It's not a bad thing. I like being surrounded by other freaks."

"I'm certainly an outcast and a freak," Aleksander stated. "I have to admit I never considered opening D'Vaire as a sanctuary, but I'm not opposed to the idea. What does everyone else think?"

"Considering how awesome it's been since Latarian, Ayden, and Blodwen got here, I'm on board. It'd be nice to fill up some of the millions of guest rooms in this house. I'm having so much fun helping our newest D'Vaires decorate their spaces, and I can always make more pajamas," Larissa remarked.

"Between Dravyn and me, there's certainly plenty of food. We have tons of resources. Aleksander, you've made us very rich. Why not give some of that back to the Council community by helping people like us? We freaks should unite," Noirin said.

"If Larissa likes the idea, then so do I," Madeline added.

"We have the space, and it'd be nice to help," Dravyn tacked on.

Ayden was overjoyed that the dragons were so receptive to opening a sanctuary. He grinned and even bounced a little in his seat. "I'm so glad you guys like the idea."

"You're going to have to speak with Brogan about it," Noirin warned.

"I'll give him a call. In the meantime, I think we should start working on finding out how to do this. Blodwen, thoughts?" Aleksander asked.

"We need to petition the Council, and they'll put it through their process. That means it'll go before the leaders. We will be invited to the Main Assembly Hall for any questions they have, and then they'll vote," Blodwen replied. "I haven't done a petition before, but I'm sure Ayden and I can figure it out."

"I'll help however I can," Ayden assured her.

"Great. Since no one objected, we'll get moving on it," Aleksander said. "If you guys need help, let us know and we'll do what we can to assist you. Ayden, did you have any other issues or concerns?"

Still beaming, Ayden shook his head. "Nope."

"How about you Blodwen? Any issues or concerns?"

"Not at all. I just wanted to take a second to thank you guys for letting me come to D'Vaire. It feels like I've spent my whole life waiting to be here," Blodwen said.

"That was incredibly beautiful, and we feel lucky to have you. All three of you. Is there anything else we need to discuss?" Aleksander asked. Once it was clear there were no problems, he got to his feet. "All right guys, meeting's adjourned. I'm going to call Brogan but since he's rarely here anymore, I doubt he'll offer any resistance. Enjoy your evening, everybody."

Ayden stood and was immediately embraced by Blodwen. He grinned and ignored the glare of his witch. Relieved that his idea wasn't laughed at or worse, Ayden promised himself he would do everything he could to create a sanctuary. It was just what he was searching for all those centuries trapped in the cottage—to have a purpose or meaning to his life. Ayden was grateful Fate had led him to where he belonged.

———————

9

Duke Brogan D'Vairedraconis threw his arm over his face to cover his eyes. He was lying on a bed in yet another hotel room. That had essentially been his life for the last several years. Traveling from city to city had seemed like such a promising idea when he was safely at home. The loneliness of being ostracized for over six centuries had eaten away at him....So to find his mate, he'd left his family.

It wasn't an easy decision and as time passed, the guilt of being away dogged him. He was shirking his duty as a duke, and not having them around was like missing a limb. They weren't just some people he met up with occasionally to talk about old times; each D'Vaire was a close friend and confidante. Aleksander was the person who knew him best, and now Brogan hardly called him anymore because he hated that he'd run away.

Brogan had visited many places and met many people. He'd learned quickly that being a D'Vaire may have been amazing at home, but it was still considered cursed among dragonkind. So, he only offered his last name and title when necessary. *Another brick of shame to add to the rest*, he thought with a sigh. He'd failed in his mission to find his other half, and he was tired of feeling adrift.

Deciding to grow up and be a man, Brogan lifted his arm and fished out his cell phone. He stared at it for several minutes before he gathered the courage to locate Aleksander's contact information and hit the call button.

"Did you find him?" was how Aleksander greeted Brogan.

"No, I haven't found my mate."

"I figured after all this time not hearing from my best friend, the only reason you'd call would be to tell me you finally met him."

"I'm sorry."

"I was just getting ready to call you," Aleksander said.

"Something wrong?"

"Nope, but I have some pretty big news."

"You met your mate? What, did she just walk up to the door and say hello? I know you didn't leave the house."

"I not only left the house, I went to Council Headquarters and met the Emperor but no, I didn't meet my mate."

To say Brogan was shocked was an understatement. Aleksander had grown more and more wary of people as time had passed and rarely left the sanctity of D'Vaire. "How did you get the opportunity to meet the Emperor? And please tell me you had Dravyn with you."

"Nah, he would've hated that. I just contacted his office and got on his schedule, but it's why I went that's the big story."

"Aleksander?"

"What?"

"You're a king. You didn't take a fucking duke with you?"

"Brogan, it doesn't matter. No one did anything but stare at me. Besides, you're the duke in charge of security, and I don't even know where the fuck you are."

"I'm sorry."

"Stop apologizing, damn it, and let me tell you why I went to meet the Emperor."

"Okay, tell me."

"A warlock showed up at our doorstep with her familiar. Well, they're called witches now, but you know what I mean. She and her familiar were in an enchanted cottage for six centuries and didn't even know they're the last of their kind."

"Strangers walked up to the door, and you took them to the Emperor? You should've slammed the door in their faces."

"Sure, right," Aleksander retorted sarcastically. "Anyway... Latarian of Mallent arrived and she's on a mission now to clear her grandfather Carvallius's name."

Brogan sat straight up. "Did you just say Carvallius? The same fucker who destroyed his people? His granddaughter's in our house?"

"Yeah, and I'll be honest—she's temperamental, but her familiar, Ayden, is awesome. I think he's enjoying our house and having some space from her. I have a feeling it's not going to be long before Ayden spreads his wings and shakes off the shackles of being isolated for all those centuries."

Shaking his head to clear the rage, Brogan said, "Okay, I can't even deal with her familiar. I don't even know what that is really, so the fact that there's one under our roof is disturbing. I'd like to remind you that we were in the castle one night when a group of people decided to kill the Emperors. You've probably got a couple of traitors living there. You're not safe."

"Seriously, Brogan, it's not 1369. No one's plotting murder around here. We're going to be too busy for that. We added a necromancer while we were at Council Headquarters, and she's going to help Ayden with a huge project I'm getting really excited about."

"For Fate's sake Aleksander, did you invite everyone you passed to come and live at D'Vaire? Shit, this is why you should've had Dravyn with you. Now you've got three strangers putting you in danger."

"Relax, we're all fine. We've decided to petition the Council to open up D'Vaire as a sanctuary for freaks or outcasts like all of us."

Brogan couldn't reply. Fear and rage choked him as he thought about strangers trampling into his home and putting the people he loved in peril. After taking several deep breaths, Brogan made a decision. "I have to come home."

"Exciting, right? You really should be here. Things will get busy if we get approved. You won't be bored, I'm sure. Maybe you'll even meet your mate."

"I'm pretty sure Fate's decided I'm either not ready or she's given up on me entirely."

"That's not a very positive attitude."

"I'm not feeling very positive right now."

"Is everything okay?" Aleksander's question was full of concern, and Brogan missed him even more.

"I'm fine. I promise."

"Just come home. Enough of this nonsense. Your family needs you."

"I need you guys too," Brogan replied as the sadness and guilt washed over him. "I've missed you all so fucking much."

"We missed you too. Now pack your shit and get back here."

"Yes, Your Highness."

"I'm hanging up, Your Grace."

"Tell everybody I'll be there tomorrow."

"You got it."

They said their good-byes, and Brogan set his phone down on the bed. There was so much on his mind, and he couldn't figure out where to start first in clearing it. One thing was for sure—no one was going to touch a hair on the head of any D'Vaire. Aleksander's big heart might have resulted in a bunch of strangers underfoot, but Brogan was going to keep a close eye on them, except for the familiar. He wasn't comfortable with the idea of Ayden being in his house, so he was going to stay well away from him.

When he nearly popped a lung blowing up a balloon, Ayden pulled it from his mouth and tied the end into a knot.

"Hey, Squirt. What's with the balloon?" Aleksander asked as he strolled into the kitchen.

"Larissa's decorating the house for Brogan," Ayden told him. The elusive Duke Brogan was returning to his home after several years away, and Ayden was looking forward to meeting him. He was sure he'd be as friendly and warm as the rest of his family. Ayden wondered if he was planning on staying for a while or if he was going to be traveling again soon.

Aleksander's brow furrowed in confusion. "Larissa, why do we need balloons and stuff? Brogan lives here."

"I thought it'd be a nice way to welcome him back," she offered. "Come on, give us a hand."

"You know what the best part of the celebration is?" Ayden asked his king.

"What's that, Squirt?"

"Noir made a cake."

"The last thing you need is another sweet," Latarian snapped from the large living space next to the kitchen where the preparations for Brogan's arrival were in full swing.

"I like it," Ayden said, feeling brave enough to stand up for himself. He no longer had to fear her lash, and he hoped it meant they could forge the friendship he'd always wanted. It was supposed to be an essential part of the relationship between familiar and witch that they'd missed out on during their isolation. Now free to be himself, Ayden was going to do his best to mend their fences.

"What's wrong with sweets, Latarian?" Aleksander asked.

"Nothing at all, I suppose. I simply cannot abide them. I do not understand how my familiar can be so very different from me in that regard."

"It's okay, Latarian. We don't need to have all the same likes and dislikes. What's your favorite food?" Ayden asked as he picked up another navy balloon. It was the color of Brogan's dragon, which pleased Ayden. It was his favorite color, and he planned to ask Brogan if he could use his dragon scales in his room decor once they got to be friends.

"I prefer salted things," Latarian responded. She'd opted not to assist with Brogan's party and was instead pretending to read in the living room. The witch hadn't picked up a book until they'd arrived at

D'Vaire, and her true purpose was to conceal her interest in the large television someone turned on.

"I think I hear a car," Larissa announced as she raced toward the door.

"Good. Does that mean we can stop blowing these damn things up?" Aleksander asked.

"One step closer to cake," Ayden replied as he handed the last of the balloons up to Blodwen, who dutifully hung them next to the banner they'd handwritten earlier.

From the kitchen, Ayden heard Larissa open the door and chat excitedly with a male voice. Seconds later, the body that had lacked sexuality for his entire life changed in a flash. Familiars responded only to their mates, and as Ayden's cock filled with blood, his eyes went wide with shock. He got a bit light-headed with excitement as Duke Brogan D'Vairedraconis walked into the room.

Brogan was tall, barely an inch shorter than Aleksander's six feet six inches, and he wore a smile that flaunted a set of faint dimples. Movie-star handsome, he had eyes the color of Ayden's much-loved navy wallpaper. His hair fell just over his forehead in short, boyish, brown curls and Ayden stared at him, slack-jawed.

Brogan's nostrils flared, and he lost his grin as he spotted Ayden. Their gazes locked, and Ayden could read nothing from his expression. Aleksander grabbed his attention and introduced Brogan to both Blodwen and Latarian. Ayden's intense reaction lessened, and he eagerly awaited his chance to meet his other half. *Blodwen was right. Fate didn't forget me*, he thought happily as Brogan sauntered over to him.

"This is Latarian's familiar, Ayden D'Vaire," Aleksander said.

Brogan lifted his hand to shake and then appeared to think better of it, because he lowered it back to his side. "Hi."

The word was brusque, and Ayden wasn't sure how to react. Brogan was obviously not pleased with him. "Hello," was all Ayden managed to utter in return.

The pair of dragons walked away, and Ayden stood there stupidly without a clue what to say or do. Ayden didn't have any concept of

how long he was lost in his thoughts but when he sought out his
mate again, Brogan had pulled Aleksander off to the side slightly.
Knowing it was rude but desperate for some notion of what Brogan
was feeling, he gathered an invisible globe of magic and let it fly over
to them so he could listen to their conversation.

"Ayden's the familiar?" Brogan asked.

"Yeah, I've told you that a few times now. What's your deal?"

"Is he real?"

"What do you mean is he real? He's standing over there, isn't he?"
Aleksander asked, sounding annoyed.

"He's tied to Latarian. Do they always have to be in the
same room?"

"What? No."

"He's got all the normal parts though, right?"

"Brogan, what the actual fuck?"

"He's really small. Maybe a couple of inches over five feet at the
most. Did she make him that way?"

"For the love of Fate, she summoned him. She didn't bake him in
a factory. What's your deal?"

"Aleksander?"

"What?"

"I'm freaking the fuck out," Brogan said with terror resonating in
his voice.

"Why? What's wrong?"

"The familiar? He's my mate."

Aleksander's face morphed into a bright smile, and he slapped
Brogan on the back. "Congratulations."

"I guess."

Deciding he didn't want to hear anything else Brogan might have
to say, Ayden destroyed his listening globe. The fury he'd tamped
down his whole life roared out of nowhere. *I would rather not have a
mate at all than have one who finds me so lacking,* Ayden thought as the
rage flowed through his veins. Ayden might be odd in his inability to
be a normal familiar, but those were the types of things your mate
was supposed to understand. Fate supposedly picked out someone

who was your perfect complement, so Ayden couldn't understand why Brogan was afraid to even touch his hand to shake it.

Ayden blew out a breath and set aside his desire for the cake he'd yearned for all day. He was done celebrating Brogan's return, so he marched out of the kitchen. It didn't take him long to stomp his way into his bedroom and when he got inside, he slammed the door behind him. For over six centuries he'd been forced to be who Latarian wanted, and when he hadn't met her standards, she'd whipped him.

Fate should have offered him a mate who accepted him from the start. Disgusted with life in general, Ayden swore he wasn't going to do anything from this point forward but be true to who he was. Forget Latarian and her lash as well as Brogan and his desire for someone taller and less magical. Ayden would be who he wanted, and anyone who didn't approve could get the hell out of his way.

10

L atarian had to admit she did not hate everything about the Draconis Court of D'Vaire. She detested giving up the name Mallent, but there were advantages to forming an alliance with a rich dragon. When she woke up each morning, it was on a soft mattress with lovely scented bedding to keep her comfortable while she slept. Larissa decorated her chamber in subtle shades of purple, and Latarian was fond of the design. The space itself was enormous, and the tiny cottage she'd shared with Ayden for all those centuries would have easily fit inside with room to spare.

There was running water, which Latarian could scorch her skin with and when she ventured out to fill her belly, the food was a far cry from the tasteless morsels Ayden had cooked each day. Aleksander's coffers were obviously deep and if anyone expressed a need, he opened his pockets to make their dreams come true, but it rankled that Latarian had to answer to a dragon king. That was not her destiny; she'd been promised she would be related to the Grand Warlock.

Instead, someone had murdered her grandfather, and the grief and anger churned in her with each day that passed. The entire world had decided he was guilty of destroying the warlocks. He was allied with the Cwylld elven, but she simply could not believe he would allow them to kill their own people. He'd told her he did not even know the secret of their magic nullifying power; how could he have assisted them?

She wanted to scream and rail against the baseless accusations, but no one wanted to listen. They'd all decided he was guilty, and Blodwen hadn't managed to find a single soul who cared to discuss it with her. If that were not enough to drive her mad, she no longer had any control over Ayden. Latarian would be the first to say she enjoyed having space away from him. He was annoying on his best day and a trial on his worst, so to not have to converse with someone lesser than she was a welcome respite.

Except she missed having someone at her beck and call, eager to please for fear of her lash. The beatings themselves were an almost daily task, and while she'd taken pleasure in his pain, it often caused her skin to sweat, which she detested. Latarian was happy without duties, and that was another part of D'Vaire she enjoyed. She wasn't expected to lift a finger, and she found that to her liking.

Latarian could not fully immerse herself in her new life until the past was resolved. She would keep as much of the fourteenth century with her until Carvallius of Mallent was once again the envy of all magickind. Once that was done, she would make sure Aleksander handed over a great deal of coin; then she would leave D'Vaire far behind her. The Council would make her the Grand Witch, and others would offer whatever they could to satisfy her.

Lost in her thoughts, Latarian almost jumped out of her skin when Ayden took a seat next to her. "Mind yourself. You gave me a fright."

"I'm sorry."

"What ails you?"

Ayden lifted his head and when their eyes met, his were swirling with emotion. She truly didn't want to be bothered with whatever piddling concern he had, but she doubted he would go away before he confessed all. "You really want to talk about it?"

"Ayden, do not anger me. Tell me what has upset you, so I may go back to my own tasks."

"Latarian, Duke Brogan's my mate."

Latarian's heart skipped a beat in fright. Her grandfather's voice washed over her startled brain—reminding her that the one thing she must not do was allow Ayden to find his other half. "What?" was all she managed to say.

"I don't think he's happy about it. He has a big problem with the fact that I'm a familiar."

"These dragons think much too highly of themselves," Latarian said. She tried to recall if Carvallius had ever told her *why* Ayden should not mate, but it was a hopeless cause. If there were ever any specifics, she would have surely remembered. What did Ayden's other half mean for her? Would it affect their bond in any way? She simply could not abide the thought of losing her power.

"A familiar is a person just like everybody else," Ayden mumbled.

"Not quite so valuable as a witch."

"Yeah, I guess."

"Perhaps Fate has matched you poorly," Latarian remarked as her mind raced from one tragic thought to another. For so long, she'd simply forgotten he was Dra'Kaedan of Leolinnia. It scared her to think what would happen if anyone ever discovered his identity. A shiver raced over her skin as she contemplated the things she'd read in Aleksander's history book. Dra'Kaedan had a twin who was also missing. What if he was still alive and somehow located his brother?

"You look pale. Are you okay?" Ayden asked.

"I am fine," she snapped. "It is you with the problem. I would have you keep your distance from this dragon if he is not a good mate." The only plan she could put together was to do everything she could to make sure Ayden didn't bond with the duke.

"I thought I wouldn't get a mate since all the other familiars were dead. Blodwen said Fate would find me one anyway, but what good is it if he's freaked out by what I am?"

"Ayden, Fate has done the best she can, given the circumstances.

There are no familiars left, and therefore you will have a poor match. Who can understand your role in life but you?"

"True, but maybe he just needs to get to know me."

Latarian had to do something she detested and stifle her deepest wish to forbid Ayden to mate with Brogan. The Council made it illegal to come between two people, and the ultimate penalty was death. She wouldn't pay with her life nor would she tell Ayden of his identity. She'd have to remind him of all the pitfalls of being with the duke without overstepping. It angered her that she must toe the line; she didn't like catering to anyone's feelings but her own. "I am sure you will know what to do with more time," she said and was quite proud that she was able to do so without gritting her teeth.

"You're right. Thanks, Latarian."

Ayden popped up from the sofa and took off to whatever destination he had in mind while Latarian tried to get a handle on herself. They had asked Fate to send them someplace safe; she simply could not believe anything too dire was going to happen. The grimmest outcome would be her losing her power, and she'd do everything to ensure that didn't come to pass.

Brogan was upset with the world in general. He'd finally come home and had even met his mate—but who, and more importantly, *what* was he? Was Brogan destined to share his mate with his witch? He had no idea how any of it worked, and it frightened him. All his life he'd wanted to find his other half, and Ayden's appearance surprised him. The guy was tiny with a messy mop of red hair. Brogan had always been drawn to blonds. When he'd fantasized about his partner, the guy had golden curls and blue eyes. Though Fate had opted for something different, Brogan wouldn't deny he found Ayden attractive.

He'd also dreamed of a man who had a disposition like his own. Brogan wanted someone fiery and strong, who knew what they wanted and took it. He'd hoped that kind of attitude would bleed over to their bedroom, and to Brogan that was a steamy fantasy he would sign up for any day of the week. Unfortunately, Ayden appeared to be on the shy side, and Brogan wondered if he'd spent his whole life doing whatever Latarian told him without question. He guessed that was how the familiar-to-witch relationship worked.

Being mated to someone who was quiet and rarely thought for themselves made Brogan wish he'd stayed away from D'Vaire. Brogan shook off the crazy ideas his brain was crafting. He didn't know how the familiar thing worked and yes, it was daunting to think about, but this was his other half. There was no question; he needed to get to know Ayden and discover what their future truly held.

Gathering his courage, Brogan left his bedroom and headed toward the kitchen. Once there, he found Ayden sitting on a stool, eating a piece of cake.

"Good morning," he offered the familiar, hoping it was still morning. He hadn't checked the clock before picking his destination.

Ayden's unreadable gaze lifted to his. "Morning."

"Uh...sleep well?" Brogan asked. Then his brain leaked out of his ear as words tripped over his tongue. "I guess familiars sleep. Right?"

Ayden's jaw clenched. "I slept."

"Every night?"

"Yeah, every night," Ayden bit out.

Brogan was irritating the guy, but he couldn't stop his mouth from running out of control. "You have all your working parts?"

"My *what*?"

Shaking his head vehemently, Brogan said, "Never mind, sorry."

"How did you sleep?" Ayden asked in an overly polite manner as he set his fork down.

"Not good. Not good at all."

"I'm terribly sorry to hear that. Was something on your mind? Perhaps a change in your life you still haven't owned up to?"

"Huh?"

Ayden's dark green eyes narrowed in irritation. "Still pretending we aren't mates?"

"Uh...no?" He had meant it as a statement, but it had definitely come out sounding like a question. Brogan wished the floor would open and swallow him.

Ayden slid off his stool and carried his plate and fork over to the dishwasher while Brogan stood there in a complete stupor. "I won't apologize for being a familiar," he stated once he was facing Brogan.

"Can you understand why it freaks me out?"

Crossing his arms over his chest, Ayden studied him for several seconds. "No, but maybe if you took the time to get to know me, you'd understand I'm just like everybody else."

"Except you're still a familiar. A small one," Brogan said and wanted to slap himself. He didn't know why he was so stuck on *what* Ayden was instead of trying to learn more about who he was.

"I'll always be one. I suggest you try getting used to it."

"I suppose I'll have to."

"Nobody has to do anything, Brogan," Ayden said after baring his teeth.

Brogan needed to do as Ayden suggested and try to get to know more about him. Knowledge was power, and perhaps his mind would move away from the rut he was apparently stuck in. "You've got magic, right? Or do you have to ask Latarian's permission to use it? You're like her sidekick or whatever. What can you do on your own?"

"Would you like to see what I can do?"

"Yeah. Yeah, sure."

"Allow me to show you," Ayden taunted, then set Brogan's pants on fire.

"What the hell?" Brogan bellowed as he stamped his feet to put out the tiny flames. He got no response; Ayden had left the kitchen altogether. Snatching a towel from a drawer, Brogan beat on the denim he was wearing until he put himself out. Ayden's retribution left him with only minor burns that were already healing due to his shifter blood. Had he thought Ayden subservient or unable to think on his own? Though he would've preferred not to have his favorite dark jeans ruined, Brogan laughed long and loud.

For whatever reason, the dumbest things imaginable had slipped past his lips, and he'd probably insulted him more than he even understood. There was no doubt about it; he deserved Ayden's ire. Their first chat together hadn't eased his trepidation about their matebond, but at least Ayden would let him know his feelings on a subject. *It might help to keep a fire extinguisher close at hand if I am unable to control my mouth in the future,* he thought with some humor. He didn't know exactly what Fate had gotten him into, but at least he no longer needed to wander the streets searching for his other half while missing his family.

His place was at D'Vaire, and he planned on staying close at hand to keep his eye on all the newest additions to their family, including the little spitfire who'd turned him into a dragon match. With a rueful shake of his head, Brogan headed back to his room to change. He idly wondered if he'd need to invest in a new wardrobe before he and Ayden figured out their future. If he couldn't pull his head out of his ass, he might have to put a serious dent in his wallet.

11

After he set Brogan's jeans on fire, Ayden teleported to his bedroom and put his face into his hands. He had no idea what possessed him to lose his temper and gather his magic to use it on his mate. Brogan's questions were rude, but to harm his other half was in defiance of Fate herself. The havoc inside Ayden had shocked him when he'd grown angry at Brogan. It was like discovering a part of himself somehow lost in time, which made zero sense. Up until he'd arrived at D'Vaire, his life had been very simple.

Perhaps all that isolation made it difficult for me to relate to others, he thought as he lifted his head and dropped his arms to his sides. Ayden hadn't struggled around the rest of the D'Vaires, so it must be some kind of reaction to Brogan himself. Whatever it was, Ayden had grown emboldened in his presence. The sheer force of his reaction was intoxicating, but it was wrong to hurt Brogan.

Setting aside Brogan's inability to converse politely, Ayden's actions were unkind and there would be a price to pay for it. Taking a deep breath, Ayden was grateful that it was Aleksander he'd face instead of Latarian. Knowing that a punishment only grew worse when he allowed himself to draw it out, Ayden left his room and wandered down the hallway to his king's office. He was pleased that he didn't run into Brogan on his way.

"Hey, Squirt. What's up?" Aleksander asked once he arrived in the doorway. He was smiling, so Ayden assumed he hadn't heard about the incident in the kitchen yet.

Ayden straightened his shoulders and stood in front of Aleksander's large desk. "I grew angry with Brogan and set him on fire."

Aleksander didn't react with the anger he'd expected. Instead, King D'Vairedraconis blinked his exotic eyes once and then twice. "You did what?"

"I was eating some cake and he came in. We had an unpleasant conversation, and I'm afraid I lost my temper. I used my magic to set his jeans on fire."

"I guess my first question is, did he survive?" Aleksander asked with humor evident in his voice.

"Of course. It took a lot of magic to set my mate on fire, and all I managed were some tiny flames near his ankles. I'm very sorry, and I'll apologize to him as well, but I wanted to come to you first. You're my king, and I need to be punished for my transgression," Ayden said.

Before Aleksander could say a word, Brogan strode into the room and raised a brow at Ayden. He plopped down onto a dragonskin couch. "Ah, the little pyro."

"I was just apologizing to Aleksander for my actions. I owe you an apology as well. You were very rude to me, but setting you on fire wasn't fair."

"Probably not, but you're right. I was rude to you. I'm sorry too," Brogan replied.

"Thank you for understanding. Do you accept my apology?" Ayden asked once again feeling brave and daring.

"Sure. Let's try not to do that in the future, though. I only have so many pairs of jeans. Do you do that a lot? Set people on fire?"

"You're the first. Most people don't refer to me as a thing or call me Latarian's sidekick," Ayden tossed back.

"You're not like the rest of us though," Brogan retorted.

Deciding he didn't want to face two punishments in one day, Ayden returned his attention to Aleksander. No one was more shocked than Ayden when he said, "I'm going to hurt him if I stay here. Can you tell me if you're going to accept my apology and what price I'm going to pay for my actions?"

"I do accept your apology," Aleksander replied. "Though I didn't really need one. This is between the two of you. I'm not going to interfere in a matebond. I'm not going to reprimand you, because I think Brogan might be insane."

"I'm not insane. I'm adjusting to Fate's choice," Brogan argued.

Ayden slapped his hands onto his hips. "Don't you think I'm doing the same thing? I always imagined myself with a familiar, not some dragon who can't seem to cope with anyone not exactly like him."

"That's not true. A familiar is not a normal thing."

"I'm not a *thing*," Ayden shouted. He was beyond caring if he was being rude or what punishment he'd face. This was the person Fate picked for him, and the man refused to believe he was a person with feelings.

"So, you had a normal childhood and stuff like everybody else?"

"I was summoned. I didn't have a childhood. I've always been an adult," Ayden snarled.

"Latarian's not like your mother, then?"

It was impossible for Ayden to imagine Latarian being anyone's parent. She liked to please herself and was cantankerous on her best day. "Absolutely not."

"I don't have to share you with her?"

"I don't understand what that means," Ayden replied. "We're connected as warlock—I mean *witch*—and familiar, but that's it. We have to be in proximity to each other because of our magical connection, but she doesn't even resupply my power like other sorcerers." Something Ayden had only learned when he'd met the Prism Wizard...but he didn't tack that on. Nor did he mention that it was Carvallius who'd bound them so tight. If he got too far from Latarian, the spells carved into his back almost ripped him apart with pain.

"Do you share a room?"

"For Fate's sake, Brogan, walk down the hall. Madeline made them plaques for their doors like everybody else. They have separate damn rooms," Aleksander remarked, and Ayden almost jumped at the sound of his voice. He had become so lost in his temper he'd forgotten he wasn't alone with the big dragon staring at him from the sofa.

"Look, this isn't easy for me. I thought Fate paired you up, and then you lived happily ever after. I wasn't expecting all these complications."

"That's ridiculous. You've got to get to know one another and work to build a relationship," Aleksander stated with a frown.

Ayden bit his lip as the rush of anger blew past him like a breeze. He wasn't sure what to do or what to say, but he wanted to trust his gut instead of molding himself to who Latarian thought he should be. "I'm sorry you're disappointed. Maybe I am too."

"I know I'm being a jerk. I don't want to be," Brogan responded softly. "We'll figure this out, and we'll make our matebond work. You have my word."

Still unsure of himself, Ayden nodded, then left Aleksander's office to try and clear his head. He decided on the living room and found Latarian. No one knew him better than his witch, so Ayden took a seat next to her. She was in her usual spot on the couch, pretending not to watch television. The only time she wasn't parked there was during mealtimes.

"Latarian, do you have a minute to talk?"

She smiled and shut her book. "I am always happy to offer you my counsel."

"I had a couple of conversations today with Brogan, and neither of them went well. I thought meeting my mate would be different."

"There is a great disparity between these shifters and magickind."

Ayden gave a negligent shrug of his shoulders as he scooted farther back into the cushions of the sofa. "He doesn't understand that I'm a person like everyone else. I don't know why familiars are so different in his mind."

"It is not so surprising to find he would take issue with a familiar. They are a rarity—at least the ones that belong to witches. Think on it, Ayden. You are now the only living one. Certainly, you must demand Fate match you with someone worthy of your value."

"Fate thinks he is, or she wouldn't have matched us."

"Have I not always seen to your needs, Ayden?"

For a moment, Ayden bit down hard on his tongue. Not once had she asked him what he needed. All his life, he'd been expected to see to her. It was as if she thought he was the thing that loomed in Brogan's mind, but she was being sympathetic, and he was clueless about his next move, so he just nodded.

"There is a spell that can free you."

"What?"

She bobbed her head enthusiastically and a large chunk of hair fell into her face, which she quickly shoved aside. "You believe you are the only one who knows spells?"

"I have your memories. I know all the spells you do."

"No, this one was taught to me by Grandfather after you were summoned."

"What does it do?"

"Exactly as I told you. It breaks the bonds of mates. Fate is a wonderful presence in our lives, but she does err, Ayden."

Ayden had no clue what to think. He hadn't considered the existence of such a spell. It didn't sit well with him. Whether she'd provided the words or not, it still felt like it was in defiance of her wishes. "I'm reluctant to anger Fate."

"You wish to stay with this silly dragon instead?"

"I hardly know him. Maybe if we spend some time together, he'll get over this aversion he has to familiars."

"It is a rather large gamble to take, Ayden. Listen, you may take time to think on it, but I will warn you. The spell is best cast before you are bound by blood or dragon bite. Once your souls have combined, there is no turning back. You will be stuck with a man who believes you are not worthy of him."

"I'll take it into consideration," Ayden said as he got to his feet. "Thanks, Latarian."

"We must stick together. We are all we have left with my grandfather gone."

He smiled in response to her kind words—it was so unlike her to be compassionate. Not wanting to be holed up inside, Ayden went through the kitchen and out to the deck, where he ran into Blodwen. She'd become a great friend to him in the brief time he'd known her, so he grabbed a seat and unloaded his entire morning on her shoulders.

"Ayden, this spell idea sounds crazy. You just met Brogan and yeah, he's freaking out, but matebonds take time. I mean, think about it. If his mate were someone else, he'd probably be the one feeling misunderstood. The D'Vaires have been ostracized, and he might've wound up with a dragon who thought he was cursed. There's always going to be some issue—it's two people combining their entire lives and trying to build something together. There's a lot you need to learn about each other."

"I didn't think about it like that," Ayden confessed.

"I'm going to be on your side no matter what decision you make. Know that, okay? My advice would be not to rush into anything one way or another. You have all the time in the world. You live under the same roof, and you guys can move slow. Figure out if Fate might be smarter than you think."

"I guess you're right. I'm torn between what's right, but it does make sense to spend some time with him."

"Hey, you can always set him on fire again."

Ayden's cheeks heated with embarrassment. "I can't believe I did that."

"Honestly, I'm sorry I missed it. You need to stand up for yourself and not worry about the consequences," Blodwen assured him. She was several hundred years younger than he was, but she had a wealth of life experience Ayden was missing. He trusted her not to lead him astray.

"I probably shouldn't do that again."

Blodwen chuckled. "If you want some practice, try doing it to Latarian."

"We share magic. I can't."

"How do you know if you don't try?"

Ayden bit his lip, then made his great confession. "I did. Many times when I was first summoned. It took a great deal of time and many whippings before I learned the patience to deal with her."

"Oh Ayden, I wish your witch wasn't such a bitch."

Allowing the brave side of himself to surface again, he smirked. "Me too."

12

B rogan took several days to get his head on straight. Ayden was his mate, and he needed to figure out how to move past his issues with that fact. He liked the fire he'd shown, although he would prefer it not to be so literal, and he was attracted to him from the start. Everyone around him thought he was crazy for having any objection to Ayden being a familiar, so he needed to get to the root of his problem. There was only one way to do that, and it was to spend time with him.

He didn't know why he'd expected to fall instantly in love the minute they clapped eyes on each other. Brogan doubted that happened all that often outside of books and movies. It would've been nice if he and Ayden had experienced that kind of romance, but that didn't mean their relationship was impossible. Wandering out of his room to grab breakfast, he found Ayden inhaling a massive stack of pancakes.

"Good morning," Brogan offered as a sense of déjà vu rang through his mind. One thing was for sure—Ayden liked to eat.

"Morning," Ayden replied, in between bites.

"Look, I want to apologize for once again offending you the other day. I really do want to learn more about familiars."

"You're still freaked out about it."

"Truthfully, yeah, but I'm getting more comfortable with the idea. You've figured out by now that most races keep to themselves. I don't know that much about magickind in general and let's face it, you're part of a race we all believed was extinct."

"That's true. I wish I could get freaked out about your whole turning into a fire-breathing dragon thing just to make us even, but I've seen Blodwen without her make-up, and that pretty much made me lose the ability to feel real fear."

The necromancer had strolled in during his speech, and she poked Ayden in the ribs as she sat down next to him. "Please, I've seen you drunk. It doesn't get scarier than that."

"Now this sounds like a story I need to hear," Brogan interjected. It was nice to see the friendship between the pair, and he hoped someday he'd be able to joke with Ayden in the same manner.

"No, you really don't," Ayden responded with a glare at his friend.

"Let's just say that Ayden decided it was a perfect opportunity to let out his inner songbird."

"He sang?"

"Oh yes, an entire concert full of songs. He has a pretty great voice."

"Blodwen," Ayden growled in warning.

"I'm confused. If he has a good voice, what was scary about it?" Brogan asked.

"Nothing. She exaggerates," Ayden stated quickly with another menacing frown in Blodwen's direction.

"Nope. Definitely wasn't the singing that was the problem. It was the striptease that went along with it that frightened the hell out of me," she said, in between giggles.

"Now that I would pay to see," Brogan remarked. One thing he had noticed right from the beginning was Ayden's sexiness, and he'd spent many hours contemplating his round ass since their meeting.

"Well, apparently Blodwen felt the same way, because I woke up with a whole game's worth of play money shoved in my underwear," Ayden countered.

"You did an excellent job," Blodwen praised through her laughter.

Ayden left his stool to offer her a courtly bow. "My thanks."

"Remind me to spike your glass at dinner tonight," Brogan told his mate with a wink.

"I don't think so," Ayden replied as he retook his seat.

"Wanna go out and grab some lunch with me today? We could do a bit of shopping after."

Ayden cocked his head to the side with a considering look on his face. "I don't want to freak you out, but I have to stay within a certain range of Latarian. I'd like to spend some time with you, except I can't promise that she'd be willing to leave the house."

"Okay, it's nice out...what if we took a walk and grabbed some sandwiches to eat outside? I'll even make them."

"I'm going to need at least three," Ayden told him.

"You going to have room for that after eating all those pancakes?"

"Yep."

Brogan pulled out the fixings for their picnic and got to work making their sandwiches. "So, here's the deal. I'm going to make all three of your sandwiches, and your gift to me in return is to not set me on fire today."

"I accept the terms of your treaty," Ayden responded as he polished off what was left of his meal. He crossed the room to put his stuff in the dishwasher, and Brogan didn't think anyone would fault him for keeping his eyes locked on Ayden's ass as he bent over. It was a pity when he straightened and leaned against the counter. Finishing up his task of seeing them fed, Brogan listened with half an ear as Ayden and Blodwen chatted.

When he was done, he turned to Ayden. "Ready to go?"

"Yeah."

"Have fun, gentlemen," Blodwen said as they walked out the back door. Ayden waved at her and they crossed the deck to step foot on the extensive grounds of King D'Vaire's domain.

"How about some basic questions?" Brogan asked as he slipped the cooler bag he'd stuck their sandwiches in over his shoulder.

"Okay, shoot."

"How old are you?"

"I was summoned a few weeks before Latarian and I left for the cottage in 1367. So, six and a half centuries, give or take. You?"

Brogan relaxed his shoulders and slowed his pace. His legs were a lot longer than Ayden's, and he didn't want the poor guy to have to run to keep up with him. "I'm about a century older than you. I shifted for the first time in 1369 when I was about a hundred years old."

"When did you guys get ostracized by everybody?" Ayden asked.

"All of us are within a couple of years of each other in age. We all shifted for the first time on the same day. Courts usually have one day a year or every couple of years when all the drakelings get their wings. When our king saw Aleksander's dragon, he called him cursed and told him to get out. It was basically a downward spiral from there," Brogan explained. He didn't want to go into the details of the deaths of the Emperors or the fact that the king who'd ostracized them was Aleksander's father. It was his best friend's story to tell, and he rarely spoke of it. As far as Brogan and the rest of the D'Vaires were concerned, it was all much better forgotten.

"I know he's very large, but why are two colors so strange to people?"

"Every other dragon only has one. People freak out when they see something new or different."

"Like me."

Brogan let out a breath. "Yeah, like you."

Silence fell over the pair as they continued their slow amble over the landscape. Brogan couldn't discern if it was a companionable quiet or not; he simply didn't know enough about Ayden to be able to glean anything about his mood. That thought reminded him their walk was supposed to allow them to learn more of each other, and they couldn't do that if they didn't speak.

"Tell me about Latarian," Brogan blurted out.

Ayden glanced up at him and his dark green gaze was unreadable, as was his expression. "What do you want to know?"

"You guys have to stay in close proximity, so you must know each other really well. My best friend is Aleksander. I was wondering if that's how you see Latarian's role in your life. You said she's not like your mother or anything."

The familiar at his side broke eye contact and focused on his feet. "We know each other well," was all he said.

"I'm sorry. We don't have to talk about her. It's just I'm trying to figure this out in my head and maybe if I knew more, I wouldn't be so freaked out."

"No, it's fine. I'm just...well. I'm an adequate familiar at best, so it hasn't been easy for Latarian to build a friendship with me, though I know it's something we both want."

"What does that mean?"

Ayden once again quieted for several minutes. When he spoke again, his words were measured and almost stilted. "A familiar is supposed to see to their witch's needs without question. I often fail to do that. For some reason, my brain seems unable to function as a normal familiar's should."

"I'm not sure what to say. I don't want to piss you off, but that doesn't seem fair. Are you saying you're not allowed to voice your opinion or make your own decisions?" Brogan asked. That was exactly what he was afraid of, a man being told what to do or what to say. Brogan didn't know how to handle that, and he couldn't figure out how it would affect their relationship. He wanted a partner, not someone who had to run to a witch to make up his mind.

"Aleksander has made it clear that under his roof I'm able to be freer in my thoughts and the things I say, but I know it doesn't please Latarian, which makes me feel guilty. I should want the same things she wants for me. I don't understand why I'm not capable of that. There's almost a living being inside me that comes out of nowhere. A person who wants to argue or set a person on fire," Ayden replied with a wry grin at Brogan.

"If my view means anything, I'd prefer you to be yourself. I like when you're joking around with Blodwen or anyone else in the house. I'll confess, I think it's sexy when you stand up for yourself, even if I did have to toss out my favorite jeans."

Ayden's eyes twinkled with humor. "I did feel bad, but I also enjoyed it. I'm not sure what that says about me as a person."

"That you don't appreciate people who insult you. That's it, Ayden. It just means that somewhere inside of you is a fiery side. Unfortunately for me, that sometimes translates literally, and I have to go shopping for new pants."

Ayden rubbed his lips with two fingers to hide his smile, which made Brogan laugh. "I liked the rush of power. Being fiery might be addictive."

"Oh, trust me, it is. Okay, tell me this. What's the worst thing about Court D'Vaire? You know, besides having a mate who's trying to get over his fear of magic."

"Blodwen watches horrible television shows. She likes to watch true crime stuff, and mostly I find it gross. It's rather ironic since she's afraid to summon her sentinel."

"Maybe someday, she'll grow used to the idea."

"So, you're okay with a sentinel around but not a familiar?" Ayden asked saucily.

Brogan winked at him. "I'm finding it easier to handle the familiar."

"The familiar in question is glad to hear it. I like being magickind."

"Being a dragon's pretty awesome too. Trust me. I've never dreamed of being anything else but what I am."

Ayden's mouth twisted. "If we're being honest, I've dreamed of being a warlock instead of a familiar. I can even understand Carvallius's longing to be Grand Warlock, although I can barely stomach the fact that I was a Mallent. For our people to all die for his greed is untenable."

"But doesn't Latarian think he's innocent?"

"She may believe what she wishes. Carvallius was allied with Cwylld and she knows it. The last day we spoke with him, he said he was going to speak with Grand Warlock T'Eirick to stop the war, but I found it difficult to believe he had the best of intentions. I didn't know him well, so I could be wrong."

"His journals were pretty straightforward. He was desperate to be Grand Warlock."

"I've found myself wondering what happened to the missing twins of the Grand Warlock," Ayden confessed. Brogan came to a stop and handed Ayden a sandwich from the bag, then helped himself to one.

"We should've brought a blanket or a towel or something," Brogan muttered as he lowered his body to the ground. Seconds later a navy cloth appeared underneath him. "Magic's pretty handy."

"I like it."

"I'm beginning to see its benefits. So, the twins, huh? Are you going to become some kind of familiar super-sleuth and find the clues to solve a mystery over six centuries old?" Brogan asked.

"I wish. I also wonder if there are others hiding around the world."

"Anything's possible, right?"

"If a dragon can handle Fate giving him a familiar as a mate then yes, I suppose so," Ayden teased.

"I have a feeling with enough time to be yourself, you're going to be trouble."

Ayden's grin charmed him. "I hope so."

Brogan swallowed a bite of his sandwich. "I was afraid of that."

The sexy little familiar next to him threw his head back and laughed. Brogan had a sudden urge to sink his teeth in his throat. He was getting over his issue with Ayden being a familiar. Ayden was a person, and it was embarrassing that Brogan hadn't understood that from the start. Being at D'Vaire was a good thing for Ayden. It allowed him to find out who he truly was, and Brogan would do whatever he could to help him.

It was beginning to feel like Brogan could forge a relationship with Ayden, and he was going to put his trust in Fate. She'd finally answered his call to find his other half, and he needed to be respectful of that gift. Brogan's dragon wanted to bite Ayden, which was proof he was already on board, and he trusted his beast's instincts. He hoped this was the beginning of something beautiful, and he was eager for the future.

13

"Ready for a super fun movie night?" Brogan asked his mate with a grin.

"You're a dork. Did you get snacks?"

"Of course. I have yet to see you go without food for more than fifteen minutes."

Ayden thought he'd gone at least thirty minutes without food since he had come to D'Vaire. It was so nice to be able to eat whatever he wanted in whatever quantity he wished. Hunger pains were a part of his past, and he refused to go back. It was one of the many things he preferred to keep in the history column.

"You're a filthy liar," he told Brogan. He needed to stop focusing on what he used to be and stay in the present, which would be easy as his entire evening was going to be spent with Brogan.

"First a dork, then a liar. Am I blushing from your praise?" the dragon asked as they walked to the kitchen to pick up their supplies. Brogan had invited Ayden to watch a couple of movies with him, and he was excited at the opportunity. They'd spent a little time together over the past few days, and Ayden appreciated that Brogan continued to encourage him to say whatever came to mind. He was embracing the inner voice inside him that preferred things on his own terms.

"No, but your arm's going to be sore from my punch in a second," Ayden responded. He wasn't planning on striking his mate, but he did enjoy their banter.

"Really? Because I don't see a ladder anywhere around here," Brogan teased as he grabbed some popcorn and chips for them. Ayden snatched a couple of sodas and made sure to remember a few napkins too.

"Oh, short jokes now? Just for that, I'm not sharing my popcorn."

"How are you going to stop me?"

All this talk of food was making Ayden ravenous, even though they'd just finished dinner. "I see we've completely forgotten that I have the ability to use your pants to roast marshmallows."

"You set me on fire again, and I might have to spank you." Ayden had absolutely no idea why Brogan's threat turned him on, but he couldn't deny that his cock was hardening in his jeans. It flustered him. He didn't want Brogan to notice his rapidly growing erection, so it was time to get to the den and get a movie started.

"Yeah, right. I thought we were watching movies?" Ayden asked as he quickly left the kitchen and headed down the hall.

"Changing the subject. Interesting. By all means, lead the way," Brogan replied as he trailed behind his mate. Ayden's cheeks heated at Brogan's words, but he let it go. He wasn't ready to figure out why the idea of Brogan smacking his ass made him horny. They finally made it to the den and settled down next to each other on one of the dark couches in the room. Across their laps, they balanced the popcorn and Brogan hit the remote.

Ayden watched the TV without seeing a single thing. All he could concentrate on was Brogan. They hadn't sat this close before, and he found it intoxicating. Their thighs were pressed together, and Brogan's delicious scent filled Ayden's nostrils. After Ayden finished the last of the popcorn, Brogan lifted the bowl out of the way and set it down on a nearby table. Brogan made no move to put any distance between them, and Ayden stayed put. He admitted to himself that he was loving every second of their evening so far.

The first movie ended, and Brogan stood to replace the DVD with their second film of the night. When he was done, instead of returning to Ayden's side Brogan walked back and fluffed the two throw pillows that were resting against the arm of the sofa.

"Want to get a bit more comfortable?"

Ayden was desperate to explore these feelings of arousal, but he didn't want to appear overeager, so he simply replied, "Sure."

Brogan gestured for him to get to his feet, and Ayden did as he was asked. Once Ayden was up, Brogan lay down on the couch and smiled at him in welcome. Ayden lowered himself down onto the sofa, and Brogan pulled him close until he lay flush against the front of his body. They were spooned together, and Ayden thought their bodies fit perfectly despite the height difference. Brogan draped his arm over Ayden's middle and once again pressed the remote.

Ayden couldn't care less about whatever was playing on the television; he was surrounded by six feet five inches of delicious male. His jeans grew uncomfortably tight as his cock filled. Brogan didn't help matters when he rubbed his hand over Ayden's belly through the thin cotton of his T-shirt. Brogan shifted slightly behind him and his mouth brushed Ayden's neck. He tilted his head to the side to give Brogan better access and bit his lip to stop his moan from escaping.

"No, baby. I want to hear every little sound you make," Brogan whispered hotly in his ear. His palm slipped under the hem of Ayden's top, and he continued the slow circles, only more intense on his bare skin. He placed kiss after kiss near Ayden's collar, and there was no stopping the sounds they created. Ayden was whining with need, and he desperately wanted more from Brogan.

"Roll onto your back." Apparently, Ayden wasn't the only one unsatisfied with what little they were doing. After complying with Brogan's orders, Ayden gazed into a pair of navy eyes filled with desire. Brogan leaned in and brushed their lips together, then dipped his tongue inside to taste. Without any experience to rely upon, Ayden simply followed Brogan's lead as they made out.

So absorbed with mouth on mouth, Ayden didn't realize Brogan's hand had moved from his midsection to his chest until his nipple was grazed by his mate's clever fingers. It sent little shocks all through his body and down to his rigid cock. Gasping with pleasure, Ayden curved closer to Brogan, and his mate responded by toying with the hardened peak. He had no idea such a small action could be so erotic, but Ayden was under Brogan's spell. All he wanted was to feel more and explore the possibilities that existed between two people.

After what seemed like forever, Brogan's palm moved down to roam across his stomach. Brogan pushed Ayden's T-shirt toward his chin, and Ayden broke another seemingly endless kiss to get the damn thing out of the way. Brogan helped him tug it over his head, and together they tossed it to the floor. After they were pressed close again on the sofa, Brogan nuzzled behind his ear.

"You smell so good," Brogan whispered. Ayden dragged in a breath as Brogan popped open the button of his jeans. He licked his way back into Ayden's mouth as his knuckles brushed over Ayden's hard shaft. Brogan dragged his zipper down, and Ayden was grateful to finally have some relief for his aching dick.

It was becoming difficult for Ayden to process thought. He burned from the inside out, and his entire being was focused on how Brogan was making him feel. Ayden wanted badly to acquaint himself with Brogan's body, but he was nearly frozen in place.

All Ayden could manage was to grab his arm as Brogan slid his hand into Ayden's briefs. Brogan stroked his cock, and Ayden closed his eyes to absorb the incredible sensation. It was his first taste of sex with a partner, and he was forever hooked. Brogan was broadening his horizons, and his back arched as tingles raced down his spine. It was too soon, but Ayden's release would not be denied. Brogan gave his shaft the tiniest squeeze...and Ayden exploded. He shouted out his climax as he filled his underwear with come.

When sanity returned, Ayden was still trying to catch his breath, and Brogan was nibbling his neck. Mortification made his cheeks burn. He was still mostly dressed, and he'd barely touched Brogan, whose hardness was poking his thigh. Ayden had to do something to make up for his stunningly quick orgasm, so he used a cleansing spell and started to roll over. Brogan caught on fast and freed his grip on Ayden's dick, allowing him to turn toward him.

Brogan captured his mouth, and Ayden kissed him back eagerly while he undid the dragon's jeans.

"Yeah, touch me," Brogan murmured after letting out a low moan.

Deciding it wouldn't be good to allow himself to get nervous, Ayden simply moved forward to complete his task. He wanted to see Brogan's cock, and he was desperate to reciprocate for the amazing orgasm Brogan had given him. Once Brogan's zipper was down, Brogan sat up without any warning and nearly toppled Ayden to the floor. After ripping off his T-shirt, he shoved his pants and underwear halfway down his thighs; then he lowered himself to the sofa, on his back.

Ayden smiled at the delectable scene in front of him. Brogan was thick and so rigid, he was leaking onto his belly. He was as mouthwatering to Ayden as a fat slice of cake. Letting the brave and fierce part of himself have full reign, he shuffled around so he was kneeling next to him. While he would've liked to taste Brogan, he didn't know how to give a blowjob, so it had to wait until Brogan wasn't so desperate. Instead Ayden licked his palm, then wrapped his hand around Brogan's dick.

"Jerk me hard. I need to come," Brogan groaned out as Ayden got to work. He liked the tenseness in Brogan's body. His muscles rippled as he writhed slightly on the couch. The navy eyes of his mate were hidden behind his lids, and the breath was being forced through his lungs and back out his slack mouth. Ayden stroked him with a single-minded intention and the cords of Brogan's neck stood out as he clutched the couch cushions beneath him.

Ayden's own blood heated despite his recent orgasm as his lucky gaze feasted on the sight before him. Brogan roared out Ayden's name as white ropes shot out over his hand. He continued to milk Brogan's cock as the dragon slowly relaxed.

"You gonna let go of that anytime tonight?" Brogan asked as he uncurled his fingers from where he was clenching the sofa.

"Maybe," Ayden replied as he reluctantly released him. Still trapped in a haze of lust, he scooted back and leaned over Brogan. He braced a hand against Brogan's side and lapped up his come.

Brogan chuckled and ran a hand over Ayden's hair. "Taste good?"

"Hmm," Ayden murmured. "As good as frosting."

"High praise coming from you."

"I hope you appreciate what good company you're in," Ayden teased as he finished licking Brogan clean. The dragon tugged him down to lie over him, took his mouth in a deep kiss, then wrapped him in his arms.

"Someday I'm going to make your every dream come true."

"Your dick, frosting, and cake all together?"

"We're really starting to get to know one another, aren't we?"

Ayden snuggled a little closer. He was glad Brogan wasn't mentioning how fast he had come in his undies. It was humiliating, and he hoped the next time they had sex he would improve his performance. Ayden figured they should probably get dressed, but he was reluctant to move. A little voice in his head hoped to hell Brogan had remembered to lock the damn door. "You're a dragon, but I like you anyway," he joked as he threw up an invisible magical barrier to give them privacy just in case.

"You're a small familiar thingy, but I like you too."

Lifting his head to meet Brogan's eyes, he was thankful there was nothing in them but satisfaction and humor. "I guess you've gotten used to me being magical."

"You're just Ayden."

"I'm glad you noticed," Ayden replied as he rested his cheek against Brogan's chest. He liked being the person who'd always lurked below the surface and was happy Brogan did too. Time would tell if he'd be able to be a good familiar and mate while still being true to himself. Ayden hoped he was up to the challenge.

14

Latarian paced the floor of her lovely bedroom as she tried not to panic. Over the last couple of weeks, Ayden was almost always in the company of the dragon Fate paired him with. The familiar was smiling all the time, and he was losing all the meekness she'd worked so hard to instill in him over the centuries. The bravery grew in his eyes each day, and he was acting more like Dra'Kaedan of Leolinnia—the precious son of T'Eirick and Saura destined to be the Grand Warlock. Such thoughts filled her with anxiety and rage.

Lifting a beautiful vase Larissa had filled with roses, Latarian smashed it into the wooden planks beneath her. It did nothing to cool her rising temper or quell her unease. In fact, her ire intensified as she didn't have Ayden at her beck and call to clean the mess she'd made. She murmured a phrase and within moments, her magic mended the vessel. With several choice curse words, she gathered up the flowers and dropped them back where they belonged. She set the entire thing where Larissa had originally put it and let out a shriek.

No one had any respect for her, least of all Ayden. If his ignoring her was not enough, there wasn't a single soul interested in clearing Carvallius's name. She couldn't bear life as the granddaughter of the biggest enemy of the Council of Sorcery and Shifters. There had to be a way to fix all her horrible circumstances, but Latarian was at a loss. She didn't want to spend her days coming up with clever schemes. Why could she not wake up the following morn and have things as they once were?

With her patience at an end, Latarian lamented the fact that she could not simply cast the spell to break Brogan and Ayden's mate-bond. She needed their blood to complete it, and with all the friendliness between the pair, neither would consent. Latarian shut down the voice that told her it might not work at all. Yes, her grandfather had found it in a demonic text, but she was sure with the amount of power Dra'Kaedan unwillingly handed her, she could overcome that tiny obstacle.

Whether she liked it or not—and she did *not*—Latarian was going to have to form a plan. She needed to return Ayden to the mouse who'd attended her over the centuries and get him away from Brogan. The problem was, she didn't have the first clue where to start. ...But Fate had awarded her a great deal of intelligence—surely, she could fix this mess. With a nod to herself, Latarian left her room to seek out Ayden. If she were lucky, the perfect solution would present itself while they spoke.

She ventured out the door and headed for the kitchens. *Ayden is forever cramming things into his mouth,* she thought as she strode down the hallway as fast as her legs would carry her. As luck would have it when she arrived, Ayden was there and cleaning his dishes.

"Ayden, might I have a word with you?"

He turned toward her with a bright smile, which only infuriated her more. She didn't want him to be so cheerful. Ayden was supposed to be resigned to his role as a familiar, not dancing upon the ceiling.

"Sure."

"A bit of privacy, perhaps? We could chat in my room," she suggested. It was imperative she had him alone, so she could speak freely. These D'Vaires were fond of reminding her not to be rude and a whole load of other nonsense she detested.

"Okay."

Latarian strode out of the room with Ayden nearly skipping along-side her. The fact that he wasn't walking behind her as she'd taught him made the blood in her veins boil. It didn't take long to get back to her bedroom, and she enclosed them both inside. To prevent any dragon from happening along and disrupting them, she threw up a magical barrier and soundproofed the space. Already she'd used more magic this day than she normally did in a month. It was one more thing to irritate her; she had power but hated crafting the phrases to complete spells.

"Are you well, Ayden?" Latarian asked as she took a seat on her lavender chaise. Without asking, Ayden dropped down into the chair next to it, which made her jaw clench.

"Yeah, I am. Are you?"

"I find myself most vexed."

"I'm sorry. What's wrong?"

Latarian narrowed her eyes briefly, then forced the muscles of her face to relax. "Let's leave it aside for a moment. How are things going with the dragon?"

Ayden grinned and it annoyed Latarian. "I think things are going really well. We didn't get off on the best foot, but he seems okay with me being a familiar now."

"Is he?" Latarian asked. She didn't like what she was learning; she had been counting on Brogan not recovering from his aversion to Ayden's status as a familiar.

"Yeah, he told me the other night I'm just Ayden. I was happy to hear it."

"Do you not feel you are being dishonest with him about who you truly are?"

"What do you mean?"

"You haven't been acting as a familiar should since he arrived. You've allowed these dragons to undo all the training we did together over the centuries."

The smile fell from Ayden's face, pleasing her. "You know I've always had that part of me that wants to push boundaries, and Brogan has encouraged me to be myself. I think to do that, I have to accept that I *do* have a temper. I like to ask questions and think my own thoughts."

"That is inappropriate for a familiar, is it not? Your role is to be influenced by your witch. Your opinions are my opinions. You are giving in to the temptation of acting wrongly as a familiar. We worked hard to quell your bad tendencies, and now you've become the very thing I most feared. A familiar who does not know his place."

Ayden's gaze hit the ground, and his shoulders slumped. It filled her with joy to see her words having some effect upon him. "Why would I have this desire to be fiery inside me if I wasn't supposed to ever allow it to come forward?"

"From the moment you were summoned, there was something off about you. I recognized it immediately and knew the only way to fix you was to manage your tendency to act inappropriately."

"But Brogan likes that side of me. He's encouraged me to let it out."

"He's a *dragon*, Ayden. He has no concept of witches or familiars. All he's doing is allowing you to betray your people. You are the last of your kind. Do you wish to represent them this way? Acting as if you are above yourself and shaming them as they view you from across the veil?"

He lifted his head, and Latarian suppressed her smile at the dampness in his eyes. "Of course not. I don't want to do anything to disgrace familiars."

"Then you must return to being the familiar I taught you to be. You must rise above that voice in your head that insists you act wrongly."

"What if Brogan changes his mind and goes back to being afraid of what I am?"

"If he should turn on you, then he is not the mate for you and we will cast the spell to free you, so you may find a partner who can appreciate what it means to be a familiar. We will always have each other, Ayden. It is you and I who must stick together through these challenging times and do what is best for our people. These dragons have provided us with things, but we cannot stay here forever. Our destiny is to bring the glory of the Coven of Witches back to the world."

"You don't plan on staying here at D'Vaire?"

"How can I? There will be a great many people who wish to meet with me once I am given the title of Grand Witch. I am most eager for it, but I have yet to find willing souls to help us clear Grandfather's name."

"I do want to do what is best for witches."

"Then you must prove to me that you are willing to be a good familiar."

"I do want to be a good familiar," Ayden whispered.

"Then you must put your witch above every other one of your piddling concerns. I am what is most important in your life."

"Of course, you're important to me."

"Then we have a great deal of work to do to restore you to the Ayden I know lives inside you. The familiar who is obedient and hardworking."

"I promise I'll do a better job."

"Let us begin where we started all those centuries ago. Go on, you know what to do."

He didn't look particularly pleased, but Ayden rose slowly. "Where is it?"

"I put it in the trunk at the foot of the bed," she informed him as she got to her feet.

Ayden crossed the room and opened the chest. He found the whip, handed it over, then yanked off his T-shirt. Without a word, he turned and placed his hands on the tall bedpost. Latarian couldn't contain her smile this time as she swung and brought the lash hard against his skin. She loved the sound as it cracked through the air and the metallic smell of the blood as it flew from the first of many wounds she gave him. He healed almost instantly, which spurred her on to mar his flesh again. The tension in his body and the pain she was inflicting had her lifting her arm over and over.

She lost track of time and space as she beat him. Her fear of losing her power lessened with each violent blow. His grunts grew louder and the sweat pooled between her breasts, dampening her gown, and still she struck him. Latarian thrashed Ayden until his body trembled, and she lacked the energy to continue. Tossing her weapon to the ground, she took stock of her surroundings and the crimson soaking his waistband was most satisfactory. She had managed to make him bleed a great deal, which was a miracle given the extent of Carvallius's spells on his back, and it pleased her tremendously.

"Clean your clothing," she ordered. Though she would've loved to see it as a reminder of his capitulation for the rest of the day, it would anger the dragons.

A wisp of magic flowed over him, and the stains disappeared.

"Go on, put the lash away. You'll need to cleanse my dress as well," she stated as she noticed the splashes of her handiwork on the lavender cloth.

When he turned and bent down to grab the whip, she was pleased by the tear stains on his cheeks. He would not soon forget her efforts. After he replaced the lash and cast the spell to make her dress once again pristine, he pulled his T-shirt back on. Latarian retreated to her chaise as the idea of a nap beckoned. *I overexerted myself for his benefit*, she thought. He came to stand near her and his face was full of misery.

"You will not tell King Aleksander of this. He does not understand your role, nor does anyone else here. I am the only one who knows how a familiar should act. Remember that when you decide to allow that hostile part of you to overcome your good sense. I do not enjoy beating you," she said. It was a half-truth. She enjoyed his pain but wasn't fond of the effort it took from her.

"I won't tell anyone. I'm going to do a better job of being a familiar."

"See that you do."

"I don't want you to cast the spell to break my matebond, though. I think Brogan likes me, and he'll get used to me being the familiar I should be."

Were Latarian not already so weary, she would have risen and slapped him. He was supposed to have seen the error of Fate's match, not become determined to make things work with the dragon. Had all her effort been for naught? "Remember that we cannot stay here forever. Your dragon may not be willing to give up his title to be the Grand Witch Familiar-mate."

Ayden shrugged as his head bowed. "I guess I can talk to him about it."

"Be sure he is ready to accept you as you are first. There is no sense in bringing the future into it yet. I will be your counsel, and you should seek me out as you build your relationship with this dragon. It is my responsibility to see to you as is yours to me. You've had your freedom. Now it is time to return to your proper place."

"Okay," he whispered.

"Go on now. I need to rest."

Once he was gone from the room, she laid her head against the cushion behind her. Latarian was unsure what Ayden would do, but she had to wrestle back control of him. It wouldn't do to return to life as a novice; power was as necessary to her as breath in her lungs.

15

Ayden soaked his pillow in tears, and it didn't make him feel any better. He couldn't understand what was wrong with him or why he'd been summoned as such a mess. All his life he'd struggled, and when he finally took a few baby steps toward allowing his true personality out, he wound up disgracing his people. Brogan wanted him to be himself, but who was that? Was it the guy Ayden preferred who spoke his mind, or was that nothing more than the bad behavior Latarian claimed it to be?

She'd beat him mercilessly. Ayden had feared Latarian wasn't ever going to be over her desire to continue lashing him. A wave of relief had flooded his entire being when she'd tired, and the pain stopped. If he set out to once again be in the role she preferred for him, he would have to get used to those punishments being part of his day. It was a good thing Carvallius gave him a mending spell; he'd be mortified if Brogan found out what a failure Ayden was as a person.

Since crying wasn't doing anything but giving him a headache, Ayden got a hold of himself. He lifted his body from the bed and ambled into the bathroom to clean his face. Once he was done, he chose to leave his room altogether. When he got to the living room he found Blodwen watching her channel of crime stories.

"Hey," he said as he sauntered over to her and tried to ignore the television.

"Where'd you run off to? I thought you were going to eat, and then we were going to get to work," Blodwen replied as she hit the remote, making the screen go dark.

"Oh, I was talking to Latarian."

Blodwen pursed her lips. "What did Miss Witch have to say?"

"Not much," he lied. "We should probably not say mean stuff behind her back, though."

"I'm sorry. I don't mean to make things weird. I know you're stuck with her."

"She's helped me my whole life."

"For her benefit, I'm sure."

Desperate to change the subject, Ayden asked, "Did you want to work on the sanctuary stuff?"

"Sure, unless you want to hang out with Brogan."

The last thing Ayden wanted to do was see Brogan. He needed some time to remember he was supposed to be a familiar, and Brogan tempted him to be lured into the dark place inside him that did crazy things like spout his opinion or set people on fire. "No, I can see him later or something."

Blodwen got to her feet and slipped her arm through his. "Did you guys have a fight?"

"No, why would you think that?" Ayden asked as they journeyed toward her room.

"I don't know. You've got this kind of sad aura about you. The first thing that jumped to mind was that something had happened between you."

"Nothing happened."

"That's good. I know it has to be a relief that things are working out so well with Brogan now. I still can't believe he was freaked out because you're a familiar. I'm glad he's encouraged you to be yourself."

Ayden didn't know who that was anymore. "I hope he understands my relationship with Latarian."

Blodwen opened the door to her space and once they were inside closed it again. She went over to a lovely gray desk and flicked her laptop on. "You mean, you hope he understands that you're wonderful, but she's a pain in your side that won't ever go away?"

The day before, Ayden might have laughed at her teasing, but now it made him feel guilty to disrespect his witch. "She's not so bad."

"Ayden, you're too nice."

"What do we need to do to start our petition for the sanctuary?"

"That's where I'm running into trouble. This website that has all the information for what you need to include is so boring, I've only managed to get through a little bit a day. I don't want to overlook anything, so I'm making copious notes."

"You know this stuff way better than I do, but I'd like to help."

"Well, read over my notes, and let me know if it makes sense. Then, you can help by sitting here with me while I'm reading this shit and slap me awake so we can get this show on the road. I want to get this sanctuary moving forward."

He took Blodwen's notebook from her and perused it. "Me too. I think it's going to be wonderful. I hope I'll get to see it in action."

"I'm determined to find a way to get this thing up and running," Blodwen responded as patted his knee. "We'll do it. No worries."

Ayden was concerned that Latarian would drag him from D'Vaire before the sanctuary was created, but he didn't want to say that to Blodwen, so he just nodded. It hadn't occurred to him that Latarian would ever want to go. His heart ached at the thought of saying goodbye to Blodwen and all the dragons. Would Brogan be willing to leave? He had spent years traveling away from D'Vaire but that was temporary, and he'd always had his family to return to. *Maybe it would be best if I free him, so he doesn't have to make that decision*, he thought as sorrow settled over him.

He was still learning about Brogan, but their relationship was growing each day. Before his session with Latarian, he was confident they were on the right path. Now things were going to change. Ayden had to be true to the familiar he was and stop allowing himself to be drawn into unpleasant habits. Shrugging off the weight of his future, Ayden focused on the task at hand. He might not have the chance to stay and watch the sanctuary grow, but he'd do everything to make this a reality for the incredible D'Vaire dragons.

"You ready to do this?" Brogan asked as he showed off by shuffling the cards into a bridge before they cascaded together seamlessly.

"I don't know any card games," Ayden responded as he sat across from him in the den with a blank expression on his face.

"Hey, that's what I'm here for. I'll teach you," Brogan said as he distributed the cards evenly between the two of them. "We're going to start with a super easy one. It's called War."

"War?"

"Yep, all you have to do is turn over the top card and if it's higher than mine, you take both cards. Whoever winds up with the entire deck is the winner."

"What if we have the same card?"

Brogan winked at him saucily. "I love how clever you are. Okay, that's the war part. If that happens, then we'll each put one card face-down and then a second one up. It keeps repeating until somebody wins."

Ayden was silent as he flipped over the top card on his stack. He was barely making eye contact with Brogan. For the last few days, Ayden had been uncharacteristically meek when he wasn't making excuses not to hang out together. Brogan didn't give two shits about their card game; he wanted to know what was up with his mate. They played for several seconds, so Brogan could marshal his thoughts and decide how best to approach the subject.

"You're winning," Brogan said. "Nice job."

"I've only gotten six of your cards."

"While I've only won one of yours. That puts you in the lead."

"Okay."

After it was quiet for several minutes minus the sound of their cards, Brogan noticed Ayden was ignoring the bowl of chips he'd set out. "You aren't eating."

"I just had dinner twenty minutes ago."

"When has that ever stopped you?"

"It's better behavior for me to only eat at mealtimes."

"That's an interesting viewpoint. What made you decide that?"

Ayden shrugged but didn't otherwise answer.

"I know we got off to a bad start, but we're friends now right?" Brogan asked. When Ayden simply nodded, Brogan was grateful he'd bypassed a soda for a beer. Lifting the bottle, he took a long drink as he studied the redhead in front of him. He was staring down at his cards, and it was driving Brogan crazy.

"Tell me what you think friends do."

Ayden lifted his head with a perplexed expression on his face. "You want to know what a friend is?"

"I want to know your opinion about friendship."

"Um...a friend is someone you care for. A person you like to hang out with and can rely upon to help you when you need it, I guess."

"Maybe even someone you'd come to if you had a problem, right?"

After flipping over another card, Ayden bobbed his head, which caused one chunk of hair to fall over his forehead. Brogan reached out and smoothed it back. Ayden's entire body went still, and he stared up at Brogan with an indecipherable look.

Brogan narrowed his eyes in growing frustration. "What's going on with you?"

"Nothing. We're playing cards."

"You're not acting like yourself. I know the mate thing is still a work in progress, but at the very least, we're friends. I mean, I've had my hand on your dick, so I don't know why you'd freeze because I touched your hair," Brogan retorted with irritation. He was mystified by Ayden's behavior, and he wasn't getting anywhere in under-standing why the familiar had put this sudden distance between them.

"This is me," Ayden said quietly with his words measured. "I'm a familiar, and I need to always be true to what is expected of me. I thought you understood that."

"Oh no, we're not going back to that shit. I told you I was okay with magickind. Yeah, I freaked out, and I apologize for that. It was wrong of me, but you aren't acting like the guy who licked come off my chest."

"I don't know why you keep bringing that up," Ayden replied. His tone may have been level, but Brogan was glad there was a banked fire growing in his eyes.

"Because we both enjoyed it, and now you're acting like some docile little mouse. That's not my Ayden."

"I'm not your Ayden. I'm a familiar. I'm Latarian's Ayden."

"Other people don't have to share their mates with someone else."

"Other people aren't mated to familiars. Another familiar would understand my role," Ayden bit out. It was an almost euphoric feeling to get under Ayden's skin. It might help him break through this strange barrier he'd erected, so Brogan could figure out why he was behaving so strangely.

"I'm not going to apologize for being a dragon. We were doing okay up until the last few days when you started spending less time with me. When we're together you're reserved, and not the fiery Ayden I know is inside you."

Ayden slammed his hand down on the table and stood. "That Ayden is unacceptable. He's everything that's wrong with me. A familiar isn't supposed to look past their own role and want more. My duty is to my witch."

Equally incensed, Brogan got to his feet. "Where does that leave us?"

After taking a deep breath, Ayden's turbulent gaze met his. "I don't like the idea of going against Fate. She matched you and me in her belief that we're good for one another, but there are many differences between us. Some of them may be insurmountable. If we don't want to be together, there's a solution."

"What the hell are you talking about?"

"Latarian knows a spell that can break our matebond. We would be free to have Fate pair us with someone else."

Brogan's dragon roared in fury inside of him. Closing his eyes, he struggled for control of the beast who couldn't stomach the idea of having their mate taken from them. Once he was sure he wouldn't shift inside the den, he lifted his lashes and pinned Ayden with a hard look. "Break our bond?"

"The idea's unsettling to me, but we need to keep it in mind."

"Did you ask her for the spell?" Brogan demanded.

"Brogan—"

"Answer the fucking question," he bellowed.

"No," Ayden snarled back. "I didn't even know a spell like that existed."

"Come with me," Brogan ordered as he turned to leave the room.

"Where are we going?"

It was not Ayden Brogan was furious with, so he held out his hand to the pissed off familiar. "You and I are going to have a little chat with someone in the living room."

Ayden's brows snapped together in confusion, but he put his palm in Brogan's, which helped calm the raging beast inside him. In a flash, Brogan understood exactly what change had come over his other half, and he wasn't going to tolerate anyone messing with his matebond, even if it was Ayden's witch.

16

Ayden was trying his best to scurry behind Brogan, but the dragon wasn't having it. He kept stopping and wouldn't move again until Ayden was at his side. It was making the short trip to the living room take an inordinate amount of time. He was so ashamed of his behavior. It didn't matter how hard he tried when he was around Brogan, his temper flared. Perhaps Latarian was right, and being with the dragon wasn't the best thing for him. If there was any hope of him being a good familiar, he had to resist the fire inside him, and Brogan's very presence seemed to beckon it.

When they finally got to their destination, Latarian was sitting on the sofa as she normally did while she was awake and not lecturing Ayden or whipping him in private. Blodwen was also sprawled over a couch watching television as were the other ladies of D'Vaire. The only family members missing were Dravyn and Aleksander, so Ayden assumed it was not either of them Brogan was searching for.

"Latarian," Brogan boomed out, and Ayden shrunk inside his skin. The dragon had no idea that he was sentencing Ayden to a harsher lashing the next day by disturbing his witch.

She lifted her chin and lowered her book to her lap. Ayden

wondered why she was still bothering with her ruse; she didn't even flip the pages, so she wasn't fooling anyone. "Can I assist you?"

"You're damn right you can," Brogan shot out. "You can explain to me why the fuck you offered to break my matebond with Ayden."

Ayden tried in vain to pull his hand out of Brogan's, but he wouldn't let go. He didn't squeeze enough to make it painful, but escape was impossible, so he settled for trying to scoot behind him.

"I do have such a spell. It is available to all who might find it necessary."

"That goes against Fate," Brogan snapped.

"No one and nothing is perfect, including Fate," Latarian responded. She didn't sound perturbed, but when she rested her eyes on Ayden the storm clouds brewing in them did not bode well for him.

"Are you aware that interfering in a matebond is punishable by death?" Brogan yelled.

"I am not interfering in anything. My duty is first and foremost to the wellbeing of my familiar. I simply made all options known to him. It takes only a moment of your time and a drop of your blood."

"It's not an option," Brogan roared. "I won't tolerate this bullshit."

"I will do what is right for Ayden, even if it hurts your feelings, dragon. He requires someone who understands him. A person who will motivate him to be a good familiar and not fall into unpleasant habits," Latarian explained haughtily.

"I think Ayden can figure those things out for himself," Blodwen interjected as she muted her show.

"She's right, Latarian. Those kinds of things need to be decided between Ayden and Brogan," Noirin said.

"None of you know what a familiar is. You don't understand him, and you certainly cannot comprehend our bond. He requires my insight to decide his fate," Latarian snapped.

Two tall dark-haired men strode into the room, and the entire D'Vaire family was now going to understand what a failure Ayden was. The inner voice inside of him wanted to tell Latarian to butt out and mind her own business. Fate gave him Brogan, and she needed to respect that, but he did his best to ignore the fire in his gut.

"What's going on?" Aleksander asked.

Brogan whipped his head toward their king and pointed at Latarian. "She's interfering in my matebond."

This entire situation was humiliating, and if Ayden was a good familiar, they wouldn't be standing in the living room having a shouting match over Latarian's offer to help.

"Tell me how," Aleksander commanded, every inch the D'Vaire ruler.

Brogan explained the spell, and one black brow raised at the news. Aleksander turned to Latarian and stared at her for several seconds, then gave his attention to Ayden, who was still standing as far behind Brogan as he could manage.

"Ayden, come here," Aleksander directed in a gentle voice. Brogan squeezed his hand, then released him.

Ayden stepped around Brogan and stood in front of King D'Vaire.

"Did you ask Latarian for a spell to break your matebond with Brogan?" Aleksander asked.

Knowing he had to tread carefully, Ayden was quiet for several minutes as he weighed his words. "Latarian has only my best interests in mind."

"You didn't answer my question," Aleksander said.

Ayden struggled to figure out how to respond. This was the king who took care of the entire court, and Ayden didn't want to defy him by being dishonest, but he was supposed to always put Latarian before himself. The inferno inside him was screaming and yelling that it was his chance to tell Aleksander everything. He wanted to explain that Latarian was going to take him away from this wondrous place and how she insisted the only way he could be fair to her was to submit to sessions with her lash.

For six centuries, he'd been molded into her idea of what he should be without ever knowing who he was or if her punishments were fair. He'd had no one to ask, and he still lacked that ability since he didn't want to betray his dead brethren. Tears threatened and in the end, all Ayden could manage was a shrug. The magic danced over his skin as he struggled to contain not only his ire but his power. It was as if he was standing in shackles and dying to get out while the rest of the world wasn't privy to his struggle.

Aleksander reached out and squeezed his shoulder. "I'm not going to pretend I understand the unique relationship between witch and familiar but as your king, I have a duty to see to your happiness. That's not for me....It's for all of you. Whether you're a familiar, witch, necromancer, or dragon, you need to search inside yourself and unlock those things that fuel you. Ayden, I want you to have everything imaginable, but I can't give you joy. That must come from within. Tell me what you want."

"I don't know," Ayden responded miserably as he lost his fight with his emotions.

"Why don't you know?" Brogan asked softly. None of the fury he'd walked into the room with was evident in his voice.

"Because he's a familiar and must rely upon my counsel, not that I expect any of you dragons to understand. You spend each day enticing him to act in a way that shames him and our people. You've confused him and led him astray. I am the only one who knows what is best for him," Latarian asserted.

"I find it difficult to believe that an entire race of people—in this case, familiars—are supposed to give up their hopes and dreams. I fail to see any fairness in having them forsake their own desires and have to ask someone else what's best for them," Blodwen said.

Latarian stared down her nose at Blodwen. "You have a sentinel you keep imprisoned because of your own silly fears. I'm sure you're more in touch with the idea of lesser beings and sorcerers than you will admit."

"As long as you call D'Vaire home, you will be civil toward each other," Aleksander barked.

"Ayden, you know what it takes to be a good familiar, even if you often fail to reach that goal," Latarian remarked. "I trust you will make the right decision."

"Why don't you stop trying to manipulate him?" Brogan demanded.

"Ultimately, what happens between Brogan and Ayden is their business," Aleksander stated. "Ayden, I know this is difficult for you. You've had to adjust to a great deal since you arrived at D'Vaire—a new way of life and the reality of finding out your race is nearly extinct. Then Fate offers you your other half. I think it's understandable that your head's a mess. Am I right?"

Ayden blew out a breath that fluttered his hair. "Yes, my head's been spinning for weeks."

"I know this might not be a popular decision for everyone involved, but I think what you need Ayden, is some time. I think space to clear your mind would be helpful, so you can figure out what you want without any influences. That means I want you to keep your distance from both Latarian and Brogan."

"Aleksander—"

"Not forever, Brogan, just a few days," Aleksander said. "That means no afternoon meetings in Latarian's room either. Is that understood?"

Latarian's fists clenched. "Of course, Aleksander."

"I'm not fond of handing down penalties, but if either of you disturb Ayden in any way, there *will* be hell to pay. Ayden, I'm counting on you to be honest with me."

"I will," Ayden promised. He was grateful to Aleksander for awarding him with this gift. He did not necessarily want time away from Brogan, but to have distance from Latarian was such a beautiful thought; he nearly fainted with the ecstasy.

"Good, then why don't you go off to your room? Noir, maybe you could bring him some snacks," Aleksander suggested.

"I might've made a cake today," Noirin said as she got up and headed to the kitchen. Ayden's heart melted at the kindness of the D'Vaire dragons and without a word, he raced to his bedroom to obey his king.

"I should call the Order of the Fallen Knights to tell them about my matebond being interfered with," Brogan complained as he dropped down onto one of the couches in Aleksander's office.

His best friend's smile was unrepentant. "Going to tell on me or Latarian?"

"Both of you," he griped.

Aleksander took a long drink from his beer. "I can see the misery all over Ayden's face, and you're the one who's been yapping in my ear for days about him not being himself. For six hundred years, the only voice he's had in his head is Latarian's. I think she's probably freaking out over losing control of him and is doing what she can to interfere."

"If you think she's interfering, why isn't she being punished?"

"Because we need to tread carefully here. This is the grand-daughter of Carvallius, who's convinced he's innocent. It's the whole *Wizard of Oz* thing. Is she a good witch or a bad one? She likes all the luxuries of being out of that cottage but if I start stepping too hard on her, she's going to leave. If she goes, so does Ayden. He has no choice."

Brogan's head dropped back against the cushion. "She'd do it too."

"Did Ayden give you any clue why he's suddenly acting like a mouse?"

"Not really. He wants to be a good familiar. I'm not sure what that has to do with not thinking for yourself since he's the one who told me that wasn't part of it."

"You mean like you thought it was at the beginning."

"You know what the problem with family is, Aleksander?"

"Yes, they never forget shit, especially when it's the bad stuff."

"Exactly," Brogan said, then lifted his head to meet Aleksander's eyes. "I'm only willing to give Ayden a week of space."

"You aren't the person I'm trying to keep him from, so I can live with that as long as he's not complaining. He's got to figure out what he wants without Latarian trying to control him."

"What afternoon meetings were you talking about?" Brogan

asked as he replayed the conversation they'd all just had in the living room over in his head.

"It's just interesting that you're suddenly having trouble getting Ayden to spend any time with you, and I just happened to see him slipping out of Latarian's room this afternoon. He looked pretty miserable until he noticed me. Then his face showed nothing at all."

"I can't even imagine the shit she's saying to him."

Aleksander gulped more of his beverage. "Let's just hope she's only using words."

"Fuck, Aleksander. Don't put that in my head. I'd lose my shit if I thought she was hurting him," Brogan said as he shook his head to clear the images Aleksander had created. He assured himself a woman who didn't do anything all day but sit in front of a television she pretended not to watch couldn't be that dangerous. "I just want Ayden back. The one who smiles, teases, and knows what he wants."

"He needs to reconcile who he wants to be without Latarian's influence. Of course she doesn't like that side of him—she'd control the world if she could."

"Must be a Mallent thing."

Aleksander cocked a brow. "Your mate's a Mallent."

"No, he's a D'Vaire, and I'm his dragon."

"I'm kind of missing that Brogan who was freaking out over the familiar thingy Fate so cruelly paired him with."

"You're such a dickhead."

The only response Brogan got from his barb was the rich laughter of his best friend.

17

The problem, as far as Ayden was concerned, was that he already knew what he wanted. Given the choice, he would embrace the side of him that wanted to stand tall and let his wishes be known. He wanted to get pissed off when things didn't seem right or fair to him and be able to speak his mind when it suited him. When he sat down and thought about it, he couldn't understand why that part of him was so different from everything Latarian had instilled in him. He was taught to trust and believe in Fate, so why would she give him such a powerful side he couldn't touch?

Under the strict rules Latarian insisted upon beat a heart of courage that wanted to change the world. He wanted to embrace his sorcery, the deep well Fate granted him, and test how far he could stretch it. Ayden wished to live with only the repercussions doled out by his own conscience. He was a good person, one who sought to help others, and he yearned to accept his own strength. The reality was, Ayden wasn't comfortable with a familiar's lot in life—at least not Latarian's version of one.

When he allowed himself to think without constraints, which was possible with the distance Aleksander demanded he have from Latarian, he asked questions he would never dare say to her face. She was the granddaughter of a traitor—a man who saw his own needs as more important than the entire Coven of Warlocks. He'd read plenty since they'd journeyed to D'Vaire, and Carvallius put higher value on his desire to be Grand Warlock than he did the lives of his own people. She'd been raised by him because her mother and father were dead. Latarian hadn't spoken of her parents, but Ayden discovered it was Carvallius who was suspected to have killed them.

Would a woman raised by a man like Carvallius really be the authority on how anyone should act? Perhaps Ayden wasn't being true to himself because of her desire to have him meek when that wasn't his destiny. One thing was for certain; he couldn't stomach the idea of having his matebond erased. He was *not* going to allow it. Ayden wanted to spend time with Brogan and move forward. What he hadn't experienced in over six centuries of life was love, and he wanted it desperately. In a perfect world, his choice would be to stay at D'Vaire and help the family he wanted to be a part of grow a sanctuary where people who didn't fit in could find refuge.

Unfortunately, nothing was perfect, and there were limits to his desires. He could demand that Latarian stay out of his matebond, because he trusted Aleksander to stand up for the rules of the Council, but he couldn't make her stay with the dragons. It would be cruel of Ayden to expect Brogan to give up the people he cared for, and he refused to put him in that position. His brain screamed out, and he wanted to set himself on fire for even thinking about walking away, which left Ayden right back where he'd started—in an endless loop of madness with no easy solution.

Kicking off the covers, Ayden got out of bed. He'd tossed and turned for hours; sleep was going to continue to evade him. It was way too early for breakfast, and that gave him a tantalizing idea. With the entire household asleep, he could go outside and switch into his little dragon form. In the past, it'd helped him clear his thoughts, and he was eager to get out of his mind before he lost it completely.

With great care, Ayden tucked the navy-and-white comforter into place. Once he was done, he fished out some clothes from his dresser and headed into the bathroom. It only took him a few minutes to take a quick shower. After he was dried and dressed, he slipped from his bedroom and used magic to cancel out any noise his sneakered feet might make on the floor. He opened the back door and went outside. Since it was not a real entity inside him, he didn't have to worry about ruining what he was wearing. It was a good thing, because he wasn't comfortable getting naked in the backyard. Taking no time to second-guess himself, Ayden murmured, "*Telavolerian draca dolcornulan.*" It was an ancient warlock language, and he still had no idea how he'd learned the words, but they always worked. His vision grew sharper; then in a flash, his body shrunk down into a tiny dragon. Flapping his wings, he headed for the garden, so he could enjoy Dravyn's flowers as he left his troubles behind.

Brogan wasn't enjoying his separation from Ayden. He'd just started to get to know him, and now he had to worry about some witch ripping him away. It pissed him off, and he'd spent too much of his life in isolation anticipating the day Fate matched him with his other half. There was finally a window to his happiness, and Latarian was trying to slam it shut before Brogan could even appreciate his gift. He understood Aleksander's desire to give Ayden space, though. It was difficult for anyone to be in a tug of war, and Ayden needed to figure out for himself what he wanted.

As for Brogan, he had to wait and hope Ayden wanted to embrace the relationship they were building as well as the fiery part of him he was taught to deny. After punching his pillow about five times and still not finding a comfortable spot to fall back to sleep on, Brogan gave up. He wasn't going to waste time worrying over the future. He would accept the choice Ayden made and go from there. In the meantime, he needed to give his dragon plenty of time to fly. His beast was antsy over the possibility of losing their mate, and Brogan was shifting at least once a day.

Saving his shower for after his flight, Brogan shoved his legs into a pair of jeans and yanked a T-shirt over his head. He didn't bother with shoes; he was going to have to strip down as soon as he got to the deck. Leaving his room, he enjoyed the peace and solitude the early morning brought as he strode through the house. After crossing the width of the kitchen, he opened the back door and sauntered out. He reached up to undress when something in the garden caught his attention.

There was a big-ass blue bird flying above Dravyn's roses. He blinked, but the scene in front of him remained unchanged. Though he was sleep-deprived, he was still pretty sure he wasn't hallucinating. He allowed the navy of his irises to bleed into the white of his eyes, switching them to their dragon counterpart. With his vision clearer, he took a few steps closer as he tried to make sense of the scene in front of him.

Brogan left the deck and discovered it was not a bird at all. In fact, it looked like a dragon. It was a dragon. The smallest one he'd ever seen—but that was not the strangest part. What was truly fascinating was that the little invader was a doppelganger for Brogan's beast.

"What the hell?" Brogan muttered loudly after he marched closer. The dragon hit the ground and rolled into a rose bush.

"Ow," the shrub said.

Brogan's sight shifted back to normal, and he ran toward where the beast had landed. His now-human orbs grew as large as saucers in shock as his mate emerged from under the leaves and flowers.

"What the hell?" he repeated.

"You can't tell anyone I can do that," Ayden ordered him in a tremulous voice.

"Roll into rosebushes?"

"No, change into a dragon."

"You aren't a shifter. How can you do that?"

"I don't know. It's a spell I've always known," Ayden confessed.

"Why is it a secret?"

"I don't know, Brogan. I've read every book I can get my hands on, and I haven't found any other sorcerer who can do that."

"How long have you been able to do it?"

"The spell is the first thing I knew when I was summoned."

Brogan leaned closer to him, so happy to be in his company after the last several days of only seeing him across the room at mealtimes. "Can I tell you something about your dragon?"

"Um...yeah. I guess."

"I've seen it before."

Ayden's head jerked back. "What?"

"Your dragon, he's very familiar to me."

"You're acting weird."

"You've learned by now we're all weird. It's a D'Vaire thing, but don't sidetrack me. I want to talk about your dragon. It's a perfect replica of mine."

For a moment Ayden's brows drew together, and then he opened his mouth, presumably to speak, but he snapped it shut again. He cocked his head to the side and stared for several seconds. "You have my dragon?"

"Nope, I'm a century older than you. You have my dragon," Brogan said as he stroked the soft skin of Ayden's cheek. "Fate made you just for me. Fiery. Dragony. Mine."

"Aleksander," a female voice Brogan knew all too well screeched loud enough to rattle the glass of the many windows of their home. "Get out here this instant. This dragon has broken the rules."

The back door opened, and Ayden slipped his hand into Brogan's. Aleksander marched out in a crazy pair of Larissa-made pajamas with his face dark as thunder. After he stomped over to them with Latarian on his heels he frowned. "Brogan? Ayden? What's going on? I thought we agreed it would be best to have some space."

"It was a happy accident," Brogan informed him. "I came outside to fly and found out I wasn't the only one who—"

"Brogan," Ayden shot out in warning as he pulled his arm away. Brogan peeked down at the scowling familiar but couldn't suppress his urge to shout from the rooftops that they had matching dragons.

"You are upsetting my familiar with your very presence. Since we are all here, I don't see why we should not cast the spell to separate you," Latarian interjected.

"You...*butt out*," Brogan retorted as he pointed a menacing finger in her direction. He'd had enough of Latarian, and she could take her spell and shove it.

"Ayden, Brogan was outside to fly, and you just decided to take a stroll in the gardens at five in the morning?" Aleksander asked, skepticism dripping into his voice.

"No, it's like I was saying Ayden was—"

"Brogan, you *promised*," Ayden bit out. The green in his eyes was disappearing as the navy underneath took over. It was something Brogan witnessed only once before, and it was when he'd had his dick in his hand. He wasn't sure how someone's irises could change that way, but he liked the reminder of their passion together.

"It's okay. You don't have to keep it a secret anymore."

"I get to decide when I want to give away my secrets," Ayden returned, the ire in his tone rising.

"Will you trust me?"

"This has nothing to with trust. It's my secret, not yours," Ayden shouted with his fists clenched at his sides.

"This is nonsense. Ayden has no secrets from me. Go on, Ayden, use your magic to create a dagger so we can get this over with," Latarian demanded.

"That's enough out of you," Brogan snarled. "He does have a secret. One he's kept since he was summoned so you don't know shit. He can—"

"Damn it, Brogan," Ayden growled as he stamped one foot.

"Would you calm down? So, you have a dragon form? What's the big fucking deal?"

"The big fucking deal is that was my secret, and you had no right to tell anyone," Ayden yelled.

"I should've known you would do something such as this, Ayden. You've always been clever and fond of books. This was a way to keep me here was it not? It will not work. I am not destined to live in a house full of dragon shifters," Latarian stated.

"You aren't going to take my mate from D'Vaire, and weren't you listening? He's had his dragon form—a perfect replica of mine by the way—since the moment you summoned him," Brogan snapped.

"Everybody calm down. It's too damn early in the morning for all this screaming," Aleksander retorted. "I understand D'Vaire might not be your idea of paradise, Latarian, but ultimately I'd like Ayden and Brogan to get to decide their future. I think you and I should have a long talk about what it'll take to keep you here. I know it's a big sacrifice to ask you to stay, but I'm sure we can figure out something to keep you happy."

"I do not know if such a thing is possible, but I will think on a list of things I believe will enhance my life here at D'Vaire," Latarian arrogantly replied.

"You're not taking my mate from me," Brogan said as he tried to keep his dragon calm.

"Do I get a say in any of this?" Ayden demanded and while Brogan wasn't happy that he'd pissed him off, it was nice to see him back to the fiery familiar he adored.

"Of course you do," Aleksander calmly replied. "Tell me what's on your mind."

Ayden glared at Brogan. "I'd prefer someone who didn't blatantly disregard my feelings and give away my secrets."

Brogan threw up his hands in exasperation. "I'm sorry. Sue me for being excited that you have my dragon."

"I'd like to see it if you don't mind," Aleksander threw in.

Ayden let out a growl from deep in his throat; then he diligently returned to his tiny dragon form. It brought a smile to Brogan's face to see a miniature version of the beast that shared his soul.

"Fuck, he really is an exact replica of you. That's incredible. Thanks for sharing that with me, Ayden," Aleksander said.

"It is nothing but trickery," Latarian replied as her lips pursed in disapproval.

It was soon apparent that Ayden was finished with the conversation. He reappeared in his familiar guise and then shimmered out of the backyard. Brogan hoped he'd teleported back to his room and not another continent. It was unfair of Brogan to tell everyone about his dragon, even if he was proud of his mate. He had some serious making up to do, and he trusted Aleksander would find a way to please an obstinate witch, so they could keep Ayden at D'Vaire. Lifting his head to the sky, he wondered why Fate stuck him with such a large thorn in his side. It was a good thing he was already convinced Ayden would be well worth the headache of dealing with Latarian.

18

Latarian believed she'd done an excellent job of dealing with the unexpected crisis that had opened up before her very eyes. For one blissful second, she was sure that when Aleksander witnessed Brogan and Ayden breaking his rules, he would demand she split them apart. Clearly, she'd overestimated the intelligence of these shifters, because Aleksander hadn't offered any kind of punishment at all. Fury had burned through her, and she was ready to hurt someone when Brogan announced that Ayden had a dragon form.

Dra'Kaedan and his brother Dre'Kariston were born with that ability. It was why they had such unusual names. Grand Warlock T'Eirick and Grand Summoner Saura had shouted from the very rooftops about the births of their sons and their special capacity to become small dragons. It accounted for the "Dra" in Dra'Kaedan and the "Dre" of Dre'Kariston. Both came from the ancient word for dragon. If there were any others, they'd kept their secret hidden—but Latarian doubted the Leolinnia twins were gifted something so rare that it was unique to only the two of them.

A cold sweat had formed down the entirety of Latarian's spine as she'd stood in the garden. If any of the imbeciles around here put any thought into Ayden's dragon and did any research into the missing twins, she could very well be doomed. She shuddered to think about what might befall her if Ayden's identity was indeed discovered. It'd taken an hour of pacing to calm down, and it was only when she reminded herself of the stupidity of the people around her that the blood warmed in her veins.

Dra'Kaedan would remain as Ayden and no one would be the wiser, she decided. Idly she wondered what had become of the twin, Dre'Kariston. Carvallius had plans for him, but the history books told nothing of his whereabouts. As Dra'Kaedan had, he'd simply disappeared. With a shrug, she gave up thinking about Dra'Kaedan's brother. If he were alive somewhere, it meant nothing to her.

Now that she'd recovered from her fright, she thought of the other problems facing her. Ayden was likely lost to her. She doubted she'd have the opportunity again to beat him into submission, and a part of her was glad. It was such a nuisance to have to continually correct his behavior. He really was quite detestable, but that didn't mean she was going to walk away. After all, they had no choice but to stay near. Her grandfather's spells caused Ayden horrific pain if he strayed too far.

It made her laugh to think of it. If she wanted to be particularly cruel, she could simply teleport away and leave him writhing on the floor, but the world still believed Carvallius was evil. It was unlikely she'd find welcome refuge anyplace but with these idiotic dragons. The good news was, Aleksander was willing to do whatever it took to keep her at his home. He was eager to promise her everything, so Brogan could have access to the revolting Ayden. She didn't see why she shouldn't take advantage of his offer.

The one thing she would never give up was her power, so if Aleksander wasn't accommodating enough, she'd leave without any further discussion—Ayden's plans be damned. The Order of the Fallen Knights couldn't stop her; she'd simply return to the land of her birth where they had no authority. Castle Mallent remained, according to what she'd learned, but it was a crumbling structure with the ground blackened. With enough of Aleksander's coin, she could have it restored. She'd leave the Council behind and watch with immense joy as Ayden pined for the dragon he could not have.

It might be the best plan as Latarian was still unsure what would happen if Ayden did complete his matebond. She certainly didn't need his presence in her life, but his deep well of sorcery she couldn't do without. What if it broke the link Carvallius had crafted, and Ayden was thrust into a place between the veil? Dra'Kaedan was too strong for it to kill him, so at some point he'd return. Would he have any memory of Latarian and what had been done to him? She wasn't sure, but he might not take kindly to her if that were the case. She was a Mallent, so he might even blame her for the demise of his family.

Latarian was surprised she hadn't worn out the floor with all her pacing of late. She was stuck in turmoil no matter how she examined the situation. She wished she could choke Ayden for suggesting they should scry and leave the cottage. As dreadful a hole as it was, life was much simpler, and Latarian longed for a time when she had less preying on her mind. Forcing herself to sit, she picked up a pen and tapped it to her lip.

She didn't particularly care for all the things Aleksander's money could buy, given that he had no way of restoring Castle Mallent, but she did so love a person willing to dance to her tune. This part of her predicament she could certainly get used to, she mused as she scratched out the first list of her life. She promised herself she would rest as soon as she finished; she did not appreciate having to go to such lengths to get even the simplest things done.

Ayden was slowly going insane. Several days had passed since his inopportune flight in Dravyn's garden, and he didn't know what to do. It wasn't a new feeling, he mused as he lay on his bed. If he wasn't struggling to figure out who he truly was, then he was wondering if Latarian would allow him to stay at D'Vaire. The witch had started negotiations with Aleksander and from the prim smile she wore when she left his office each day, Latarian was enjoying every moment of this game.

That insight and knowledge of her personality had settled one thing in Ayden's mind. She might have spent centuries trying to break him down, but she did not have the power to change his nature. He wanted to be the person that lurked inside him. Ayden wasn't going to allow insecurity to rule his life or allow her hatred of his true personality to keep him from it. She could wound him, and she might even be able to drag him kicking and screaming from D'Vaire, but he would not be broken. Ayden had found his fire, and he was so much more than her whipping boy.

In the garden a rush of fury had raced over him, and he'd exulted in not holding back when he'd become upset. He was going to remember that moment when she glowered or spat curt words. She could only make him cower if he gave in to her demands, and he wasn't going to do it any longer. Familiars were intended to be a friend or companion to their witch, and he needed to stand his ground. With that weight lifted off his shoulders, it should have been easy to move forward with Brogan, but it wasn't.

He had grown upset with him over breaking his word, but he was not so uncompromising that he'd allow that to be a barrier to happiness. What pulled him from Brogan's side was Latarian's threat to leave D'Vaire. When he reflected on their life together, he examined it through the eyes of his tougher side instead of accepting her words at face value. The reality was, she wasn't a kind person, and she probably reveled in being able to wave over his head the idea of separation. Aleksander could promise her his entire kingdom, and she might still wake up one morning on a whim and travel far away, giving Ayden no choice but to follow.

For Ayden, it left him with a difficult decision. Did he risk moving forward, stripping away the walls between him and Brogan to learn everything he could about him? Could he allow his heart to grow fond of him, knowing their love might not endure the test of time? He supposed questions like that were always asked between mates. Brogan was undaunted by such menial problems. He'd been camped outside of Ayden's room for days. Whenever Ayden opened the door, there he was, stretched out on the floor, staring up at him with determined eyes. It was as unsettling as it was flattering.

With a rush of determination, Ayden resolved not to be a prisoner to his bedroom. He pushed himself off the mattress and in a matter of seconds, turned the knob to leave. As he'd expected, there was a giant dragon sprawled against the wall.

"Hey," Brogan said, wariness in his navy gaze.

"Hey."

"Can we talk?"

"Are we even allowed to yet?"

"It depends on you. You've had over a week now to think on your own. How're you feeling about everything?"

Ayden shrugged. "I think I've figured me out. I know who I want to be. It's going to take work to shake off my shackles, though."

"No one should've ever shackled you, baby."

"I'm not sure *us* is a good idea," Ayden said apologetically.

"I think it's something we need to talk about."

Reaching up to scratch his head, Ayden lifted his shoulders a second time.

"I'm not going away. I know you're pissed at me, but I'm not giving us up without a fight. We need to talk before anything's decided."

Knowing the dragon was serious, Ayden nodded. "I promised Blodwen I'd go to her room and help her with some stuff. Maybe we could talk after dinner?"

"Go on, help her. I'll go grab a shower and see you at dinner."

"Okay," Ayden replied. He waved at Brogan, then headed to the next door over and knocked.

Blodwen opened it and pulled him inside. "You made it past your guard," she teased.

"I can't believe he's still hanging out there. I don't think he's left to sleep or anything," Ayden told her as they crossed the space and piled on her bed. She had her laptop and the partially completed sanctuary application spread out over the coverlet.

"At least you know he's serious about being together and getting you to forgive him."

"I'm not angry at him anymore. What difference does it make if everyone knows I have a magical dragon form? It's not that I don't want to be with him. I just don't know what to do. Latarian could make me leave and then what? Either lose my mate or force him to make a choice between me and his family."

"Her lazy ass isn't going anywhere. Aleksander's going to give her every damn thing she wants, and Fate love him, because I don't know how he hasn't killed her yet."

"My gut tells me you're right, but my heart's scared."

"Okay so don't judge me but I was watching a show..."

Ayden rolled his eyes. "Blodwen, I don't want to know about your gross crime shows."

"I'll have you know this was a comedy. I can't watch the murder stuff before I go to sleep, or I'll have nightmares."

"I watch it during the day and have nightmares," Ayden muttered.

"Anyway," she drawled out with an annoyed expression. "Sit your sexy dragon down and together you guys can make a list of pros and cons. You'd get to talk things over and even learn some shit about each other. It'll help you both decide if it's worth the risk to move forward."

The more Ayden thought about the idea, the more he liked it. He smiled at his clever friend. "That's genius. I've already agreed to talk to him after dinner. I'll just get a pen and some paper, and we'll work it out. Like you said, we can ask questions and either this is going to work, or it won't."

"Don't you hold back. Just be yourself. Not the Ayden Latarian wants," Blodwen instructed as she poked him lightly in the chest. "Be the Ayden inside of here. He's a great guy with a fiery spirit. You're awesome. I promise."

"Okay. I like that Ayden too."

"Good. Slap a hand on your hip and give the world hell."

"I'm so glad I fell over you that day," Ayden said.

"Best day of my life. Now let's get this sanctuary shit done, so we can have a house full of awesome people who are freaks like us."

"It's going to be so damn awesome."

"Yeah, and maybe we'll even find some people crazy enough to want to hang around Latarian, so she'll stop fixating on being a pain in your ass."

Ayden grinned and only experienced a twinge of guilt as he agreed with her. "It'd take someone pretty special to want to befriend Latarian."

Blodwen leaned in and her gray eyes widened. "Here's one for you. Somewhere on this planet is her mate."

"It's funny because she's a witch, so she's not lacking sexuality like a familiar, but I don't even know if she prefers women or men."

"Well, you did spend over six centuries trapped in an isolated cottage, so there's that."

Ayden chuckled. "Good point."

"Do you really even want to know?"

"My brain simply stops whenever I try to go there, but you know what I do want?"

"Tell me, Ayden D'Vaire. What's one thing you want? You know, besides that sexy dragon lying in the hall."

"I'd like for you to meet your mate."

Her smile was gorgeous. "Who knows? Maybe he'll even knock on the door just like you did."

"Not if we don't finish this application."

"Let's do this shit," Blodwen replied, then turned her attention to her computer. Ayden was grateful to have someone who didn't judge him or expect him to be anyone but who he wanted. To be Blodwen's friend, he didn't have to make any tough decisions; all he had to do was simply be. He refused to think about her out of his life, and it was a similar struggle when Brogan came to mind. Later he would sit down and find out if Brogan was worth the risk of a broken heart since Latarian couldn't be counted on to keep her word. A voice in his heart, the one he was beginning to trust, told him he already knew the answer.

19

Taking a seat on the big couch in Aleksander's office, Ayden set a pad of paper on his lap and glanced up at the dragon sitting next to him. Brogan had circles under his eyes, but at least he smelled a damn sight better.

"Blodwen suggested we make a list of pros and cons about us being mates. We can then discuss it and make a decision together about our future," Ayden explained.

"Okay, that sounds like a promising idea to me."

"All right. I'll start. Con—"

"You're starting with a con? Not much of an optimist, are you?"

"Nope, I've lived my whole life with Latarian. Con—"

"Wait."

"What now?"

"I think we should discuss whether each item is a pro or con before we write it down," Brogan suggested.

"Not happening or we'll never get through this. We write it down. When it's your turn, you can dispute a con with a corresponding pro or vice versa."

"You've really worked this out, haven't you?"

"Yep, strained my little brain cells all through dinner," Ayden retorted, and Brogan let out a laugh. "Back to business. Con—Brogan gave away Ayden's secret dragon form."

"I'm sorry. I really am. I shouldn't have betrayed your trust, but I think it's amazing and if I promise to never tell another of your secrets, can we remove that con?"

"No, you know the rules."

Brogan furrowed his brow. "Technically, I don't believe I agreed to them."

Ayden's self-assurance grew as he allowed his fiery side to take over him. "I'm pretty sure I didn't ask if you did. Now, it's your turn."

"Pro—Ayden has a secret dragon form."

"I think you're wasting your turn. Do we need to write down that you like that about me?"

"It's my turn and I get to use it as I want," Brogan retorted with a grin.

"Fine, then it's my turn again. Con—"

"Again with a con?"

Ayden let out a chuckle at Brogan's penchant for interrupting him. "Yes, now hush. Con—Brogan is uncomfortable that Ayden is a familiar."

"Nope, that should be past tense. I was uncomfortable in the beginning because I didn't know anything about witches. I traveled a lot, but you know how it is by now. There's still a great deal of space between magickind and shifters. I spent most of my life ostracized and talking to the five people in my family. When we left our previous court, it was 1369 and we didn't even know sorcery existed. I didn't pay enough attention when we joined the Council because the only familiars I'd ever heard of were mage elementals. Have you seen those things? They're like swirls of air or hunks of rock."

"But I look like a warlock, so you knew I wasn't one of those."

"Why not just say you appear human-like?"

Ayden leaned toward him. "Because warlocks have larger brains."

"I knew you looked like a warlock or witch, but it took me awhile to wrap my brain around the familiar thing. It didn't take me long to get over the creep factor. I was convinced I'd have to share you with

Latarian in the beginning and she hasn't made things easy, but I don't have any problem with what you are now."

"None at all?"

"Not when you're like this. Your eyes are sparkling, and I can see your confidence," Brogan told him. "I still have questions about your people, but I have no objections."

"What kind of questions?"

"Like do you have any other form besides a dragon?"

"All witches and their familiars have what we call a 'true form' which we use for deep casting or ceremonies. I've never used it because it's just been Latarian and me. Being Latarian's familiar, it's just a bunch of pale green markings on my skin," Ayden explained. "For whatever reason, her markings don't reflect her level of power so Latarian hates it."

"Okay, I'd still like to see it someday. What schools of magic do you have? That's what they're called, right?"

"Yes, witches can have them all. Depends on how much they want to study," Ayden informed him.

"All?"

"Uh huh. You can choose light spells or dark spells. All you have to do is take the time to study. The only exception is for necromantic spells, because we're taught that goes against Fate. Witches don't raise the dead."

"So Latarian studied and then taught you all the spells when you were summoned?

"I added to what she knew by studying, but I was summoned with all her knowledge and memories."

"Wow."

"Yeah, and since she's a woman, I know things I wish I didn't," Ayden confessed as Brogan roared with laughter.

"You were made by her magic. What happens if you were to run out somehow?"

"I die. Familiars just go poof and disappear."

Brogan's eyebrows shot up to his hairline in surprise. "Seriously?"

"Yeah, but it's not something I worry about. I have a deep pool of power."

"How long do witches live? How long is your life-span?"

"Weaker witches have a similar life-span to yours. The more magic, the longer you live. For me, I'm strong enough to have eternity."

"Wait," Brogan stated as he closed his eyes for several seconds. When he opened them, they were full of shock. "You're immortal?"

"Yep."

"So, if we were to complete our matebond…"

Ayden grinned. "Yes, you would be too."

"Okay, I'm going to set that aside because my brain can't even process it. We're going to move on. Your eyes turn blue sometimes."

"I can't explain that. It happens if I cast a strong spell or my emotions get intense."

"It's really hot."

"I don't think that's the reason I have it."

"It not just hot…it's sexy. It happens when you get aroused. By the time you came, there wasn't any green left at all," Brogan informed him in a warm voice.

Ayden decided they needed to get back on track. He wasn't ready to talk about the night when he'd embarrassed himself by filling his briefs after Brogan barely touched him. "Zip it. Are you done with your questions, or can we get back to our list?"

"I suppose I'm done for now, but I do reserve the right to question you at my discretion."

"Whatever," Ayden retorted with a roll of his eyes. "Your turn. Pro—"

"Hold on there, it's my turn. I get to decide if it's a pro or con."

"No, we have to put a pro to correspond with the con of your former uncomfortable feelings about me being a familiar. So, pro—Brogan has overcome his disgust for Ayden."

"Disgust's a hard word, but at least we have that straightened out."

"Right. Con—"

"No way. You've done two cons and I haven't even had a real turn yet. You have to do a pro," Brogan informed him.

"Why?"

"I just explained it. Write a pro down."

"Fine, but it might take me awhile to think of one," Ayden teased as he tapped the pen on his paper.

"Then I should have a turn."

"No way."

"I already thought of a perfectly good con. I could write it down," Brogan suggested as he made a move to grab the pen. Ayden moved his hand out of reach.

"My pen. My rules."

"Fine, I'm tired. I'll just take a nap while you take your sweet-ass time," Brogan retorted. He leaned his head against the couch and feigned sleep by letting out ridiculously loud snores. The corner of Ayden's mouth lifted in a half smile at the dragon's antics.

"Pro—we already have the same last name."

Brogan sat up straight again. "That's terrible. Of course we have the same last name. We live in the same dragon court."

"I didn't have enough time to think of a better one."

"That's nice. My turn. Con—Ayden likes to set people on fire."

"Pro—Brogan's a shifter who can heal quickly."

"You're turning into a real little shit," Brogan said, and Ayden laughed. He liked being able to tease his mate and was glad the dragon was fine with it as well.

"It's your turn."

"Right. Pro—"

"You're already switching to your pro list?" Ayden asked, happy to be the one with the chance to interrupt.

"I like to mix it up. Pro—Ayden's a good kisser."

Ayden refused to blush. "Con—"

"Nope, you're supposed to say, 'Pro—Brogan's a good kisser,' " Brogan told him seriously.

"I'm afraid I can't say that. I don't have enough evidence to make that determination." Ayden hoped Brogan accepted the gauntlet he'd just thrown out.

"I believe I can help you with your data collection."

"Okay."

Brogan leaned toward him and used one finger to lift Ayden's chin. They stared into each other's eyes for several moments, and there was amusement and lust in the dragon's navy depths. Without a word he brushed their lips together, then set his mouth firmly over Ayden's. He licked his way in, and their kiss became all-consuming. Ayden's heart pounded in his chest and his body responded eagerly as Brogan caressed his jaw. He wanted to feel the way he had the night in the den and his blood traveled south.

When Brogan lifted his head and put some space once again between them, Ayden couldn't process a single thought. Gathering his scattered wits, he cleared his throat. "Pro—Brogan's an excellent kisser."

"Change mine to Ayden's a fucking fantastic kisser," Brogan demanded as he reached over to grab the pen.

To keep Brogan from snatching it, Ayden smacked his hand. "No way. There are no edits."

"Ow," Brogan complained. "You put excellent and I only put good."

"It's not a competition."

"The hell it's not. Fix it."

"No, that's not happening. Your turn."

Brogan let out an overly dramatic sigh. "Fine."

"Pro or con?" Ayden prompted.

"Give me a second. All my brain cells are in my dick—thanks to your hot mouth."

Ayden was flattered to have that kind of impact on Brogan. "I'm pretty sure your brain cells can't travel like that."

"I think I know my dick a little better than you do."

"Well, whose fault is that?"

Brogan's eyes widened; then he let out peals of laughter. "Okay, here's mine," he said after he got his hilarity under control. "Pro—inside of Ayden is a fiery temper."

"You said pro, but that's always been a con for me."

"I consider it a pro and so should you."

"Why?"

"It shows you have a passionate nature."

Once again, the heat headed toward Ayden's cheeks. He hadn't looked at it quite like that. It'd always been a surging beast inside him, but perhaps Brogan was right. "Oh."

"Did I make you speechless?"

Ayden shrugged. "Technically I did say, 'Oh.' "

"Okay, time for you to list a pro."

"No way, I did a pro last time. Con—Ayden's not Brogan's type."

Brogan frowned. "I'm pretty sure we haven't discussed types. How do you know you aren't mine?"

Ayden was going to have to admit to eavesdropping on his conversation the first night when Brogan returned home. His bad behavior was embarrassing, but they needed to clear the air about everything between them. "After we met, you told Aleksander I was very small. You didn't seem pleased by that."

"How do you know that?"

"I used magic to listen to your conversation. You were also concerned I wasn't anatomically correct, but you know...you've touched...I mean—"

"I've jerked your dick so good—is that what you're trying to say?"

"Yeah."

Brogan winked. "I like all your parts. As for your height, all my previous partners were dragons. They tend to be tall, so I was shocked that you were only a couple of inches over five feet. It doesn't matter though. I still find you very attractive."

Ayden didn't appreciate hearing about Brogan's previous lovers, but he supposed that was natural. Fate gave him to Ayden, and the last thing he wanted was to visualize other men in his place. Shaking off those horrid thoughts, Ayden returned to the subject at hand. "The con's still accurate. I'm not your type."

"It doesn't matter. You're my mate, and I find you very desirable. That makes you my type. What about you? Am I your type? What kinds of things attracted you in the past?"

"I didn't have one," Ayden confided.

"You don't have to be shy. Tell me about the men you were with. Tall? Short? Blond? What?"

"None."

"What's that mean?"

"What do you think that means? Familiars lack sexuality until they meet their mates. Which turned out to be a good thing since I spent almost my entire life stuck in a cottage with Latarian."

"I didn't know that. I'm sorry, baby. I didn't realize you were a virgin. You don't kiss like one."

Ayden peered down at the floor and hunched his shoulders. "Now maybe you'll understand why I embarrassed myself in the den that night."

"I have zero clue what you're talking about."

His head popped up, and his brows snapped together in annoyance. "Did you forget that I came in my pants after you barely touched me?"

"Listen, you don't have a damn thing to be embarrassed about. Do you have any idea how incredible it made me feel to make you come so fast? I love knowing I drove you that crazy. I seem to recall emptying my balls not long after you did. No one's ever kissed me the way you do. Pro—Brogan doesn't give a shit about types."

So busy staring at Brogan in wonder, Ayden just sat there until Brogan bumped their shoulders together.

"Write it down, Ayden."

Shaking himself out of his stupor, Ayden did as he was told. It was his turn, and he couldn't think of another con. Latarian would do as she pleased, but he wasn't going to put her on the list they'd created together. However, he couldn't ignore the impact she might have on their future. "I don't have any more cons, but I'm scared."

"I am too," Brogan confessed. "I think we're supposed to be. This is too important for it not to be scary. We'll take our time and get to know one another. Fate brought us together, but we have to figure out how it works."

"What if Latarian wants to leave?"

"Is that what scares you the most?"

"I don't want you to have to choose between your mate and your family," Ayden confided.

"It won't be you forcing me into that corner. Let's not freak out over that now, though. We should concentrate on moving forward one step at a time."

Ayden bobbed his head in agreement. It was all they could do. "Okay."

"Total honesty and communication from here on out. I'll tell you if something's on my mind and you do the same."

"I'm going to reserve the right to set you on fire again if you piss me off," Ayden teased.

"Note to self—to avoid being scorched, don't piss off Ayden."

With a grin, Ayden stood. "Now that we have everything settled, I'm heading to my room."

"Same for me. I'm exhausted."

"Why were you camped out in front of my room anyway?"

"I knew you were angry at me for giving away your secret, and I didn't want you to rush into any decision without speaking to me first. I couldn't get the thought out of my head that you'd ask me to give you my blood to break our matebond."

"I'm a long way from being convinced it's even an option."

Brogan got to his feet and flexed his spine. "Good. I can't keep that up. Do you know how many achy body parts I have?"

Reaching out and laying a hand on Brogan, Ayden murmured a healing spell and one to ensure his mate had a restful sleep.

"Thanks. I feel amazing," Brogan told him with a gorgeous smile.

"You're welcome. Thanks for showering before our meeting. You were really stinky."

"I'm going to have to burn the clothes I was wearing."

Ayden smirked. "I can take care of that for you."

"Little pyro. Give me a hug so we can both get some sleep."

Taking a step forward, Ayden leaned into Brogan and their arms came around each other. "This is nice."

"We fit perfectly, baby."

"Can I get a good-night kiss now?" Ayden asked.

Brogan touched his lips gently to Ayden's forehead, then released him and put several feet of space between them. "Good night."

"That wasn't a kiss."

"Sure, it was."

"Not like the ones we've had before."

"We've decided to take things slow. It's going to take some time to work up to that kind of kiss," Brogan said as he headed to the doorway. "See you in the morning."

Ayden stood there stupidly as Brogan left him alone. He hadn't expected after all the progress they'd made to move forward, to lose the kisses he'd only had the pleasure of experiencing a few times. Refusing to be daunted, Ayden lifted his chin, proud he was true to himself all evening. He was going to continue to spread his wings, and he was glad Brogan would be at his side. Mating was a scary thing, and there were no guarantees in their future, but Ayden was committed to giving it his all.

For the past several days, Brogan had dedicated himself to spending as much time as possible with Ayden. While he would've liked to be alone with him, that wasn't a good idea for his libido, so they'd stuck to family gatherings only. He didn't know why the hell it hadn't occurred to him that Ayden was a virgin, but now it was important that he respect his innocence. It also made him nervous as hell; he wanted Ayden's forays into sex to be positive ones, and he was putting a lot of pressure on himself to get it right. His dragon was thrilled—his beast didn't want anyone to put their grubby hands on their mate, but he wasn't the one who had to make love to Ayden, so Brogan was ignoring his desire to take him to bed immediately.

From the moment he met Ayden, their relationship had rested on a precipice and with the threat of Latarian looming over them, that wasn't going to change. It was important to keep his mind far from those dangers and simply focus on the here and now. Ayden bursting out of the shell Latarian had put him in was helping significantly with that issue. Brogan was enjoying every minute in his company. Eager to be with him, Brogan grabbed a shower and then dressed.

After leaving his room and heading to the kitchen, he wasn't surprised to find Ayden sitting at one of the stools, shoving waffles into his face like they were about to go extinct.

"Good morning, mate," Brogan said as he took a seat next to him. He grabbed a plate from the stack Noirin left out for the household.

Reaching out his fork to grab some waffles from the giant stack on the serving plate, he was stopped by a hand on his arm. "Those are all mine," Ayden informed him.

"Fuck off, I'm starving."

"Too bad. *Mine*," Ayden growled at him.

"Your name isn't on them," Brogan retorted and helped himself to breakfast.

"It is now."

Brogan glanced down and each of the three waffles he'd put on his plate had Ayden's name emblazoned across them. Laughing at the crazy familiar, Brogan smothered them with syrup. "Did you honestly think that would stop me from eating them?"

Ayden shrugged. "It was worth a shot."

"Why do you eat so much anyway? You got a tapeworm or something?"

"No, I did tell you I was nonsexual before meeting you. Familiars can reproduce on their own and a few weeks before you arrived, I decided I wanted a baby. I'm eating for two."

"You're full of shit. You're just a pig."

"So true," Ayden responded cheerfully.

"Got any plans for the day?"

"Yeah, I promised Blodwen my morning."

"Can you promise me your afternoon?"

"Well, that would depend on what your plans are."

All Brogan was concerned with was spending time with Ayden; he was game for anything he suggested. "Not sure yet, you got any ideas?"

"Hey, guys," Blodwen greeted them as she entered the kitchen and sat on the other side of Ayden.

"You gonna write your name on her waffles too?" Brogan teased.

"He better not. I'll turn his to smoke," Blodwen said as she grabbed breakfast for herself.

Ayden let out a gasp. "Cruel necro."

"Nasty little witch helper," Blodwen threw back.

"Zip it. Brogan and I were talking," Ayden teased.

"You tell people to shut up a lot," Blodwen retorted.

"Yeah, what I don't understand is why no one listens," the familiar remarked.

Blodwen leaned back on her stool and caught Brogan's eye. "So, Brogan, what were you and Ayden talking about?"

"Don't mind me," Ayden interjected.

Brogan gave Ayden a little pat on the head and earned himself a glare. "Don't worry, we won't. Ayden and I were talking about what to do this afternoon."

"Oh cool, what did you decide?" she asked.

"Nothing yet. Ayden's too busy stuffing himself to think properly."

Ignoring Brogan, Ayden turned to Blodwen. "What are you doing this afternoon?"

"The ladies of the house are going shopping for fabric and clothes."

"Oh, that sounds fun. Have a good time. I'd like to go but I made plans with Brogan, and I'd have to convince Latarian to go."

After taking the last bite of his waffles, Brogan slid off his stool. He grabbed Ayden's dishes and rinsed off their stuff, then placed it all in the dishwasher. When he was done, he walked around the counter and held out his hand to Ayden. "Come on," he said as he wiggled his fingers.

"Huh?"

"Take my hand, and let's go."

He got a puzzled look; then Ayden hopped off his stool and slid his palm into Brogan's. They headed down to the hall to Aleksander's office where he was hanging out with his cousin Noirin.

"Good morning, Your Highness," Brogan stated.

Aleksander threw up his middle finger at his best friend. "What the hell do you want, *Your Grace*?"

"Assistance."

"That's nice. What did you do to Ayden?"

Brogan frowned in confusion. "What do you mean? He's standing right here."

"He's holding your hand, and it appears not to be under duress," Aleksander teased.

"What's with everybody today? I'm short but I'm not invisible," Ayden interjected with a wave of his unoccupied hand down his torso to emphasize his point. "I'm standing right here."

Refusing to give in to his mirth, Brogan lifted his chin. "Baby, let me handle this."

"Brogan, just ask Bigfoot for whatever assistance you believe he can provide."

"Bigfoot?" Brogan asked.

"Yeah, Aleksander's abnormally large."

"Nope, you're just abnormally small, Squirt," Aleksander said.

Ayden cocked out one hip. "At least I don't have to wait for it to rain to take a shower."

"At least I don't need a ladder to get on the toilet," Aleksander fired back.

"You do realize I'm barely an inch shorter than Aleksander, right?" Brogan asked Ayden.

"Don't spoil my fun," Ayden instructed, and Brogan bit back a grin. This was the Ayden he liked, the one who said whatever came to his mind and whose potent spirit was unmistakable.

"Right. Well, here's the deal. Ayden and I would like to accompany the ladies going shopping this afternoon. Can you arrange that with Latarian?" Brogan requested.

Aleksander nodded but didn't appear thrilled about it. He met with Latarian to go over how to keep her at D'Vaire daily, but Brogan was short on details about how things were progressing. Brogan had faith Aleksander would do his best and trusted it to be good enough. "I'm not going," Aleksander stated.

"No one invited you, honey," Noirin told him in a singsong voice.

Somehow King Aleksander D'Vairedraconis was still sane, although he wasn't sure how long that was going to last. He woke up each morning reminding himself that Ayden had endured the company of Latarian of Mallent for over six centuries without anyone else around, and he'd done it at her mercy. She might prefer to flounce around in long gowns in varying shades of purple and request things like flowers, but there was nothing gentle about her. There was avarice in her eyes, and the taunting smile she wore told Aleksander she enjoyed the process of making demands more than getting the things on her list.

After all, the stuff she requested was silly in nature. A soft throw for her bed, another cushion for her sofa, and several pairs of new shoes. He was generous with his family and she was a D'Vaire now; her bank account had a tidy sum in it. She could've purchased all those items on her own, but the woman didn't want to do a damn thing for herself. Noirin had left his office after confessing Latarian requested all her personal items be purchased by Aleksander's cousin. Latarian couldn't be bothered to pick out her own soap or shampoo.

She believed she was clever in telling Noirin she needed her to buy them because it was too confusing for someone who'd walked out fresh from the fourteenth century, but Ayden didn't have the same difficulty. The familiar had picked up everything in his new life with great ease. As Aleksander leaned back in his chair and girded himself for another irritating conversation with the only witch on the planet, he thought about Ayden.

Brogan might have his mind in a whirl over discovering they were mates, but Aleksander wasn't muddled in the same fashion. He'd witnessed all the nasty looks Latarian had thrown at Ayden since the pair walked through the door. She might profess to hold her relationship with her familiar above all else, but it was evident to Aleksander that she could barely stand Ayden. She'd spent centuries manipu-

lating him into believing her ideas of how he should act and when
Ayden started behaving more like himself, something had changed.

One day he was once again standing behind her and dropping his
gaze to the floor. There was no doubt in his mind that Latarian had
used some sort of physical punishment to alter his outlook. She had
no other hold on him; he wasn't like the other familiars. Aleksander
hadn't missed the Prism Wizard's shock when he'd learned that
Ayden produced his own magic. So, what was it that kept him to her
side if not the threat of violence? He wasn't sure, and he had no
evidence, but if Aleksander found out anything of the sort was going
on under his roof, there would be hell to pay.

Aleksander hoped with time Ayden would get comfortable
enough to tell someone, likely Brogan, about it. Then Aleksander
could figure out a way to punish Latarian without compromising the
relationship between Ayden and Brogan. It pissed him off on every
level that a person would use someone's matebond to force the
people around them to play to their tune. There was no doubt about
it—Aleksander did *not* like Latarian. That troubled him. He wasn't
simply King D'Vaire; he was part of a family. The core of their court
was a common love for one another, but he couldn't feign feelings he
didn't have. When Latarian sauntered into his office, it took all his
considerable control not to curl his lips into a sneer.

"Good morning, Latarian. Did you have breakfast yet?"

"I cannot abide those...waffles. You simply must tell your servants
to do better when it comes to meals."

"My what?"

"Your servants. The woman in the kitchen—she's rather
outspoken."

"Latarian, I don't have servants. I've never had them, and I never
will," Aleksander retorted. He took considerable pride in that fact
and wouldn't be the kind of king he'd once lived under. "Noirin's my
cousin, and she happens to enjoy cooking. I don't have any say in
what she prepares. She's free to make whatever pleases her."

"So, we are all to suffer at her whim?"

"I'd suggest if you don't like what she serves you, fix something for yourself. She's nice enough to keep the kitchen stocked with all kinds of things. I know you've added things to her grocery list before."

"Aleksander, you simply must understand how difficult it is for someone adjusting to this century."

"I know. We've been over this a few times. It's important that you try, though. Noir's only helping you while you figure things out."

"I assure you, I am doing all I can to learn of your world."

"I'm sure you are," Aleksander said, proud he kept his tone level. "I just talked to Brogan and Ayden. They'd like to go shopping this afternoon with the ladies. What can I offer you to allow them to go?"

"I would have to spend the entire afternoon traipsing from one establishment to another?"

"I understand there's a courtyard around the shopping area. You could relax there if you prefer," Aleksander replied. He hadn't seen it for himself—he rarely left his home, but he'd heard from his family that it was pleasant.

"I see. I suppose I could rest there if I had food and drink. Perhaps Larissa might be persuaded to purchase more cloth to make garments for me? I do so hate making do with so few dresses."

"I'll speak with her. I'm sure she'd be happy to, and I'll ask Noir to make you a snack," Aleksander said. All the D'Vaires had already assured Aleksander they'd do anything they could to help with Latarian. They were fond of Ayden, and they didn't want Brogan to lose his mate to a conniving witch.

"Very well, then. I shall accompany them, but I do not wish to be gone for more than an hour or two."

"I'm not comfortable limiting their trip, but I will ask them to be as quick as they can."

Latarian rolled her eyes; then they lit up with a mix of greed and spite. "Shall we move on to our other negotiations?"

"Sure. How's your list coming along?"

"The thought that occurred to me as I tried to find rest was that I am in need of much coin if I am to stay here at D'Vaire."

"Have you even looked at how much is already in your account?"

"Truly Aleksander, how would I even know how to do such a thing? I need coin I can hold in my hand."

"Everything's done electronically in the Council now. They don't issue coins or paper money. They haven't for a few years."

Her skin turned ashen, and she stared for several minutes; then she suddenly rose to her feet. "I see. I must think on this."

Without giving Aleksander any time to respond, she disappeared. He was glad the Council of Sorcery and Shifters had embraced technology and done away with the trappings of physical currency. Aleksander was certain she'd planned on building herself a little stockpile of riches in her room before running off to wherever in the world she decided would be better for her than D'Vaire. Perhaps she was finally realizing that she needed this place, and Aleksander hoped it boded well for Ayden. His best friend had waited forever for the familiar, and Aleksander wanted Brogan to be happy. He'd missed him over the past few years of his wandering, and Aleksander wanted everyone he loved to stay close.

21

"Of all the damnable luck," Latarian shrieked in the comfort of her room. She did not want anyone in the house to know how very angry she was. Her plan had been a simple one. Aleksander was willing to hand over anything she wanted and in doing so, had opened a world of possibilities for her. Then a few days ago in his office, he'd calmly explained to her that coins and paper money no longer existed within the Council. It was as if even in death, the Leolinnia family was screwing up her life. Grand Warlock T'Eirick and Grand Summoner had come up with the idea for this ridiculous Council, and now their rules were ruining everything.

How could she leave D'Vaire with no money? To use the currency Aleksander had given her, she would be required to use her identification card. Somehow the gold was accessed with it. Latarian had no notion of how, and she would not take the time to learn. Castle Mallent wasn't a part of the Council; it was on another continent, and the land likely belonged to the rival Consilium Veneficus. She could not bring back its glory and demand her rightful place in the world without having some way to pay for it.

This was all the fault of Ayden. He'd wanted to come to this blasted place after scrying. His stupid mate had shown up, and now he was hardly recognizable from the familiar she'd held sway over for so long. Ayden sauntered around with a chip on his shoulder, eating sweets and walking with the confidence of someone far higher in station. He was reveling in what she'd always told him was his bad side, but it was the personality of the man he used to be. Her fists clenched as she thought about how badly she wanted to hurt him. To punish him for not being respectful of her and pretending she no longer existed.

He didn't know she'd stolen his power—he believed it was she who'd summoned him. Why was he not grateful? Latarian's slippered feet crossed over the wooden planks of her bedroom repeatedly as her thoughts turned darker. She had to accept that she might very well be stuck at D'Vaire after all. With no coin, her only other choice would be to return to that hateful cottage, and she simply couldn't do it. It might give her the opportunity to lash Ayden until he screamed, but that was no consolation for being stuck in his company forever.

Still, there was no reason she need tell these stupid dragons of the pickle she found herself in. Aleksander was being most accommodating, and she took pleasure in the irritation in his strange eyes. His jaw would clench, and it was obvious he hated to capitulate. Fate made him a king, but Latarian was the last of her kind. Someday she would be Grand Witch and far above his station as the mere leader of some tragically ostracized dragon court. Aleksander was willing to do anything to keep Brogan happy, and though she could hardly understand how anyone would believe he'd find that with Ayden, she was going to make the most of her situation.

Any trinket on television that caught her eye, she'd add to her list and demand he purchase. The poor sap did it without complaint, and it was the only thing that soothed her bad temper. Rarely did she get the chance anymore to speak to Ayden, and that suited her fine. All the time he spent with the dragon warned her; he would someday complete his matebond—if for no other reason than to spite her and all the care she'd given him since he'd become her familiar.

She'd simply stopped thinking on what would happen if he did. Her grandfather was so vague in his warning that she'd come to realize her worry might be unnecessary. It might have no effect on her at all. Carvallius had a deep hatred for all the Leolinnias, and he would have wished for Dra'Kaedan to have no measure of happiness. Perhaps he simply wanted him to miss out on his mate as another form of punishment like causing him great pain if he ventured too far from Latarian's side. Dra'Kaedan's family was so often cruel to him, and so his bad feelings toward them made perfect sense to Latarian.

Latarian wished that possibility had occurred to her from the onset; it would've saved her a great deal of grief. She'd likely been making herself upset over nothing other than Carvallius's desire to keep Dra'Kaedan lonely. While such thoughts were a comfort to Latarian, it did not fix her circumstances. This dragon court was in the middle of nowhere, and she'd languished for too long, but what choices were left to her? That damn Blodwen had failed in her mission to locate people to help clear Carvallius's name so Latarian might find allies. The necromancer didn't seem to like Latarian much, and she could offer no other proof than pointing at a computer screen to back up her claim of contacting all these wizards around the globe.

As far as Latarian could tell, Blodwen had simply typed up a few words and considered the task complete. Everywhere Latarian turned, she was faced with incompetence. *Oh, how I wish the world were full of people with my intelligence and drive*, she thought. It would make life so much more tenable if she were surrounded by clever ideas and ambition. Instead she was stuck with a house full of idiots, her only consolation making a fool of their king. She wished her grandfather hadn't managed to get himself killed. Should she have him at her side, things would be quite different. After stamping her feet several times to shake off the worst of her anger, she sat herself down for her daily chore of list making. She swore Ayden would pay for putting her through all this someday.

∽

It was late on Saturday, and Brogan was relaxing in the living room with joy in his heart. Truth be told, he was relishing just about every-thing in his life. Refusing to waste time on Latarian, Brogan was concentrating on Ayden. While the familiar was particular about spending his mornings with Blodwen helping her with something or other, Brogan had his afternoons and evenings.

They hung out with the other D'Vaires, and then Brogan would escort Ayden to his room. He'd hug his mate, give his cheek a peck, and head to his own space. Determined to move ahead on a schedule dictated by Ayden, it pleased him the previous night when his mate had stamped his foot and let out a growl as Brogan sauntered away. Ayden might be irritated, but Brogan was confident Ayden wasn't being pushed into intimacy too soon.

He doubted the familiar was going to put up with teasing much longer, and Brogan's cock hardened at the thought of doing more with him. Grabbing a throw pillow to cover his erection, Brogan snuck a glance at Ayden. Instead of watching the movie, Ayden was staring at him through narrowed eyes.

Brogan grinned. "What?"

"I didn't say anything."

"You're staring at me."

"So?" Ayden demanded.

"Got a problem?"

"Yeah, you."

Mustering up as innocent a look as he could manage, Brogan asked, "Me? What did I do?"

"Why do you keep giving me those stupid kisses?"

"I can stop if you'd like."

"What I'd like is a real kiss."

"I've been giving you real kisses," Brogan said. There was irrita-tion in Ayden's green eyes as they slipped into blue. Ayden's fiery disposition turned him on. If he couldn't enjoy Ayden between the sheets, at least he got the pleasure of riling him up.

"No, I'm talking about kisses on the mouth."

"Okay, this movie's just about over anyway. Ready to head to your room?"

He'd barely gotten the words out when Ayden hopped off the couch. "Yeah."

Since they were the last ones in the living room, Brogan shut off the TV and grabbed Ayden's hand. It didn't take them long to stroll to Ayden's door and once they did, Brogan pulled him close. He lived for those moments of being able to hold him tight. After several minutes he finally pulled away, pressed his mouth to Ayden's briefly, and ended their embrace. Turning to go to his own room, Brogan stopped when Ayden grabbed his arm.

"Where the hell do you think you're going?" Ayden demanded. His eyes were pure navy, and Brogan nearly laughed at the pissed off expression on his face.

"To bed."

"Nope, you promised me a real kiss."

"I gave you a real kiss," Brogan countered.

"Stop smiling and kiss me."

With a shrug all for Ayden's benefit, he brushed their lips together a second time and then straightened. "Good night."

"Damn it, use your tongue," Ayden demanded.

Brogan chuckled and tugged Ayden into his arms. Then he licked his face.

"Gross, I meant put your tongue *in* my mouth."

Obeying the familiar to the letter, Brogan stuck his tongue out and thrust it into Ayden's mouth. He didn't move a muscle and after a few seconds, Ayden pushed at him.

"Let go of me, so I can set you on fire," Ayden ordered with a murderous glare.

"Sorry, I couldn't help myself."

"Maturity, Brogan. It's not only for humans."

Not bothering to respond to his mate's jab, Brogan stopped fooling around. When their lips met this time, Brogan kissed him deeply. Just as he'd done the night in the den weeks ago, Ayden upended his world. Sliding his hand down to caress the plump curve of Ayden's ass, his mate let out a moan. If they weren't in the hallway, Brogan would try and coax more of those delicious sounds from him, which was why it was the perfect place to maintain the slow seduction Ayden deserved.

When that reminder slapped into his brain, he forced his palm upward, so it rested on Ayden's back. Raising his head, he tried not to notice that he was poking Ayden with his dick. There was an equally hard shaft against his thigh and while his beast roared in triumph, Brogan had to leave Ayden before he did something stupid. Reluctantly, he left his arms and put plenty of space between them. Ayden was staring up at him with dark eyes full of need. Brogan wanted so badly to take him to bed, but he wouldn't allow Ayden to be rushed.

"Good night," he whispered, then turned and walked away. He couldn't take one more second of holding back when Ayden was so close, and there was no way he was going to be able to sleep without jerking off. That was nothing new. His hand and his cock were having a torrid affair at this point in his matebond. It didn't irritate him; Ayden's comfort came first, and he would take as much time as necessary to make sure they were both ready for him to lose his innocence. The truth was, Brogan was still scared shitless about easing Ayden deeper into intimacy, and he was waiting for his own confidence to grow.

Meanwhile, Ayden was learning to be himself, and nothing could've pleased Brogan more. Latarian might have convinced him he needed to hold his tongue, but Brogan wouldn't stand for it. Each day Ayden stood a little taller—*well, as tall as someone who was only two or three inches over five feet could stand*, Brogan thought with considerable humor as he let himself into his bedroom.

As he stripped down to take care of the aching shaft that wasn't going to go away on its own, Brogan looked forward to spending more time with Ayden. For so long he'd waited for Fate to match him, and he didn't have a single complaint about the enticing familiar. Naked, Brogan flopped down onto his mattress, dumped some slick into his hand, and wrapped his cock with his fist. He dredged up the memory of Ayden's ass in his hand, and it wasn't going to take more than a stroke or two to come. Ayden was just too damn tempting.

22

Ayden had a great deal to smile about. Latarian was giving him plenty of space, and no one had corrected his behavior since he'd unleashed his fiery side. In fact, he was encouraged to keep it up and to follow his instincts. Without Latarian's lash or reprimands, Ayden was a different kind of familiar altogether. He was discovering it wasn't in his nature to hold back questions or allow someone else to speak for him. Ayden knew what he wanted, and he was working on discovering how to get it.

A perfect example was the dragon Fate picked for him. The previous night he'd finally gotten more than a simple peck on the cheek. It meant the world to Ayden that Brogan wanted to make sure he was comfortable, but he was ready to try more. If his other half decided to revert to innocent kisses, he was going to do something truly evil to him. Perhaps an itchy rash or maybe golf-ball-sized hemorrhoids. No, Ayden decided he'd cover Brogan in oozing sores. With a shake of his head, he tossed that idea aside. While that would be awful for Brogan, it'd be nasty for everyone else too, and he didn't want to lose his lunch.

"You have a very devious smile on your face. What are you planning?" Brogan asked as he entered the living room. It was early afternoon and Latarian was off wasting Aleksander's time with her paltry demands, so Ayden was watching television while he waited for his dragon.

"Actually, I was thinking about doing something horrible to you if you give me another of those pecks."

After sitting down next to him, Brogan leaned close and brushed their lips together. It was the first time he'd kissed him during the day since the "go slow" idea had entered Brogan's head, and that made Ayden smile. "Exactly like that. I want tongue kisses."

"Duly noted, but if I promise to use my tongue at night, then I reserve the right to kiss you as many times as I want, however I want, during the day."

Ayden pretended to mull it over, but he'd be a fool to turn down such an offer. The more the merrier as far as Ayden was concerned, and he hoped it led to more. He was tired of jerking off alone. "Fine."

"It's a deal, then. Now, what's on the agenda for us this afternoon?"

"How the hell do I know? I was too busy thinking of giant hemorrhoids on your ass to plan anything."

"That's really sick."

"I know," Ayden responded gleefully.

"I guess we're stuck on this couch staring at each other, then."

"Guess so."

"I'm bored," Brogan declared.

"Me too."

"Wanna set Noirin on fire?" his dragon suggested.

"Don't talk crazy. The woman feeds me. No."

"I could shift into my dragon and set you on fire so we'd be even."

"That will only happen in your dreams. You know, you've asked a ton of shit about me, but I haven't gotten the chance to question you."

Brogan grinned. "Well, I'm good-looking, ridiculously smart, excellent in bed, and I can't cook for shit. Me in a nutshell."

"You forgot humble," Ayden pointed out to his obviously secure-in-his-own-skin mate.

"Nah, I was never very good at playing down my numerous attributes."

"Tell me about your parents."

"Okay. Well, we weren't close. I grew up as a peasant. My parents weren't mean or awful—they just worked, ate, and slept. It wasn't an easy existence being so poor, and I suppose I grew up kind of lonely. I didn't have friends because the other drakelings around my age thought I was puny and made fun of me for it."

Ayden found that hard to believe; his mate was massive. "You were puny?"

"For a drakeling, yes. I grew slower than the others but by my late teens, my life was drastically different."

"How?"

"Aleksander. He was riding his horse one day and saw the kids beating the snot out of me."

"Why were they beating you up?" Ayden asked, ready to build a time machine and go beat up some shifters.

"They caught me kissing another boy. He was older and when they found us, he told them I'd forced myself on him. The truth was, he initiated it but I wasn't an unwilling participant. I knew I was attracted to boys but kept it to myself because gay dragons weren't welcome in our court. Aleksander broke up the fight and befriended me. I spent most of my time with him after that."

"So, you and Aleksander became best friends right from the start?"

"Yeah. Though, and if you ever tell him this I'll deny it to my last breath, I had a massive crush on him for years. I still think it's a shame he's not gay."

"I can understand that. He's hot."

"You aren't supposed to notice other men, mate."

"He lives here. You want me to cover my eyes when he walks into the room?"

"No, but I must find you a blindfold."

Clearly Brogan is insane, Ayden thought with a chuckle. "You need to be medicated."

"So says the person who wants to give me giant hemorrhoids and has already set me on fire."

"We can share a padded room," Ayden assured him.

"Deal. So, what else do you want to know about me?"

"Um. I know you like to travel. Are you planning any trips in the future?" Ayden didn't know what Brogan wanted to do with his future, and getting Latarian to cooperate with anything was virtually impossible. He simply couldn't imagine her hopping from one destination to another. She preferred to park herself in one spot and belt out orders.

"Ayden, I started traveling because I couldn't stay here any longer. I was lonely, even around the people I loved, and I wanted to find my mate. I thought if I went out into the world, I might find him. If I travel again, it'll be because we decide there's someplace we want to see. If you want to stay here, I'll be just as happy."

"I didn't know you were traveling to find your mate."

Brogan wore a mystified expression. "Of course I was. I think that's what most shifters and magickind want—to find their other half."

"Did you have boyfriends and stuff?" Once the question fell from his lips, Ayden wanted to smack some sense into his skull, but Brogan didn't appear to mind the invasion into his privacy.

"I had lovers, Ayden, not relationships."

"You just wanted to get laid, then?"

"Yes, and so did the men I was with. That's how our society works. Casual sex happens, and the Council does an excellent job of providing clubs with private spaces, so it can be done with a minimum of fuss."

"I understand," Ayden said as his nose crinkled. "It's weird for me —I guess because I didn't get horny before I met you. I don't really want to think about you with someone else, though."

Brogan bumped him with one brawny shoulder. "Then don't think about it. It's not like I'm going to be running out to get laid now. I've met my mate. I won't be one of those shifters who cheats."

Ayden's temper roared to life, and he nearly lifted his hands to check for steam rising from his ears. "Shifters can cheat?"

"Um...yeah. Sorry, I thought you knew," Brogan responded sheepishly. "But like I said, you have nothing to worry about. I wouldn't do that to you."

Tamping down his urge to grab Brogan's dick and never let it go, Ayden allowed sanity to reassert itself. "You haven't given me any reason to think you're not going to keep your word. I trust you."

"Thanks. You won't regret it," Brogan promised.

"Before you met me, did you ever try and imagine what your mate would be like?"

"Sometimes. I'm shallow, so I wanted him to be good-looking. I like to laugh, so I hoped he'd have a good sense of humor. I dreamed of someone who'd love my family because my preference is to be with them. I consider myself very lucky because I got a mate who has everything on my shopping list. How about you?"

"I honestly didn't consider it. We were trapped so long, my only thoughts were about getting out of that cottage. I suppose if I had to make a list, the one thing I'd put on it would be to have someone taller than me. Life isn't easy for us short people."

"I know, I've seen your struggles with shelves, but I like your height. You fit just right in my arms."

"Kind of cheesy," Ayden decided.

"How about I love the delicious fit of your sexy, toned physique against the tall manliness of mine?"

"Too wordy."

"Okay, last choice. Your body feels amazing against me."

"Still has some cheese factor, but I'll take it," Ayden declared.

"Brat."

"I have no regrets," Ayden informed him.

His dragon grinned. "Somehow I'm not surprised."

"We all have to be good at something. I'm learning to be excellent at saying whatever comes to mind."

"You're a good kisser," Brogan countered. "You could spend more time doing that and less time being bratty."

"Yeah, I've been trying, but my mate's a pain in the ass and doesn't give me much opportunity."

"So, what you're saying is that you wait for him to make all the moves?"

Ayden was dumbstruck. That was exactly what he'd been doing. He couldn't believe he'd let Brogan dictate their progress until the previous night, when he'd finally demanded that the man give him more. If life was about embracing what he wanted, Ayden craved nothing more than Brogan.

Without a word, Ayden leaned forward and kissed his mate. It was no gentle peck—his tongue dueled with Brogan's, and the dragon took control. He hauled Ayden close and massaged his back with his large paws as their mouths made love. Ayden wound his arms around Brogan's neck as moans tumbled past his lips. Long before Ayden was ready, Brogan pulled away.

"I like it when you take charge," Brogan told him.

"I wasn't finished."

"You keep kissing me like that, and I'm going to forget we're in the living room."

"Please, Madeline and Larissa make out in here all the time."

Brogan's brow furrowed in irritation. "Good for them. I don't like sitting in here making out. My dick's pressing against my zipper, and it fucking hurts."

Ayden jumped off the couch. "Let's go to my room, then."

"Taking it slow, remember that?" Brogan reminded him from where he still sat on the sofa.

"Damn it, why did we agree to something so stupid?" Ayden demanded and slapped his hands onto his hips.

Brogan narrowed his eyes in frustration as he stood. "Because you have no experience."

"I'm over six centuries old. How long are you going to make me wait?"

"Long enough to make sure you're ready."

Tilting his head back, Ayden's eyes met an angry set of navy ones, but he was an expert on what he was ready for, and he wasn't going to tolerate anyone else making rules or guidelines for him. He'd had enough of that in his lifetime. "I think I know when I'm ready."

"How? Huh? You've never been in a relationship, so how do you know?"

"I know myself, don't I?" Ayden yelled.

"What the hell's going on in here?" Aleksander asked as he stalked into the living room.

Ayden was lost in his anger and he didn't think, he just acted. Lifting his finger, he aimed it in Brogan's direction. "We're both hard, and he won't do a damn thing about it."

"I'm out," Aleksander responded as he turned on his heel and exited in the same direction he'd just come from. "I'll be in my room if anyone needs me. You two can figure this one out on your own."

There was a tense silence in the living room for several minutes; then Brogan bent over in half from the force of his laughter.

It made heat bloom in Ayden's cheeks. "I can't believe I said that to him."

Brogan straightened, and their eyes met. "He's heard worse. Don't worry. Look, I know you want more, but we need to stick to the plan. This is too important to make mistakes."

"I'm ready for more."

"How about I'll allow kissing and maybe a little more to be determined on a case-by-case basis," Brogan offered as he took a step closer to Ayden and grinned.

Bridging the distance between them, Ayden walked forward until their toes bumped. "You'll allow? It doesn't work that way unless you want to be covered in oozing sores."

"I think that's more disgusting than the enormous damage you wanted to do to my ass earlier."

"Give me one of those pecks you're so fond of, and let's go get a snack. We can talk about that little more you mentioned," Ayden said as he held out his hand.

Brogan grabbed it and leaned down to touch their lips together. "We ate lunch less than thirty minutes ago."

"Do you have a point?"

23

Century after century of Brogan's life had passed and with each one, he'd ached more for his other half. Dreams had filled his mind about the man who would become the center of his world, but nothing had prepared him for the reality of Fate's gift. Ayden made him feel fully alive for the first time since his shift from drakeling to dragon. For a beast as large as his, it was a dangerous thing to undertake. Man and animal did not always manage to accept each other, and there was nothing like your own demise to get someone's blood pumping.

Being with Ayden was like that for Brogan—walking the exquisite tightrope between complete failure and the rush of hitting the sky with your wings unfurled. Ecstasy and agony. Ayden's wit and personality raised his spirit, and then he'd have moments of absolute fear when Brogan thought about him being torn away. He no longer knew how he'd manage to go on without him.

Night was another kind of torture since they were still at the kissing and petting stage, but Brogan was determined to bring Ayden into things slowly. Brogan was his first, which made it important that Ayden enjoy every level of seduction. When they were together though, he was surrounded by the joy of his presence. He was falling for the familiar with the red mop of hair and color-changing eyes.

He glanced over at Ayden, who was sitting close by and eyeing him intently again. It was something Brogan was getting used to, but he was unnerved—though it had more to do with the proximity of the bed wreaking havoc on his brain. Somehow, Ayden had convinced him watching a movie would best be done in his bedroom. His mind kept creating all too real pictures of the various positions he could have Ayden in and no matter how hard he tried, he couldn't convince his hormones to shut up and watch the television.

"You're staring at me again," he told Ayden.

"You're more interesting to watch than this crappy movie."

"It does suck."

"Then why is it still on?" Ayden asked.

"Because there isn't anything else on."

"Turn that crap off," Ayden ordered, and Brogan hit the remote, ending their torment.

"What are we going to do now?"

"Arts and crafts?"

"I suck at arts and crafts."

"You could go get me a snack," Ayden suggested.

"You've had chips and popcorn, and that's just in the last hour."

"Fine. Get naked."

"Huh?" Brogan managed, stunned by Ayden's request.

"I said, 'Get naked.' You know, remove all articles of clothing."

Brogan wasn't sure whether to continue to sit there in shock or rip his clothes off as fast as possible, but his dick wasn't conflicted. It wanted relief and not from Brogan's palm this time around. "Why would I do that?"

"Because I want to see you naked."

It was crystal clear that Ayden was ready to move past just kissing and fondling. Brogan nearly shouted for joy; Ayden vocalizing his demands was just what he wanted. "I see. So, you expect me to sit here in the nude while you do what exactly?"

"I suppose I could take my clothes off as well," Ayden's tone suggested he was reluctant, but those witchy green eyes quickly going blue were saying something entirely different. They were hungry, and Brogan hoped Ayden wasn't thinking about his next meal. He just never knew with his mate; he appeared to worship at the altar of food.

"I like that idea. You go first."

"Nope. My idea. Get naked."

While Brogan was always willing to argue with his increasingly volatile mate, he decided it was time to give in quickly and gracefully. "If you insist."

Brogan got to his feet slowly and pulled his T-shirt over his head. Ayden stared without blinking as Brogan reached for the snap of his jeans. Having no desire to delay getting Ayden out of his clothes, Brogan was swift to lower his zipper. He yanked his pants and boxers down in one smooth motion. Stepping out of them, he tore off his socks. Ayden swiped his tongue over his top lip as he stared. He obviously approved of the view.

"Your turn," Brogan reminded him softly.

Ayden reacted by springing off the couch like a rocket. He moved so fast to get out of his clothing Brogan couldn't have said where he started, but it was impossible to miss where he finished. Standing before him was a sexy familiar with a half-hard cock rising from a nest of red curls. Long in comparison to what the diminutive Ayden should have been packing, Brogan noticed it didn't lack girth either. It was growing stiffer and darker under Brogan's riveted gaze, and his own dick was ready to play as well.

"Baby, your body's incredible," Brogan growled.

"Same goes. Enough chatter. Kiss me."

Brogan chuckled at Ayden's orders and then took a step forward, bringing them close enough that they were nearly touching. "Come here," he requested huskily.

Ayden complied by closing the tiny gap between them and snaking his arms around Brogan. After he followed Ayden's example by holding him tight, Brogan leaned down and brought their mouths together.

"Is that what you wanted? A kiss?" Brogan teased.

"No, I want you on the bed."

Brogan regretfully stepped away from the tempting man in front of him and after taking his hand, led him to the bed. If he'd wanted a slow slide into seduction, he was doomed to disappointment. They clambered up onto the mattress and were in each other's arms again seconds later.

"Why do I have to keep telling you to kiss me? I thought you had experience and knew how to do this," Ayden complained. Brogan took pride in the breathlessness in his voice and decided words were unnecessary.

He wasn't going to let Ayden talk either, so he captured his mouth again. The feel of their bodies so close together, the taste of his kiss, and his intoxicating scent were setting Brogan on fire. Their height difference made it tricky to line their cocks up, but Brogan wasn't deterred. He palmed Ayden's luscious backside and pulled him closer and higher. Ayden undulated against him and moaned loudly.

The friction was just what he needed; he rolled them so Ayden was above him. The familiar's hips snapping forward as he moved against him. Brogan slipped his hand closer to Ayden's crack and let one finger smooth over his entrance. Ayden gyrated against him faster and then lifted his head. His cheeks were bright with color from their exertions, and his face was contorted almost as if he was in pain. Brogan's name was a sigh through his lips as he froze above him.

There was a telltale wetness between them as Ayden came. Spreading his legs so he could bend his knees, Brogan grabbed Ayden's ass with both hands as he ground against him. It took only a few seconds for his own shout of glory to follow, and he covered Ayden in his seed.

The first thing he heard when his heart was no longer thundering in his ears was Ayden's voice. "I did it again," he murmured against Brogan's chest.

"Yes, you did. You look so sexy when you come, baby." Brogan coasted his palms up Ayden's back. He was still trying to catch his breath after easily the best orgasm of his life.

Ayden's head popped up from his chest. "No, I came too soon," he grumbled.

"Where'd you learn this crap? That was fucking fantastic."

"I've watched porn, and I've read a bunch of romance novels. Those dudes always have plenty of stamina."

Brogan tugged him closer to his mouth, so he could kiss him. "I don't give a shit what happens in any book or video. I've never come that hard, and it was mostly from watching you. Just knock this shit off about not lasting a week or whatever unrealistic nonsense you have in your head. We're the only ones who get to decide if we're pleased or not. I can assure you I was."

"Okay," Ayden replied quietly.

"I mean it, Ayden. I don't want you beating yourself up about this again."

"Okay," the familiar repeated.

The last thing he wanted was for Ayden to retreat during love-making into the skittish part of his personality Latarian had created because he was afraid he couldn't hold his climax for six weeks or whatever. "Do you understand me?" Brogan roared into his face.

"Stop spitting on me," Ayden shouted back. "I said okay."

Brogan scrutinized a pair of navy eyes with both satisfaction and annoyance in their depths; then he burst into laughter. "I guess we wouldn't be us if we had normal pillow talk after sex."

"Shut it. You're the one who started yelling at me."

He swept his lips over Ayden's once and then because it felt so good, he did it a second time. "You know I don't have any complaints, right?"

"Yeah, now let go of me. We're sticky and this shit is starting to dry. You want me to use a cleansing spell?"

"We'd have more fun in the shower."

Ayden grinned and rolled off him. "Fine, but you're washing my back."

"That's an option only available if you'll allow me to scrub that fine ass."

"Contingent upon me being able to wash your dick," Ayden countered as he hopped off the bed.

At a more leisurely pace, Brogan rose from the mattress. "Best get the balls while you're there."

With a shrug, Ayden grabbed his hand. "If you insist."

Ayden handed Brogan a towel as he stepped out of the shower. They'd washed, gotten each other dirty again, and then cleaned each other a second time. Brogan had wrapped his big hand around Ayden's cock and once again he'd come quickly, but he decided he wasn't going to let it bother him anymore. His dragon hadn't lasted long after Ayden fisted his dick. Either this was normal when the two of them got together, or neither one of them had any stamina. The result left them breathless and satisfied, so why should he care about the quickness of it all? Not having to spend his night jerking off was one of the crucial factors, and being with Brogan was mind-blowing.

His dick was huge, and Ayden almost tackled him onto the bed just so he could touch the damn thing again. The size of it did give him a moment's pause when he thought about it in his ass, but they had to complete their matebond ceremony first, so there was time to get used to the idea. His magic would attack if they tried to have intercourse before their blood mixed. He wasn't going to waste time dwelling on his fear. Fate had supposedly matched them in every way possible. *Just because it looks like a physical impossibility is no reason to panic*, Ayden assured himself.

"Wow, are those scars?" Brogan's question interrupted his runaway thoughts. He'd finally caught sight of the silver markings that decorated most of his back.

"Yes."

"How can you scar when you can heal yourself? These look like symbols, Ayden," Brogan said as he got closer and ran his hand over them.

Trying not to purr at his touch, Ayden explained, "They are symbols. Spells, actually. I guess the best way to describe them is unmagic burns. I was told they're neither light nor dark, which makes them impossible to remove. Carvallius gave them to me."

Brogan was still coasting his fingertips over Ayden's skin, and it was wonderful. "There are a lot of them."

"Each symbol represents a spell that's either constantly cast or useful in a certain situation."

"A certain situation?"

"Yeah, like a stranger attacking me. Shit like that. My magic strikes first and then asks questions."

"Does it hurt?"

"Yeah, but you get used to it."

Ayden turned to face a frowning dragon. Brogan was displeased, but there was nothing either one of them could do about it.

"They look kind of cool, I guess."

"Can I get dressed now?"

"I prefer you naked."

After extricating himself from Brogan, who would've probably spent all night rubbing his back, Ayden pulled a purple pair of pajama bottoms decorated with bright yellow sheep from his dresser. He added a matching yellow T-shirt. "Too bad. I love my pajamas."

"Larissa does find the most interesting fabrics. No underwear?"

"Not when I sleep," Ayden replied as he climbed into bed. Brogan headed for his pile of clothes, but Ayden wasn't sleeping alone.

"Get your ass in bed so we can go to sleep. I'm tired."

At Ayden's command, Brogan tossed his towel into the bathroom and climbed into bed gloriously naked. After Brogan got settled on his back, Ayden sprawled himself over his chest. His dragon was warm, and those strong arms of his enveloped him almost instantly. Ayden was going to get used to this. He didn't want to spend any more nights wishing Brogan was close. Not only would his dick be happy but so would he.

"Turn out the damn light already," Ayden ordered.

"Good night, baby. Thank you for tonight. You really were amazing," Brogan whispered to him after plunging them into darkness.

"So were you. Night." They'd had an incredible evening, and Ayden anticipated many more in their future.

24

yden woke up with Brogan lying beneath him, sharing his immense heat, and he luxuriated in the fact that they were moving forward in the right direction.

"You drool in your sleep," the big dragon stated in a sleep-roughened voice. *Okay, so no relationship is going to be perfect*, Ayden thought with a great deal of amusement.

"I do not," Ayden denied as he lifted from his comfortable position on Brogan's chest to look him in the eye.

"Then explain the wet spot on my chest."

"Maybe you have a sweating problem."

Brogan's eyebrow quirked. "In one spot?"

"A few overactive pores? Maybe you should see a doctor about it. No...wait, you're a shifter. Do you go to a vet?" Ayden teased with a smile.

"Ha ha," Brogan replied dryly while palming the back of Ayden's head to drag him forward for a kiss.

"I like waking up with you," he said against Ayden's mouth.

"I was thinking the same thing until you accused me of having overactive salivary glands."

"At least I didn't make fun of your stanky morning breath."

While Ayden was charmed by Brogan's grin, he'd gone all night without eating. "Whatever, I'm starving."

"Nothing new there. Let me grab a shower and get some clothes from my room. Then we can work on getting you fed."

"You should just bring your stuff in here."

"Are you inviting me to move into your room?" Brogan asked, sounding genuinely surprised by the offer.

"Well, we aren't moving into yours. It's ugly."

Brogan scowled in outrage. "It's not ugly."

"The hell it's not. What do you even call that color on the walls? It looks like someone painted it with ear wax and then smeared crap all over it."

"I was experimenting with sponge painting," Brogan replied indignantly.

"I regret to inform you that it failed," Ayden stated as he rolled off Brogan. Once his bare feet were on the floor, he grabbed Brogan's hand to drag him to the shower. They got clean and filled their bellies in the kitchen after they were dressed. After breakfast, they took on the arduous task of packing up Brogan's belongings and dragging them down the hall to Ayden's room. It was exciting for Ayden to think about moving one step closer to being a committed couple, and he hoped Aleksander was up to the task of pleasing Latarian. He wasn't sure he could stomach the idea of losing any of his new life.

It was unfair to dump such an enormous responsibility onto King D'Vaire's shoulders, but Ayden didn't have any other options. He had nothing to offer Latarian, and she didn't care enough about his feelings to consider them. All those centuries he'd tried to be her friend were a waste of time; she was only concerned with what people could do for her.

That knowledge made Ayden furious at himself. He had endured countless beatings for his bad behavior. If he'd understood there was no way to close the gap between them, he would've given in to his true personality—the consequences be damned. Ayden had learned too much about her real nature since they'd arrived in Arizona and was convinced she would've whipped him no matter what choices he made. Being himself was preferable to conforming to her idea of who Ayden should be for over six hundred years.

He had no regrets about the changes he'd made to himself. Ayden was a firebrand, and he wasn't going to pretend not to be for anyone's sake. Free of Latarian's haranguing, he was becoming someone he was proud of, and he wasn't going to allow her to stop him. She might have the power to tear him away from this incredible place and even his mate, but her control of his personality was over. He promised himself nothing would stand in his way of building a deeper connection to Brogan.

The dragon wanted to be with him, and Ayden cherished that because it was the same thing in his own heart. They might have a ways to go yet, but Brogan was making all the pain he endured worth it. Fate hadn't paired him with a kind witch, but she'd made up for it by giving him a man whose very presence made Ayden strive to be a better person.

He didn't mind the sparring they did. Like Brogan, it fired him up and when his ire cooled, his hormones rushed in to suggest strongly that Ayden jump on him until they were both satisfied. Ayden was going to ride that wave as his heart grew fonder of his other half. It surprised him how fast love had bloomed, but Brogan had lured him in with his stalwart and fun-loving personality. Like Brogan, Ayden found his mate's passionate nature a temptation he refused to resist.

Brogan was stunned by Ayden's invitation to move in together, but he recovered quickly. After all, it was exactly what he wanted. Ayden was the center of his world and the closer they grew, the better. Unfortunately, they'd walked into his bedroom and quickly discovered that if they wanted to get this done efficiently, it was going to take more than two people.

"This room really is hideous," Ayden muttered as he surveyed the space. He pulled open the door of the closet and sighed. "For Fate's sake, how much shit do you have shoved in this closet?"

"I've just been tossing crap in there in between trips."

Ayden turned and when their eyes met, the familiar's were full of exasperation. "This is going to take forever."

"No, it's not," Aleksander said as he appeared in the doorway with the other D'Vaires—minus the witch, who was probably parked in her spot on the sofa.

"Oh, thank goodness, the cavalry's here," Ayden replied. "We're going to need to stage an intervention. I think Brogan's a hoarder."

"Wow, that closet is almost stacked to the ceiling," Blodwen remarked as the necromancer walked over and stood next to Ayden.

"Brogan, have you thrown away anything in your life?" Noirin asked.

Brogan twisted his lips in annoyance. "I've been gone most of the last few years. I'd come home and toss my crap in there before heading out again."

"If there are any dead animals in here, I'm gone," Blodwen said as she reached out to gingerly poke a small box.

"We'll make one of these dragons eat it," Ayden promised.

"Here's the thing, Squirt. Dragons aren't really big on eating vermin," Aleksander commented. "Are we saving all this shit?"

Ayden whipped around to face Brogan. "Are we? I mean, you can't want all of this, right?"

"No, not all of it. I need to go through it," Brogan responded.

"Take a seat on the bed, Brogan," Noirin directed. "I'll grab some garbage bags. We'll hand the stuff to you, and you can ditch or donate whatever you don't want to keep."

Brogan did what he was told without an argument because Noirin wasn't a woman easily ignored, and he appreciated all their help. "Sure, let's get started."

Aleksander reached over the heads of the two magickind in front of the closet, grabbed a box and passed it to Brogan. After Brogan opened it, Aleksander leaned down so they were at eye level. "It's also your responsibility to snack on any creepy crawlies we find."

"Fuck off," Brogan retorted with a glare at his best friend.

"We know the clothes are being moved, right? Ayden, let's start emptying this dresser," Blodwen suggested. As the pair moved to the tall highboy, Brogan cringed a little on the inside.

When Ayden exploded, Brogan wasn't surprised. "I can't even—" he yelled, then toppled back onto his ass. He'd tried to open a drawer that was so stuffed it wouldn't budge an inch.

"Oh dear," Blodwen muttered as she helped Ayden up. "Are you okay?"

"I'm fine," Ayden snarled as he scowled at Brogan. "I'm considering accidentally setting this room on fire."

"It's not an accident if you announce it before you do it," Brogan bravely pointed out.

Ayden's eyes narrowed in irritation. "Perhaps I can distract you, and then you'll believe it was an accident."

"It's possible," Brogan responded as he waggled his brows. "There are quite a few things you could do that would blow...my mind."

The familiar smirked. "Maybe later."

Blodwen tugged on the drawer and the whole dresser rattled. "Fuck this. I'm using magic," she grumbled. A puff of black smoke appeared, and every drawer slid open. Brogan was embarrassed by the things cascading onto the floor after being trapped inside for so long.

"This is a hot mess," Noirin stated as she handed Brogan a large trash bag. He was happy Aleksander had handed him a box of things he could do without. It made him feel marginally better that he had stuff to toss while everyone believed he was at the very least a horrible pack rat.

Things settled down as he combed through his junk, and Brogan forced himself to think clinically about his choices. He didn't need a room full of old memories. Some of the things were fond reminders of places he'd traveled to, and he set those aside to share with Ayden later. As for the rest, most of it was silly souvenirs he couldn't believe he'd wasted money on. The entire group of D'Vaires were doing what they could to assist, and Noirin set up roles for everyone.

Blodwen and Ayden were hunting for clothing and still tackling the contents of the dresser. After a while, the only sound in the room was the two chatting, and Brogan didn't have any issue listening in—Blodwen and Ayden were talking loud enough for everybody in the space to hear.

"Do I really need to ask how things are going?" Blodwen teased as she grinned at Ayden.

"It was my idea to move in together," he replied. The pride in his voice made Brogan feel about ten feet tall.

"Are you happy?"

Ayden turned back and gave Brogan a beautiful smile. "I'm very happy," he said; then his expression flipped to a frown. "But to be completely truthful, I'd be happier if Brogan wasn't such a pack rat. Mate, I just found a stack of paper napkins in this box. Really?" Ayden waved around the cellophane-wrapped package to emphasize his point.

Brogan laughed. "*Whoops*," he responded. He had zero explanation for why he'd even purchased them.

Noirin grabbed them from Ayden's hand. "At least these won't go to waste. Neither will these pencils you apparently bought in Seattle since that's what's written all over them. Dare I ask why you purchased seventeen of them?"

After shrugging because he honestly had no clue, Brogan returned to his task of going through his things and tried to ignore all the sarcastic comments flying around about his collection of odd crap. The important thing was, he was moving in with Ayden and he was going to focus on that until they were done, so his ego could recover from all the insults being muttered about him from every corner of the room.

It was easier to move than Ayden would've expected—after seeing the nightmare of Brogan's space—and to organize their things. The dragon had been willing to get rid of most of the crap he'd accumulated, and they'd found homes for the things he wanted to save.

Ayden enjoyed learning more about the places Brogan had traveled to and his adventures far from D'Vaire.

As the days passed, their relationship continued to grow, and Ayden loved each day with him. Latarian went to Aleksander with her lists, but she was getting low on ideas or the process was boring her, because she no longer made daily visits to his office. Ayden wasn't sure if he should be happy Aleksander had to spend less time in her presence or terrified she was so discontent they would be packing their bags.

He hadn't spoken to her since before they moved in together, so there was nothing for Ayden to go on. Ayden simply focused on Brogan and waited for whatever happened next. He despised the magical bond between them that forced him into limbo but there was no resolution, so he set his useless anger aside.

Ayden and Brogan developed a pattern of retiring to their shared room after dinner to be together. Normally it meant snacks, movies, or games, but sometimes it was all about passion. As the sun had already set, Ayden was lying on Brogan while they watched television. He was half-asleep, wondering how to coax Brogan into bed, when the dragon said, "I want to suck your dick."

Ayden's eyes widened in surprise and he sat up to face him. "Now?"

"Yeah, now."

"On the couch?" he asked stupidly.

"Exactly," Brogan affirmed, then slid out from underneath him. He lowered himself onto the floor on his knees. "Lose the shirt."

Ayden yanked off his T-shirt as all the blood in his body redirected to his cock. The idea of Brogan giving him a blowjob was so sexy he could hardly stand it. Brogan grabbed Ayden's legs and tugged him, so he was sprawled out in front of him. The dragon unsnapped his jeans and tugged his zipper down. Ayden was fine with getting naked for him; he lifted his hips and Brogan pulled his clothes off.

"You aren't naked," Ayden complained.

"Hmm...sorry," Brogan replied as he ran a finger down Ayden's hardening shaft. "I got distracted by the view."

"There you go with another cheesy line," Ayden accused in a breathless voice.

Brogan stood and within a few seconds, his shirt and jeans were lying on top of Ayden's on the floor. "Deal with it. I like looking at my sexy mate."

Lowering his body so he was hovering a few feet above Ayden with one strong arm bracing his weight, Brogan captured his mouth, leaving him unable to reply. They kissed long and deep until Ayden nearly came from that alone. Then Brogan trailed his lips over Ayden's chin and down his chest.

The dragon let go of the couch and returned to his knees as he ran his tongue over Ayden's belly. As for Ayden, he was only capable of lying there and closing his eyes in mindless pleasure. His dick leaked, and Brogan lapped up every drop from his stomach but didn't touch his length at all. Instead, he spread Ayden's legs wider and continued with his drugging kisses over one hip.

"So sexy," Brogan murmured against his skin. "All mine."

Ayden nodded enthusiastically as he gripped the sofa cushions. Brogan laid his palms on Ayden's thighs and smoothed them up toward his waist.

"You ready?"

"Uh huh," Ayden managed. Brogan stopped teasing and sucked Ayden's length down his throat. His cheeks hollowed as he swallowed around the head of Ayden's dick. Ayden's eyes fell shut as his body bowed. Brogan was giving him the most intense pleasure yet, and he continued to use his warm, wet mouth over his length. He rocked his hips helplessly, and Brogan didn't object. The dragon slid one hand down and toyed with Ayden's balls.

That shattered all of Ayden's control, and he let out a yell as Brogan deep throated him again. He filled Brogan's mouth with come, and his mate continued to suckle him until his orgasm was complete. When he finally softened, Brogan let him slide through his lips; then he got up from the floor and kneeled over Ayden. He used one hand to balance himself next to Ayden's head, then used his free one to wrap his fingers around his own sex.

Ayden reached out and stroked his hands over any part of his mate he could reach as Brogan jerked himself above him. It only took a few furious tugs; then white ropes shot out over Ayden's belly and chest. When he was done, Brogan once again kneeled on the floor. He laid his head on Ayden's thigh as his breathing leveled out. Ayden ran his hands through Brogan's soft curls and hoped for many more nights just like this one.

25

It was the middle of the afternoon and Ayden wasn't sure how it happened, but he was at loose ends. Brogan was chatting with Aleksander in his office, and the ladies of D'Vaire were off shopping. Ayden had opted not to drag Aleksander into another negotiation for an outing, and somewhere in the mansion Latarian was also finding some way to amuse herself—or so he hoped.

As for Ayden, he didn't know how to deal with so much idle time. He'd be glad when they finished their sanctuary petition—something he and Blodwen were sure would be ready by their next family meeting on Monday. He hoped they'd get approved, and his days would be filled with helping, however he could. He trusted that their family would be inundated with applications as soon as the Council allowed them to open their doors.

In the meantime, Ayden decided he needed hobbies besides having sex with Brogan. Of course, that was incredible, and he'd do it constantly if possible but that probably wasn't healthy, so he needed more of a life. He was bored of the television, so Ayden shut it off and got to his feet. Aleksander had given him enough funds that he could indulge by buying a new book, he assured himself.

"I am surprised to find you not wrapped around that dragon," Latarian said as she strode into the space.

Ayden wanted to slap himself for not retreating to his room a few minutes earlier. He was determined to be polite despite the glower on her face. "Brogan's hanging out with Aleksander."

"Why are you not with them? I have barely seen you without him for weeks now."

"Because it's important that we have interests outside of each other."

"Are you not afraid that with time to think, the dragon will realize he can do much better than a familiar incapable of behaving as one should?"

"Brogan happens to like my personality."

"Is he the only one that matters, then? You care not for the feelings of your witch?"

"Latarian—"

She took a step closer to him so there was only a foot of space between them as she cut his words off with one raised hand. Ayden refused to give up any ground, and he wasn't going to be afraid of physical repercussions either.

"You have to be the most selfish familiar to walk this earth," she accused. "All you care for is having inappropriate relations with that dragon. Were you not taught to wait until after your mating ceremony?"

"It's not the fourteenth century anymore. Plenty of mates move in together before their ceremony." Ayden didn't know if Brogan had any plans to have one soon or ever, but he was not going to explain that to Latarian, and he certainly wasn't going to entertain a discussion about his sex life.

"You disgust me," she sneered. "You are embarrassing yourself and our people."

"That's not true."

"History books speak of my grandfather as a traitor. They're wrong. Not that you care but you, Ayden, are a traitor. You've turned your back on the Coven of Witches."

"Being with your mate doesn't make you a traitor," Ayden countered. His fury rose but he didn't want to have a yelling match with Latarian, because it solved nothing. She refused to see things from his point of view, and hers was impossible to comprehend.

"You should watch your tone with me. These dragons will not always be able to protect you," she snarled.

"The hell they won't," Brogan thundered as he stormed into the room behind her. "That's enough out of you, Latarian. You can leave Ayden alone. He's dealt with enough of your shit over the centuries."

"Brogan, please," Ayden interjected.

"I'm not going to stand here and listen to her say awful shit to your face."

"I know you're angry, but I'd appreciate it if you'd let Latarian and me talk alone."

"No, absolutely not," Brogan retorted.

Ayden ground his teeth together as his anger rose. First, he had a horrible witch insulting him and now an overprotective dragon. The leash on his temper snapped. "You need to leave us alone," he barked at Brogan. "We're having a discussion, and you aren't part of it."

Brogan's fists clenched, and Ayden didn't like the mix of hurt and fury in his eyes, but he needed to deal with Latarian himself. Then he and Brogan could duke it out.

"Fine," Brogan bit out as he turned on his heel and left the living room.

Latarian pursed her lips and said mockingly, "Your pet dragon was quite upset. Perhaps you should be wary of separating yourself from him. Without a protector, you might find yourself reacquainted with my lash."

"I'm not scared of you," Ayden snapped. "You can't hurt me, because I won't allow it. I did before. I thought the problem was me. I wanted to be your friend. I longed to have a loving and caring relationship with you, just the way it should be between warlocks and their familiars. But that wasn't ever going to happen, and it has nothing to do with my temper. It's because of you. All you gave me was cruelty while trying to morph me into someone I'm not. I'm sorry you don't like me the way I am, but I can't worry about that anymore. Being with Brogan feels right, and so does standing up to you."

"We shall see, will we not? How brave will you feel when we leave this place behind us? You won't have your dragon, and I'll have the world at my feet. You will pay for saying such things to me and we are witches now, not warlocks."

Thinking of Latarian as the leader of their people didn't suit Ayden, so he ignored her lesson on what word should be used to describe them. "You don't want to admit it, but you need D'Vaire. You don't even know how to function in the world, and you refuse to learn. How long do you think you'd last without someone to do everything for you? With no money? The only thing you could do would be to return to our little cottage, and we both know you hate it there."

Latarian lifted her chin. "Believe what you will Ayden, but you will not have the chance to enjoy this dragon fairy tale of yours forever."

Before Ayden could reply, she shimmered out of the room. She must have really been pissed to have used magic to teleport away, but Ayden wasn't going to feel guilty about the things he'd said to her. They were long overdue. Not willing to dwell on it, Ayden took a few deep breaths to calm himself before he sought out his dragon. Brogan was probably furious, but Ayden wasn't going to allow anyone to fight his battles, and he fully intended to make that clear to him.

Brogan stomped into the bedroom he shared with Ayden as he fumed over the altercation he'd just had with him and that bitch Latarian. His rage grew as all he could envision was Ayden losing all the progress he'd made in finding his fire. He ached for Ayden; Brogan could only guess how difficult he found it to be caught between who he was and who Latarian expected him to be. For all those centuries he'd lived a lie, being forced to submit to a selfish, greedy woman. He wanted better for his mate, and it tore him apart to think of him retreating to that person who truly only existed in Latarian's mind.

He understood why the Coven of Warlocks hadn't created the Council with the penalty of death for coming between two mates. The strange relationship between warlocks and their familiars would have led to the entire demise of their race. If anyone else used his relationship as a tool to hurt Ayden, he would have called the Order of the Fallen Knights in a heartbeat. It rankled that Latarian was able to act however she wanted with no repercussions. There was no leader of her people to appeal to and as dragons, they weren't sure what parts of the things she did were acceptable and which were not. When you were dealing with the only living witch, it was clear that she was the one with all the cards.

Before he could decide whether to go and yell at Aleksander about it for a while, the door swung open to reveal a familiar with eyes missing their normal green hue. Ayden was pissed, and Brogan was pleased. The anger sure beat the sadness that used to follow him when he was around Latarian, he mused as Ayden marched over to him.

"I don't appreciate you trying to tell Latarian off. I can do that myself," Ayden said as he folded his arms over his chest.

"If I see someone yelling at you, I'm going to fucking say something."

"I can handle my own battles."

"You don't think I know that?" Brogan countered.

"If you knew that, why would you come barreling into my conversation?"

"Look, I'm a duke. I take that seriously, and it happens to be in my nature to be over-protective. That side of me doesn't have an off switch."

Ayden blew out a frustrated breath. "I've spent too much time with someone else speaking for me. I won't allow it any longer."

All the wind slipped out of Brogan's sails, and his ire cooled. He was fully aware of what a struggle Ayden went through to be himself. "Baby, I'll try my best, but you aren't the only one whose temper flares fast. I can't say I'll always be successful."

Ayden's arms dropped to his sides and his mouth twisted; then his face settled back to normal. Brogan couldn't tell if he was still ready to rage or if his words were penetrating through his skull, so he was pleased when a little smile emerged. "I guess we both have some adjusting to do, huh?"

"I'd say centuries of isolation have hampered our people skills." Ayden shrugged. "So now what?"

"We start by updating our pro and con list."

"We do?"

"Yep," Brogan said as went over to the desk and fished it out from where Ayden stowed it for safekeeping. "Pro—Ayden can stand on his own two feet."

"Give me that. Your handwriting sucks," Ayden retorted. Brogan chuckled and handed it over along with a pen, so Ayden could update it. "Con—sometimes Brogan wants to step in."

"Sometimes Brogan wants to step in, so Ayden doesn't have to deal with it," Brogan corrected.

Ayden planted himself on the bed to write and rolled his eyes. "Pro—Ayden and Brogan are working on their people skills."

"Con—neither of them has been in a relationship before, and they have no clue what they're doing."

"True, but we're doing pretty good," Ayden murmured as his pen scribbled across the page. "Pro—they'll learn what they need to know together."

"Great, I think we're done."

"No, we're not. We need a con."

"Hmm," Brogan said as he sat next to Ayden. He pointed at the page. "Put con—arguments can't be solved in bed while naked."

"But I have another pro for that," Ayden responded as he wrote.

"What's that?"

"Pro—make-up sex."

Brogan grinned. "Good one."

"We're going to need a con."

"I'm going to need some time to think about it. Maybe you should give me a kiss for inspiration."

Ayden tossed the notebook and his pen onto the area rug, then launched himself into Brogan's waiting arms. They fused their mouths together, and Brogan nipped Ayden's bottom lip before their tongues met. He fell backward onto the mattress, taking Ayden along with him, and gripped his ass with both hands. Brogan would fight with him a thousand times a day if it meant being able to return to their bedroom to enjoy the passion that always simmered just below their skin for each other. Emptying his mind, he gave himself over to his desire and concentrated on the moaning man in his arms. His only concern was how long it was going to take them to get out of their clothes.

The night before, Ayden had confessed his desire to learn how to effectively give a blowjob. What else could Brogan do but make his cock a willing participant for lessons? Humor switched to passion as Ayden worked his hands between them and slid down his zipper. With Ayden's brand of determination, Brogan doubted he would take long to become a master, and he sent up his thanks to Fate for giving him such a rare gift. He treasured everything about Ayden in and out of bed.

"Focus on sex," Ayden demanded as he sat up and tugged on Brogan's jeans.

Properly chastised for his rambling thoughts, Brogan lifted his hips and helped his mate get him naked. Then he moved higher on the mattress, spread his legs, and gently coached Ayden into giving him the best blowjob of his life. He might have struggled to swallow him all down but when Brogan reached for him to reciprocate, Ayden bashfully admitted he'd already come. With a smile, Brogan brought their mouths together and enjoyed the taste of himself mixed with Ayden's unique flavor. Brogan explored leisurely as he pulled Ayden close and doubted there was a better way to spend an afternoon.

26

When his family's weekly meeting rolled around, Brogan didn't think it was possible to be in a better mood. It had everything to with the familiar sitting next to him who was grinning mischievously. He'd worn the expression for most of the afternoon and Brogan had no clue why, but he liked it. He was hoping he'd find out his secret soon enough but first, he had to get him alone, which was next on the agenda—after Aleksander made sure everyone was on the same page.

As if his best friend could read his mind, the D'Vaire king strolled in and took a seat. "Thanks for taking the time to meet tonight," Aleksander stated with a smile. "Blodwen and Ayden have asked to talk to everybody. Get on up here, guys."

Brogan lifted a brow at Ayden, who patted his thigh and then darted up and strode over to stand next to Blodwen, who'd already parked herself next to Aleksander. She handed Ayden a stack of papers, and he waved them around.

"We're only one decision away from being able to send our petition to become a sanctuary to the Council," Ayden announced.

For a split second, Brogan's heart simply stopped. Then his eyes fell shut as his brain conjured up images of hordes of people stomping into his home and hurting the people he loved, including the excited familiar standing next to Blodwen. All the weeks since he'd been home, the sanctuary had slipped right from his mind. He'd become so wrapped up in his relationship and dealing with the issue of Latarian, it had fallen to the back burner.

"All we have to do is decide what we want to name it," Blodwen added while Brogan's head spun.

He couldn't believe he'd forgotten. It made sense now why Ayden disappeared into Blodwen's room every morning. The pair had obviously worked hard to fill out the petition, which wasn't going to make Brogan's objection a happy one, but it couldn't be helped.

"Before we start tossing out ideas, we need to discuss this," Brogan interjected.

"Discuss what?" Ayden asked. "The name? Yeah, I think everyone should get to come up with something we can vote on."

"Not the name. The sanctuary," Brogan corrected.

Ayden's face fell, and his brows drew together in confusion. "I don't understand."

"Brogan, you have questions?" Aleksander asked.

"I don't have a question. I have a complete and unequivocal protest."

"What?" Ayden demanded his voice flat.

"I apologize for not bringing this up sooner," Brogan said. "I cut my trip short as soon as I learned about the sanctuary, but when I got in and I met you I forgot all about it. When no one brought it up at our meetings, I suppose I figured it'd been vetoed. You guys want to help people who've been rejected by their own kind, and many of them will be just like Blodwen—yearning for somewhere to fit in. Unfortunately, not all people who live on the fringes of their race are shunned due to their differences. Some of them are pushed aside because they're unpredictable and dangerous. We'd be endangering the lives of everyone here by welcoming them into our home."

"I don't understand how you can be against helping people," Ayden responded. There was hurt in his voice, and Brogan hated that he was the cause. There was also an edge he understood was Ayden's temper, and he preferred that to the first.

"Brogan has a valid point. We didn't consider the possibility of bringing people to D'Vaire who have the intention or propensity for harm," Aleksander chimed in.

"Well, we can accept only people who aren't dangerous," Ayden suggested as he handed the stack of papers back to Blodwen, so he could cross his arms over his chest.

"How do we know if they are or not before they get here? It's my job as a duke to keep us safe. I can't do that with a bunch of people running around we don't know," Brogan replied, careful to keep his tone neutral.

Ayden's now navy eyes narrowed. "I'm not trying to be mean, but you weren't even here when Latarian and I got here."

"You know why I started traveling," Brogan stated.

"Yes, I do. But it still doesn't negate the fact that anyone could've walked up to the door and charged in," Ayden retorted. "It's exactly what we did."

"Fate sent you here for me," Brogan bit out.

"We asked Fate to help us find a safe place because we didn't know where Carvallius was," Ayden snapped.

"She surely made an error in sending us here. None of you dragons know a thing about my grandfather or our people," Latarian threw out. "Look how you've managed to ruin my familiar."

Unwilling to deal with Latarian's shit, Brogan ignored her and stood so he could try to get through to her irate familiar. "Nothing in this house happens unless all of us agree. That's been Aleksander's rule from the start. There's no way I'm going to allow this to happen."

"Maybe we can find a compromise," Blodwen suggested.

Ayden pursed his lips and gazed at her for several long heart-beats, then turned back to Brogan. "We'll just add an application."

"We can't just have a checkbox that asks them if they have violent tendencies," Brogan argued.

"I know, but we could check their background. We could contact their current leader and verify their need for sanctuary," Ayden suggested.

"We'd need Council permission to do that. There are no cross-race sanctuaries, and there's no guarantee we'd get the Council to agree to let us open the doors anyway. Every other sanctuary has people placed in them by the fallen knights," Brogan responded. He had investigated how things were normally done the night he'd spoken with Aleksander and was glad he could recall everything. "We might not get to hand our little application to anyone. We probably won't even know the person's name until they show up on the doorstep. The other ones are large courts, circles, packs—nothing at all like us. There are nine people in this house to defend and maintain order."

"Latarian and I have more power than nearly all of magickind," Ayden bit out. "We have security covered. No one can even walk up to the door without us knowing it."

"I must say that I've had reservations about this idea from the start. I agree with Brogan. Our own safety should be considered. We would not want to open ourselves to danger."

Brogan wasn't sure whether to laugh or cry. The last thing he wanted was to have Latarian on his side. It wouldn't do a damn thing to help convince Ayden his idea wasn't a bad one, but it was simply not possible for them. "No one's infallible, Ayden. It only takes a second to end someone's life. In a single flash, any one of us could be dead. The price of opening a sanctuary has too steep of a cost."

"I think you're overinflating the potential danger," Ayden countered as his cheeks flushed with furious color. "If we added the application and did background checks, it would minimize our risk."

With a heavy heart, Brogan shook his head. "It's not enough. No one's life in this room is more important to me than a stranger. Fate brought you and Latarian here, and Blodwen's arrival stemmed from a happy accident, but we don't need a bunch of refugees bringing potential violence to our doorstep."

"You're not even considering the options," Ayden accused. "I can't believe how closeminded you're being."

"I don't think you're seeing the reality of the dangers you'd be putting us all in," Brogan returned.

"I understand that the world's full of dangerous people. My entire race was wiped out. I know evil exists," Ayden growled. "I know we're smart and can do our best to minimize the possibility of inviting homicidal maniacs into our home."

"Under zero circumstances am I willing to risk the lives of our family," Brogan stated in a voice that rose with each word. It was impossible to get Ayden to listen to reason and while he appreciated his tenacity, Brogan wasn't going to change his mind.

"You're being unreasonable," Ayden shouted back. "You're not even thinking about all the people we'd be saving from horrible lives."

"I'm thinking of *our* lives," Brogan yelled.

Aleksander got to his feet, and Brogan turned his attention to his king. "Gentlemen, we're getting nowhere. Both of you are passionate about your position, and I think it'd be best for us all to take a step back. We can think it over and perhaps in the future, we can find a reasonable compromise. I'm afraid for now, we're going to have to shelve the idea of a sanctuary. Ayden and Blodwen, I do appreciate all of your hard work. I think we all need to cool off a bit, so I'm going to adjourn our meeting. Enjoy the rest of your evenings."

"That's great," Ayden snarled. "Just great. I hope you're happy, Brogan."

With the threat of danger removed, Brogan's temper cooled. "I just want everyone to be safe."

Ayden's expression was wounded as he stomped out of the room.

"Blodwen, I'm really sorry for all the effort you put into this," Brogan offered the necromancer.

"Thanks. I'd suggest you go talk with your mate." Blodwen's gray eyes were irritated, and so was her tone.

She was right, so Brogan left the living room and headed toward the bedroom he shared with Ayden. He assumed that was where his other half had gone and was unsurprised to find himself locked out.

"Ayden, open the door," he requested after he rapped on it.

"*Go away,*" Ayden roared from inside.

"Not happening...so open up or I'll break it the fuck down."

Seconds later, the door was nearly ripped off the hinges by a furious familiar. "I don't want to talk to you right now."

Brogan barreled past him after slamming the wood back into the frame. "Too bad. We're going to work this out."

"I can't believe you'd destroy our sanctuary idea. I've been working on that forever, and it's very important to me and you don't even care."

"I know you mean well, but it's too big of a risk."

"That's your opinion," Ayden shot back.

"Yes, and just like yours, mine counts for something."

"You've made mine count for nothing. You killed the sanctuary. All I wanted was to help, and you've made that impossible. Why doesn't that matter?"

"Of course it matters, but how could I live with myself if something happened to anyone in this house? How the hell am I supposed to put you at risk? Ayden, what the fuck would I do if someone hurt you or worse?" Brogan demanded as he closed the distance between them.

"You don't know if that'll happen."

"How many ways can I say that it doesn't matter? If it's even a remote possibility, I can't handle it. I love you, Ayden. I can't imagine my world without you. I love your passionate nature and that you eat everything except the tablecloth. I love that I get to fight with you and especially what comes after when we make up."

Ayden stood there for several seconds, and Brogan couldn't decipher his expression. Then the corner of his mouth lifted in a half smile. He closed the distance between them, wrapped his arms around Brogan, and laid his head against his chest. "Blodwen and I will think of some way to make the sanctuary safe."

"Hey, you little shit. That's not what you're supposed to say right now."

Ayden chuckled. "I love you too."

Brogan slid his hands down and gave Ayden's ass a pat. "Ready for a matebond ceremony and dragon bite?"

"Yeah, we have to do the ceremony first, or my magic will attack you. You'd be dead before I finally got your dick in my ass."

"I'm on board to fuck you, but not if it means dying," Brogan replied. He was pretty sure his nerves could handle Ayden's virginity —mostly sure anyway.

Ayden pulled away until their eyes met. "Thanks for saying I'm not worth dying for."

"I didn't mean it like that, although I hope I never have to prove that one."

"That makes two of us."

"Get the notebook out. It's time to update the list again."

"It is?" Ayden asked in surprise.

"Yep. Pro—Ayden loves me."

With a roll of his eyes, Ayden shook his head. "Nope, we aren't adding that."

"How isn't that a pro?"

"Hello, what would be the corresponding con?"

"Hmm, I hate to concede, but you have a point."

Ayden smirked. "Of course I do. I'm the brains of this operation."

"Oh, no. You're the sexy one. I'm the brains."

"Agree to disagree. Now can we please get to the make-up sex?"

Brogan bent his knees and pulled Ayden up with the palms he still had on his ass, so he could kiss him. Ayden's arms circled his neck as his legs wound around his waist. Once he'd tongued him until Ayden was panting, Brogan corrected him. "Not just make-up sex but celebration sex."

"Wrong. Celebration sex would include cake."

"Stop thinking about food and concentrate on my dick."

"Spoilsport."

27

A yden pulled on a beautiful cloak trimmed in Brogan's dragon scales. He admired himself in the mirror and smiled. It was almost too good to be true that after the rough start he'd had with Brogan, it was finally the day of their mating ceremony. He was in love with Brogan, and he was excited about meshing their lives. Ayden wasn't going to think about the obstacles in their path. Latarian would always be there ready to strike to make her impact on their future, and Ayden hadn't forgotten about the sanctuary. He was no longer angry at Brogan; he'd turned over all that fire to determination. There had to be some way to make it safe, so Brogan would change his mind. He simply refused to believe otherwise.

Leaving the sanctity of his bedroom, he jogged down the hallway to get to the throne room. The long flaps of velvet decorated with all his magic schools slapped against the back of his calves and he had to right his coronet, but Ayden didn't care. He'd been waiting for this day from the moment he was summoned. The door was wide open when Ayden arrived, and Brogan was standing near Aleksander. His outfit was like Ayden's, only his cloak was missing a hood because he was a shifter and not a sorcerer.

Strolling up to him, Brogan winked; then Aleksander got his attention. "Ready to begin?

Both men nodded fervently, which made Ayden chuckle.

"Draconis Court of D'Vaire. Today we witness the joining of Duke Brogan D'Vairedraconis to Duke-mate Ayden D'Vaire, using the combined traditions of magickind and dragons. Gentlemen, please raise your left hands," Aleksander said.

After Ayden and Brogan complied, Aleksander spoke. "Duke Brogan was granted his title on the first day Fate created our court. Since that day, he's been dedicated to keeping each of us under his protective wings. Duke-mate Ayden was sent here by Fate. She beckoned him to seek us out for refuge, and he found that as well as love. He was summoned into the Coven of Witches and is the last surviving familiar."

Blodwen stepped forward with a stunning athame done in a silver metal. She sliced a cut across Ayden's left palm. It bled a single drop; then the wound closed.

A chill settled around Ayden's heart at how fast his magic responded. "How are we supposed to do this? My body heals itself too fast."

"Relax. We'll figure it out," Brogan assured him.

Panic filled him and with it, anger rose. Carvallius etched his back full of spells, and there was no way to undo his handiwork. "I can't turn off my magic. How are we going to do this?"

"I haven't figured that out yet," Brogan replied.

Turning to where everyone was gathered, Ayden didn't miss the small smile playing around Latarian's mouth. Whatever grip he had on his temper snapped. "How the hell am I supposed to bond with my mate?" he demanded in a shout.

"There has to be a way," Brogan said gently as he rubbed Ayden's arm.

Blodwen waved to get their attention, but all Ayden could focus on was the terror choking him of being deprived of his mate. "Um, guys—"

"This isn't fair," Ayden shouted. "I didn't consent to these spells, and now they're ruining my life."

"Ayden, calm down. We'll think of something," Aleksander insisted.

"Ayden—"

He didn't want to hear any more reassurances, even if they were from Blodwen. "It's easy for you guys to tell me to be calm, but Brogan's right in front of me and I can't have him."

"Come on, baby. I'm not going anywhere, and I'll always be yours."

"I can't keep the cut open long enough to mix our blood," Ayden yelled.

"*Guys*," Blodwen shouted.

"What?" Ayden roared back at her.

"About time," she muttered as she wiggled her shoulders a little in indignation. "I could poison the blade. It'd keep your magic busy long enough to keep it open. We'll cut Brogan first, and you guys slap your palms together fast, okay?"

Ayden was eternally grateful they had a necromancer in their family. "Thanks. That'd be perfect. Please do it."

Blodwen handed the dagger to Dravyn, who cut Brogan. When he gave it back to her, she turned the blade a pale green and then opened a fresh cut on Ayden's palm. They pushed their hands together, and both men grinned as their blood mixed. There was a slight battle inside of Ayden as his magic warred with Blodwen's poison but mostly, he experienced the beauty of their hearts nearly combining in full. It set his body and mind at ease. No moment in his life had ever been so right. He couldn't wait until Brogan finished the bond when he bit him later.

"Witch familiar to Draconis. Duke to Duke-mate. Their souls are now tied and their lives now linked. May their hearts always stay united so that they will never want another," Aleksander said. "A dragon claims his mate through the teeth of his beast. Once complete, it leaves behind no mark for the world to bear witness. In draconic tradition, Duke Brogan and Duke-mate Ayden will now exchange bands."

Noirin handed them each a ring made of an enchanted metal crafted by Madeline that would allow Brogan to keep it on, even when he shifted. It was done in the blue-black of Aleksander's dragon and in the center was a thick stripe of the navy that symbolized their matching dragons.

"Chosen by Fate and accepted by my heart as true, I accept you as my mate," Brogan said as he pushed the exquisite piece of jewelry onto Ayden's finger.

With a smile, Ayden did the same for Brogan. "Chosen by Fate and accepted by my heart as true, I accept you as my mate."

"By the traditions of witchcraft and Draconis, you are now mates. You may now kiss the bride," Aleksander stated solemnly.

"Not funny. I'm not his bride," Ayden said to his king.

"I wasn't talking to you," Aleksander returned, and Ayden roared with laughter at the disgruntled expression on Brogan's face.

The dragon shifter tugged Ayden into his arms and kissed his smirk. Ayden held on tight and allowed Brogan to deepen the caress, to the delight of their family who clapped noisily.

When Ayden pulled away, he smiled brightly. "That's done. Time for cake."

"Ah yes, Ayden's second true love—food," Brogan drawled out.

"Damn right, first love. Let's go."

Hours later, Ayden was finally alone with Brogan. He'd lost count of how many slices of cake he stuffed in his belly while they'd celebrated with their family. Ayden's focus was now getting his dragon bite to complete their bond and having Brogan fill him. He'd dreamed of it, but he had to admit there was some worry over getting the deed done for the first time. However, Brogan was having considerably more trouble handling his nerves. Brogan was pacing the long length of their spacious bedroom, and there was sweat glistening on his forehead.

"Hey, you okay?" Ayden asked as he folded his arms over his chest. He was already naked and in their bed, but his dragon had yet to notice. As for Brogan, he was still in the T-shirt and jeans he'd changed into after their ceremony.

"Huh?" Brogan responded distractedly as he came to a stop.

"I asked if you were all right."

Brogan swiped his forearm over his brow mopping up the moisture. "Oh yeah...sure. Fine. Good. You?"

"Are you coming to bed?"

"Uh...yeah," he responded without moving.

"Brogan?"

"What?"

"Get naked and get your giant dragon ass into our bed," Ayden ordered. He was desperate to get him close, and his own anxiety melted away. Brogan was worked up enough for them both.

"I don't have a giant ass," Brogan informed him indignantly. "I have a great ass. It's not as perfect as yours, but I've never had any complaints."

"I don't want to hear about the other men who've appreciated your ass. Not tonight. Not ever."

"You're the only one that counts. I'm just saying my ass is great, and I know you like it. I've seen you staring at it plenty of times."

"I didn't say I don't like your giant ass. I told you to get it over here and lose the pants."

Brogan stared at him for a few seconds; then he appeared to get a hold of himself. Or at least Ayden hoped he did as the dragon finally pulled his clothes off and tossed them onto the floor. He climbed into bed next to Ayden and after lying down, propped his head on his elbow. "I don't want to fuck this up. I want tonight to be perfect."

"I just want you to fuck me."

His mate's faintly dimpled smile appeared. "Give me a kiss."

Leaning forward until their lips touched, Ayden was thrilled when Brogan pulled him closer. As their tongues danced, Brogan's hands smoothed over his back and then slid down to cup his ass. Ayden's cock hardened as they did nothing but make love with their mouths. Brogan's palms kneaded his cheeks, and Ayden's breath came out in big pants. It never took him long to respond to Brogan, and this night was no exception.

Moans and whimpers escaped as Ayden tried to press closer to get some friction on his dick, but Brogan had him locked in place with several inches of space between them. Grabbing some of the soft curls on Brogan's head, Ayden's neck arched as the dragon worked his way down his throat.

"Brogan," he murmured.

"What's the matter?"

"Touch me."

Brogan squeezed his ass. "I am touching you."

Ayden let out a growl, but his dragon only chuckled in response. He rolled onto his back, forcing Brogan to shuffle closer. Brogan responded by letting go of his backside and smoothing a hand up his thigh. Ayden spread his legs wide and bent his knees as he practically humped the air above him, so desperate for relief.

Brogan got up and crawled down until he was staring at Ayden's aching sex. He leaned down and swiped his tongue over Ayden's balls. Clutching the sheets in his hands, Ayden reminded himself that it was too soon to come. Brogan rubbed one slicked digit over his hole as he covered his dick in soft kisses. Ayden had no clue where he'd found the lube, and he didn't care—as long as there was plenty there to get the job of fucking him done.

One finger slid into him and then stopped, giving Ayden plenty of time to adjust to the unfamiliar feeling of having something inside him. Assessing it, Ayden decided he liked it.

"More," he managed.

Brogan moved it in and out of his hole as he continued to suckle his balls and press his lips everywhere he could reach. Forever passed as Brogan patiently worked him. Ayden let out a groan when Brogan wrapped his lips around the tip of his cock. When he pushed two digits inside him and crooked them against Ayden's prostate, a shout tore from his dry throat while Brogan continued to suckle him.

Pleasure coursed through him, and Brogan was making every nerve in his body sing with joy. Ayden writhed as his mind warred with his hormones and he struggled not to climax. Brogan must have figured out his dilemma, because he skipped that delightful place inside him and continued to open him. Ayden let out a sigh as he relaxed slightly, able to enjoy Brogan's mastery.

Before long, Brogan worked three of his clever fingers into him and pumped them in and out enthusiastically as he lapped his tongue over Ayden's shaft. When he was finally satisfied that Ayden was ready, he lifted his head and pulled his hand free. Ayden released the death grip he had on the sheets as Brogan moved up to bring their mouths together in a sweet kiss.

"I want you to get on top," he whispered against his lips.

"Okay," Ayden breathily agreed. He would do anything to finish what Brogan had started.

They switched positions and as soon as Brogan was settled on the mattress, Ayden straddled him. Brogan cupped the back of his head and pulled him down for a kiss. "Ready?"

Ayden loved the need in Brogan's navy eyes and imagined his own were full of the same. "Absolutely."

Brogan slicked up his cock and then smoothed more lube in and around Ayden's entrance. He grabbed the base of his sex and guided Ayden into the right position to take him in. Ayden could feel the thick head of Brogan's dick against him and slowly lowered his body. Brogan steadied him with a hand on his waist and murmured words of encouragement.

Ayden's hole stretched as Brogan entered him, and he was discovering that his shaft was a great deal different than three fingers.

"Relax, it'll get better. I promise," Brogan whispered. His other half read the apprehension on his face and Ayden was grateful when the head finally popped through the first barrier. The fullness was bizarre, and a part of him was unsure if this was still a smart plan.

"Oh really? When was the last time you had a dick up your ass?"

he demanded, knowing damn well Brogan had probably not bottomed for anyone. He always took charge in the bedroom, and Ayden couldn't imagine him giving up his innate need for control to do anything other than top. Brogan arched upward to join them faster, and Ayden's cock wilted under the onslaught as he adjusted to Brogan's strange invasion.

"I haven't, but I've had sex before. It'll start feeling better once I'm all the way in," the dragon replied with an edge to his voice. Ayden was irritated at his attitude.

"Do you really think it's a good idea to bring up other men right now? What the hell is wrong with you? That's the second time tonight," he growled as Brogan continued to fill him.

"Of course not. My point is I speak from experience. I know you'll like this once you get used to it. You're so fucking responsive."

"News flash—I don't like this. I feel full and weird, and your dick's way too big. It's never going to fit."

"I won't fit?"

Ayden shook his head. "No way."

"I've got news for you."

"What?" Ayden snapped irritably.

"I'm all the way inside you, baby."

Ayden wanted to call him a liar, but Brogan's pubes were tickling his ass. The dragon released his waist and massaged his thighs. The muscles loosened, and Ayden sucked in a breath; then he let it out slowly. The tension left his body as Brogan used one big hand to grab Ayden's dick. With their eyes locked, Brogan stroked his length smoothly, and Ayden reevaluated the thickness inside him. It wasn't nearly as unpleasant as he feared, and it didn't take long for the palm expertly working his cock to lure him into responding.

He hardened in Brogan's grasp, and he had the urge to move. Ayden braced himself on Brogan's broad chest and lifted himself, then eased back down again. He moaned as he repeated the action.

"Feels good, yeah?" Brogan asked as he gripped his hip and they found a workable rhythm.

Brogan was jerking him and as he fucked himself on his dragon's cock, Ayden glanced down to see his flushed cheeks. Peeking over his bottom lip was a set of fangs, and Brogan was ready to bite. Ayden moved faster and faster as he raced toward completion. Somehow, he'd managed to angle himself so Brogan was hitting him directly in the prostate with each stroke, and Ayden was nearly sobbing with the need to come.

Without any warning, Brogan released his flank and grabbed the back of his neck. Instead of the kiss he might have expected, Brogan reared up and sank his teeth into Ayden's throat. No sound escaped him as pleasure exploded and overwhelmed him. Thanks to Brogan, he was familiar with ecstasy, but this went way beyond anything he'd experienced before. Satisfaction was too tame a word to describe their souls uniting. Ayden's seed splashed between them as Brogan's come filled him.

Love swamped him as he and Brogan were united in every way possible. Overwhelmed, Ayden clung to his sweaty dragon who'd already licked his wound closed. Brogan pulled him upward, so their damp foreheads rested together as he wrapped him securely in his strong arms. Like Ayden, he was doing his best to catch his breath.

"I love you," Brogan whispered as he pressed his lips to the corner of Ayden's mouth.

"I love you too," Ayden replied as he kissed him back. There was nothing either of them could say in the profoundness of the moment. Their fates were intertwined, and Ayden cherished every aspect of their completed matebond.

28

Dre'Kariston of Leolinnia walked into the grubby apartment he shared with his familiar, Derwin, and flopped down onto the sofa. For over six hundred years, he'd hidden his identity and every day, it got more difficult. His power grew, so he'd had to find a creative way to conceal it. Over time and with a great deal of effort, he'd built a suppression spell. It was important that no one discovered he was one of the last warlocks, but it was painful and both he and his familiar hated it.

There was no choice in his mind; the Cwylld elven were still out there somewhere, and he couldn't take any chances. When the time was right, and his twin was found, perhaps he could change his destiny. Until then, he worked menial jobs as Ari Leonard and none of the humans who employed him knew he was an imposter. It should've been easier to survive with two people bringing in an income, but Derwin refused to work. Their money had proven too difficult to replicate with magic, which frustrated one of the strongest sorcerers alive.

"Did you bring dinner?" Derwin asked when he stalked into the living area of their tiny home.

Lifting his arm, Dre'Kariston waved the bag of greasy food in his hand, which Derwin snatched. "Enjoy."

"There's only one burger in here," his familiar complained with a frown.

"Use a duplication spell," Dre'Kariston told him as he dragged a hand through his hair. He had altered his appearance many times since the death of his parents, and he missed the black curls he'd once sported. His latest look was a muted brown which waved softly —it was nearly impossible to conceal the natural twist of his locks.

"I hate using magic. I don't know why you can't remember to bring enough fucking food back."

"Give me a break. I worked all day." Dre'Kariston was tired, and his always cantankerous familiar would have found something else to complain about if he'd remembered to bring two hamburgers. Since the day Dre'Kariston summoned Derwin, he'd been unhappy. Dre'Kariston was only eighteen at the time, which was several years too early, but he would've died without his assistance. Wounded and with his magic tormented by evil, Dre'Kariston spent the last six hundred or so years apologizing for his decision.

"I'm surprised you didn't run right into your room to check your necklace," Derwin remarked after he'd polished off his fries. "Though I don't know why you bother. Dra'Kaedan's dead, just like the rest of our people."

Dre'Kariston's jaw clenched. "My brother isn't dead. He's missing. My necklace still glows."

"The dragon's been spinning this whole time."

The emblem was supposed to point in Dra'Kaedan's direction so they could always find each other, but it hadn't worked properly since the day his twin disappeared. Their father hadn't given it that ability when he'd created it, so no one understood what it meant. Derwin was convinced it backfired when Dra'Kaedan perished, but Dre'Kariston refused to believe his best friend was dead.

Refusing to get into a spitting match with Derwin, Dre'Kariston pulled himself from the sofa and wandered to his bedroom. He tossed his uniform onto the bed and changed into a comfortable pair of jeans and a black T-shirt. Dre'Kariston preferred darkness but was stuck with the light power he was born with. He couldn't give in to the lure of the other side of magic with so few living warlocks, and Derwin hated even discussing switching sides.

When he was dressed, he closed his eyes to gather his strength. It wasn't easy to be alone, and he ached to know Dra'Kaedan's fate, but the necklace would fail him as it always did. Opening the drawer of his nightstand, he grabbed a fresh cotton wristband to cover the silver mark Fate gave him to symbolize his rank of Grand Summoner. It was the only proof he had that his brother might be alive somewhere. Fate should've changed the dragon in a circle to gold and marked him as Grand Warlock without his older brother around, but she had not. Derwin was convinced it was because there weren't enough of their people living to bother with a leader, which didn't do much to fuel Dre'Kariston's confidence.

Fishing out the box with both his and Dra'Kaedan's necklaces, he let out a sigh as he lifted the lid. Inside was the same thing as always: a gilded chain next to a silver one—both with a medallion that glowed a faint navy. It was the color of their magical dragons and as usual, the one Grand Warlock T'Eirick of Leolinnia had placed in the center was spinning in circles. Dre'Kariston wanted to punch a wall, but his anger was futile. He went to close it and then blinked. Staring down, he did it a second time, but there was no way to deny the damn thing had stopped moving.

"Derwin," he yelled.

"What?" Derwin roared back.

Dre'Kariston raced into the living room just as the necklace started to spin again. "Fuck."

"What's your problem?"

"It stopped. For a second it wasn't moving."

"Bullshit."

"Look," Dre'Kariston demanded as he pointed at it. "It's doing it again."

"Now you're going to make us chase a ghost, aren't you?"

"He's not dead, dammit."

"He is, or he's been shirking his duties all these years," Derwin snarled.

"Get your stuff. We're going to follow this," Dre'Kariston demanded as he jogged back to his room and tossed his things into a bag. He laid the necklace on the bed and as he moved around the space grabbing his clothes, it spun and stopped a half dozen times.

For days, Dre'Kariston teleported across the world, trying to figure out where his necklace was leading him. Although his mood was buoyant in the beginning, it hadn't remained that way. Perhaps it was the fatigue or Derwin's constant yammering, but he was pretty sure he wasn't going to find his brother at the end of the road. Derwin insisted on stopping each night at a hotel and they'd watched on the news that a woman called Latarian was the last living witch.

Dre'Kariston supposed since no one knew he was alive, it was sensible that they'd switched to the feminine version of his race, but it rankled. With Dra'Kaedan missing, he was the temporary leader of his people, and they should remain warlocks. He hadn't heard Latarian's name before, but Derwin was convinced that the necklace was leading them to her location. She was living with dragons, and so they'd decided to track her directly there instead of continuing the dizzying journey Dra'Kaedan's emblem was trying to send them on. They found themselves in an isolated part of Arizona, and as they walked up a long driveway after teleporting past a giant gate, his senses detected a warlock and familiar inside.

It was not his brother. The pair inside the large mansion had the combined power, which would be close to what Dra'Kaedan should have today. It would be double if it was his twin and his familiar. Still, he was happy to find another of his kind after all this time, and he adjusted his baseball cap as he trudged toward the door. They stopped for a moment so Dre'Kariston could gather his wits.

Derwin scowled as he banged on the wood in front of them. It didn't take long before a tall man opened it. His hair was brown and his eyes the same navy Dre'Kariston had when he wasn't hiding under a glamour spell.

"Hi, can I help you?"

"I hope so. Does Latarian live here?" Dre'Kariston asked.

"Who wants to know?"

"My name's Ari and this is Derwin. We heard there's a warlock alive and that she lives at a place called Court D'Vaire. This is Court D'Vaire, right?"

"This is Court D'Vaire."

Before Dre'Kariston could reply, a man an inch or two shorter than himself popped out from behind the first. His hair was red, and his eyes were dark green. Dre'Kariston's senses recognized him as a familiar and he smiled. More than six centuries had passed since he was in the presence of one of his people.

"Are you a warlock?" the familiar asked.

Dre'Kariston's grin widened. "Yes, I'm a warlock."

"I'm Ari's familiar. Who are you?" Derwin asked.

"My name's Ayden. I'm Latarian's familiar."

Dre'Kariston studied Ayden's face and didn't see his brother anywhere. His search for his sibling was far from over, but Dre'Kariston hoped he could find refuge with the dragons. Though he was tired of running, he wasn't ready to give up his anonymity. There was no way to know who he could trust and who he could not.

"Latarian's in the living room. Come on inside, and you can tell us why you aren't dead like the other witches," the tall guy remarked as he stepped aside to allow them to enter.

They followed him in as Ayden spoke. "Everyone else is a lot nicer than he is, but in case you want to talk to him, his name's Brogan."

"Brogan, who was at the door?" a dragon king asked. His eyes held the unmistakable silver ring of his rank though there was another of gold, which was odd. The man was extraordinarily handsome, his black hair mixed with blue and strong elegant features.

"This is Ari and Derwin. They're here to talk to Latarian."

A female warlock rose to her feet and crossed the room to stand in front of Dre'Kariston. She wore a bright smile and her lavender clothing was straight out of a history book. "You must be here to give me news of my grandfather. I am pleased to see you. I am most anxious to clear his name."

Dre'Kariston didn't have a single clue what she was talking about. "Your grandfather?"

"I am the granddaughter of Carvallius of Mallent. I assumed you were here in response to one of the many letters Blodwen sent out on my behalf."

The rage and fury from hearing the name Carvallius didn't surprise him. Carvallius destroyed his people, murdered his parents, and Dre'Kariston had come close to losing his own life battling him. He wasn't sure he wanted to be anywhere near his granddaughter, no matter how friendly her familiar was.

"Emails," a necromancer corrected.

"Yeah...uh, good luck with that. No, we're here because I'm a warlock," Dre'Kariston explained, shaking off his anger. "My familiar and I didn't realize until we heard of you that any other warlocks had survived."

"We are called witches now," Latarian corrected and flounced over to a sofa where she promptly sat.

Dre'Kariston would be damned if he'd call himself a witch. His brother ruled their people, wherever the fuck he was, and so they would always be warlocks in his mind. If Dra'Kaedan was dead, it was Dre'Kariston who would lead their people, and he could assure everyone he was very much a male.

"I'm King Aleksander D'Vairedraconis," the stunning ruler said as he shook their hands and introduced them to the other dragons in the house. "It's nice to meet you, Ari and Derwin. Have you been in hiding? Latarian and Ayden were sent to an enchanted cottage before the war started."

Noirin, a woman whose hair was also a mix of colors, although her black was accented with violet, set out cookies and beverages. Dre'Kariston was invited to take a seat, which he did after snatching a drink.

"When the war broke out, my parents forced me to hide. I started off in a small cottage, but I lost patience waiting to be told it was okay to come home. When I went back, everyone was dead. I hid from the Cwylld, knowing they'd kill me too, and learned to mask my power. We mixed with humans until we learned that we weren't alone. I'm hoping you might contact the Council on my behalf. I'd like to stop running from place to place," Dre'Kariston revealed. He wasn't ready to tell them everything about himself or the past, but he'd be damned if Latarian of fucking Mallent would be the de facto ruler of the warlocks.

"I'd be happy to contact the Emperor. If you'd like, I could ask his permission for you to stay here with us," King D'Vaire offered.

Dre'Kariston considered Derwin, who offered him a smile. The familiar had waited centuries to stop pretending, and he was probably going to harangue Dre'Kariston about using their titles soon. "Thank you. We'd be honored," Dre'Kariston said, returning his attention to the dragon king.

"Aleksander, I feel I must caution you. We do not even know these people. Do you think it is wise to invite them to live with us?" Latarian asked.

"We know them just as well as we knew you when you arrived, and Aleksander invited you to stay," Brogan retorted. Latarian didn't appear to be a popular addition to their home. No one would ask her to leave; Dre'Kariston hadn't missed that her familiar was mated to Brogan. It made him think of his still-missing brother who'd been determined to have a dragon shifter of his own. Someday he hoped when he found Dra'Kaedan, he'd have the same love match this pair radiated.

Ayden was curled up in Brogan's lap, and the dragon dropped a kiss onto the familiar's mop of red hair. It was beautiful and Dre'Kariston envied them; Fate hadn't only withheld his brother from him but his other half as well. Perhaps with them finally in one spot, he could use Court D'Vaire as a base to continue to follow Dra'Kaedan's necklace to find him. He refused to give up on him and wished the warlocks they'd located were the right ones.

As Dre'Kariston examined the luxurious home of the dragons, he imagined Derwin would soon be filled with excitement over the idea of getting his own piece of the wealth. His familiar had longed for things since his summoning. Perhaps a comfortable home would soothe some of his rough edges, so they might be able to build the friendship he'd always wanted but first, he needed a long nap and some fuel. His mission to find the Grand Warlock was far from over.

29

"Guess what the Emperor said when I told him about Ari and Derwin?" Aleksander asked.

Brogan lifted a brow at his best friend. "Look at you, all friendly with the Emperor. You actually got him on the phone?"

"Yeah, he's a nice guy. His assistant, Wesley, didn't even keep me waiting that long. He had no issue with us adding our new witch and familiar, but he offered a suggestion."

"You're wearing a creepy grin. I'm scared to ask."

"He thought it might be nice to turn D'Vaire into a sanctuary," Aleksander revealed as he broke out into laughter.

Brogan grunted. "It's too dangerous."

"Somehow, I doubt you're going to risk having your mate unhappy with you forever. You'll cave."

"Oh, fuck you." Brogan got to his feet and ignored his cackling king. Leaving his office so he didn't punch him, Brogan wandered down the hall. Everyone in the house wanted the sanctuary and while he was fine taking in whatever witches showed up on their doorstep, he wasn't risking his family for any stranger the Council decided to send them.

He grinned when he got to the large living room and found

Ayden there. Striding over to the couch, he took a seat and lifted Ayden into his lap. His mate smiled, then returned his attention to their newest D'Vaires. Brogan dropped a kiss on his head as he did the same.

"Those are beautiful rings you wear on your left hands. Do they signify something special?" Ari asked.

"It's a mating band," Ayden replied. "It's a tradition for shifters."

"A familiar mated to a dragon—it's pretty incredible. As far as I know, a first for our people," Ari commented.

"I think it's awesome. I thought I was going to wind up mated to a mage elemental without any other familiars around. I don't want to wind up with some kind of thing as a mate," Derwin remarked.

Ayden turned to Brogan with a pointed look. It didn't faze Brogan; he'd come a long way from the fool who'd struggled to understand what Ayden was. His other half was a person just like anyone else, no matter his race.

"I'm sure you won't wind up with a thing. Fate made sure Ayden knew his other half would be a dragon," Brogan confessed. He was proud of Ayden's unique ability and planned to spread the news far and wide. "He has a spell to turn himself into a dragon and it's an exact replica of my beast."

"No way," Derwin shouted as he got to his feet and did a hop. Brogan had no idea if he was excited or about to pee his pants.

Ari, on the other hand, had a thoughtful expression on his face. "Does Latarian have a similar ability?"

Though Latarian was in the room, she was ignoring their group completely and had her book in her lap. It was Ayden who responded to Ari's question. "No, just me. I've looked through every book I can and can't find any spell to turn into a dragon. Have you ever heard of anyone with that ability?"

Derwin clapped his hands. "Yes."

"Derwin and I both possess the ability to change into dragons," Ari clarified.

Brogan's eyebrows rose in surprise. "Really? How did you get the ability?"

"I was born with it and when I summoned Derwin, he was capable of changing into one as well. Both of our beasts are distinctive. Like you, I haven't been able to find others with the ability," Ari confided.

Derwin sat down and his face went blank. "Why can't your warlock do it? That doesn't make sense. You shouldn't have abilities unless she has them as well."

"I am a witch, not a warlock," Latarian interjected. "Ayden's obsessed with reading, and he discovered a way to curry favor with these dragons. He has always been too clever for his own good. Just because it was never in a book doesn't mean there aren't dozens of witches with the ability to morph into dragons."

Ari and Derwin exchanged glances but neither said a word.

The room grew awkwardly silent for several minutes. Ayden broke it with a question for their newest additions. "I'd like to see your dragons. What color are they?"

"Blue," Derwin answered.

"Maybe we should put an ad online for all blue dragons to mail us photos of their beasts so we can find your mates," Brogan teased.

"I'm happy to allow Fate to match me up when the time is right," Ari responded.

"I'm so glad you guys are here, but I'm going to have to call it a night. I'm exhausted," Ayden apologized as he scrambled off Brogan's lap.

"You were tired this morning too after we slept in, and it's barely nine o'clock," Brogan responded as he got to his feet, fully prepared to follow his other half to bed.

"I'll probably wake up in the middle of the night since it's so early, but I'm ready to fall asleep," Ayden revealed as Brogan took his hand.

They said their good-nights to everyone and strode down the hallway. Once inside their private space, he made plans to wear his mate out a little more, but Ayden was drooling on his pillow before Brogan even finished brushing his teeth.

With a sigh, Brogan climbed into bed and pulled Ayden, so he was lying across his chest. He was becoming accustomed to curling up with Ayden, and he doubted he still had the ability to fall asleep without him. It'd been an exciting day, and Brogan hoped Ayden was replenished by morning. He had a feeling Ayden would need all his energy to keep up with Ari and Derwin. *Not to mention keeping up with the demands of a horny dragon,* Brogan thought as he kissed the top of Ayden's head. Closing his eyes, he willed sleep to come.

Ayden didn't feel rested the next morning. Several days passed with Ayden spending more time in bed than out of it. It was five days after Ari and Derwin arrived that Brogan became convinced Ayden was somehow ill. Magickind suffered from few maladies, and most of them were related to birth defects, so Brogan had no clue why Ayden needed so much sleep. He might have been able to overlook his fatigue, but Ayden had started to refuse food.

For a man who all but planned his day around meals, it was chilling. Brogan had no clue what to expect next or how worried he should be. Was this something Ayden could recover from? His brain flatly rejected the idea of Ayden not being able to fight off whatever was happening inside his body. He wasn't going to allow anything to take away his mate, and that included unseen foes.

When Monday night rolled around, Brogan attended their weekly D'Vaire meeting alone. The minute after Aleksander sat down and thanked them for coming Brogan got his attention. "Aleksander, Ayden's sick."

"He's already gone to bed?"

"Yes, he was only up for a handful of hours today," Brogan confessed.

"Did he eat anything at all today?" Noirin asked gently. She'd spent most of the last two days baking up numerous sweets to try and tempt him to no avail.

Brogan frowned. "No, he just kept saying he wasn't hungry."

"I've never heard of an illness like this among warlock familiars, but it's obvious there's something very wrong," Ari stated. Though he and Derwin arrived only days before, the pair spent most of Ayden's time awake with him. It didn't surprise Brogan; his mate was impossible not to like.

"We are called witches," Latarian corrected with an aggrieved sniff. "I find it odd that Ayden has fallen ill just as you two have arrived."

"Are you trying to imply that I'm responsible for him being sick?" Ari demanded, with flushed cheeks over her accusation. Brogan didn't want to believe he had anything to do with it, but the timing was difficult to ignore.

"What else could explain his malady?" Latarian demanded. "He has never shown these symptoms before."

"I am *not* making him sick," Ari bit out.

Latarian pursed her lips. "You must know you will not get away with it if you are responsible. After all, to come between a mated pair the punishment I'm told is death."

Ari's fists clenched but he didn't say a word. Brogan relaxed slightly at his behavior; surely someone who was guilty wouldn't react that way. In the end, Brogan wasn't going to focus on anything but getting Ayden better. He'd worry about whose neck to wring for being responsible after Ayden returned to his normal self.

"We need to contact someone to help him," Brogan demanded.

"I think we should start with the Prism Wizard. He was very helpful when we met him and as a history scholar, he'd know where to begin," Aleksander stated.

"He will also lead us to the authorities if his illness is not caused by natural means," Latarian added.

"I would do nothing to harm anyone here," Ari growled. His voice was tight with indignation, and his eyes were blazing with fury.

"No one's accusing you of hurting Ayden. Our concern right now should be getting him healthy. I'm going to go leave a message for the Prism Wizard," Aleksander stated as he stood.

Brogan thanked him, then darted out of the room. He wanted to get back to Ayden and see if he needed anything. It was late enough that there was no way Ayden would be up again. After undressing, Brogan crawled into bed with his dozing mate.

"Brogan?" Ayden asked groggily as Brogan pulled him over to lie across his chest.

"Who else would be getting into our bed naked?"

"I think I've got a list written down somewhere," Ayden teased. "I'll find it for you in the morning."

Brogan rolled his eyes, but he was pleased Ayden's sense of humor was still intact. "Very funny. Aleksander's working on getting a hold of the Prism Wizard. We need to find out why you're so tired and have no appetite."

"I'm not supposed to get sick. The spells on my back heal me constantly."

"Latarian thinks it's Ari's fault. She's convinced that he's doing something to make you sick."

"Why would Ari want to make me sick?"

"I have no idea."

"That doesn't make any sense. I'd believe it of Latarian before I would Ari," Ayden scoffed.

While Brogan was far from convinced Ari was the cause of Ayden's illness, he wasn't ready to cross off any possibilities. "He did get here just as you got sick."

"I still don't think it's him."

"I just hope the Prism Wizard can help."

"Me too. I knew I'd probably be spending more time in bed after we were mated, but I didn't think it'd be for extra sleep," Ayden complained with a wide yawn.

Brogan stroked a hand over his hair, then dropped a kiss on the top of his head. "Stop thinking with your dick."

"He's kinda lonely, you know."

Smoothing his palm down Ayden's back, Brogan stared up at the barely discernable ceiling. "We'll catch up once you're better."

Ayden let out another yawn and the sheets rustled as he cuddled closer to Brogan. "I hope so. I waited a long time for sex."

"I waited a long time for *you*."

"Don't get sentimental on me. I'm talking about dicks here."

The corner of Brogan's mouth lifted in a half-hearted attempt to smile. His worry and fear grew with every minute that Ayden's illness went on, but it was important to shield him from all that, so he kept the mood light. "I love you, my little hornball."

Ayden laid a kiss onto Brogan's chest. "I love you, my giant hornball."

Brogan rubbed his back as Ayden drifted off to sleep. Closing his own eyes, Brogan willed it to drag him under, but it wouldn't come. Through the night Brogan was tormented with visions of Ayden growing weaker and the light of dawn peeked through the tightly drawn curtains before exhaustion finally won out. When he dreamed, it was of chasing down an unknown foe poised and ready to snatch Ayden away. Shield and sword in hand, he battled demons until he woke an hour later, determined to stop at nothing to get his Ayden back.

30

"Prism Wizard, thank you so much for coming," Brogan said once he was introduced to the leader of the Spectra Wizardry. The man hadn't hesitated to teleport to their home the morning after Aleksander called him, and Brogan was grateful he was willing to help them.

"Please call me Vadimas. I'm happy to be of service. Let's go see what we have here." He and Aleksander escorted him down to the bedroom Ayden and Brogan shared; the familiar hadn't found the energy yet to rise.

When they got there, Blodwen, Ari and his familiar, along with Latarian were keeping his mate company.

"Ayden, how are you feeling?" Vadimas asked as Brogan sat down on the bed next to his mate.

"I can't get enough sleep, and I have no appetite," Ayden explained. His face was washed out, and his lids were half-closed with weariness covering a good portion of his eyes.

Latarian pointed a finger at Ari. "You might find it interesting that my familiar's illness began just as *he* arrived."

Vadimas studied Ari for a few seconds, then returned his attention to Ayden. "I rarely believe in coincidences, but in this case, I can tell you Ari's arrival as you fell ill is just that. I don't know what illness this is yet, but I can tell you it's coming from your own magic."

"Are you saying Ayden is making himself ill?" Latarian demanded. "Ayden, you have done your best to draw as much attention to yourself since our arrival. Is it truly necessary to feign illness as well?"

Ayden glared at her but didn't say a word.

The Prism Wizard glanced at Latarian. "I didn't say it was your familiar's fault. All I can tell you is that his magic is attacking him. We need to figure out a way to stop it. The fatigue and lack of appetite are only symptoms. The real problem is that his power's draining and without it, he will perish. I don't believe a Council hospital will be able to assist—modern medicine has never treated any of your kind."

Brogan closed his eyes as a cold chill washed over him. When he opened them, there was shock written all over Ayden's face. "Are you saying that Ayden's dying?"

"Indeed, but I don't intend to allow that to happen," Vadimas stated, and Brogan appreciated the determination in his voice.

Ari's brows drew together in confusion. "He's a familiar. His magic's naturally drained whenever he casts a spell. Can't Latarian just provide him with the power he's lost?"

"I do not give Ayden magic. He has his own," Latarian scoffed. "My own goes straight through him without replenishing his well."

"But...he's a familiar. I don't understand. That's not how it works," Ari argued.

"It's odd, but apparently this pair have a unique relationship. He has his own magical source, and did you notice he is the more powerful of the two?" Vadimas asked Ari.

"When I arrived, I thought she kept him so full of magical power that it was confusing my senses," Ari confided.

"No, he's stronger than her," Vadimas said. "I understand he also knows more schools of magic."

"I thought the point of this was to make Ayden better, not to quibble over why you believe us to be different," Latarian snapped.

Brogan hated to agree with her, but they could worry about the odd stuff later. He wanted Ayden healed.

"Of course, you're correct. We can discuss this at another time. Has anything unusual besides Ari and Derwin's arrival happened since the symptoms started? Is there anything you can think of that might've caused Ayden's magic to start attacking him?" Vadimas asked as he made eye contact with everyone in the room. He seemed to expect all of them to volunteer any information that might help him figure out this mystery.

"Ayden has recently mated with this dragon," Latarian announced. "Perhaps his magic is rejecting his mating. A familiar should be mated with another. It's unnatural to be with a shifter." At that moment Brogan remembered why he did not like Ayden's witch.

"Fate chooses our mates, so there's nothing unnatural about any pairing. Your mating was just as the symptoms started?" Vadimas asked.

Brogan instinctively scooted a bit closer to Ayden. The familiar peeled himself from the mattress so he could snuggle against Brogan's chest. Brogan wrapped his arms around him and held him tight. Neither one of them liked the idea that their matebond could be making Ayden sick.

"Yes...you don't think our mating caused this do you?" Brogan asked. "If his magic's rejecting us, I'd be willing to let Latarian cast her spell to break our matebond."

They were the hardest words Brogan had ever uttered, and his dragon was roaring in protest, but he'd take whatever measures necessary to save Ayden's life.

Ayden struggled to sit up, his green eyes going blue with emotion. "No way. There's absolutely no way we're ending our matebond. You can't even use the spell since our blood has already mixed."

"We could give it a shot. I'm not going to just sit here and let you die."

"This is ridiculous. Our mating's *not* making me sick." Ayden's voice had risen with each word, but Brogan wasn't going to allow his stubbornness to result in his death.

"You don't know that."

"The idea's absurd," Ayden shouted. "Matebonds don't kill people."

Brogan opened his mouth to reply when a bolt of lightning landed just a few inches from Ayden's small blanket-covered feet. Everyone in the room was in varying degrees of shock, except for the Prism Wizard whose arms were folded over his chest, and there was annoyance written across his wizened face.

"You have to teach me how to do that," Aleksander enthused. "Every time they start yelling, I can start tossing out thunderbolts."

Vadimas cracked a grin. "Unfortunately, shifters lack the ability to use magic—otherwise I'd be happy to teach it to you. As for your disagreement, I must side with Ayden. I can't fathom any circumstance where a matebond would result in illness. Latarian, I'm quite curious about your ability to break their connection. Could you tell me more about it?"

Latarian mumbled the words of the spell and Vadimas's face remained impassive, offering Brogan no insight on his thoughts. Giving Ayden his most apologetic look, Brogan pulled him back against his chest and then kissed the top of his head.

"I'm not sure who taught you that, but it won't work for you," Vadimas finally said.

"My power is unmatched. It will work," Latarian responded. Brogan rolled his eyes. Ayden's magic was stronger than hers, and he had no idea how to measure Ari's since he didn't have that kind of ability.

"I'm afraid power has nothing to do with it. That spell requires demonic blood which you clearly don't have. I'm not even sure if any of them still exist, and there's no written history of it being used successfully," Vadimas remarked. "Is there anything else besides the mating, which we've already ruled out, that could be suspect?"

Brogan wracked his brain, but he didn't know of anything new in their lives that could account for Ayden's illness. He did recall how they'd struggled to complete their matebond because of the silver marks etched into Ayden's skin.

"Ayden's back is covered in unmagic spells. Could they be harming him?" Brogan blurted out.

"Unmagic? May I see them?" Vadimas requested.

Ayden pulled away from Brogan and tugged up his T-shirt so Vadimas could view them. The wizard leader's face was impassive for a few seconds as he studied Ayden's back. Brogan let his gaze slide over to the other occupants of the room. Aleksander gave nothing away while Latarian appeared utterly bored with the entire affair. Then his eyes fell on Blodwen, Ari, and Derwin. All three were wearing matching expressions of pure horror.

Before Brogan could make any sense of their reactions, Vadimas lifted his hand in midair as if he wanted to touch them but something, possibly fear, kept him from doing so. "Ayden, how did you come about these spells?"

"Carvallius cast them."

"I've never seen symbols like this before. Do you know what each spell is?"

"No, but I was told they're all for healing and protection for me and Latarian."

Vadimas straightened and lowered his arm. "Latarian, do you have similar marks? Did your grandfather perhaps give you a key to all of these spells?"

"I have no need of them," Latarian stated. "My grandfather knew it was important for my safety that Ayden use his magic to benefit me as is his duty."

"Familiars have no duty to constantly cast spells that a warlock's more than capable of casting on their own. Those aren't unmagic spells. There's no such thing as unmagic. Those marks on Ayden's back are dark as night," Ari snapped. His words were full of barely leashed rage, and his mouth was twisted in disgust.

"Ari is correct. These spells are the result of dark magic," Vadimas said. The concern in his eyes was impossible to miss. "Without knowing what they all mean, we can't determine if they're the culprit. I'm afraid we can't remove them, as it could be harmful. I'm going to call Arch Lich Chander Daray. He's the authority on dark magic. Hopefully, he can unravel this mystery."

"We most certainly will not be removing them," Latarian declared, her tone frosty. "My grandfather put those there for me, and I will allow no one to alter his magic."

"Your familiar has the right to decide if they stay or go," Ari shot back.

"Once again, our new friend is correct. It's Ayden's decision, but we need the Arch Lich's expertise. Ari, I'd love to chat with you when we have Ayden settled," Vadimas said, then left the room to make his call.

"I hope the Arch Lich can help, but I have to confess I'm scared of meeting him," Blodwen whispered.

"It's the whole sentinel thing, right?" Brogan asked.

"Yeah, he has two, but he only keeps one with him at a time. I've only seen sentinels from far away, never up close," she responded.

Brogan had no time to reply as Vadimas reopened the door and walked in with two men not far behind him. Both were wearing all gray. The shorter of the pair had on a dark charcoal suit while his shirt and tie were the color of steel. Over it, his cloak was beautifully decorated with black and silver filigree. Brogan had seen photos of the Arch Lich in the past—he'd run the Council for over four hundred years before stepping down, so he had no trouble recognizing him. His face was deceptively young-looking. Chander could easily pass for a teenager if not for the shrewd pewter eyes that were studying Ayden behind a pair of wire-rimmed glasses.

Over the rather unruly brown curls of Arch Lich Chander's head was his sentinel. The assassin had pale skin and was a full head taller than the man he was bound to protect. He was dressed in an undecorated cloak over a military-style shirt and pants. Hanging on either side of his waist was a shiny dagger. They were obviously poisoned; each of them glowed a bright green.

"Everyone, this is Arch Lich Chander Daray and his sentinel Baxter," Vadimas said, then ran down the list of all the people in the room.

"Blodwen, it's a pleasure to meet you," the Arch Lich offered. "I'm sorry you felt so misplaced in the Order of Necromancia, but I'm glad you're somewhere that I hope brings you happiness."

She blushed prettily at the leader of her race, but her gaze never left the sentinel who stood still just inside the doorway scanning the room with his light eyes. "Thank you. I'm very happy here."

"May I see your back?" the Arch Lich asked and once again Ayden lifted his T-shirt.

Chander leaned in. "Definitely dark," he muttered. "Some of them look somewhat familiar, but warlocks used differed spells than necromancers. Vadimas, we'll have to see if we can find any records left behind by the warlocks to figure this out."

"Chand, take a picture of his back, so we have something to compare to whatever we can uncover," his sentinel suggested.

The Arch Lich dutifully tugged his phone out of his pocket and snapped a few photos. "Great idea, Bax. Don't worry, we'll figure this out. Is this normal for familiars to have spells cast upon them like this?"

Ari scowled. "No. There are very firm rules about the way we treat familiars, and forcing them to cast continuous magic is pure laziness. One of the duties once held by the Grand Summoner was to oversee the familiars and make sure they weren't abused. I'm sure Grand Summoner Saura would've had Carvallius, and perhaps Latarian as well, punished for such a thing."

"I have done nothing wrong," Latarian snapped.

Ignoring her, Chander kept his attention on Ari. "I didn't know Saura well, but I found her to be an intelligent and fiery woman. I have no trouble believing that. I have to say, this bothers me. I wouldn't expect my sentinel to be subjected to this. Ayden, did you give permission for these spells to be cast?"

Despite his fatigue, Ayden shook his head vigorously. "No, I wasn't asked, and I've always wanted to know what they meant, but no one would tell me."

"Okay, we'll make sure we get them off, then. My gut's telling me that these spells are somehow responsible," Chander said.

"This is absurd. I object," Latarian stated as she got to her feet and surprised Brogan by teleporting out of the room.

"The Coven of Warlocks no longer belong to the Council, as we believed them extinct, and Grand Warlock T'Eirick didn't live long enough for the rules of their race to be ratified into the Council, in any case. So I don't know if there's an enforceable punishment for this, but you have a right to make your own decisions," Chander remarked after Latarian departed.

"Right now all I care about is feeling better," Ayden interjected.

"We'll get there," Chander promised; then their guests left the room to find what information they could to help Brogan's mate.

"He seemed nice," Blodwen said once they were all out the door.

"Yeah, he did. I hope they figure this shit out fast. I don't want you getting any sicker," Brogan told Ayden.

"What did you guys think of his sentinel?" Blodwen asked.

"I think he seemed nice too, but also scary," Derwin offered.

"I wouldn't use the word scary. More like intimidating. And isn't that kind of the point?" Ari asked.

"I guess," Blodwen whispered.

"I'm just glad they're all here. I'm sorry they did this to you, Ayden. It has to be why you're sick," Ari commented, his eyes full of sorrow. Brogan was glad Ari and Derwin had found their way to his home. It meant a lot to Ayden to have them here, even if he lacked the energy to do more than chat in between naps.

Brogan squeezed his mate a little and brushed his lips over his hair. "Once you're better, we're going to discuss how we can have her punished for this."

Ayden let out a yawn, then drifted off to sleep. Brogan shoved aside his anger at Latarian and focused on finding the confidence he needed to endure the wait of the sorcerers trying to solve the puzzle of Ayden's back. Even in death, Carvallius was still wreaking havoc over his people.

31

Latarian paced her bedchamber as her thoughts raced from anger to fear and back once again to fury. Her emotions had been churned up for the last few days as Ayden appeared to be growing weaker. She was at a loss for what to do. These powerful sorcerers were trying to discover what Carvallius's spells meant and, despite her many objections, were intent on removing them. She did not know why life forever treated her so unfairly. What was she supposed to do without her power? Fate was ever cruel to her, and she could not fathom the purpose.

Since she had grown to adulthood, she'd done her best to follow the dictates taught to her as a child. Had she not spent over a century and a half with a measly sum of magic? Then when she finally had what she craved most, she was sent off to a cottage to toil away six hundred or so more years in the company of tiresome Ayden. To Latarian, it was most harsh that she would suffer so. Whatever would she do now? Where would she go?

She had yet to solve the problem of gold. It was not as if she could simply flee to some grand place and begin anew. *Under no circumstances will I return to that hateful cottage*, she thought with rising rage. Latarian had nothing left but to hope the Prism Wizard and the Arch

Lich were not as clever as she and Carvallius were. Surely Ayden was not rejecting the spells after having them for so long. It could not be possible. It had to be the dragon's fault.

Stamping her foot and taking a moment to let out a shriek, Latarian once again lamented scrying and coming to this horrid patch of sand in the middle of Arizona. Was this what Carvallius had warned her about? That his spells could not continue should Ayden meet his mate? She fumed with derision. What a fine pickle her grandfather had left her in. Latarian had no idea what would happen if the spells were broken. She wondered if Ayden would disappear and Dra'Kaedan would take his place. He may very well wish to see her dead, and she would perish innocent of all crimes.

She believed Ari was somehow responsible for Ayden's illness. Despite Vadimas's assurance, she didn't think his arrival was nothing more than coincidence. Latarian had full use of her senses, and he was powerful. Not nearly as strong as her, but there was something strange about him, as if he masked the extent of his witchcraft. Perhaps he was clever enough to craft a spell to trick sorcerers into thinking he had less than his fair share. Latarian doubted it was possible, but he was not pleasant.

He refused to use the word witch when she was clearly his superior, and he was too quick to point out the differences between her familiar and his. He had a magical dragon, so the Leolinnia twins were no longer unique among witchkind. If her magic wasn't light, she would've used it to end his miserable existence, but she could not go dark as long as she was tied to Dra'Kaedan. To her way of thinking, his magic was so pure that it was obnoxious. No matter how she examined the situation, things didn't bode well for her.

That big shifter wouldn't let anyone be alone with Ayden. She had no hope to persuade him to keep these men from breaking the bond between them by removing the marks upon his skin. She detested dragons and everyone else in this stupid house, but none more than Ayden himself. From the moment they'd peered down at that mirror and viewed the word D'Vairedraconis, her world had started to crumble.

In the end, there was only one person responsible for all of this, and his name was Dra'Kaedan of Leolinnia. Were she forced to escape this place, she vowed somehow to get revenge upon him for destroying her life. Latarian yanked on her hair until it pained her as she thought about slinking away with no real options for her future. She needed her grandfather and his inventive ways of helping her. He would know what to do and how to make sure her power was not lost to her. If everyone wasn't so absurdly irritated with Ayden's spells, Latarian might have suggested they fix them to not make him sick while keeping them connected.

Speaking of such a thing was an impossibility. To move forward with that plan would be revealing too much about him, and more questions might be asked of her. Ones she could not comfortably answer if she wanted to save her neck. Determined to think of some cunning plan for her plight, Latarian lay down upon her bed and closed her eyes.

She'd expended a great deal of energy working off her emotions, and she needed a quick rest before her mind found the solution she required. Her hands fisted at her sides as she thought of the lazy familiar lying abed with his body weakening. *Oh, how I wish I could lash him until he has a reason to feel so tired*, she thought as she relaxed her muscles for slumber. As her mind drifted toward sleep, she held tight upon her rage for Dra'Kaedan. He would pay for every second of worry forced upon her.

The next week passed by in mostly a blur for Ayden. The Arch Lich, the Prism Wizard, and everyone except for Latarian were doing everything they could to help but so far, they hadn't unlocked the mystery of the spells Carvallius had carved on him all those centuries ago. Latarian carried on as if nothing out of the ordinary was happening in the house. She visited Ayden often but with so many people around, he wasn't left alone with her. It was something he was grateful for; he didn't have the energy for her—or anything else, for that matter.

After washing his hands, Ayden took stock of himself in the mirror and noticed through bleary eyes that they were no longer green. They were all blue but not the navy that once signaled a strong spell or heightened emotions. It was an azure so light, they almost lacked any color at all. His power was waning, and they were going to run out of time before anyone figured out how to save him.

Dragging himself into the bedroom, Ayden collapsed onto the bed. Brogan would be returning soon with the breakfast he'd force him to eat. He'd let his mate pull the covers over him; he was too damn tired to bother. Ayden didn't want to think of Brogan, because he was leaving him soon. It broke his heart; he was going to lose the man he loved, and there wasn't anything he could do to prevent it. He didn't even have the energy to help search the ancient tomes to translate the spells forced on him so many centuries ago. It was so soon after his summoning that he lacked memory of the event.

Fate offered him no choices. That was nothing new—before arriving in Arizona, all he'd experienced was cruelty. The D'Vaires gave him joy and somehow, against all odds, he'd found the perfect mate. Ayden could hardly believe he wasn't given a single day to bask in that miracle after their matebond. He was grateful that she hadn't matched him with another magickind. It would be particularly cruel to know that by dying he would be dragging his other half across the veil with him.

For himself, Ayden refused to shed tears, and he wouldn't feel sorry for himself. He was lucky to have found love, and he had a dragon who adored him, but he couldn't rest or find any kind of peace until he got Brogan to promise him one thing. Shifters could live past the death of their mate but only if they didn't succumb to heartsickness. Ayden needed Brogan to survive.

"Hey, why'd you get up? I would've helped you." Ayden hadn't heard Brogan enter the room and set down a tray full of food he didn't want. Instead of tucking him under the covers, Brogan lifted him into his arms and walked across the room to sit in one of the comfy navy printed chairs near the window.

"I had to pee," Ayden explained. He was cocooned and safe in Brogan's strong arms. It was one of the many things about his dragon he cherished, his desire to always keep him close.

"Chander and Vadimas were really excited at breakfast. Did you want to eat now or wait a bit? They've figured out some of the symbols. They think they're going to have a breakthrough soon," his mate spoke softly to him as he kissed his head.

"Food can wait. Brogan, we need to talk." This was not going to be easy for either one of them, but Ayden no longer had the luxury of time.

"What's wrong?"

His mate's beautiful dark eyes were full of love and worry. "I need you to promise me something."

"Anything."

"Promise me that when I go, you won't let it stop you." Nothing mattered more to Ayden than Brogan surviving his heartbreak after he crossed the veil.

"Where are you going to go? You can hardly even walk. Or are you planning on walking out on me after they get those marks off you?" Brogan joked, and Ayden lifted his hands up to his man's cheeks. Losing that faintly dimpled grin that was so dear to Ayden, Brogan's expression grew serious.

"I don't have much magic left. Look at me—it's almost gone. I need you to promise me that when I die, you won't let the heartbreak destroy you."

"You aren't going to die. They're so close. I'm not going to lose you, so you don't have to worry about anything destroying me," Brogan assured him and pressed his mouth to Ayden's forehead in a soft kiss.

"Promise me anyway. Promise me that if I die, you won't. I need to know you'll survive...that you'll go on living. I need you to be happy." When a tear slipped out, Ayden tried hard to stem the tide, but his weeping wouldn't subside. It was not his sad fate he lamented but what Brogan would endure. If he could cast a spell to save him from the struggle of his grief, he'd do it in a second.

Brogan raised his head toward the ceiling and then lowered his chin. Like Ayden, his cheeks were wet. "I can't do that," he murmured.

"Please. *Please* do this for me," Ayden whispered back. He kissed his lips gently as they cried.

"I don't—I don't want to live if you aren't here."

"I *need* you to live for me. I did nothing but exist before I met you, and now I can't bear to think of a world without you in it. I beg you, please make me this promise."

"Okay. Okay, but you aren't going to die. You promise me that you'll hold on as long as you can....Because they *are* going to figure this out." Brogan's words were just as stilted as his own.

"I'm not leaving you until the last drop of magic leaves me. I love you so much." Ayden slid his hands from Brogan's face to wrap them around his neck.

"I love you, too." He punctuated his words with another kiss, then leaned their heads together. Letting his eyes fall closed, Ayden gathered his resolve. *No more tears*, he promised himself as he enjoyed the closeness of the dragon he adored. His life was nearly done, but he'd fill every moment with what mattered most, and that was undoubtedly Brogan. He'd promised him eternity, and Fate had reduced it to a matter of weeks.

Ayden didn't know if he had another full day to cherish the devotion they'd built, but he was glad he was magickind. The only thing he had left would be to watch over Brogan in death. All the power draining from his body would be restored, and he'd spend each day scrying, begging Fate for any scrap of Brogan's life she'd permit him to see. Their matebond would shatter until they could be reunited on the other side of the veil, but he wanted Brogan to find happiness. For himself, all he could do was curse Carvallius for destroying him.

32

B rogan was finishing up his dinner when a disheveled pair of Council leaders burst into the dining room.

"We got it. We figured it out," Vadimas announced, but he wasn't smiling.

"It's the spells on his back," Chander explained. "One of them has the mark of death. We don't know exactly what they all are, but they must be removed. However, we need a strong dark sorcerer to tackle it."

"Chander can't do it because those spells will attack anyone who tries to get rid of them, and his sentinels will be unable to ignore their innate instinct not to strike back," Vadimas said.

"So how do we find someone who can do it?" Aleksander asked.

"I'm not sure. There are so few that practice dark magic outside of necromancers," Chander responded.

"Maybe I could—" Blodwen's soft voice was drowned out by the Council leaders.

"A demon would be perfect, but I have no clue how to find one," Chander complained.

"Tristis elves are dark but lack sorcery," Vadimas added.

Blodwen straightened her shoulders. "I think—"

"There are dark casters outside the Council, I believe," Chander suggested.

"Yes, but can we trust them, and will they help?" Vadimas questioned.

"I really think—"

"*Hey*," Chander's second sentinel, Benton, yelled.

Chander scowled. "What are you yelling about, Ben?"

"Blodwen's been trying to talk to you two, but you keep interrupting her," he explained and both sorcerers gave her their full attention.

"I swear I need a whistle," she grumbled. "I haven't summoned my sentinel, so we aren't fully bound. If you think I am powerful enough, I'm willing to try."

"If power's an issue, I can help since Chander can't risk it," Ari offered. "It'll be painful as we'll be mixing warlock and necromancer magic."

"I don't care about that. I want to help Ayden," Blodwen assured him.

"Wonderful. Let's go fix our familiar," Vadimas exclaimed, and Brogan wasted no time following them to his bedroom. Without any surprise, he found his mate sleeping, so Brogan sat down next to him and gently roused him. When Ayden lifted his lashes, his irises were devoid of any color at all.

"They've figured it out. Blodwen's going to take the spells off your back now. Chander's put together an attack plan so she has a roadmap to follow," Brogan told him and was not entirely sure his words registered.

The familiar's eyes had yet to focus on him, but when Ayden spoke, it was clear he was still lucid. "Will it hurt her?"

"It may hurt a bit, but we'll be quick about it," Vadimas explained.

Brogan cupped Ayden's cheek in his hand and grinned. "I told you they'd figure it out."

"You were right. That's a first," Ayden said with a weak smile of his own.

"I love you, baby."

"I love you, too." Brogan brought their lips together and kissed him softly. He helped peel Ayden's T-shirt off, and they made sure he was comfortable as he lay down on his stomach with his back exposed. As much as he wanted to touch Ayden to comfort him during the process, the magic could seriously harm him. He had to make do with kneeling on the floor next to the bed so Brogan could at least meet his eyes as Ayden endured what was to come. Blodwen removed the first spell, and Ayden grimaced, but Ari was filling the room with powerful healing magic. Several more spells were removed, and Blodwen and Ayden were both sweating.

Blodwen blew her hair out of her eyes impatiently. "This one won't come off. I've tried three times."

"There's an ancient mark of the warlock. Maybe we need Latarian. Perhaps this spell connects them. She might need to be here for it to work," Chander suggested and Vadimas ran down the hall and was back almost immediately with the witch in tow.

"I want no part of this," Latarian declared. "Those spells are not hurting him. No one has gained my permission to take them away."

"I need her quiet to do this," Blodwen demanded as she filled the room with her dark magic once again. Derwin waved a hand in Latarian's direction, and she flew into the closest chair with her mouth moving, though no sound came out.

Necromantic and witch magic cascaded around the room as Blodwen removed spell after spell. Over an hour later, both her and Ayden were worse for the wear. Sweat dampened their hair, and there was strain on both of their faces, but there was also a great deal of determination.

As each mark disappeared, Ayden's back became less and less colorful. They were down to the very last one, and Blodwen took a moment to swipe a few stray tresses out of her face. Noirin offered her a bottle of water as if she were a boxer between rounds, and considering the battle she'd endured, it was an apt comparison. Brogan offered his exhausted mate a wink, and Ayden responded with one of his own and he mouthed the words, *I love you*; then Blodwen gave Ari the signal that she was ready to continue.

Pale streaks crossed the room as dark smoke surrounded Ayden, Blodwen cursed as Carvallius's handiwork fought her magic. Ari raised his hands high, and the entire floor lit up as he poured his power toward Ayden. Despite the brilliant show, Brogan kept his eyes on his mate as Blodwen swore viciously.

Suddenly a howling wind swirled in the room, and Ayden's red hair flew above his head. Then it was Ayden's entire body that rose to float in the air. Blodwen and Ari were both knocked to the floor, but they continued to cast. Ayden's colorless eyes met Brogan's, and they were teeming with sadness as the space around him filled with a blinding light.

It forced Brogan's eyes to close of their own accord and when he could finally open them again, everything was eerily silent. He had to know how Ayden was faring, but he didn't see him anywhere. Brogan blinked furiously and still, Ayden didn't appear as his brain coped with the struggle to understand where he'd gone.

"I'm sorry. I'm so sorry," Blodwen said, repeating the litany over and over.

Aleksander hunkered down on to the floor next to him and when he placed his hand on Brogan's shoulder to get his attention, there were tears running down his cheeks.

"I'm so sorry, Brogan. We were just too late," Vadimas whispered.

As the room filled with the sounds of weeping, Brogan's mind scrolled back to a conversation he'd once had with Ayden. He'd explained that when familiars ran out of magic, they simply disappear. They had failed. Ayden wasn't missing. His mate was dead.

Brogan opened his mouth in a desperate bid to breathe. The other people in the room were offering heartfelt condolences, but Brogan couldn't process their words. He was stuck with a single thought he couldn't get past. Like a loop, all he could think was that Ayden was on the other side of the veil. His little mate with the pretty eyes that went navy with passion and the giant heart desperate to help was never coming back.

"I didn't mean to hurt him," Blodwen choked out.

With words as wooden as his heart, Brogan said, "It's not your fault."

"I do not know why you are all carrying on this way," Latarian shrieked. "It is me you should be offering condolences to. I have lost my familiar."

Brogan wanted to slap her. It was her fault; she'd allowed her grandfather to carve spells into Ayden. His loss was so great, he could do nothing but sit on the floor and wonder if he'd ever find a way to go on. Ari fished something out of his pocket and his face went ashen. When his eyes met Brogan's, they were as broken as he was.

"*Enough,*" Ari roared at Latarian. "Not another word out of you. I hate to do this right now. I don't want to upset Brogan any further, but I can't listen to this shit."

Ari's jaw clenched as he grappled with his pain, and Brogan didn't care what he said. Ayden wouldn't return so there was nothing that could pain him further. The light in Brogan was gone just like the spunky familiar.

"What are you babbling about?" Latarian demanded.

"History tells of two twin boys born to Grand Warlock T'Eirick and Grand Summoner Saura. You've all heard of them?" Ari demanded.

Brogan automatically nodded.

"The twins were named Dra'Kaedan and Dre'Kariston. At birth, they were the most powerful warlocks in existence. The eldest was Dra'Kaedan, and he was the stronger of the two. He had beautiful golden curls and eyes of pure navy. The younger one had the same eyes, but his hair was dark as night. Their names were unusual because they were born with an ability to change into magical dragons. Draca is an ancient word for dragon, and their parents wanted everyone to know how special their sons were since someday they'd rule their people. The boys were born with a faint symbol on their wrist showing Fate's destiny."

Latarian stomped her foot heavily against the wooden floor. "What is the point of this stupid tale? How can we trust any word you say?"

Ari waved a hand over himself and his hair twisted into black curls. His irises darkened to midnight, and his features evened out to form an extremely handsome man. Derwin's countenance changed in a similar fashion. After pushing up one sleeve, Ari ripped off a sweat-band from his wrist to reveal a bright silver circle with a dragon's head in the center.

"I apologize for my deceit. My name isn't Ari Leonard," he said as he lifted his chin. "I am Grand Summoner Dre'Kariston of Leolinnia, and the man who died in this room tonight was no familiar named Ayden. He was Grand Warlock Dra'Kaedan."

Brogan managed to blink. He was so deep into shock he had no other available response. His Ayden was the Grand Warlock?

"My familiar died this day, not your brother," Latarian screeched.

"He speaks the truth," Derwin shouted back.

Ari—or more accurately, Dre'Kariston—threw the object in his hand at Latarian's feet. "That necklace was placed around my neck as a baby. It contained an essence of my twin and until a few minutes ago glowed blue. Dra'Kaedan disappeared weeks before the war started, and we searched endlessly for him. My necklace should've led me to him. It was enchanted with a dragon's head that should've pointed in his direction. When he vanished, it spun wildly and was no longer any help. It tried again in the last couple of weeks, but it's been unreliable at best, and now the glow is gone because he's *dead*. I don't know why the mark on my wrist hasn't turned gold yet but perhaps these things take time. Fate has a great deal to manage."

Latarian lifted a shoulder. "So your silly necklace no longer glows. We must take your word that it ever did. How could my familiar be your brother?"

Dre'Kariston's furious eyes latched on her, and Brogan was surprised Latarian didn't catch fire from the hatred blazing in them. "Explain why your hair is darker red, your eyes are lighter, and your power is now at a novice's level."

Brogan tore his gaze from Ayden—*Dra'Kaedan's*—brother and noticed that his observations were correct. Her features were also different, and her tresses were stick-straight instead of wavy.

"My familiar is dead," she spat out. "How can you not expect there to be changes?"

"You should be stronger, not weaker, and now I know your grandfather had everything to do with his disappearance."

"You lie," she shouted.

Dre'Kariston reached into his jeans and pulled out another necklace. It was gold and unlike Dre'Kariston's medallion glowed a faint navy. He let it dangle from his fingers and it swung almost hypnotically. "This is Dra'Kaedan's necklace. Can you guess how I got it?"

"For all I know, you murdered your brother and are now trying to make my grandfather take the blame," Latarian scoffed.

Brogan's knees ached from kneeling, but he didn't move an inch. A part of him thought that if he just stayed still long enough, there was a chance his mate would return to the spot where he'd disappeared from. He didn't care if his name was Ayden or Dra'Kaedan, he wanted him back.

Dre'Kariston swallowed loudly, his eyes red and awash with tears. "I loved my brother. I wouldn't have done anything to hurt him. I know it was Carvallius because I found Dra'Kaedan's necklace in his pocket after his death."

"His *death*? How would you know of it unless you were there? You killed my grandfather did you not? You are the only murderer in this room," Latarian accused, her face mottled with color.

"You're right," Dre'Kariston confirmed softly. "I did kill him. My parents made me hide, and Carvallius used Dra'Kaedan's necklace to track me down. He attacked me, and I battled back. I didn't know when I got here that Ayden was my brother. I didn't see any of my twin in his face, and he didn't recognize me."

"The oddities make sense now that you've told us his real identity," Vadimas offered quietly.

Latarian's gaze glowed ripe with fury. "How could you murder my grandfather?"

"How could I? It was my *pleasure*. Look what he's done to our people. To my parents. And you used my brother for centuries. You and Carvallius filled his back with evil magic, and now he's dead. You came between him and his mate, and as you were so keen to tell me, that's punishable by death," Dre'Kariston sneered.

Brogan was stunned. Thoughts lined up in his head, and Ayden was nothing more than a mirage. The familiar had never existed at all. He'd been mated to Grand Warlock Dra'Kaedan of Leolinnia. A teenager who was abducted and forced into servitude for over six centuries by a crazy woman and her evil grandfather. "He was Dra'Kaedan?" Brogan blurted out.

The room was silent except for the sounds of mourning as the truth settled around the occupants. It was the Arch Lich's sentinel Benton who took a menacing step toward Latarian. "Why didn't you tell us his real identity when he got sick? We might've been able to save him before he grew too weak to survive the removal of the spells."

"I had no reason to believe he would be hurt," Latarian stated with a shrug. "All my grandfather gave me was a vague warning that he should not be allowed to mate."

Surging to his feet, Brogan strode over to Latarian and she shrank down in the chair. He loomed over her fighting his dragon's desire to rip out her throat. "Why didn't you tell me who he was? You stole my mate. *His death is your fault.*"

Chander laid a hand on his arm. "Brogan, she'll pay for this. We'll take her to the fallen knights in the morning. They'll decide what to do with her, and I can't imagine they'll take this lightly."

The Arch Lich was trying to calm him down, and Brogan straightened to put space between him and Latarian. He didn't give a shit what happened to her. Dra'Kaedan wasn't coming back, and he would *never* forgive her. How could he? His life was ruined.

"It had to be the addition of the matebond. It is far stronger than anything. The dark spells were no longer able to keep Latarian and Dra'Kaedan bound," Vadimas surmised. *She had every opportunity to tell us the truth, and my mate would still be alive,* Brogan thought bitterly.

"I know I should've told you the truth about me as soon as I arrived, but I didn't even know evil spells like that existed. It's still difficult for me to believe. Dra'Kaedan was so powerful, I couldn't have imagined he could be twisted into her familiar. I wish I'd said something," Dre'Kariston choked out. He walked over and grabbed Brogan's hand. He dropped Dra'Kaedan's glowing gold necklace into his palm. Brogan curled his fingers into a fist around the necklace that had once hung from his mate's neck.

"He would've wanted you to have it, and this way you can always find me," Dre'Kariston vowed. "I owe you a debt I can never repay, but please know I would've given my own life to keep him here with you."

"Thank you," was all Brogan could manage as he stared at his mate's twin, searching for similarities to the man he loved, but they were impossible to find.

Dre'Kariston's smile was sad. "He was obsessed with dragons. His clothes, his bedding, and his tapestries were all covered with them. Shortly before he disappeared, we had guests in my parents' castle who told us as we dined that dragons were real. After that, he was convinced we were both going to be mated to dragons. It was his fondest wish."

Losing any control he had on his emotions, Brogan's grief grew until he was overwhelmed by it. He needed to be alone; he could no longer deal with the pain. Without a word to anyone, he ran from the room and headed straight outside. Carefully, he set down Dra'Kaedan's necklace on the deck and then allowed his dragon to take over. His clothes ripped from his body as his limbs stretched and formed into his beast. Quickly flapping his wings, he soared into the sky and filled it with fire. Inside of him was a loss so deep and vast, neither he or his dragon would ever be the same.

33

E veryone in the house was so mired in grief, they had only escorted Latarian to her bedroom and the sentinel had given her a stern warning to stay put or else he would track her down. Latarian had appeared appropriately subdued and allowed him to lock her into her space. Fools, she thought as she gathered her belongings. They knew she had no funds and now little power, but it didn't mean she wasn't clever. Latarian would be damned if she was going to stay and wait for the Order of the Fallen Knights to carry her off.

She'd done nothing wrong. Fate denied her power, and she was related to a genius capable of fixing that issue. Latarian had gone to her grandfather one day after hearing him complain of the Leolinnias and had suggested they use Dra'Kaedan as her familiar. Carvallius had somehow arranged it, and now all his hard work was for naught. These damn people had ripped his spells off Dra'Kaedan's back and left her with nothing.

Without giving herself a moment to reconsider, she teleported to her ancient home of Castle Mallent. The land was unowned by the Council of Sorcery and Shifters, so neither the Arch Lich's sentinel or the fallen knights could venture here to arrest her. It was now up to her to solve her problems, and it infuriated her. She didn't want to sit around thinking of stratagems. Her life with the dragons had been more than tolerable, though she hated them.

There was tasty food to eat, clothes on her back, and a roof over her head. Now she had a crumbling castle, and the entire fault could be laid at Dra'Kaedan's feet. His mate was swamped in tears, believing him dead, which just showed how stupid they all were. The Grand Warlock was not beyond life but simply stuck between the veil as he recovered from the marks ripped from his skin. He would be back, and Latarian couldn't wait. She vowed vengeance upon his curly head as well as his brother's. She did not care how long it took; she would find a way to make them pay for all the indignities forced upon her.

Latarian stood on blackened ground surrounded by crumbling stones and had no idea where to find her next meal, but she would not be cowed. Her destiny wasn't to be a novice just because her power was stolen from her. It might take some time to change her circumstances, but she was ever a resourceful soul. The last thing she would do was scurry to that hated tiny cottage where Ayden had served her. The world owed her for all the pain and suffering heaped upon her person. Latarian would see that the D'Vaires paid—but first, she needed to find a place to lay her head at night. With a tormented sigh, she put one foot in front of the other and demanded that Fate do something to fix the intolerable situation.

For three days, Brogan flew. He fought against a dragon who wanted to fall from the sky and end their torment. He'd made a promise to Ayden—Dra'Kaedan, he reminded himself—and he wouldn't let him down. His feet softly hit the ground as he let his scales turn back to skin. Brogan turned to find Dravyn standing there, armed with a pile of fresh clothing for him.

Brogan grabbed the stack and tugged them on. "Thanks, Dray."

Dravyn handed him Dra'Kaedan's necklace, which he tucked into the pocket of his jeans. "I thought I'd build a gazebo. He liked to walk the gardens."

"I think he would've liked that, thanks."

"Noir's making breakfast."

Following Dravyn inside, he closed the door behind them and found himself in a room eerily quiet. "What's wrong?"

Aleksander stood. "Latarian's disappeared. Vadimas and Chander notified the fallen knights before they headed back to Las Vegas."

Brogan shrugged. Latarian was of no consequence to him any longer. There was no punishment that would bring his mate back. "I don't care."

Sitting down, Brogan ate the tasteless food Noirin placed in front of him. Nothing in his life would ever feel the same as it had when his other half was still alive.

"I'm sorry, Brogan. Is there anything I can do to help you?" Blodwen asked as her eyes filled with tears. Brogan hated that she blamed herself for what happened to Ayden—no, he had to think of him as Dra'Kaedan, he mentally corrected himself.

"Please stop apologizing. Your magic was what offered us that last bit of hope. It's not your fault it didn't work."

"I wish I'd spoken up sooner about who I really was. Maybe—"

Brogan cut off Dre'Kariston's words with a single raised hand. "It was Carvallius and Latarian who hurt him. Ayden...Dra'Kaedan wouldn't have wanted any of you to blame yourselves. We need to focus on positive things. He made me promise I wouldn't die of heartbreak. I'm going to need all of you to help me keep my word."

"Of course," Aleksander promised. "Whatever you need. We'll all be here for you."

His chin quivered as he struggled with his despair. He could count on his best friend and the rest of his family to keep him sane. "Thanks...I want to remember him in a good way and not how I lost him."

Larissa smiled, though it did not quite reach her eyes. "It'll be easy to remember the good things about him. He was wonderful. He loved everything, and he had such a big heart."

"He sure did. One morning, he wanted a way for the world to see how wonderful you guys are. He thought about all the other people like me who were different and decided the Council should send them here, and the idea of the sanctuary was born," Blodwen remembered.

It was impossible to forget the sanctuary Dra'Kaedan had wanted. His anger over Brogan's objections loomed fresh in his mind. *Oh, how I am going to miss my little firebrand*, he thought helplessly.

"He was so pissed at me but determined to find a way to convince me it'd be safe for all of us. If I had to do it over again, I would've agreed just so he'd have what he wanted. I would've lavished all my attention and every dollar I have to make him happy," Brogan said quietly. He would give up everything he was and all he had just to hold him one more time. To pull him onto his lap and kiss his hair.

"I wish we'd figured out a plan to ensure our safety. That sanctuary was so important to him," Blodwen added.

Brogan thought about the gazebo Dravyn wanted to build and it would be a beautiful memorial for his mate, but opening a sanctuary would be an even bigger way to keep his memory alive. "Dre'Kariston, how powerful are you?"

"Twice what Latarian thought she had since my brother's magic pool was split over the two of them. I'm so grateful I no longer need to hide it. It was painful to keep it contained."

"So, how do you rate amongst all magickind?" Brogan asked.

"With my brother gone, I'm the most powerful sorcerer alive."

Knowing how strong Dre'Kariston was helped Brogan come to a decision. "Good. I want to open the sanctuary."

Aleksander's face was full of concern. "Are you sure that's a good idea? I certainly want to help people, and I haven't changed my mind, but are you sure now is the best time to consider it?"

"Nothing will bring him back, Aleksander. I need something to focus on to keep my promise to him. This is the perfect time."

Dre'Kariston's mouth lifted on one side. "Dra'Kaedan's Coven. He never got to have his."

"Perfect. That's what we'll call it," Brogan said with a determined nod.

~

Brogan worked tirelessly with Blodwen and Dre'Kariston to hammer out their sanctuary proposal. All the changes were for security, and the application Dra'Kaedan suggested was created. They'd ask the Council to give them permission to select their own candidates and do their own background checks. The D'Vaires had no idea if it was feasible, but if they couldn't have it their way, then they were all content with putting the idea on the shelf permanently.

The work filled his days, and his nights were spent mostly staring at the ceiling of his bedroom. Sleep eluded him, even though he was exhausted. He couldn't get used to not having Dra'Kaedan lying across him at night. Everyone kept on him to eat, to focus on the positive, and he did his best but when he was alone, it was difficult to keep a brave face. It was grueling to try and go through the motions of everyday life when everything triggered memories that brought him to his knees.

He'd done their laundry the day before and cried as he folded his mate's colorful pajamas. The sheets on their bed were washed as well, but Brogan hadn't been able to put Dra'Kaedan's pillowcase in the washing machine. It smelled too much like him, so he'd stuffed it under his pillow to take out when he needed to feel close to him. Last night he'd lain all night with it draped over his face.

Promising his mate to not allow heartsickness to take over was proving to be even more difficult than he'd imagined. He was beginning to seriously doubt if he could keep his word. No longer bound to Dra'Kaedan, he'd lost his immortality but even for a short-lived dragon, Brogan still had at least one or two thousand more years to survive before they were reunited on the other side of the veil.

He didn't think it was possible to spend that long without Dra'Kaedan. So he kept up his façade of being okay and he worked on the sanctuary to make sure no one ever forgot that Dra'Kaedan had lived. Brogan was slowly preparing himself for another lonely day when there was a knock on his door.

"Ready to grab some breakfast and get this proposal finished?" Blodwen asked when he opened it.

"Sure," he replied and followed her down the hall. Expecting the morning meal, Brogan was surprised when they got to the kitchen and he was beckoned outside.

"What's going on?" Brogan asked Aleksander as soon as he joined them.

"Dravyn and I finished the gazebo. Madeline made the plaque," his king explained as Brogan absorbed the scene in front of him. The gazebo was beautiful. It was the same wood as the deck of their house and as he stepped closer, he noticed inside were thick navy cushions on the bench seats that wrapped around the walls of the structure. Hanging over the entrance was Madeline's sign. It was crafted with the same metal combination she'd used for their rings and it read simply, DRA'KAEDAN.

"Thank you. Thank all of you...it's beautiful. He would've loved it. Truly," Brogan said as he tried not to choke on the emotion welling up inside him. Soon he was in a giant D'Vaire family hug, and there was no point in holding back his tears because everyone was crying as they all tried to cope with the devastating loss of their little non-familiar.

Somehow, he struggled through breakfast and later that morning, they put the finishing touches on the proposal that would hopefully add Dra'Kaedan's Coven to Court D'Vaire. They opted to wait until the next day to send it in. Before then, they were going to celebrate Dra'Kaedan's life and his idea that had fueled all the challenging work they'd just completed.

By nightfall, Noirin had made a cake and while Brogan wanted to keep his family satisfied that he was holding his own, there was no way he was going to be able to eat any of it without breaking down. In fact, he refused all sweets and wouldn't even look at popcorn, not that it really mattered since he'd ceased to enjoy food when Dra'Kaedan died.

He was happy that the proposal was done, and he was curious as to what the Council would make of it, but he wondered how he would fill his days now that it was completed. It had only taken him an hour of feigned revelry before it was time for him to go to bed. Most likely he wouldn't get much rest, but he couldn't fake his smile any longer. Brogan changed into pajamas, a blue pair aptly covered in bright pink ghosts, and then climbed into his empty bed.

Larissa had made the damn things for him for decades, but he'd only started donning them in the past week because they made him feel closer to Dra'Kaedan, who'd worn them without fail. Pulling out his mate's pillowcase, he slid it over his nose to cherish his scent and decided he'd sleep in the following day. He had a week's worth of exhaustion to catch up on and nothing to keep him occupied. Switching off the light and closing his eyes, Brogan tugged a pillow to lay over his chest and tried to pretend his life wasn't over.

34

"T'Eirick, it's been nearly a week since Dra'Kaedan's mate got out of bed." Saura's voice was tight with concern as she came to stand at her other half's ghostly side.

"I know, but Dra'Kaedan's not awake yet," T'Eirick replied, wrapping Saura into his arms.

"If Brogan dies, so does our son. As much as I yearn to spend time with our children, I have no wish for Dra'Kaedan to join us permanently on this side of the veil."

"Saura, he hovers between life and death. He's much too weak to return to his mate now."

"It's a risk we must take."

"What would you have me do?"

Pursing her lips in frustration, she said, "Send Dra'Kaedan home."

"It would mean losing our magic."

"What use do we have for it? If Dra'Kaedan hadn't been missing, we would've given it to them right after we died," Saura countered. "Once we located him with that horrible girl, we certainly weren't going to increase her power by sending what we have over the veil to our twins."

"It's too much magic for Dra'Kaedan alone."

"We'll do as we originally planned. It'll be split between him and Dre'Kariston."

"It'll be painful for Dre'Kariston. Unlike his brother, he's very much alive."

Saura was growing impatient with her mate's stalling. "T'Eirick, he's perfectly capable of healing away his pain. Besides, he'll be so grateful to have his brother back, I'm sure he won't care."

"What if this doesn't work?"

Smiling, Saura thought over all they'd learned since their deaths centuries ago. They'd met many spirits and expanded their minds with new spells and abilities. "Then we're not the warlocks I believed us to be. Come on, we'll cast the spell to restore our son's life. It's the only way to save him and Brogan."

Hand-in-hand, they gathered the Coven of Warlocks butchered centuries before by the Cwylld elven. Her heart broke for all the missing familiars who'd struck out on their own after death. It was something she hadn't seen coming, and she grieved for the split between her people but there was nothing she could do. They were now the Coven of Familiars with their own leaders, and they wanted nothing to do with their former sorcerers.

Once their coven was assembled, T'Eirick addressed the crowd of eager faces. "My successor, Grand Warlock Dra'Kaedan D'Vaire, is stuck in the veil which separates life from death. His mate has done his best to endure the loss of him, but he's losing his fight. We're unsure if Brogan will live long enough to save them. It's up to us to restore Dra'Kaedan by giving him and Grand Summoner Dre'Kariston the power that belongs to Saura and me. The twins are the only hope for the survival of our people. Do you wish to help us?"

There was a thunderous roar as the warlocks cheered and clapped loudly. Saura reveled at the beauty of the scene in front of her, then tossed her blonde curls over her shoulder. "Carvallius robbed us of life, and yet we endure. I look around and see men and women who fought bravely against the relentless elves who chased us down. Not one of you ever lay down and gave up. I know we face overwhelming odds in succeeding, but I also know the hearts of you. We will find a way to save the Grand Warlock and his mate."

T'Eirick grinned at her as their people shouted out ideas and words of encouragement. Saura's heart swelled with pride over the amazing people that she'd been honored to die alongside. She'd breathed her last breath surrounded by so many of the smiling faces now determined to help Saura save her son, so he wouldn't join them as a ghost.

Once the chatter died down, T'Eirick lifted his arms high. "Are you ready to return the Grand Warlock to life?"

Saura was tugged against T'Eirick in a tight hug as once again, the spirits around them bellowed out their willingness to help them succeed. After T'Eirick released her, they split up and organized the energized crowd. It took no time at all to create a large circle with their hands interlocked. They would combine their power to push their magic pools into their children. Saura nearly collapsed in shock when out of nowhere the entire Coven of Familiars showed up and, without a word, stood alongside them. They appeared willing to put their rift behind them, if only for a few minutes, to save her eldest son.

T'Eirick's eyes widened and with a nearly imperceptible shrug, he took her hand. Her mate raised his chin and his face was solemn. The excited covens went still as their former leader spoke. "Fate, hear our call. Saura and I cede our power to Grand Warlock Dra'Kaedan and Grand Summoner Dre'Kariston. They live among dragons at the Draconis Court of D'Vaire and we ask in your grace you watch over their entire new family. We shall all serve our leaders, though we are no more than spirits."

After T'Eirick closed his eyes, Saura did the same, and the air around them crackled with the surge of so many souls combined. Saura dug deep inside and tugged as hard as she could on her soul. With a smile on her face, Saura ignored the agony of being ripped apart and pushed her power outward. Focusing on the two bright lights she and T'Eirick had created out of pure love, Saura shoved her magic toward them.

Dre'Kariston was easy to find, resting in his room in Arizona, and a tingle raced over her skin as her sorcery bled into her youngest son. Dra'Kaedan was a different story; his presence was little more than a wraith, and there was no body to look upon her firstborn child. Saura wasn't deterred.

She focused on the memories of Dra'Kaedan inside her and let out a shout as Saura found the piece of him that straddled the thin line of the veil. She refused to falter as she gave up the core of herself to save Dra'Kaedan, and she thanked Fate as her plan came to fruition. Darkness passed over her, and she tumbled to the ground. Her last thought as she fainted was astonishment that she could manage such a thing while dead.

Pain so close to being unbearable traveled down every inch of Ayden. He wanted to scream, to demand Blodwen stop casting so he could have a moment to breathe as she removed the spells on his back. Then, his brain remembered she was successful. For one moment he was Latarian's familiar and the next he was ripped violently away from her. He was given no time to enjoy it. Eyes open, he'd gazed into the navy ones of his mate as Ayden was tugged across the veil. He'd wanted to stop and tell him good-bye—to murmur his love—but he was too weak.

Confusion was unmistakable on Brogan's face; the dragon hadn't understood that he was dying. Slowly but still way too fast, he'd slipped into the unknown. His soul had cried out for Brogan as a strange calmness floated over him. The grief of his other half being gone hadn't lessened, but it was overwhelmed by the knowledge drifting into him. It was then that memories danced through his mind. Strange remembrances of a life before Latarian.

Mystifying fragments assaulted him. Two people he knew were his parents, which made little sense at first. *Familiars don't have parents*, he'd argued with himself, but it was an undeniable truth that Grand Warlock T'Eirick and Grand Summoner Saura were responsible for his birth. There was no summoning by a novice named Latarian. Already unable to reconcile that, he saw more—pictures of his family and the joy they'd shared together.

More than a mom and a dad, he had a brother too. A twin named Dre'Kariston. Once they were inseparable, and no one had known him better. He couldn't revel in those thoughts as dark ones of being knocked out and waking up in Carvallius's castle had invaded. A madman conspiring with his granddaughter to rob him of not only his power but his identity. Ayden, they had called him, but that was not him. He was Dra'Kaedan of Leolinnia, the Grand Warlock.

Then he heard her voice. "Dra'Kaedan," his mother said. "You must wake up. Brogan needs you."

Forcing his heavy lids open, tears welled as he stared into the beloved faces of his parents. He hadn't seen them in over six hundred years, and yet they remained the same. Saura's blonde hair twisted in curls to her waist, and his father's blue eyes were the same serious, intelligent gaze he remembered. Then the words she'd spoken registered and fear clutched his heart. "Brogan, where is he?"

"He believes you're dead. He's struggling to survive without you," Saura told him gently, then leaned down and kissed his forehead.

He scowled in confusion. "I *am* dead."

"No, you're not," T'Eirick corrected. "You existed between the veil, and your magic would've restored you on its own, but we couldn't wait. We didn't want Brogan succumbing to heartsickness and killing you both. We gave you and Dre'Kariston our magic to speed up the process."

"Dre'Kariston's still alive?"

T'Eirick smiled and squeezed his hand. "You met him. He's with your dragon, he was disguised, and you knew him as Ari."

His wits were already scattered, but there were new spells and abilities being layered into his memories.

"Your father's giving you all we've learned in death. Use the knowledge wisely, dear. We don't have much time. Remember that we love you. So much. You're always in our thoughts. Give Dre'Kariston hugs and kisses from both of us. Go now, *live*, and love that dragon of yours."

She flickered from view as did his father, so Dra'Kaedan forced his weary body upright. "I love you," he yelled to them as they faded away. His last glimpse of them was his mother blowing him a kiss, and tears slipped down his cheeks. He'd been stuck in a cottage with Latarian when they were robbed of life by both Carvallius's greed and an elven tribe hell-bent on annihilating everyone of warlock blood. Dra'Kaedan's heart mourned them as if they had died this day instead of centuries ago.

He put his head into his hands and wept. His body swayed with weakness and the air around him changed. It grew warmer and the stone slab under him was somehow soft as a cushion. Struggling to contain his emotions while trying to figure out what was going on, Dra'Kaedan lifted his head and found himself in a place he didn't recognize. Dashing the wetness from his face, he grew concerned. His magic was too drained to be of any help if he were in danger.

Placing his palms down next to him on a large navy pillow, he forced his trembling legs to hold him upright and lurched forward two steps to the entrance of whatever the hell structure he was inside of. When he got there, he leaned his weight against one pole and a grin popped out at the sight in front of him. It was his house in Arizona where he'd met Brogan. His mate was somewhere inside, though he'd never make it that far to join him.

Tilting his head upward, he noticed a metal sign. In bold letters, he read his own name. Not Ayden, as the D'Vaires thought he was, but Dra'Kaedan. *At least they figured out my identity*, he thought as he nearly stumbled backward. Putting his tired body onto the seat, he settled back to wait for someone to find him. Dre'Kariston couldn't have missed all the magic their parents had forced onto him; hopefully they'd investigate and rescue him.

His eyes slipped shut as fatigue tugged on his consciousness. A smile creeped over him as he wondered what his mate would think of his new look. Too exhausted to ponder the possibilities, Dra'Kaedan lay down. He'd feel better once he got some rest. As he slid into sleep, he hoped to hell Brogan got there soon; he didn't want him hurting for one more moment.

There is a stain on the ceiling, Brogan thought as he lay in bed. It was right above the bathroom door. Had someone missed it when the room was painted? Brogan wasn't sure—the rest of the ceiling was pristine, but that was the spot he stayed focused on. His stomach let out a rumbling sound, and he couldn't remember the last time he'd eaten. Rolling over onto his hip, he ignored it. As he reached up to scratch his chin, there was a knock on the bedroom door, but he paid no attention to it either.

All he could handle was the sadness tearing him apart, and the only way to combat it was to stare above him. He'd made a promise to his mate to survive, and doing that took all his concentration. He missed Dra'Kaedan so much. Brogan wondered how different their lives together would've been if he'd known his real identity. Helpless to resist, the corner of his mouth lifted as he thought about how stupidly he'd reacted when he had met Ayden the familiar.

The knocking continued so Brogan called out, "Trying to sleep, can you come back later?"

Apparently choosing to ignore him, the door banged open to reveal Dre'Kariston. His eyes were wide with shock, but that wasn't what had Brogan sitting up. His mate's brother was shimmering, his entire being was lit up with a golden aura.

"*Brogan,*" he shouted. "Brogan. I'm glowing."

"Yeah, I see that. What's going on?"

Dre'Kariston ran to the bed and nearly shoved his silver chain up Brogan's nose. "My necklace. The glow is back!" he yelled as Derwin raced in behind him.

Grabbing Dre'Kariston's hand, he tugged it down to find the dragon medallion radiating blue. "I don't understand," Brogan said slowly. With Dra'Kaedan gone, there was no reason for the necklace imbued with his essence to be alight.

"I don't either," Dre'Kariston bellowed. "My whole damn body hurts. *Seriously hurts.* I'm casting all the healing shit I can and still, it's torture all the way to my bones. My power. It's stronger too."

"What should we do?"

Dre'Kariston swung the chain hypnotically. "The dragon's lit up. We should follow it."

Without giving Brogan any time to respond, Dre'Kariston dashed through the doorway. Brogan threw off the covers to follow him. Confusion filled his brain as he thought about Dre'Kariston's glow and his necklace. Trailing the bright warlock down the hallway, his broken heart wondered if Dra'Kaedan had somehow figured out a way to communicate from the other side. Brogan ached for even a moment to speak with him. Dre'Kariston ran faster, and Brogan had no choice but to sprint after him.

When they got to the living room, Dre'Kariston smacked into Aleksander. "Hey, you okay?" their king asked as he steadied Dre'Kariston to keep him from toppling over.

"My necklace is glowing," Dre'Kariston shouted as he weaved around Aleksander with Brogan on his heels. The warlock tore open the door and leaped across the backyard like a gazelle. Then he stopped dead in his tracks because like Dre'Kariston, the gazebo they'd erected in memory of Dra'Kaedan was faintly iridescent.

"What the hell?" he blurted out.

"I don't know," Dre'Kariston said as he crept closer to the wooden structure. Brogan was two steps behind him when he heard his voice again, only it was much softer than before. "*Oh, praise Fate.*"

"What's going on?" Brogan asked.

"Come here," Dre'Kariston invited, the words a reverent whisper.

Dre'Kariston stepped into the gazebo, and Brogan followed him in. When he got to the doorway, he went still. The world spun, and he clutched two of the pillars that held the roof up as he stared down at the cushions. Curled up on the navy fabric was a stunning blond man. Golden curls fell over his forehead, and he had a strong, chiseled jaw. His nose was straight and slightly turned up at the tip.

Those features were new, but his soul recognized the man in front of him.

Taking one large step and falling to his knees, Brogan trailed a hand over the bouncy tresses as the tears slid unbidden down his cheeks. He pressed his lips to every part of his face he could reach and thanked Fate over and over again for the miracle of being able to do so. He smoothed a hand down his body over a dark blue cloak intricately embroidered in gold.

"It's my brother," Dre'Kariston choked out as he sat down next to Dra'Kaedan, and like Brogan, couldn't resist touching him.

"How's this possible?" Brogan whispered. He was so afraid it was nothing more than a dream and he hoped if it was he never woke up.

"Dra'Kaedan's in here," Dre'Kariston yelled out, which startled Brogan. He turned slightly as a sound registered behind him to find his entire family gathered in the backyard. "Did you hear me? He's not dead."

"I heard you. You're shouting loud enough," a voice muttered irritably.

"You're awake," Dre'Kariston said. "How aren't you dead?"

"Tomorrow," Dra'Kaedan responded as he held out a hand which Brogan immediately grabbed. "I don't have the energy to explain it now."

"I'm so glad you're here," Brogan managed.

"I would've done anything to return to you," Dra'Kaedan replied as he lifted his lashes to reveal an exhausted pair of navy eyes. "I love you."

"I love you too," Brogan responded as he leaned forward and scooped Dra'Kaedan from his resting spot. His mate wrapped his arms around his neck, and Brogan wanted to cry all over again at the feel of his lips against his skin. Standing so he could carry him inside, he walked out of the gazebo.

"I've missed you, little brother," Dra'Kaedan murmured over his shoulder.

"I missed you too," Dre'Kariston replied, only steps behind

Brogan. The entire D'Vaire clan gave him room, so he could get his precious bundle inside.

Dra'Kaedan's eyes fell shut, and Brogan hurried into the house. His knees were shaky, and Brogan still wasn't convinced what was happening was real, but Dra'Kaedan needed a bed. Once inside, he raced into their space and then gently laid him down on the mattress. The love of his life didn't move a muscle as he was already fast asleep. His strength appeared to have deserted him.

After tugging off his gorgeous cloak, Brogan carefully laid it over a chair. Dra'Kaedan was barefoot and wearing a simple navy tunic and pants in linen. Brogan didn't know how much time passed as he stood there watching him, but he barely dared to blink. In his mind, he'd always envisioned his mate as a gorgeous, blue-eyed blond. It was surreal to see that dream in the flesh, though he hadn't needed a certain visage to adore him. It had always been the force of his personality that beckoned Brogan. Unaware that his weeping continued, Brogan finally lowered his own fatigued body down next to Dra'Kaedan and tugged him over his chest.

There was a deep fear inside of him that he'd wake up once again without Dra'Kaedan at his side, but he was exhausted beyond reason. He whispered all the tender words of love inside his heart and brushed his lips over his springy curls. Closing his eyes, Brogan held on tight and hoped this was more than a cruel joke of fate.

35

With a jaw-popping yawn, Dra'Kaedan opened his eyes to find himself alone in his big bed. He scowled as he tried to free his mind of cobwebs. His memory was sluggish as he was still recuperating, but he would only get better. The man he wanted above all else was nowhere to be found, which frustrated Dra'Kaedan. He'd barely had a moment the night before to tell him anything more than he loved him. The sound of water reached his ears and he smiled. Brogan was in the shower and not so very far away.

With no desire to be up and about quite yet, he tried to reconcile the two different people in his mind. There was Ayden—the familiar whipped into knowing his place but always wishing he could be the fiery person inside him. Then there was Dra'Kaedan. The man he truly was—who not only embraced the fire but stood tall while charging forward with no worries about being thought of as too bold. After all, he was the Grand Warlock. Grief hit him as he thought about how he'd attained that title along with the gold circle with the dragon head on his wrist.

His parents and all his people destroyed. It wasn't something he'd ever allow anyone to forget, but there was one bright light and it was knowing that just down the hall rested his brother. Once inseparable from his twin, he was going to make sure they repaired that relationship after so much time apart, but when the door to the bathroom swung open, all Dra'Kaedan could think of was his dragon. Clean shaven and fully dressed, Dra'Kaedan licked his lips at the delicious man Fate had paired him with.

"Good morning," he offered from where he lay on the bed. His thin pants were twisted around his knees, but he was feeling too lazy to remedy the situation, and he wasn't done staring at Brogan.

"It certainly is," Brogan responded with his faintly dimpled smile. "How are you feeling? You don't look as wiped as you did last night."

"Better. I feel better, and you smell a whole lot better."

Brogan sat on the edge of the bed next to him with a laugh as he ran his hand over Dra'Kaedan's tangled curls. "You look good as a blond."

"You aren't shocked to see me like this. How'd you find out who I was?"

"Your twin. He realized who you were when his necklace stopped glowing."

"You okay with me being Dra'Kaedan instead of Latarian's runty familiar, Ayden?"

"Instead of runty? You're still runty. Your face and hair are different, but you didn't get any taller." Brogan's grin curled his toes with pleasure, and Dra'Kaedan beamed back at him. They simply stared at each other, and it was just for the bliss of being back together. Before either of them spoke, there was a knock on their bedroom door.

After giving him a wink, Brogan stood and answered it to reveal the entire Court D'Vaire. They didn't ask to be invited in, they simply strolled in and took up positions around the bed. Dre'Kariston and Blodwen were both armed with trays of delicious smelling food.

"Brogan, take a seat next to your mate," Noirin ordered and he obeyed without question. Breakfast was set over their laps and as Dra'Kaedan anticipated, it tasted even better than it smelled. After shoveling a few giant forkfuls into his face, Dra'Kaedan grew a little uncomfortable with all the people watching him. Brogan was evidently not of the same mind, because he kept right on inhaling his breakfast.

"What?" he demanded of his family.

"Well, brother, we're overjoyed to have you back, but would you mind explaining to us exactly how it's possible that you're sitting there? And how am I more powerful?" Dre'Kariston asked him curiously.

"I only had a few minutes with them to absorb it all, but it was our parents. I was caught somewhere between life and death. Ayden was dead, but my spirit was too spent to even wake up let alone resume my former life as a warlock. Our parents were watching over Brogan and when they feared he'd die, they gave us their power so I could return quicker," Dra'Kaedan explained.

"That would explain why the mark on my wrist never switched to gold. If you were truly dead I should've been made the Grand Warlock. Wow, it's their power that's been added to mine?" His twin sounded surprised.

"Yes. They also send their love. Mother asked me to give you hugs and kisses, but I think hugs will be enough." Dra'Kaedan smirked at his brother who returned his smile and added a wink.

"I haven't seen my twin in centuries. I not only expect but demand many hugs and a kiss or two, but I want you to stick to kissing my cheeks—I know how tempting my lips can be."

He rolled his eyes at Dre'Kariston. "Whatever."

"I envy you the time you got to spend with our parents. I miss them," Dre'Kariston said, his face solemn and so reminiscent of T'Eirick's.

"It went so fast, but it was wonderful to see them. I won't ever be able to repay the gift they've given me. I might not have woken up in time to save my mate, and now I get to spend the rest of my life with not just him but all of you," Dra'Kaedan answered as he gave Brogan's arm a squeeze.

"We love you, too, Frodo," Aleksander said with a wicked grin.

"Thanks, Lurch," Dra'Kaedan replied and shared an amused glance—first, with his king and then, with his mate.

"So, elephant in the room...I just want to say I'm so sorry that I couldn't do more to save you," Blodwen spoke quietly with unshed tears in her gray eyes. Dre'Kariston took a step closer to her and rubbed her back.

"Blodwen, if I'd lost all my power with those spells still on my back I would've died, and my parents wouldn't have been able to do a damn thing to help. You saved my life. I'm so grateful for you."

"Thank you," she managed as she went straight to the bed to give Dra'Kaedan a crushing hug.

He embraced her with the same enthusiasm. "No, thank *you*."

"We should probably tell him the bad news now," Larissa said after Blodwen returned to Dre'Kariston's side.

"Bad news?"

"Yeah, your brother told us who you were and how you disappeared. Then he told us how he killed Latarian's grandfather, but that isn't the bad news, because that guy was an evil prick. The Arch Lich said that Latarian had to pay for her crime of basically turning you into her little slave, and he was going to take her to the fallen knights, but the next morning she was gone. No one knows where that bitch went," Larissa told him without so much as a pause for breath.

"You killed Carvallius?" Dra'Kaedan was shocked but also pleased that Dre'Kariston had avenged not only him but every warlock.

His flat eyes spoke of a man who wanted to go back in time and slay Carvallius all over again. "He followed me using your necklace when our parents made me hide in a crappy cottage."

"What's with warlocks and cottages?" Aleksander asked, and they all shrugged.

"Speaking of necklaces, you probably want yours back." Brogan pulled the gold necklace that contained his brother's glowing essence from under his T-shirt. After slipping off the chain, he fastened it around Dra'Kaedan's neck. He thanked Brogan with a small kiss and rubbed the blue dragon medallion in his fingers as he shared another smile with his brother. He was glad to have it back. The last time he'd worn it was a lifetime ago before his identity was ripped away.

"Oh, and we didn't tell him about the sanctuary," Derwin announced.

"The sanctuary?" Dra'Kaedan echoed, confused.

"Brogan said we should ask the Council to make us into a sanctuary. We decided to do it for you. We made a bunch of changes, and then we sent our proposal in," Dre'Kariston explained.

Overwhelmed with the joy that bubbled up, Dra'Kaedan glanced at Brogan. "You sent in the petition?"

"We gave it a pretty cool name too, Squirt," Aleksander stated. "Our sanctuary is called Dra'Kaedan's Coven."

Heedless of the trays across their laps, Dra'Kaedan tackled Brogan and kissed him deeply. Brogan's arms locked around him, and Dra'Kaedan wrapped his own around his dragon's neck. One kiss quickly became another and then another. Dra'Kaedan was vaguely aware that their dishes had disappeared. Before he could manage to press himself closer, the bedroom door closed with a small click.

"I guess we cleared the room," Brogan murmured against his lips.

"Yeah, we'll say sorry later, but I really need you."

"My dragon and I need to bite you so damn bad."

"Before we get naked, will you exchange blood with me again?"

"Why? Are you afraid your magic will attack me?"

"No, those fucking spells were the only reason we had to worry about that. My parents gave me a bunch of knowledge they learned after they crossed the veil. They met an ancient druidic spirit who told them about a blood ritual for mates. We can ask Fate to give us visible mating marks that look almost like tattoos. We pick where we want it, and Fate decides the design. It doesn't require sorcery, so it should work for both magickind and shifters."

"That's awesome. We should do it," Brogan responded. As he crossed the room to grab their mating athame, they decided where to put them.

"At least I can bleed this time," Dra'Kaedan mused as he tugged off his shirt and kneeled across from a bare-chested Brogan. He sliced open a cut on each of their palms; then they put them together. "Draconis to warlock. Grand Warlock to Duke. Our blood has spilled, and our spirits have bonded. We ask Fate to grant us a mark from left shoulder to elbow so that the world may see we belong to only each other."

A searing pain worked down his left arm and from the grimace on Brogan's face he was experiencing the same. An image formed on Brogan's skin and Dra'Kaedan smiled at the picture of himself, complete with a gold crown and scepter that befitted his rank. He was standing under a full moon, and the D'Vaire sash was visible through his exquisite cloak. Curled at his feet was his tiny dragon form.

Glancing down at his own biceps, there was a stunning and beautiful replica of Brogan's dragon with his wings unfurled as if he was ready to take flight. It took up all the space between his shoulder to elbow, and he was going to show it off as often as possible. "Wow, it worked."

"You're fucking amazing," Brogan responded as he dragged him down to the mattress. He lay over him, keeping his weight balanced on his forearms so he didn't squish Dra'Kaedan. "I still think this is a dream. Yesterday you were dead, and I was beginning to fear I was headed there myself. I'm sorry I didn't do better to keep my promise."

Dra'Kaedan swept a hand over his cheek. "Do you honestly think I'd hold that against you?"

Brogan's troubled eyes grew misty with unshed tears. "No, but I wanted you to know I tried but losing you..."

"It's okay. I'm just glad you're not hurting anymore and that you're okay with me being Dra'Kaedan instead of Ayden. I know it's probably been a big adjustment for you."

"You were adorable as Ayden, but I have to tell you that you're fucking hot as Dra'Kaedan," Brogan confessed with a kiss.

"I guess the adjustment's been pretty smooth," Dra'Kaedan teased. As much as he would've liked to keep things light, there were things he needed Brogan to know. "I won't leave you again. My magic's scary powerful, and so is my brother's, and you're a duke who I know will always protect me. There's nothing I wouldn't do to be with you."

They stared at each other for several seconds; then Brogan spoke again. "That sounds like something that should be added to the list."

"Pro—Dra'Kaedan's absurdly powerful."

"Pro—Brogan's a duke who would never allow anyone to lay a fucking finger on his mate."

"Nice. We have no cons," Dra'Kaedan pointed out.

"Con—sometimes Brogan and Dra'Kaedan are actually going to have to leave their bedroom."

"Yeah, because I need food."

"I'm glad your appetite is back, you bottomless pit."

Dra'Kaedan's tone grew serious again. "Thank you for the sanctuary. I know you were against it."

"You were right. If we have control over who we bring in, we can make it work. We did agree that if the Council won't go for our rules, then we'll nix the idea again."

"I have another con."

Brogan's gaze was wary, but Dra'Kaedan was okay with putting the sanctuary aside if they weren't safe. Nothing was as important to him as Brogan. "Con—sometimes Brogan talks too much when Dra'Kaedan needs to get laid."

With a chuckle, Brogan captured his mouth. Their tongues searched out every crevice, memorizing along the way all they'd missed while they were apart. When they had to stop for air, Brogan dropped little kisses over his cheeks, his nose, and when Dra'Kaedan's eyes fell shut over each lid, onto his forehead.

"I love you so much," he whispered against Dra'Kaedan's skin. With his dick already aching, Dra'Kaedan worked his hands between them to tug on Brogan's zipper.

"I love you too," Dra'Kaedan murmured back.

Brogan raised up to push down his pants and underwear together in one smooth motion. He wiggled the rest of the way out of his clothes and dropped them onto the floor. The dragon reached for Dra'Kaedan's bottoms and he obliged by lifting his hips. Once Brogan tossed them aside, he stared down at Dra'Kaedan's naked body. The heat in his gaze made Dra'Kaedan's cock twitch. The dragon was clearly going to fuck him mindless.

"Your dick looks the same."

Pushing aside the haze of lust he was surrounded in, Dra'Kaedan's brows snapped together in annoyance. "Seriously? Why would my dick be any different?"

"It could've shrunk on re-entry."

His eyes narrowed. "Are you implying that you'd be dissatisfied with your mate returning to be at your side for all of eternity if his dick was smaller?"

The jerk grinned. "Being together for eternity sounds pretty good."

With a roll of his eyes, Dra'Kaedan reached for his dragon. "Just kiss me, damn it."

Brogan did as he was told, and Dra'Kaedan had a mouth full of his tongue. It was heaven, he decided as Brogan fished around in the nightstand drawer. Once he had the lube in his hand, Brogan lay alongside him and Dra'Kaedan obliged him by slinging one of his legs over his mate's. Their lips met again as Brogan slid two crafty fingers inside him.

Dra'Kaedan's body arched with pleasure as the dragon took his time stretching him and gliding over his prostate every couple of strokes. He didn't care if he was responding too fast or any of the other nonsense that had once plagued him. All he wanted was to feel the way he did when Brogan loved him.

"More," he demanded as his skin grew damp and his dick leaked on his belly. His balls were tight and while he would've liked to give in to the demands of his raging hormones, he would be damned if he'd do so before he had Brogan inside of him.

His dragon offered no argument and worked a third digit into his hole. Dra'Kaedan clutched Brogan close to him as he sucked on his tongue. Too much time had passed since they enjoyed the magic between them, and his need grew to a ferocity he couldn't have anticipated.

"Brogan...*please*. Fuck me," Dra'Kaedan begged.

His mouth disappeared as he pulled free of Dra'Kaedan and scrambled down the mattress. Dra'Kaedan spread his bent knees wide as Brogan settled between them. Desperate for something to hang on to, Dra'Kaedan grasped the sheets in two tight fists as Brogan prepared himself for sex. His thick cock gleamed as he spread the lube over it. Their eyes met, and Brogan watched him as he continued to stroke himself. Brogan couldn't miss his neediness and was purposely dragging things out to heighten his pleasure.

"*Now*," Dra'Kaedan demanded.

Brogan let out a husky chuckle as he shuffled forward until the head of his shaft pressed against the center of him. Dra'Kaedan was grateful his mate was done teasing and pushed into him steadily. When he was finally buried to the hilt, he gave Dra'Kaedan a few precious seconds to adjust and grabbed Dra'Kaedan's thighs; then Brogan drove in and out of him.

"So tight, baby. You feel so fucking good," he panted out. He pounded into him faster, much to Dra'Kaedan's delight, and he couldn't stand it. His head thrashed from side to side as he let out a shout. No one had laid a finger on his dick, but it didn't matter. His seed splashed out as his muscles locked in place with the fervor of his orgasm.

Before Dra'Kaedan was finished, Brogan leaned over him and grasped the back of his neck in one hand. Aware of his mate's intent, Dra'Kaedan arched to give him better access. Brogan's tongue swiped over his skin; then his fangs sank into him. Dra'Kaedan's body did its best to respond and to his amazement, he had a second climax, though it was considerably weaker than the first. Brogan's come filled him, and Dra'Kaedan wanted to sing with joy.

The dragon removed his teeth and slid his arms under Dra'Kaedan to pull him close. They clung to each other as Brogan pressed their foreheads together. It was a moment Dra'Kaedan added to all the incredible moments he had collected since the day he'd met Brogan. Dra'Kaedan had made it back to his side and as they lay there trying to catch their breath, he vowed to always remain there.

36

Dra'Kaedan and Brogan dozed off at some point after making love. They were both playing catch-up on sleep but pulled each other out of bed to face the world. After all, several hours had passed since breakfast, and Dra'Kaedan was starving. Somehow, they'd managed to make it through their shower without getting too carried away.

"You've got a mark on your back," Brogan said as Dra'Kaedan climbed out of the shower.

Not missing the panic in his voice, Dra'Kaedan turned to him as he handed Brogan a towel. "Don't worry, it's because of my familiar."

Brogan's navy orbs went wide with surprise. "You have a familiar?"

"I will as soon as I summon him," he responded as he dried himself and wandered into the bedroom to find clothes.

"It's weird to think of you having a familiar. I'm still getting used to the idea that you aren't one," Brogan said as he followed him.

"Yeah, it's weird for me too, but my familiar should've been summoned a long time ago. I think it's kind of cool—I'm excited to meet him."

"We should summon him with everybody around."

"Good idea."

Dra'Kaedan wiggled into his briefs, then donned a pair of jeans and a T-shirt. Brogan grabbed his hand after dressing, and they strode down the hall into the kitchen. Dra'Kaedan barely managed to stifle his scream of fear when his family popped up from behind the furniture to yell, "Surprise!"

Brogan let go of him to rub his palm over his back while Dra'Kaedan willed his heart to stop thundering in his chest. Unmoved by his distress, the D'Vaires laughed and led the pair over to the dining area to see the wide array of edibles.

For once there was something more important than stuffing his face, and Dra'Kaedan took the time to thank Dravyn and Aleksander for building the gazebo as he embraced everyone. He saved his brother for last, and they clung to each other. There were some things that words could simply not convey. His throat constricted as he thought of all they had meant to each other and all that they'd lost.

"I love you, little brother," he whispered to him.

Dre'Kariston pulled back and his face was full of mock indignation. "Little? You're the short one."

"I'm still older," he retorted as he kissed his cheek and let him go.

"Don't think you're going to get away with not being my best friend again."

"I wouldn't dream of it. We've got a lot to catch up on."

His twin smirked. "Like what I've been doing for the last six hundred or so years?"

"Exactly."

Dre'Kariston's smile fell away and he went still. "What are we going to do about Latarian?"

The entire room seemed to stop at the question, and Dra'Kaedan didn't have to consider his response. "She robbed me of centuries. I won't allow her to have one more minute of my time. Latarian has no money, no friends, and little power. All she can do is crawl into some hole and lick her wounds. The woman isn't terribly bright, no matter what she's convinced herself of otherwise, and she rarely lifts a damn finger. I'm not afraid of her. If she's stupid enough to step foot back in

Council territory, then the Order of the Fallen Knights can deal with it."

His brother smiled and gave his back a friendly slap. "Fuck those Mallents."

"Exactly," he retorted; then he turned to get acquainted with the buffet. When his plate was so brimming with food he grew concerned it would topple, Dra'Kaedan found a seat next to Brogan. As he consumed his meal, Dra'Kaedan let the happy voices of his family wash over him. Too busy eating to respond, Dra'Kaedan let Brogan field questions over their visible mating marks, and Larissa and Madeline made plans to try the ritual themselves later.

When they were done and the area once again spotless, Dra'Kaedan went into the living room and prepared to summon forth his familiar. He was determined to make it a great relationship, unlike the one forced on him. Brogan got comfortable on the couch, and Aleksander handed his mate a tablet, so he could search for possible names. When Dra'Kaedan's familiar arrived, he would need one and it was up to the warlock to make sure he got one that suited him. Dra'Kaedan was happy that Brogan wanted to help with such an important task.

In the center of the room, Dra'Kaedan smiled at Dre'Kariston and Derwin and then closed his eyes. Taking a deep breath, he mouthed the words that would turn the mark on his back to a living, breathing person. The air around him vibrated and crackled with energy as his familiar lifted from his skin. Seconds later, a blond man stood in front of him. He had only a moment to notice his hair was considerably shorter than Dra'Kaedan's before the man dropped to the ground and pounded his fists and feet against the floor as he filled the room with screams.

"What the hell?" Dra'Kaedan blurted out as his familiar had some sort of fit.

"Did you say the right words?" Dre'Kariston yelled to be heard, and Dra'Kaedan shot him a glare to let him know what he thought of his question.

"Is he dying?" Derwin wailed out as he wrung his hands with worry.

"Dying?" Dra'Kaedan barely managed to get the question out when the screeching and thrashing abruptly stopped and the man stood up.

"I am not dying," the blond informed them.

"Then what the hell's wrong with you?" It was probably rude, but Dra'Kaedan's last twenty-four hours had been momentous, and this was supposed to be an easy freaking spell.

The blond's expression was one of pure annoyance. "*Hello*, look at me."

"You look all right to me." *Great, maybe this familiar has a screw or two loose from Carvallius's dark magic*, Dra'Kaedan thought with despair.

"I'm short. I'm shorter than you, and your mate probably has to put you in a car seat when you want to travel." Aleksander roared with laughter as Dra'Kaedan pulled the corners of his mouth inward to hide his smile. Dra'Kaedan shook his head. With his personality, there was no way his familiar wouldn't be a little shit too.

"I've got the perfect name," Brogan announced from the couch.

"What is it?" the familiar asked.

"Renny," Brogan offered.

His familiar mulled it over as he cocked his head to the side. "What does it mean?"

Brogan grinned. "Small and defiant."

"I like it," Renny declared and from the smirk on his face, he appeared determined to work hard at living up to his rebellious new moniker.

"Welcome to the family, Renny D'Vaire," Aleksander said, after wiping the tears of hilarity from his cheeks.

Renny offered their king a deep bow. "Thank you, King Tut."

Dra'Kaedan tugged his new familiar into a quick hug. He looked forward to building a friendship with him and from the mischievous look in his eyes, Renny was going to be loads of fun. One thing was for certain; he would be encouraged to always be himself, and

Dra'Kaedan would burn himself in a fiery pit before he'd allow anyone to get in the way of that. Dra'Kaedan would also be damned if he ever allowed an angry lash to bite into Renny's flesh.

~

Walking into the living room, Brogan was immediately assaulted by loud music and a female singer promising to marry the night. Blodwen, Dra'Kaedan, and his brother, as well as their familiars, were grinding their bodies to the tune. Brogan nearly forgot why he'd come to find Dra'Kaedan in the first place. His eyes locked on to Dra'Kaedan's firm denim-clad ass, and he licked his lips. Dra'Kaedan was a very talented and sensual dancer. While Brogan was content to watch him all day, Dre'Kariston spotted him standing there and turned down the volume on the stereo.

"What's up?"

"Emperor Chrysander just called. The Council wants us to come to Headquarters." Brogan was disappointed that the dancing stopped as they all reacted to his announcement.

"When do we go?" Dra'Kaedan asked and came over to tug Brogan down for a kiss.

Brogan brushed their lips together twice before responding. "Tomorrow."

"Did the Emperor give Aleksander any clue about our petition?" Blodwen asked.

"Nope."

"Don't worry, we'll convince them," Dre'Kariston said. The truth was, they had no idea if they could convince the Council to allow them to run a sanctuary by their own rules, but Brogan was hopeful. After all, the Emperor had suggested the idea himself when he'd learned about their second warlock moving in.

"You should go back to what you were doing. You looked hot," Brogan told Dra'Kaedan.

"Why don't you join us?" Dra'Kaedan invited.

Brogan laughed; his ability to move in any discernible rhythm was nonexistent. "Yeah, no one wants to see me dance. Trust me, it's not pretty."

"So, you think I'm just going to perform for you?" Dra'Kaedan teased.

"Exactly. I am going to sit here and enjoy." Brogan took a seat on the couch and waved at him in a lordly manner. "Go on."

His mate slapped his hands on his hips. "So not happening."

"It's not like you haven't danced for anyone before," Dre'Kariston accused, and Dra'Kaedan fixed him with a murderous glare.

Brogan lifted a brow. "He did what?"

"Nothing. I did nothing," his mate stammered out quickly.

"Liar," Dre'Kariston taunted as he poked his twin in the arm.

Brogan leaned forward to grab him, but Dra'Kaedan backed out of reach. "Spill it."

"Well, there was—" Dre'Kariston's explanation was cut off abruptly as Dra'Kaedan set his brother on fire. Unlike Brogan's experience with the same spell, Dre'Kariston didn't take any damage. He simply stared at his brother in boredom as the flames licked around him. "Really?" Dre'Kariston drawled as he waved a hand over himself, extinguishing the blaze. "Anyway, as I was saying—"

Dra'Kaedan turned his brother into a little black puppy, halting his words.

"*Oh*, a puppy. Can we keep him?" Renny exclaimed as he dropped down to the floor to pet the canine version of Dre'Kariston.

Clearly Brogan needed to rein in his mate. "Dra'Kaedan, turn your brother back."

Dra'Kaedan let out a gusty sigh. "Fine."

Renny was knocked onto his ass as the puppy changed back into Dre'Kariston. Dra'Kaedan's familiar stuck out his bottom lip. "I liked him better as a puppy."

"Hey, shitface. Do that again, and your ass is going to be covered in giant hemorrhoids."

Brogan let out a bark of laughter at Dre'Kariston's threat. Dra'Kaedan turned to him with a smile. "Your brother threatened me nearly the same way once," Brogan explained so Dra'Kaedan's twin didn't get any ideas of retaliation.

"You going to let me tell the story, or do I need to turn you into a cactus until I'm done?" Dre'Kariston's threat filled Brogan's head with all sorts of jokes about prickers, but he feared his wrath, so he wisely stayed quiet.

"Tell the damn story," Dra'Kaedan snarled at his brother after they eyeballed each other fiercely for a full minute. Brogan tried again to snatch his mate, but he still wasn't cooperating.

"Fine. When we were in our teens, our parents made us attend dinners with guests at the castle," Dre'Kariston said as he sat down on the floor next to Renny.

"You hated them," Dra'Kaedan said as he parked himself on Dre'Kariston's other side.

Dre'Kariston smiled. "And you loved going since they always had the best food."

Surprise, surprise, Brogan thought with a roll of his eyes.

"So true," Dra'Kaedan responded.

"You don't seem antisocial to me. Why did you hate them?" Brogan asked.

Dre'Kariston's expression was one of pure disgust. "We were meant to lead our race. We were young and not yet mated. We had *suitors.*"

Dra'Kaedan laughed. "Dre'Kariston hates to flirt."

"I hate to flirt with men who are only interested in me because of my power."

"None of them bothered me," Dra'Kaedan said smugly.

"Of course not. You told anyone who would listen that you were going to mate with a dragon. You also said you were saving yourself for your dragon. I think a lot of them were afraid you were insane. If that didn't scare them away, you just stuffed your face and ignored them," Dra'Kaedan's brother explained in exasperation.

"So how did he wind up dancing for anyone?" Brogan asked.

"V'Adryann showed up," Dre'Kariston replied.

"He was hot," Dra'Kaedan added.

Brogan frowned. "Hey, you aren't supposed to say that about other men, and I thought you were nonsexual before we met."

"As a familiar I was, but warlocks aren't. Besides, it was centuries ago, and the man's dead," Dra'Kaedan argued, but Brogan continued to glare at him.

"He was a dumbass. 'Dra'Kaedan, our names rhyme. We were meant to be special to each other.' " Dre'Kariston mimicked the long-dead V'Adryann.

Dra'Kaedan chuckled and met Brogan's gaze. "I guess I've always had a thing for cheesy lines."

"That's way cheesier than anything I've ever said," Brogan defended and Dra'Kaedan agreed with a wink. "So, you danced for a dumbass?"

"Yeah, and after I did he visited the castle again," Dra'Kaedan replied and cast a rueful glance at his brother.

"Then you punched him in the nose," Dre'Kariston supplied.

"All I wanted was to look at the pretty man, but he tried to get me to kiss him. Then he tried to grab my dick under the table. He deserved it," Dra'Kaedan explained.

"I'm surprised he got away with just a punch," Brogan mused.

Dra'Kaedan's expression was pure dismay. "You know me better than that, mate. After he left that night, I cast a spell that turned his ass into such a mess, I heard he had to stand for a week straight."

"You're insane. Get over here and kiss me." Dra'Kaedan got up and pressed his lips to Brogan's as the room filled again with loud music. Pulling away from him with a smile, Dra'Kaedan joined the group of D'Vaires already moving to the beat. Brogan sat back on the sofa and prepared to spend a little time drooling over the sexy way Dra'Kaedan danced.

37

The following morning, Dra'Kaedan stood in the living room while his family gathered. They'd all decided to make the trip to Headquarters to find out what the Council had to say. Dra'Kaedan thought of the last time he'd traveled there. It was shortly after his arrival at D'Vaire, and there was no way he could've known how different his life would be now. The man he loved took his hand and he smiled up at Brogan; then Dra'Kaedan let his lashes fall to cast the teleportation spell.

After they arrived and strolled over to the security booth, they were told the Emperor was expecting them in the Main Assembly Hall. The wide doors were held open for them as they ambled in. Swiveling his head to take in the full expanse of the magnificent room, Dra'Kaedan could hardly believe his eyes. They were led to a long bench and they all silently grabbed a seat. Once his butt was parked, Dra'Kaedan resumed his gawking. The cavernous space was set in wide tiered rows to accommodate the leaders of all the races.

Their banners stood proudly behind the circular desks and on the top row, dead center in the round room, was the Emperor's spot. The dragon leader was in place and his gold crown gleamed. Clearly everything about the hall was meant to intimidate, and Dra'Kaedan wasn't immune to its effects. He had a death grip on Brogan and managed to loosen his hold slightly.

"Relax, baby," Brogan whispered close to his ear.

Dra'Kaedan almost jumped out of his skin when he heard a loud banging.

It took a moment to comprehend that the sound came from Emperor Chrysander thumping a gavel, trying to garner the attention of all the occupants of the large room.

"This Council calls forth Duke-mate Dra'Kaedan D'Vaire and Dre'Kariston D'Vaire as well as their familiars, Renny and Derwin." The Emperor's voice carried throughout the hall, thanks to the microphone in front of him. Dra'Kaedan glanced at Brogan, but he just shrugged. Without any real choice, Dra'Kaedan got to his feet to comply with the Emperor's request. The four of them were directed to stand at a wide podium not far from their seats to answer to the Council.

"Your Grace, I must begin by saying that on behalf of all the leaders of the Council, we were thrilled when we learned that you had survived your ordeal."

Dra'Kaedan assumed Aleksander had filled their leader in on recent events. "Thank you, Your Majesty."

"When I became aware of your identity—and yours, Dre'Kariston —I immediately notified this Council. Arch Lich Chander Daray pointed out our responsibility toward not only the four of you, but to any other warlocks who may remain in hiding," the Emperor stated.

"Your parents created our Council, thereby making the Coven of Warlocks the very first race to be represented. Until a few months ago, we believed your people to be extinct. When Latarian was discovered, we thought she was the only living warlock. Due to her lineage and her lack of Fate's mark as a leader, it was decided that the warlocks wouldn't rejoin this Council. Things have changed now that we know about the two of you," the Arch Lich said.

Chander gave a short nod to Emperor Chrysander, and he once again took charge of the room. "The Council of Sorcery and Shifters officially recognizes the Coven of Warlocks and as the first to join, your place in this assembly room will honor that distinction. Grand Warlock Dra'Kaedan D'Vaire, you are hereby recognized as their leader. As is the custom of your race, Grand Summoner Dre'Kariston D'Vaire will be considered an advisor and alternate ruler. Your familiars will also have access to assembly room rights, and you're all welcome to resume wearing the colors and traditional garb of your people. Gentlemen, welcome back to the Council of Sorcery and Shifters."

When the Emperor finished speaking, the entire room erupted in applause, and the leaders all got to their feet as Dra'Kaedan struggled to contain his tears. He'd thought himself content to be an honorary dragon, but to be able to represent the warlocks as a part of the Council was an unimaginable honor.

Somewhere on the other side of the veil, his parents must be proud to see their fondest wish come true—to see their sons assume their titles, and he loved knowing the warlocks would be represented once again by the government T'Eirick and Saura created.

Risking a glance at Dre'Kariston, he could tell from his locked jaw that his brother was doing his best to contain his emotions. The ovation eventually died down and once everyone was back in their seats, Dra'Kaedan gathered his wits and spoke. "We humbly accept your invitation to be a part of the Council of Sorcery and Shifters. Over six hundred years ago, my parents had a dream to unite people to better their lives, and your efforts have far surpassed their goal. My brother and I can only hope we're able to live up to the high standard our parents and all of you have set."

Emperor Chrysander smiled. "Thank you, Grand Warlock. It's been an absolute privilege to lead the Council your parents created. The Council is prepared to offer you territory for your Coven. I am assuming you wish it to be adjacent to King Aleksander."

"Your Majesty, I have no intention of living anywhere but in the Draconis Court of D'Vaire. I am a warlock, but I'm also a dragon," Dra'Kaedan proclaimed. He thought back to Brogan's wish that his mate would love his family. Dra'Kaedan considered himself every inch a D'Vaire. Like Brogan, he would never give them up.

"Grand Warlock, I'm delighted to hear it. Let's move on to the next matter. If you and your familiars will remain where you are, the Council would like to ask King Aleksander D'Vairedraconis to join you."

Aleksander quickly complied with Emperor Chrysander's request and was soon standing between the twins at the large podium.

"The Council has received a proposal from the Draconis Court of D'Vaire to add a sanctuary to their territory called Dra'Kaedan's Coven which includes several unique rules. Draconis Court of D'Vaire is ruled by King Aleksander, but he has asked that the leaders of the Coven of Warlocks also be granted permission to field questions, and I'm granting that request."

After speaking, Emperor Chrysander gave a small bang of his gavel, and Dra'Kaedan's body stiffened in preparation for the onslaught of questions. The king next to him wore a placid expression, and Dra'Kaedan admired his poise. He also respected his heart. Aleksander had known what the Council planned regarding him and his brother. Dra'Kaedan was grateful to Fate for sending him not only to Brogan but putting them in a kingdom with such a selfless, giving ruler. Before he could give in to the crazy impulse to give Aleksander a kiss, which would surely piss off his dragon, one of the elven leaders got his attention.

"Grand Warlock, I understand you wish this sanctuary to be available to every race. Historically, Council sanctuaries have only included one. Why should yours be different than all the others?" Chieftain Tristis asked.

"Chieftain, our Court's comprised of several races already, and it's our intention to invite the misfits, outcasts, or forgotten individuals to join us," Dra'Kaedan replied. He appreciated how difficult it was to struggle with someone else's perception of appropriate behavior. It was the misunderstood people who sought only to be themselves whom he wanted to invite to share his family and his home.

"Your Highness, you don't fear weakening the traditions of your court or of this Council by crafting new rules of your own?" the Tristis leader queried.

"Chieftain, my court believes in the same tenet as this Council—that we're stronger when united. The warlocks and necromancer that live under my rule honor their own traditions, but also consider themselves Draconis," Aleksander replied.

"Your Highness, you've asked to use your own application and want to conduct your own background investigations. Don't you consider the Order of the Fallen Knights capable of handling the placement of individuals into your sanctuary?" Though he appeared nonchalant as he twirled his pen while asking the question, Dra'Kaedan found Reverent Knight Drystan Kempe's fierce blue eyes intimidating.

"Reverent Knight, we want Dra'Kaedan's Coven to extend to those who aren't traditionally thought of as sanctuary applicants. While we're happy to accept anyone in need, we feel it's our calling to give what others consider freaks or unusual a caring home. By permitting us to accept candidates beyond those that the Order of the Fallen Knights recognizes as eligible, those applications would represent an extra workload for you that our family can handle," Aleksander responded. The leader of the fallen knights must've been satisfied, because he didn't add a follow-up question.

"Your Highness, I understand your court is small by any standard. Can you handle keeping a sanctuary safe?" Many of the sorcery leaders smiled at the leader of the panthers' inquiry; they understood how much power the twins wielded, though the shifters did not.

"Alpha Panthera, it's our intention to grow slowly, so we don't overwhelm ourselves. As for security, we have two dedicated dukes who are strong by any Draconis standard, as well as the strongest magickind alive, along with their familiars. They plan to ward our land to secure it from danger and even conceal our location if necessary."

"I believe Draconis Court of D'Vaire has answered the most pressing questions. Would anyone from D'Vaire like to add any final words before we ask you to exit the assembly room so we can call a vote?" the Emperor asked.

Dra'Kaedan nodded enthusiastically. "Your Majesty, a few months ago I landed on the doorstep of a loving Draconis Court once believed to be cursed. I literally fell over an outcast necromancer who was soon allowed to join us. One morning, we devised an idea to open our doors and hearts to others like us. Eventually our entire family agreed, but only after we experienced an event that showed us how incredible our races can be if we disregard our differences and work toward a common goal. The event I speak of is the only reason I stand here today. It required the efforts of Draconis shifters, wizards, warlocks, necromancers, and sentinels to combat the evil spells placed on my back by Carvallius.

"I want to thank everyone who had a part in saving my life and a very special thank you to Prism Wizard Vadimas Porfyra and Arch Lich Chander Daray and his two sentinels, Baxter and Benton, who put their own lives and responsibilities on hold to help me. Emperor Chrysander, I also want to thank you for not hesitating to add me to the Draconis Court of D'Vaire. Not only did your decision give me my mate, but it led my brother and his familiar to my side as well. The gifts bestowed on me are ones I can never repay, but with your approval of our sanctuary, it's my hope that I can pass on some of your kindness to misfits just like me."

"You're most welcome, Grand Warlock. Thank you to every D'Vaire who traveled here today. I'm going to ask you to recuse yourselves, so we can discuss your sanctuary," the Emperor stated.

The D'Vaires filed out the door. They stood just outside debating whether to eat or head home when Imperial Duke Damian came barreling down the wide hallway toward them. "This is the last vote of the day before the Council adjourns. If you'd like, you can wait in the Emperor's antechamber. He can meet you there and let you know whether the sanctuary was approved, not approved, or if they want more from you and have delayed their decision."

They accepted the invitation and traipsed after the Imperial Duke. While the future of their sanctuary hinged on the next few minutes, Dra'Kaedan refused to allow worry to overwhelm him. He gazed up at Brogan with a smile. The restoration of his race to the Council was keeping him on a cloud, and he gave his dragon a wicked look of promise. He had the perfect idea of how to celebrate. Brogan lifted a brow and patted his ass as he walked past him into the room. Dra'Kaedan's laughter trickled out; his message had obviously been well received but first, he needed to learn what the future held for Dra'Kaedan's Coven.

38

Dra'Kaedan tried his best to read the expressions of Emperor Chrysander Draconis and Reverent Knight Drystan Kempe when they joined them, but the pair was obviously used to giving nothing away. Their faces were impassive, so Dra'Kaedan had to summon patience he didn't have and wait for them to reveal their news.

"I'm glad you all decided to join me," Emperor Chrysander said as he took a seat, removed his golden crown, and placed it on his lap. "The Council had some concerns about your proposal. Namely, they feel you are unknown and with such powerful warlocks, they want some assurance that you'll keep within Council ideals."

"Your Majesty, the parents of our warlocks were creators of the Council—there should be no question of their loyalty. As for being unknowns, it wasn't their fault they remained hidden for so long," Aleksander argued, and the Emperor held up a hand to halt anything else he might want to add.

"You can forgo my title behind closed doors. I agree with you but to pacify their concerns, we had to come up with a compromise. To open Dra'Kaedan's Coven, you're required to have a member of the Order of the Fallen Knights join your court," the Emperor clarified.

"Before you get angry, I have a proposal for you," the Reverent Knight offered.

"It's insulting that the Council doesn't trust us. What kind of proposal?" Dra'Kaedan asked. He was having second thoughts about this idea if they had to live with a spy, but while it was irritating to have his loyalty questioned, Dra'Kaedan wasn't going to surrender their sanctuary for his ego.

"I have a son. He's half fallen knight, but his mother was a necromancer. She died at his birth and although I love my son very much, he doesn't fit in with our people. He has no interest in working in security or investigating crimes. He refuses to even carry a weapon. I swear he must've been a wizard in a former life, because he loves history. I've always encouraged him to do what he wants, but he's an adult now and finished with school. He's twenty-five and spends almost all his time alone, either on his computer or buried in a book. The only time he's not alone is when I'm there. I think your sanctuary would be a wonderful place for him to continue to do what he wants while at least having some friends, so he doesn't turn into a complete hermit. I haven't talked to him about it yet, but if he agrees, he'd fulfill the Council's requirement for a fallen knight to join your court."

"Your son's half necro. Does he have a sentinel?" Blodwen asked. If he did, there might be a problem with the Reverent Knight's plan—despite the kindness of Baxter and Benton, she was still terrified of them.

"Chander believes so, but he has too much fallen knight in him, and his magic appears to be too weak to summon one," Drystan replied.

That's one crisis averted, Dra'Kaedan thought as he made eye contact with Aleksander. Nothing happened at D'Vaire without them all on the same page—they needed a family vote.

"Okay, family. What do you think of allowing the Reverent Knight's son to come and live with us?" Aleksander asked.

"I have no objection," Brogan immediately replied. Dra'Kaedan gave him a grateful smile, then echoed his words.

"It's fine with me," Dravyn said quietly. Since Council tradition forced Dravyn to wear his Duke's coronet, his deep forest green eyes were, for once, unobscured by his dark hair. They were earnest and somehow gentle in his sparsely freckled face.

"As long as he doesn't mind eating whatever scraps Dra'Kaedan leaves for the rest of us, I have no problem with it." Noirin gave Dra'Kaedan a wicked grin, and her violet eyes danced in merriment.

The Reverent Knight lifted a dark brow. "Should I ask?"

"My brother's a pig. Aleksander, I have no objection either," Dre'Kariston retorted. Dra'Kaedan briefly considered turning his brother into a boar but decided it could wait until they got home.

"Me neither," Derwin nearly shouted. His brother's familiar seemed to have none of his brother's more subdued personality.

"We vote yes," Larissa said, speaking for both herself and Madeline.

"Renny, what do you think?" Brogan asked softly. Dra'Kaedan rolled his eyes at his mate's tone of voice. He was talking to Dra'Kaedan's familiar as if he was a scared child.

"I get a vote?" Renny asked, sounding surprised.

"Of course you get a vote. What kind of question is that? You live at the house, don't you?" Dra'Kaedan demanded.

"Well excuse me, Grand Warlock, but I moved in like what...two days ago? Little early for me to be making decisions, don't you think?" Renny countered flippantly.

Emperor Chrysander chuckled at Renny's outburst, then turned to Aleksander. "I really must make time to visit your family soon."

"You're always welcome. Renny, your vote?" Aleksander asked.

"Oh, yeah. Sure. Let the kid move in," Renny said with a dismissive wave of his hand.

"You're two days old. Should you really be calling anyone a kid?" Dra'Kaedan asked.

"*Duh.* Physically two days old. Mentally I am as geriatric as you."

"Gentleman, we haven't heard from Blodwen yet. Blodwen, what do you think?" Aleksander asked, bringing the argument brewing between warlock and familiar to a close.

Blodwen pulled her lips in for a moment, then stated in a firm voice, "I will do whatever it takes to make Dra'Kaedan's Coven a reality. I vote yes."

"Reverent Knight, it would seem all of Court D'Vaire is eager to meet your son," Aleksander confirmed.

"Great, I'll talk to him and see if he's willing to join you."

"If he declines, we'll figure out another compromise to satisfy you as well as the Council. I've been determined to make this sanctuary happen from the time I first suggested you consider one. I agree with what you said earlier. We need to abandon the idea of every race being an island. It's my hope that your sanctuary will become a model for all future and existing ones. Please keep me informed of any issues or problems you have as we move forward, so we can all do our best to work through them." Emperor Chrysander's words were earnest, and Dra'Kaedan was grateful their leader shared their vision.

"Your Majesty, you have our heartfelt thanks. We look forward to working with you. Reverent Knight Drystan, we really hope your son agrees. It'd be our pleasure to welcome him to our family," Aleksander offered.

The Reverent Knight caught Dra'Kaedan's eye, and his expression was fiercely determined. "Grand Warlock, the fallen knights don't ever give up when a crime has been committed. No matter how long it takes, rest assured that we'll do our best to bring Latarian to justice. She *will* pay for her crimes."

"Thank you, Reverent Knight. Your promise means a great deal to me. I spent centuries living my life according to her rules and dictates. In the end, she nearly destroyed everything I've built with my mate. I can't deny that I'd like justice, but I don't intend to waste any time thinking about her. However, if I can assist the fallen knights in any way to enable her capture, please know I'm only a phone call away," Dra'Kaedan replied and shook the hand of the fierce protector of their Council.

Brogan followed suit and while Dra'Kaedan was content to simply stop worrying over Latarian, his other half wouldn't be satisfied until she paid the ultimate price for her crimes. The Reverent Knight's reassurance that the matter wouldn't rest had to be music to Brogan's ears.

The Emperor took the time to make sure he learned everyone's names; then they all rose and said their good-byes. He reminded Dra'Kaedan and his brother that the Coven of Warlocks had to provide the Council with the rules of their race before they could add them to the system. They assured him they would work on it as soon as possible.

Dra'Kaedan imagined both the Emperor and the Reverent Knight had horribly complicated schedules and needed to get back to them. The D'Vaires didn't keep them any longer than necessary and minutes later were charging down the hallway. Dra'Kaedan remembered the amazing buffet in the cafeteria and made sure everyone understood that was where he was headed for the next hour.

Lucky for him, his family was hungry as well, so no one argued. Privately he acknowledged that if they had, he would've asked Dre'Kariston to teleport them back, so he could still stuff his face. Once they were all seated and eating, excitement reigned over the conversation as they all hoped the Reverent Knight's son decided to accept their invitation. They all wondered what he was like and what interesting things as a student of history he might be able to share with them.

Madeline then turned the conversation to her craft. "I'll have to start designing crowns appropriate for the new leaders of the Coven of Warlocks."

"Dragon," Dra'Kaedan blurted out between bites.

"What does he mean?" Madeline asked Brogan.

Brogan shrugged. "I love him, but his brain's a mystery."

"Crown," Dra'Kaedan said firmly. "Dragon."

"Oh, he wants a dragon on his crown. There's a surprise," Dre'Kariston muttered.

"Rings of rank—I forgot to ask you to make one for Ayden," Brogan said. "How did that happen? Anyway, all the warlocks will need them, and I want something to represent my mate on mine."

"Your rings will match," Dravyn remarked.

"Of course our mating rings match," Brogan responded, then gave Dra'Kaedan his attention. "I'm glad you didn't lose yours when you crossed the veil."

Dra'Kaedan grunted in agreement as he gulped down his drink to make more room for the delicious pasta he'd found at the buffet.

"I wasn't talking about mating rings," Dravyn stated. "I was referring to your rings of rank. Grand Warlock is a higher title than Duke. That makes you Grand Warlock-mate, not Duke."

Brogan's eyes widened in dismay. "Grand Warlock-mate?"

"I can feel a yelling match coming—we should probably head home before that happens," Aleksander drawled out.

"Eating," Dra'Kaedan argued.

"Do you have a problem being Grand Warlock-mate?" Renny asked sweetly. Something about his sugary tone made Dra'Kaedan want to laugh.

"No, it's just...well, I—look, Duke's my title. I'm a dragon and I've earned it. It feels strange carrying a title for a race I'm not even a part of. I like warlocks. Well, I love them actually, and I'm proud of you guys, but I guess I didn't realize I'd be Grand Warlock-mate," Brogan rushed out.

Dra'Kaedan patted his thigh. He understood how integral a title was and how it would affect Brogan if he surrendered the one Aleksander gave him. If Brogan preferred to be a duke, Dra'Kaedan didn't have any complaints. "Council rules. No Grand Warlock-mate."

"Would you mind putting your damn fork down long enough to speak in complete fucking sentences?" Dre'Kariston demanded. "No one knows what you're talking about."

With a roll of his eyes, Dra'Kaedan did as his testy sibling asked. "We can write it into the rules we submit to the Council. The Grand Warlock will carry his title without it carrying over to his mate. For now, we'll have the other titles—Grand Summoner, Grand Warlock Familiar, and Grand Summoner Familiar—all shared with their mates. When you guys meet your other halves, we can adjust if necessary. How's that sound?"

Brogan tipped his chin toward him and touched their lips together. "You sure you don't mind?"

"Not at all. We all need to be ourselves, including you," Dra'Kaedan told him. Then he grinned. "But it's your loss. My crown's going to be way nicer than your coronet."

"It's not a competition."

"The hell it's not. Now, is this shit settled, so I can finish eating?"

"The Grand Warlock's peckish," Renny said. "We must allow his royalness to stuffeth his face."

Ignoring him, Dra'Kaedan gave his attention back to his lunch. The conversation flowed around him as everyone else appeared to be finished. When his belly was finally filled, they left the restaurant behind while Dra'Kaedan promised the buffet he'd be back. It took almost no time at all to get to the teleportation area and even less for Dra'Kaedan to cast the spell to send them home. Everyone was heading toward their bedrooms when Aleksander's phone rang. They all stopped and turned to stare at him. He said little to the caller and his face showed no emotion until he hung up. Then he grinned wildly. "The Reverent Knight's son would love to join our family."

They all cheered and when Brogan leaned toward him, Dra'Kaedan gave him a smacking kiss. Dra'Kaedan's Coven was officially the newest sanctuary—and the first multi-race one—of the Council of Sorcery and Shifters. Their family was entering a new era of the Draconis Court of D'Vaire, and Dra'Kaedan couldn't wait to get started.

39

Brogan put together an excellent plan, and it was finally coming together. He set down his tray of goodies, feeling quite pleased with himself. Dra'Kaedan was washing up in the bathroom and Brogan waited impatiently for him to come out. His dick was even more eager, if the way it was straining against his zipper was any indication. He tugged off his T-shirt just as Dra'Kaedan swung open the door. He was dressed in his pajamas, and Brogan was unamused by the stick figures with their legs caught on fire. By the smug look on Dra'Kaedan's face, he was enjoying Brogan's ire at remembering the day he'd had to beat the flames out of his jeans.

"Nice pants," Brogan offered.

Dra'Kaedan's eyes narrowed, and then he sniffed loudly. "What's that smell?"

"I'll make a deal with you."

"What kind of deal?"

"You peel off those pajamas and climb up onto that bed. Then I'll tell you what you're smelling."

"It smells sweet. Did you bring me food?"

Brogan rolled his eyes and finished tugging off his clothing.

When he was naked, he sat down on the mattress and patted it. "Come on, get those jammies off."

"What's with the covered tray over there?"

"Dra'Kaedan. Get naked."

"Fine."

Brogan watched with rapt interest as the smooth skin of his chest was revealed. The dark image of his dragon over half his left arm drew his attention. He loved seeing it; it was a perfect reminder of their commitment to each other. Since Dra'Kaedan never wore underwear to bed, all he had to do was loosen the tie of his bottoms and push them down, but for some reason it was taking an inordinate amount of time. Or maybe it just seemed that way to Brogan, but he was anxious to get their evening started.

The small nest of blond curls between the warlock's legs appeared and though his cock wasn't completely hard yet, there was no mistaking his interest. Brogan's own erection grew as Dra'Kaedan's pants hit the floor and he stepped out of them. Dra'Kaedan took a few steps, so he was standing directly in front of Brogan. Though he didn't want to get distracted from his plan, Brogan grasped the back of his neck and kissed him.

"On the bed," he demanded when he released him.

Dra'Kaedan smirked as he got on the mattress and sinuously crawled toward the headboard. Brogan smacked his ass, then stood and walked toward the nightstand, where he'd placed his big tray. Sitting down next to Dra'Kaedan, he said, "You once told me celebration sex meant cake. I figure we'll never have better reasons to celebrate than we do right now. I have you back and we get our sanctuary."

Brogan whipped off the cloth he'd used to cover his tray of food and Dra'Kaedan laid a hand on his thigh. "Right? It's not like I'm going to come back from across the veil every day, and we can only have one sanctuary."

"Never again, Dra'Kaedan. I don't ever want to be put through that again."

"Kiss me."

Not wanting to get distracted, Brogan gave him a quick peck on the nose.

"Oh, here we go with these stupid kisses again."

"Behave or no cake."

"That's mean. What kind of cake?"

"Let's see. We have blue velvet, triple chocolate, and coconut."

"I think I just came. What's in the bowl?"

"Vanilla buttercream frosting."

Dra'Kaedan shifted on the mattress, and his dick was now completely erect. "What're we going to do with a bowl of frosting?"

"I can think of a lot of things we can do with a bowl of frosting," Brogan promised fervently. "Here's the plan, baby. You get cake only when I feed it to you. If you want a bite, you must be very good and if you're extra nice, I'm going to let you do whatever you want with that bowl of frosting."

Dra'Kaedan squeezed his thigh. "Do I get the frosting before or after you fuck me? Because I need to make plans too."

"I guess that depends on you."

"This is sexy. Cake, frosting, and Brogan. My three favorite things all at the same time," Dra'Kaedan enthused. His stiff length bobbed as he wiggled a little on the bed. Letting go of Brogan, he put his arms at his sides; then he closed his eyes and smiled. "Have at me, big dragon."

"Hmm...I think we're off to a good start," Brogan said as he grabbed a piece of the blue velvet and placed it against Dra'Kaedan lips. The warlock dutifully opened his mouth and Brogan slid the treat inside.

Dra'Kaedan hummed as he chewed and once he was done, Brogan kissed him. The only cake he intended to taste was on Dra'Kaedan as he didn't have the same lust for it that his mate did, but he enjoyed its sweetness as he tongued him thoroughly. When he broke for air, his body was buzzing with anticipation.

He slid his palm up Dra'Kaedan's cock. "Rather difficult to play."

"I'm being very good by spreading my legs," Dra'Kaedan

informed him as he bent his knees and made plenty of room between his feet, giving Brogan a sensational view of his balls and his pucker.

Dutifully, Brogan gifted him with a sliver of chocolate cake. As Dra'Kaedan enjoyed it, Brogan stroked his palm, up his calf and down his thigh, all the way to the crease of his leg, then pulled it away. He leaned down and bit gently on one erect nipple. Dra'Kaedan moaned and clutched the sheets as he laved it with his tongue. Every part of his mate was so responsive, and Brogan loved his reaction to each touch.

He continued to lavish the tender bud with attention as he gently twisted the other between his fingers. Dra'Kaedan panted and Brogan's lungs were just as desperate for air. Any other night and he'd already be buried inside him. Instead of giving in to the pounding need of his hormones, Brogan lifted both his mouth and hand away. He rewarded Dra'Kaedan with a piece of coconut cake.

Squeezing some lube out, he warmed it and then traced around Dra'Kaedan's hole. The warlock lifted his hips slightly, and Brogan was so pleased he gave him more blue velvet to enjoy. Dra'Kaedan lapped the frosting off Brogan and opened his eyes. The navy was rich with lust, and Brogan watched him as he pushed two digits inside of his welcoming heat.

Groaning, Dra'Kaedan let go of the bedding and threw his arms above his head. Brogan glided over his prostate as he fed more triple chocolate to Dra'Kaedan. His dick leaked onto his belly as Brogan continued to pump in and out of him. Still, Dra'Kaedan made no demands, so Brogan laid more baked goodness onto his lips. His mate eagerly ate it up in between the delightful sounds of a male being pleased.

"You're doing so fucking great, baby," he praised.

"Love you," Dra'Kaedan murmured. "Love cake."

Brogan chuckled as he gave him more of his favorite dessert while working three fingers inside him. Dra'Kaedan's skin glistened in the low light of their bedroom, and he liked watching him finding his pleasure. His mate wasn't touching him and yet, Brogan was warm inside and out. All he needed was to see the desire in the sensuous lines of Dra'Kaedan's body to be aching and ready.

When Dra'Kaedan's balls were drawn up tight and his hole was ready to be fucked, Brogan pulled his busy hand away from him. The warlock's lashes lifted and the lust in them was a lure Brogan couldn't resist. He leaned down and crushed their mouths together. He slid his tongue over Dra'Kaedan's and exulted in their combined passion. Brogan wanted to drive into him, but he'd made a promise, and Dra'Kaedan had lived up to his end of the bargain.

Regretfully he nipped Dra'Kaedan's bottom lip, then lifted his head. "The bowl of frosting is yours."

"Hot damn," Dra'Kaedan shouted as he sat up and pushed Brogan out of the way so he could grab it. Using the bowl, he gestured toward the bed. "Go on dragon, assume the position."

"What position is that?" Brogan asked warily, suddenly afraid of what he'd signed up for.

"Get that look off your face, I'm not going to do anything bad. Just lie like I was," Dra'Kaedan coaxed.

Brogan slowly did as he was told. After twisting a little on the mattress to get comfortable, he closed his eyes. "Have at me."

"Oh, I plan to."

His lids flew up as something cold was slapped against his dick. "*Motherfucker*."

Dra'Kaedan froze, he had a spoon in one hand and there was a giant glob of frosting sliding down Brogan's cock. "What's wrong?"

"Shit's cold and maybe not so rough. Or you know...no cake for you."

"Can't live without cake," Dra'Kaedan murmured; then he bent forward and used his hand to coat the frosting all over Brogan's length.

"This is going to be a sticky mess, isn't it?"

"No worries, that's what cleansing spells are for. Don't think you're going to get out of fucking me," Dra'Kaedan said as he nearly flung the bowl back onto the tray. He situated himself between Brogan's legs and then closed his mouth over Brogan's shaft.

Brogan pushed one hand into Dra'Kaedan's curls as the warlock bobbed his head. Dra'Kaedan sounded like he was purring as he sucked, and the vibration had Brogan's eyes crossing. His toes curled as he chanted in his head that he would not come. Brogan's dick didn't want to hear it, so he focused on the thought of Dra'Kaedan's tight ass and was able to get himself under control.

He wanted to give Dra'Kaedan ample opportunity to enjoy the frosting he'd smeared all over him, but Brogan wasn't made of iron. When his mate put a hand near the base of Brogan's sex and worked it in conjunction with his wicked mouth, he gently extricated himself and pushed a very irritated Dra'Kaedan away.

"Frosting," he snarled.

"We'll play again later, baby, but I need you."

Dra'Kaedan let out a growl, but he waved a hand over Brogan's shaft, cleaning it and drying it at the same time. He scrambled over and snatched the lube where Brogan had left it. All business, he slicked up Brogan in seconds; then he reached behind himself and did the same to his pucker.

With a look of fierce determination, Dra'Kaedan straddled him. Brogan steadied him with a hand on his hip, and he grabbed the base of his dick to make his entry easier. Dra'Kaedan lowered down, and Brogan smiled as his mate's body stretched around him. Moving steadily but not rushed, Dra'Kaedan didn't stop until Brogan was fully seated inside him.

Then he braced his palms on Brogan's chest and rode him. His pace was a ruthless one, and Brogan grabbed his other hip as they raced toward completion. Dra'Kaedan angled slightly and then dug his short nails into Brogan's skin. He was hitting him in his prostate if Dra'Kaedan's whimpers were anything to go by, and he focused on making sure his other half got there before he did.

Brogan was about ready to tell Dra'Kaedan to start jerking his cock when he did it of his own accord. His hand flew over his length, and then he let out a roar as his hole clamped down on Brogan like a vise. He hissed out a breath as his climax was torn from him, and he helplessly shot his seed into Dra'Kaedan's welcoming heat. They slowly stopped rocking against each other as Dra'Kaedan melted against him. He managed somehow to wrap him in his arms and dropped a kiss on his head.

"How was celebration sex?" Brogan murmured as he ran a hand over Dra'Kaedan's tousled curls.

"We're doing this again," Dra'Kaedan panted out against his chest.

"Well, you know...if you're good."

Dra'Kaedan snorted, which caused the corners of Brogan's mouth to lift. Who was he kidding? They both knew there was going to be plenty of cake-fueled sex in their future, so it would be pointless to argue. Besides, the most important part of it was that there was time ahead for them. An eternity to share the beauty of the relationship they'd built. Brogan held Dra'Kaedan snugly against him and whispered words of love to his man. He understood all too well that his life wouldn't be the same without him.

40

When Saturday morning rolled around, Brogan was lying on his side in the bed he shared with Dra'Kaedan and pressing a line of kisses down his back. Less than twenty minutes before, he'd been buried inside him while Dra'Kaedan's fingers dug into his sides, urging him on. Apparently still needing time to recover, Dra'Kaedan was sprawled out over the mattress, on his belly. When his lips reached his shoulder blade, Brogan replaced them with his palm. He smoothed it down over Dra'Kaedan's skin when someone knocked on their door. Shifting so he could press his mouth lower, they both ignored whoever wanted to interrupt their interlude.

Dra'Kaedan let out a soft sigh of contentment as Brogan's hand made it down to his firm ass. Brogan was considering how much longer it would be until they were ready to go again or if he'd need to feed his bottomless pit when whatever maniac was in the hallway banged on the wood separating the two spaces.

Lifting his head, Dra'Kaedan bellowed, "Go away."

Giving one of his mate's perfect cheeks a light smack for his rudeness, Brogan was rewarded with a small moan from Dra'Kaedan.

The warlock buried his face into the rumpled covers. "Why does that turn me on?" he muttered.

One corner of Brogan's mouth raised in amusement. "Does it? Well, maybe we should—"

Before Brogan could finish his suggestion that they explore Dra'Kaedan's desire to get spanked, the door was pounded on again.

"Who the hell is it?" Dra'Kaedan roared.

"Good morning. It's Renny," the familiar yelled cheerfully from the hallway.

"Yeah, yeah. Come back later," Dra'Kaedan shouted. "We're busy."

"Well, if you're doing what I think you are, I'll just wait. It never takes you guys longer than five or ten minutes to have sex," Renny responded, his voice still full of an overexuberance of joy.

Dra'Kaedan growled something about killing the brat as he rolled over. He kissed Brogan hard, then waved a hand over himself. A pair of pajamas appeared, masking his nakedness, and he strode over in angry stomps to whip open the door.

"What do you want, Renny?" Dra'Kaedan snarled into his familiar's face.

Renny was apparently immune to Dra'Kaedan's fury, because he sashayed into the room toward the bed. "Hi Brogan, good morning."

Glad he'd tugged the sheet over himself when Dra'Kaedan had marched across the space, he grinned at the familiar. "Hey, Renny. Morning, what's up?"

Perched on the bench at the foot at the bed, Renny waved a hand in the air nonchalantly. "Oh, Aleksander asked me to let you guys know that Drystan called."

"Why would you need to interrupt us to tell us that?" Dra'Kaedan demanded.

"Because Drystan's going to be here with his son in like fifteen or twenty minutes," Renny explained. "Aleksander wants the whole family there to greet our newest D'Vaire. So here I am."

Dra'Kaedan, who remained parked at the entrance of their room, barked, "You couldn't just say that through the door?"

Lifting up one shoulder in a negligent shrug clearly meant to irritate the steaming warlock, Renny replied, "He told me to make sure you guys knew. I thought it was best if I could see your faces when I told you. I don't know what you're doing in here and whether you're listening if I'm in the hallway."

"What the hell do you think we were doing?" Dra'Kaedan asked, then shook his head like a dog coming in from the rain. "Never mind. Don't answer that."

"*Duh*, Dra'Kaedan, I have your memories. I know how sex works."

"Thank you very much for letting us know," Brogan told Renny. "You can tell Aleksander we'll be there in time to meet Drystan's son."

"Cool," Renny exclaimed but made no move to leave the room to carry his message to their king.

Dra'Kaedan's mouth flattened into an irritated line. "We could use some time alone now, so we can get ready."

Renny got up and walked toward the warlock. "Oh sure, if you make your shower a quick one, you probably still have time to have that sex you guys wanted."

"Thanks for the advice," Dra'Kaedan deadpanned, then slammed the door behind his familiar's back. Racing back to the bed, Dra'Kaedan crawled up to where Brogan was lounging against the headboard. He gave him a deep kiss and pulled back. "He didn't say anything about breakfast."

"We probably missed it. We were pretty busy."

Dra'Kaedan nodded and hopped back onto the floor. "We'll have to snack until lunch."

Brogan tossed the sheet covering him aside and followed Dra'Kaedan into the bathroom. The warlock was already fiddling with the taps, so Brogan yanked Dra'Kaedan's pajama bottoms to the floor. Lowering to his knees, he bit gently on Dra'Kaedan's ass and then straightened.

"Are we having sex in the shower?" Dra'Kaedan demanded as he tugged off his T-shirt.

"No time."

"I hate that you're right," Dra'Kaedan complained as he stepped under the spray. Brogan followed and decided if they were going to make it out of the bathroom without fucking, he'd have to concentrate on cleaning himself only. If he got his hands on Dra'Kaedan, all bets were off.

"We don't want to miss our newest D'Vaire's arrival."

Dra'Kaedan's sigh echoed around the shower walls. "I know."

Brogan somehow managed to limit himself to kissing Dra'Kaedan only a dozen or so times under the hot spray, which gave them plenty of time to shampoo, soap, and condition. When they were clean, Brogan turned off the water and grabbed the towel Dra'Kaedan handed him. With efficient motions, he managed to get dry and then wandered into the bedroom.

Only a minute or so later, the two were dressed and on their way to the living area of the house to wait for Drystan and his son. Brogan found a seat next to Dre'Kariston and took it. The twins were still making up for all their lost time, and Brogan enjoyed seeing the pair together. Whatever made Dra'Kaedan happy brought joy to Brogan's own heart. As he tugged Dra'Kaedan down onto his lap, the Grand Warlock glared at Renny. The courageous familiar returned it with a guileless smile.

Hiding his grin, Brogan touched his lips to Dra'Kaedan's bounty of riotous curls just as the sound of the doorbell reverberated through the house. Dra'Kaedan hopped off his lap, and the entire D'Vaire clan went charging toward the entryway. With an instinct to protect—and that went double for his mate—he tried to be nonchalant as he stepped in front of Dra'Kaedan, then opened the door.

"Dragons," Dra'Kaedan muttered as Brogan got his first look at their guests.

He nodded in welcome to Drystan, then took stock of his son. His brown hair was cut short in the back but fell messily over his forehead as if he didn't care enough to style it. Behind a pair of wire-rimmed glasses, his eyes were clear sky blue that matched his father's. Like his dad, he was tall and lanky, standing perhaps an inch or two below Brogan's six feet five inches. The fallen knight and necromancer hybrid was dressed in a pair of faded jeans and a light T-shirt. He had a full backpack strapped to him.

"Everyone, this is my son, Trystan," the Reverent Knight said.

Aleksander pushed Brogan out of the way, so he could shake Trystan's hand. He offered him a smile as he greeted him. "Trystan, I'm Aleksander. Welcome to the Draconis Court of D'Vaire and Dra'Kaedan's Coven."

"Thanks so much," Trystan said. With no hesitation, Trystan walked into the house and didn't stop until he was standing directly in front of Blodwen. He thrust his hand toward her as she stared at him bug-eyed.

"Hi," she blurted out.

Trystan grinned brightly at her as she raised her arm. Instead of greeting her with the handshake Brogan had expected, he clasped her palm in his. Then he leaned forward and kissed her cheek.

"You're the only necromancer here. You must be Blodwen, right?" he asked.

Her head bobbed up and down, but her face was still a study in abject surprise.

"I'm so glad you're my mate," Trystan told her, and then she shyly smiled back at him.

Brogan's lips curled upward as Dra'Kaedan slapped his arm lightly. His brows drew together in consternation. "What the hell?"

"Do you see that?" Dra'Kaedan demanded. "*That* is how you greet your mate."

A chuckle escaped him—not only at the indignant expression on Dra'Kaedan's face but the idiot he'd been the day the warlock entered his life. He leaned down and whispered close to his ear. "I think I redeemed myself with cake sex."

Dra'Kaedan pursed his lips slightly. "That's definitely something for the list."

"What's the con?"

"Oh, that's easy. It's that you think I need to be good to get more of it."

Brogan rubbed Dra'Kaedan's chin lightly between his fingers. "You can write that down, but we both know I'm going to give you that cake no matter what."

"Because you're pretty fucking awesome."

Renny shoved Dra'Kaedan over. "You're both also completely in the fucking way."

Managing to prevent familiarcide by shuffling Dra'Kaedan out of the hallway and into the living room, Brogan allowed Aleksander the space he needed to corral the rest of the crowd, so Drystan was no longer forced to stand idly on the porch. The newly introduced pair of mates walked side by side with their hands locked as they were the last of the group to straggle in. Aleksander took up the task of acquainting Trystan with the names of all the D'Vaires. After being introduced to and greeting Trystan, Brogan tugged Dra'Kaedan onto his lap and gazed down into his beautiful navy eyes. Since the day Brogan returned to D'Vaire, his life had been turned upside down.

He had no idea how he'd managed to survive without the amazing man in his arms and was so incredibly grateful to have him back. Brogan was dedicated to making Dra'Kaedan happy because he was lost without him. The darkness had nearly claimed them both and while it would've been nice to have been spared the pain, it only made him treasure his mate more. In so many ways, they'd both experienced what it was like on the other side. Brogan endured an emotional journey that had almost consumed him while Dra'Kaedan physically crossed to straddle the veil.

Somehow with the help of Dra'Kaedan's parents, they were together again. Dra'Kaedan was his light, his love, his best friend, and unequivocally the finest part of his soul. The future bloomed in front of them, one ripe in hope and devotion. Brogan was ready for whatever Fate had in store, not only for him and the amazing warlock in his arms, but for their entire family. The doors of Dra'Kaedan's Coven would soon be flung wide open, and Brogan was eager to find out what incredible things—and people—awaited the D'Vaires.

ABOUT THE AUTHOR

Jessamyn Kingley lives in Nevada where she begs the men in her head to tell her their amazing stories which she dutifully writes it all down in what has become a small mountain of notebooks. She falls in love with each couple and swears whatever book she wrote last is her absolute favorite.

Jessamyn is married and working toward remembering to start the dishwasher without being distracted by the scent of the magical detergent. For personal enjoyment, she aids in cat rescue while slashing and gashing her way through mobs in various MMORPGs. Caffeine is her very best friend and is only cast aside briefly for the sin better known as BBQ potato chips.

Visit her website at: www.jessamynkingley.com

Follow her on Facebook at: www.facebook.com/jessamynkingley. She loves to engage with readers there.

ALSO BY JESSAMYN KINGLEY

Made in the USA
Middletown, DE
06 January 2021